BY PINCKNEY BENEDICT

Town Smokes
The Wrecking Yard
Dogs of God

dogs of god

nan a. talese

doubleday

new york

london

toronto

sydney

auckland

dogs of god

of

pinckney benedict

PUBLISHED BY NAN A. TALESE
an imprint of Doubleday, a division of
Bantam Doubleday Dell Publishing Group, Inc.
1540 Broadway, New York, New York 10036

DOUBLEDAY is a trademark of Doubleday,
a division of Bantam Doubleday Dell Publishing Group, Inc.

Book design by Marysarah Quinn

Library of Congress Cataloging-in-Publication Data

Benedict, Pinckney
    Dogs of God / Pinckney Benedict.
      p. cm.
    I. Title
PS3552.E5398D6 1994
813'.54—dc20   93-12565
                        CIP

ISBN 0-385-42022-6

1 3 5 7 9 10 8 6 4 2

FIRST EDITION

For Nan

For Mike—
With pleasure in our (now
quite long) friendship—
Congratulations on your
retirement. You made it,
pal!

I will appoint over them four kinds, says the Lord: the sword to slay, and the dogs to tear, and the fowls of the heaven, and the beasts of the earth, to devour and destroy.

—JEREMIAH 15:3

acknowledgments

The author wishes to express his thanks to the following people for their expert assistance in the writing of this book: Cleve Benedict; Laura Philpot Benedict; Dave Nalker; Mike Arthur; Jim Mazza; Colonel Richard Schmidt, USAF (Ret.); Robert Head; Nelson Cambata; Micheal Dunkin; Jim Finn; Doug Ashworth; George Angel; and Fred G. Leebron.

prologue

I'm standing there waiting to see if they've got a bell they're going to ring to start the bout, and this weedy bastard I'm fighting skips right across to my corner and hits me in the face. Only he's taller than me and doesn't get the point of the jawbone. Instead, he catches the side of my head, on the ridge of the cheek, which smarts like crazy and takes some skin off, but it can't level me. I guess he figured he could end the whole thing right there. Hell, I thought he was coming over to shake my hand.

I push him away from me, put both hands against his chest and shove, and he backs up a couple of steps, hands high and jabbing. "What the hell," I say, and he catches me in the mouth, splits both lips, then connects with a left cross to the temple: all these head shots he's scoring while I'm still figuring out the fight has started without me. He's a ridgerunner, name of Benoit I've heard, from some shitty little town farther up in the highlands. I wonder if anybody told him my name. All his buddies are yelling Rolly, Rolly *at him from behind the sawhorse barricade they've got set up around us.*

A stroke to my forehead puts me on my knees, brain sloshing against my eyeballs so that everything whites out for a second, and I can feel the wooden plank of the near sawhorse against my back. My guys are quiet, got their hands folded I guess, watching this tall skinny fuck take me to the cleaners in the first seconds of the first round. He's dancing back and forth, weaving, shifting into the light and then out of it again.

The White Mule work gloves he's got on his hands make this wet smack smack *as he drives his hooks like rocks against my skull, knocking me back and forth. Look left and there's this crowd of crazed yahoos waving their money; look right and there's the Shifletts—the old man that runs the place and his three giant sons— sucking on thin Swisher Sweets cigarillos. The boys carry ax handles with them, and the old man has an Army Colt stuck in the waistband of his pants. They're all four smiling but you don't know what that might mean. I want just one guy to yell out my name. Yell out, "Get up, Goody! Hey, on your feet and flatten this character!" But nobody does.*

I'm mad now but it might be too late to save me. Usually I get mad sometime in the middle of the third round, and I let the punishment I've taken in the last seven and a half minutes come back on the guy that did it to me. That's how I have to do it. I can't afford to wear an opponent down with pokes and jabs; the bones in my hands break too easily. One good hard shot with the right, that's what I've got. That's how I'm fifteen and oh, but not in the record books that anybody's keeping. Twelve of those are clean knockouts, too, the guy flat on his back and not moving. I'm probably the only one who knows my whole true score.

Benoit clips me on the ear and I go down onto the board floor. I can't hear anything out of the ear he hammered, but with the other I hear Seldomridge, who arranged the fight, say, "Right in the latrine." His voice is clear, and I think he must have leaned down to say it directly to me. The world slips and rattles for a minute before the holes line up against the sprockets again.

When I crack my eyes, the hillbillies are screaming Rolly, Rolly *with this new frantic note. Nobody on my side says a single thing back to them, not even booing Benoit for bad sportsmanship. We're guests here, came up from the county seat to take the woodhicks' money. They're all related up in these mountain places. They're all one big family. Impossible to tell whose side the Shifletts are on, if they're on anybody's. Rolly Benoit strides across the ring, arms down at his side, muscles in his shoulders bunched. He's shaking his head.*

The guys behind me are making plans for the evening. I can catch some of what they're saying.

. . . long way down to the valley.

. . . couple of pros . . .

. . . tonight.

. . . I'm tapped.

. . . too. This little screw-up . . .

Somebody else—it might be Seldomridge—says in a loud voice, Seventeen point two seconds.

And I'm hot to go now. Suckered. Too slow to stop Benoit. I push off the floor, shove with my legs, come out of my crouch like a lineman from his three-point stance, picking up speed in the short distance between us. Somebody on the hillbilly side calls out a warning, but Benoit is pretty deep in his victory stalk so he doesn't pay any attention.

I was a pretty mean tackle in high school, and I hit him solid in the middle of his back, just above the waist. His skin is sweaty and slick, but I keep my hold. He's not expecting me—fair's fair—and he goes down. His head catches the sawhorse near his corner as he takes the spill, and then the wooden stool that sits there. I hear both impacts, which sound the same: like the fat part of a baseball bat connecting with a pumpkin. Benoit grunts. He twitches in my arms. Then I'm lying on top of him and he's not moving.

The machine shop falls silent. I swear I can hear the ticking of somebody's wristwatch, a tight metal snip snip snip *as the second hand jumps forward from moment to moment. Somebody coughs and the sound of it is loud as a pistol shot.*

Then the ridgerunners drag me off of Rolly Benoit. They're swinging at me, trying to tear me apart, but there's too many of them. Benoit by himself was a lot more efficient than this mob. They're tugging me every which way and scratching me with their fingernails more than anything else. I get a couple of quick jabs in, feel somebody's nose smash like a ripe tomato against the canvas of my glove, but it's hard to get leverage when they're picking me up, tossing me back and forth. My right eye is swollen shut.

Seldomridge shouts something that I can't understand, and Yarrow, another guy from the valley, answers him, so I know they're in it now. I feel a kind of gratitude toward them, even though it only means we'll all take a beating. One big red-faced boy in a tan coverall, a real heavyweight, has got me pretty much to himself, the others having turned their attention elsewhere, and he's whipsawing me back and forth, holding me by my neck. I give him a shot in his fleshy brisket and he falls back, got his hands clasped against his heart like it might fall out of his chest and he wants to catch it if it does.

And I drop. My legs are made of rubber, and without the big boy holding me I flop down like a baby. I try to rise, but there is not much on me that's in working order anymore. My trunks have gotten jerked down off my ass somehow, and that is embarrassing, but what is worse I can't reach down there to drag them back up and cover myself. I can't even manage that.

Around me it is all legs in denim pants. They are standing planted like trees when they swing, and I want to laugh at their footwork. Nobody up there knows how to land a punch; nobody knows how to draw blood. Everybody that really knew how—that is, me and Benoit—is lying on the floor now. A man in muddy brogans puts his foot down on my hand, and I shift it out of his way, but he stomps it again before he moves on. One of the sawhorses goes down with a crash. The others have been shifted out of their places or dismantled for weapons so you can't tell where the ring used to be.

Rolly Benoit is looking at me from only a couple of feet away. We are laid next to each other like we're grabbing some sun at the beach, or maybe like fish, the catch-of-the-day set out on a bed of ice at the supermarket. His left eye is closed, but the right is open wide: a frozen wink. He looks surprised to be where he is. The pupil covers most of the hazel iris of the open eye, and I am near enough to see that it is ragged at its edge, not smooth like you would expect. It is the dilated pupil that gives him his startled look. He has a slight smile on his lips. Blue shadow fills a deep rectangular dent in the exact middle of his forehead.

There are hard little kernels of cracked corn scattered across the floor, among the cigarette butts and plastic wrappers and hardened wads of old gum. Benoit's got a few of the kernels stuck to his cheek and caught in his cropped hair. It makes me want to laugh at him. There are white worms of chicken shit here and there too, some with wispy pinfeathers stuck in them. At first I think it must be a slaughter plant for chickens that we're in, but then I realize that they probably fight birds in here. They might have fought them before we came in tonight: sunset-colored cocks wheeling on each other, mirror-bright splinters of razor lashed to their spurs, cupped wings swatting the air like big clumsy hands.

Somewhere not far away, Seldomridge shouts again, more like a scream this time, and then he stops. It is all hard breathing and scuffling sounds in the warehouse, like the dancing of a bunch of performing bears. I hear the old man tell his sons to break it up, and they wade contentedly into the fracas. People run to escape them. Someone steps on my chest, forcing the air out of my lungs. A couple of people step on Rolly Benoit also. The ax handles of the Shifletts rise and fall. The sound of them is like the sound of fists in eight-ounce gloves working the heavy bag.

You can stop it now, *I want to say.* It's finished here. *My eyes have both swollen tight by this point, and all I can see is the movement of shapes through a thick red curtain. Thrashing figures pass through bands of blood-colored light. The Shiflett boys grunt. I turn back to Benoit, whose face won't have changed expression, I know, so I don't need to see it. His lips must still be curved in that dumb sweet smile. We're lying together like brothers.*

Well Rolly, *I want to say,* we did it all.

Oh did we? *That is what he might say to me.*

We sure did. You sucker-punched me, but I got you back.

Oh did you? *he might say.*

You got an astonished look on your face when you went down. How did I look when you first hit me?

Pretty shocked, *he would tell me.*

Listen, *I could say,* this whole thing was a surprise to me. I don't even live around here. They brought me up to fight you because some guys heard I was pretty fierce, and you're the local hero. I never meant to hurt you this way.

Rolly again. My story's much like yours. Circumstances and accident. Except I'm only too happy to have hurt you, you know.

And so on in a companionable enough way while we wait for the Shifletts to sort things out.

After a time I am able to open my eyes again, but by then I am not in the abandoned machine shop up in Peebles County anymore, but in another place altogether.

Sometimes when I am dreaming or daydreaming I get a hand up in front of Rolly Benoit's first swing, a neat sweeping block. I take the impact on my forearm, and I'm surprised because it's a light blow, really, not the kind of a thing that would knock you down at all. And I stop the second blow too, and when I shove him he slides backward out into the middle of the ring and he waits for me there, just on his side of center, feet spread shoulder width, knees flexed. I come out to meet him, and I'm ready to start the fight.

He is a solid opponent, in shape, a tall light-heavy who looks more like a golf pro than a boxer. We are pretty evenly matched, because he has reach but I have power. At first he's jabbing me, short sharp testing punches that don't hurt much even when they do land, but then he's getting inside, and there's a seam open on the thumb of his glove. An edge of the stiff material cuts me above the right eye.

I break away, but I come right back, boring in on him, letting his midriff have it. I make it hard for him to breathe, peppering his body, bruising his ribs, tenderizing him for later in the fight. I'm using mainly the left, sparing the bones in my right hand for a real opportunity to put him away. When he covers up the rib cage I go for the head. He manages to stop my attack, scores a couple off me, dances away.

There are no breaks between rounds, but we don't need breaks. When one of us is tired, we're both tired. We breathe together. The stiffs in the audience, the ridgerunners and the fellows from the county seat, they don't know what they're watching. They don't know how to see it. Pretty soon they start drifting off, his people and my people, figuring to go visit whores or get a couple of drinks. Maybe they'll be back later to see how it all came out, or maybe not. Meanwhile, Benoit and I are trading blows out there on the wood floor, and he's got blood coming out of me, cuts over both eyes now. That just pisses me off, which is bad for him. He starts to gasp for his breath, those tender ribs costing him pretty dear.

Finally the Shifletts leave too. They shuffle off, the old man and his hulking sons, and the vapor lamps set in the high ceiling shut down with a bang, and the doors slide shut and lock. By this time Benoit and I can't dance anymore. We fight flat-footed, like a couple of pugs, just swinging away, and I don't care whether I break my hands or not. His eyes are purple, bruised shut, and mine are closing. Dark surrounds us, but the dark doesn't matter because we've blinded each other.

We stand arm's length apart, lashing out, not even trying to duck or block. The blows have taken the place of our eyes, of the light. And each lick of the gloves, mine on him, his on me, underneath that metal roof and between those sawhorses, tells us what we need to know: that we are still alive.

1

Goody knew the stench. It had been growing steadily denser, more malignant, in the week that he had occupied the rented house. It wafted over him as he lay in bed, borne through the open bedroom window on a hot gust of wind. It pulled him gasping from sleep, from another of his frequent fight dreams. He hadn't recognized it in the days previous, or he hadn't allowed himself to recognize it, but in the thin gray light of early morning he realized that he knew what was producing the gassy, fetid odor.

"Something," Goody said, rising, "something dead in the cane."

The window sash slid down a few inches when he put his hand to it, and then it stuck fast. He pounded at it, and the window loosened in its frame and slid shut with a bang. Through its rippled glass he could see the patch of cane that grew to the east of the house. The tall plants clashed and undulated as though something trapped among them were battling to get out. With the window closed, he could not hear the hollow sound they made. He knew that it was the dry east wind pushing the woody stems and that nothing was going to emerge, but he watched for another few moments anyway. He scanned the mottled sky over the canebrake, looking for the telltale cruciform shapes of vultures, but none circled. Blue anvil-shaped clouds brooded there, promising rain that he doubted would come. He dressed and left the house.

Outside, he took a handkerchief from one of his pockets and wrapped it around the lower part of his face, tying it in a clumsy knot behind his head. The cloth lay over his nose and mouth, moving slightly to and fro with his breath. He felt silly, like a kid playing at being a bandito, and he looked around to make sure that he went unobserved, though there was no other house within sight. Invisible in the stand of cane, a couple of jackdaws croaked in harsh voices at each other.

As he passed the old Pontiac musclecar parked in the yard, he trailed one hand over its dull finish, rapped his knuckles lightly against the metal of the roof. It was, he thought, the one thing that he could lay claim to, free and clear. It had carried him this far, to this small house on a failing farm, in a dusty narrow valley cloaked by the crenellated shadow of Little Hogback Mountain. The car's rocker panels were eaten up with rust; likewise the muffler; and the wide tires with their alloy rims didn't have much tread left on them. But the Le Mans ran. The fucker ran like a scalded cat, and that was something.

He had little difficulty climbing the sagging wire fence at the brake's edge. Once across, he searched for a path among the cane plants. When he didn't fine one, he forced his way into the stubborn growth. The fleshy leaves brushed the nape of his neck, and he gritted his teeth against the unpleasant sensation, like humid over-friendly hands on him. He was not a large man, and he was able to move quickly between the close-packed stalks. It was probably just a dead dog, he decided. He frequently lay awake at night and listened to the packs of feral dogs that trooped down the dry wash behind the house, delicate feet padding, blunted claws clicking against the water-smoothed stones. On moonlit nights they sang together, and often they fought. It seemed more than likely to him that some outcast dog, slaughtered by the pack, lay rotting in the cane.

It was dark in the middle of the field, where the slanting morning light hadn't yet managed to penetrate. It illuminated the tops of the highest cane plants. The stand covered several acres, and in criss-crossing it a number of times Goody failed to find any dead thing. The smell was intense, but it wasn't stronger in any one direction than in the others and so provided him no bearing. After a time he became convinced that the stench had permeated his clothing and perhaps the pores of his skin and that he carried it along with him. He thought that it had become trapped among the small hairs that lined the moist tubes of his nostrils, so that he might never get free of it. He continued to batter his way through the hardy stalks. Bright green dome-backed beetles dropped onto his hair and ran across his lips and scuttled down his collar. He slapped them off him and crushed them between his thumb and forefinger when he could catch them, but there were always more. Sweat ran down his face and stung his eyes.

"Enough of this shit," he said finally, deciding that Inchcape would have to find the source of the stench himself. Inchcape was the old man who owned the place. Goody calculated to the best of his poor ability where the nearest edge of the canefield lay and headed in that direction, anxious to be out in the sunlight again. As he went, he came upon a stretch of bent and broken cane stalks, and because it led largely along his own planned trajectory and because it made easier going, he followed it. A big flying insect droned like a bullet past his ear, and he ducked away. Around him, the cane clattered musically as the hot breeze rushed past.

The clearing that Goody found was not a wide one, and he almost stepped on the body that lay there. He took it at first for a poorly made scarecrow that had toppled from its post, but a second look at the sprawled figure told him that this was the source of the reek, and that it had been a person. The man—Goody thought that it was, had been, a man—lolled in a mess of uprooted and trampled cane. Goody drew his foot deliberately back from the withered, ruined shape on the runneled earth. He stood regarding it.

The body was spread-eagle on its back, dead face gazing sightlessly up at the darkening sky. Goody couldn't guess how long it might have been there. Its lips were drawn back in a grimace, and he could see the blackened gums and uneven yellow teeth. The teeth seemed very long. A wasp ambled into the open mouth and out again, pausing briefly on the thin lower lip. The insect fanned its delicate glassine wings and rose into the air. When it had climbed above the level of the cane stalks, the sun glinted briefly on the black, neatly articulated armor of its exoskeleton. Then it was gone. Other wasps ascended from the body and proceeded off in the same direction. A mob of flies hung over the cadaver as well. The air was filled with their insistent murmur.

The corpse's bushy hair had been gathered at the neck into a meager ponytail, held together by a wide red rubber band. Its jeans-clad left leg was twisted beneath it, and Goody noted that both long, narrow feet were bare and heavily callused, covered with rich black dirt. He looked around for shoes but saw none. Had this fellow come here under his own power, breaking his way through the cane? What had he died of? Who was he? No telling; those were questions for someone else to answer.

Goody inspected the clearing once more. He looked at the close ranks of the surrounding cane, at the broken, browning stalks on the ground, and at the churned dirt, but he didn't look closely at the body again. He didn't want to look closely at it. The sharp coppery odor of mortifying flesh made his eyes water. He wanted to sneeze. He was afraid that he might vomit, and even more afraid that, inexplicably, he might weep. The bandanna that he wore over his nose and mouth seemed suddenly to constrict his breathing. He was choking, but he did not dare to tear it away. He turned and moved hurriedly off from the corpse, taking a new vector which he hoped would soon bring him out of the cane.

He picked up the phone and dialed. After a few rings, the receiver on the other end was taken up. The voice that answered was curt and blurred with interrupted sleep.

"Mr. Inchcape?" Goody said. Silence from the answering party. "We've got a problem." More silence. "Are you there?" Goody said.

"I'm here," the voice answered.

"Fine," Goody said. "I thought for a minute maybe we had a bad connection. Listen, I wanted to tell you about this body."

"Body?"

"Yeah. There's a man in the cane over here, and he's dead. He's been dead a while, I guess, because he smells like pure hell. Do you want to call the sheriff, or should I?"

"What cane is it we're talking about, exactly?"

"To the east of my house. He died in there, it looks like."

"Was it Tannhauser's people?" The voice was meditative. Goody did not know exactly what response he had expected the old man to make, but this was not it. "Those boys ought to know better than to bring their problems down here."

"I don't know what happened to him. He was dead when I got there." Goody scowled, wondering what Inchcape could be getting at.

"Who is this, anyway?" the voice wanted to know. Suddenly Goody doubted that it was Inchcape that he had got hold of. The gruff tones might belong to Inchcape and they might not. Goody tried to recall the number that his fingers had dialed, matching it to the number he held in memory as Inchcape's.

"Goody," he said. The voice on the other end didn't reply. Listening intently, Goody thought he heard the dissonant creaking of bedsprings and, beyond that, tinny laughter from a television set in another room and, further even than that, a sound like an ocean's constant breaking against the shore. He thought it might be the sound of the phone company itself he was hearing, its thousands of miles of relays and conductors, transformers and line, wires strung on poles across the countryside, switching networks in cavernous buildings, all waiting on him to speak, or on the one whom he had reached.

After a while of unanswered listening, he broke the connection. Cradling the handset between his cheek and shoulder, he took up the slim tattered directory that sat by the phone and flipped through its limp pages to the County Services section, looking for the number of the sheriff's office.

2

"Death by misadventure," the sheriff said. His name was John Faktor, and he was a broad, squat man with a bald dome of a head that gleamed in the sun. He stood facing Goody behind the rented house. Out in the canefield, near its center, the county coroner and several sheriff's deputies pored over the body, talking to one another in loud, unintelligible voices. "Can't tell you anything for sure until I read the coroner's report, but that'd be my best guess."

Goody squinted at him.

"Misadventure," Faktor said again. "It means he met with an accident."

"Sure," Goody said. "I know that."

Faktor looked out over the field. "We'll have him off your hands in just a couple of minutes now. Don't worry."

"He never really was on my hands. It's not my place. A fellow named Inchcape owns it. He lives over to the west, on the other side of the farm. I rent the house from him."

"Well, we won't trouble you much more in any case. You been out here long?"

"Only about a week."

Faktor laughed. "Hell, he looks like he's been dead longer than

you've lived here. What do you think about that? You're moving in
your stuff, looking the place over, and all the time some drifter's
lying dead out in the field. Gives you the shivers, eh?"

"No," Goody said, "not really. He wasn't any friend or kin of
mine, I don't believe." The voices from the canefield drew closer as
the deputies moved toward the house, bringing with them the body
of the stranger.

The walk from Goody's place to Inchcape's took about a quarter of
an hour. He followed the dry wash, the stones crunching and grinding together under his tread. They made for uncertain footing. Along
the banks of the wash grew a tangled thicket of thorny bushes like a
living wall, their thin branches adorned with pale papery blooms.
Within the brush, starlings rustled and twittered and peeped, but
Goody could see of them only the flash of their wings as they moved
from branch to branch. Set here and there among the strangling roots
of the stickerbushes were little riots of herbs and colorful wildflowers:
lavender joe-pye weed, boneset and tiny feverfew; stalky pokeweed,
cardinal flower, daisies and beggarweeds. There were other plants
growing there too that he had not seen before and could not identify.

He was warm from the exertion of walking when he reached the
farm road that led to Inchcape's place. The barrier of thornbushes
dwindled and petered out along the road, and he was grateful to walk
on packed dirt rather than on the treacherous loose stones. He presently came upon Inchcape's house, a low clapboard building covered
in peeling white paint.

"Hey," he called. "Mr. Inchcape." An immense Great Pyrenees
sheepdog lay on the porch of the house. The dog's name was Tonto.
Tonto raised his head and glared at Goody with deep cunning, blue
eyes glittering out from under the ropy dreadlocks of his dense pelt.
Something that looked like a horse's shoulder blade, bone worked
clean, lay between his forefeet.

Inchcape's Mack truck stood in the sparse grass of his yard, long
dump bed cantilevered skyward. Goody peered into the sharply angled bed and found it empty, with just a little gravel clinging to the
bottom and sides. Inchcape had pretty well given up on the farm as
being too much work for too little return, and he made what money
he had by hauling loads of limestone crusher-run for the quarry at
Unus. His old rust-red Ford pickup sat on the other side of the ten-
wheeler.

Goody edged around the place that Tonto had staked out as his own. He waved a conciliatory hand at the dog. "Good Tonto," he said. "Good boy." Tonto's short tail thumped noncommittally against the floor of the porch. With a heavy sigh the dog rested his head again on his paws, looking out over the dusty expanse of Inchcape's yard and, beyond that, the fallow rolling acreage of the farm. The shoulder bone rocked slightly under his hairy chin. Goody passed inside, easing the screen door shut behind him.

Inchcape sat on the couch in his living room, wearing only a thin flannel bathrobe over a pair of lemon-colored boxer shorts. He seemed to be contemplating the scarred surface of the coffee table on which he rested his bare feet. As Goody watched from the hall, Inchcape scratched idly at his scrawny chest. "You coming in?" he said without looking up.

Goody entered the room and took a seat in a large armchair that faced Inchcape. "Saw Tonto out on the porch," Goody said. "Animal that big must make one hell of a watchdog."

"Well," Inchcape said, "he didn't keep you out, did he?" The skin of his face was leathery and deeply seamed. His eyes were the same bright blue as Tonto's. Inchcape shifted in his seat, hooked a thumb toward the porch. "His mother ate every whelp in the litter but him. He was the only one of those pups that managed to stand her off. Some people think it's a problem in the genes that makes a bitch do that, eat her little dogs, but I think she just wants the protein back. It's a terrible loss of protein, dropping a brood."

"Listen, Mr. Inchcape," Goody said. "I wanted to talk to you about what happened. Over at my house."

"Your house," Inchcape said. He had a moth-eaten grin on his face, and his gaze was unfocused. "The house you rent from me." His wandering eyes seemed to fix temporarily on Goody's face, the features of which were square and even but for a couple of fight scars: a shiny pink line down one cheek and a knot on the bridge of his sharp nose.

"That's right," Goody said. "There was a dead person over there."

Inchcape started, and his eyes went wide. "I know all about it," he said.

"You do?"

"Sure I do," Inchcape said. He laced his hands together in front of him and leaned his head against the frayed antimacassar that lay across the back of the couch. "That place has always had a bad air."

"That's pretty much cleared up, the stink," Goody said. "Since they took the body away."

"Did you know I used to live in that house?"

"I never did," Goody said.

"Well, I lived there. But I couldn't stand it after a while. Nobody that's rented that house has been able to take it for long. They all leave after a while. I knew you'd leave too, come your time."

"I don't plan to leave," Goody said. "I just want to know about the dead guy."

"It's a haunted house," Inchcape said.

Goody paused before replying, unsure whether he was being ribbed. "I wouldn't know about haunted or anything. It's just a man has died. I found him in the sugarcane."

"The fellow that built the house killed his wife," Inchcape said. "Beat her to death with a ballpeen hammer. I bought the whole place off him when he knew he was going to the pen for life. Got it for a song. But I couldn't live in that house, so I built this one." He shrugged dismissively. "Ran out of money about in the middle. So you got a nicer house, but I wouldn't live there. You got insulation against the winter. High ceilings."

"I like the house fine, Mr. Inchcape," Goody said. He leaned forward to see if he could catch the scent of liquor.

"You ever notice the patches of paint in the hallway, about so high?" Inchcape held up a hand to indicate the height he meant, four feet off the floor. "I rollered those on myself, when I first moved in. They cover the handprints where she pushed herself off the walls while he was chasing her. Hitting her in the back of the head with his hammer till the blood just flew. Making bloody handprints. I never could get the paint to match just right, so I give it up after a couple tries." Inchcape looked up at him. His eyes narrowed, became pinpoints of concentration. "You'll move. Everybody does," he said.

"I don't want to move." Goody felt a little desperate. The air was close in Mr. Inchcape's house, and growing hotter with the advancing hour. "I like it there."

"She went screaming down the hallway, him following swinging that hammer like John Henry, and as she went out into the yard she hit the screen door and took it right off its hinges. She was still running, but it was just her feet by that time. The rest of her was dead. The sheriff and his people carried her body away on that loose screen door like it was a stretcher. I never put a new one on."

Goody said nothing.

"Her husband took the hammer after he was done with it and put it back in the toolbox with his saw and all his screwdrivers and his socket wrenches. I come across it there myself. He went to take a shower. Didn't even clean off the hammer head." Inchcape took a deep breath. "When I rinsed the bathmat, it come out all blood. That was after she'd been dead I don't know how long." He belched.

"Are you all right, Mr. Inchcape?" Goody asked.

"One night while I was living there I woke up and a woman was standing over my bed looking at me. I thought maybe it was a blond-headed woman I knew from town that used to come see me, but this one had dark hair that hung over her shoulders and down her back. I knew that hair when I saw it. I had cleaned it off of that guy's hammer."

"That'll wake a person up," Goody said.

"She just stood there and looked at me with these sad eyes, and she was as real in the room as you setting right where you are." Mr. Inchcape pointed a finger in Goody's direction. "I got out of bed and I marched over here to the far side of the farm and set down the footers for the foundation of this house. Poured it the next day."

"But I didn't see any woman," Goody said.

"I don't tell tenants about the history of the place, but they find it out for themselves in the end. They've all got some complaint about creeping spirits. Television turns on and off by itself. Drawers open and invisible hands pull the clothes out, rumple the linens, clatter the silverware. That kind of a thing won't go away," Inchcape said. He shook his head.

"Why don't you lie down on the couch a minute," Goody said.

"So it don't surprise me to see you here," Inchcape said. He looked at Goody again, but the unnerving brightness had gone from his eyes. "I'm hypoglycemic, you know," he said. "But I got a terrible sweet tooth." He gestured at a drift of candy wrappers that lay on and under the coffee table: Mounds bars, Mars bars, Zagnut, all mixed together. A number of unopened chocolates lay among the crumpled papers. "I guess I made myself sick."

Goody stood and took the old man under the arm. The flesh was loose on his bones. Goody tugged at him to get him to stand. "You need to see somebody," he said. "You need to see a doctor."

"No," Inchcape said, resisting. "I just need to set a while. It'll pass."

Goody sat again. "If it's how you want it," he said, "there's nothing that I can make you do. Me, I'd want a doctor. Can I get you something? Glass of water?"

"No," Inchcape said. "There's not a thing I want at this point." He smiled mischievously. "Unless it's another piece of candy. But I guess I better not have one."

"No," Goody said. "I guess you better not."

He could see the porch through a window. Tonto occupied the same place on the warped boards. The dog raised his head, snapping at an insect that was buzzing him. His gargantuan mouth yawned open, revealing a set of glistening teeth. The jaws came together with a sharp click and, having missed the bug, swung swiftly open again. A bright shivering string of saliva connected upper mandible to lower. Tonto darted his head forward with startling speed, clapped his mouth shut on the insect, and swallowed. He shuddered and subsided, falling swiftly into a deep sleep that was to all appearances undisturbed by dreams.

"So what's this about a man in the cane?" Inchcape asked. He was blinking rapidly and he looked as though he might go to sleep himself, reclining on his couch. "You keep talking about a dead man, but you don't say what it is that you need."

Goody followed the farm road back toward his house, walking slowly. The rough trail wound its way along humped ridges and over untended meadows, through cornfields where the parched stands rustled and past wooded lots where locusts whirred in the heat. Goody knew that the bandsaw sound was just a prelude to what would come when their full season arrived. Already the sparrows and starlings sat somnolent in the trees, stuffed to bursting with the life that came boiling up out of the ground. Empty amber-colored cicada shells clung everywhere to tree trunks, fence posts, the board sides of barns and outbuildings.

In one thistle-choked paddock, a small group of cattle stood behind their collapsing fence and regarded Goody as he went by. They were a motley bunch, a few young Holstein heifers and some older beef steers with ragged, patchy hides. The pastured cattle hung their long heads over the top fence wire, their dished ears twitching to keep the flies away. Undeterred, the flies lighted on their faces, patrolled their noses, drank at the deep wells of their eyes. At some signal invisible to Goody, the cattle wheeled and moved off into the shade of a grove of elms, the heifers kicking their heels and nipping at one another, the whiteface steers drifting behind at a more sedate pace.

The road led around a bend and along the shoulder of a hill, following the route of a slow brackish creek. Tree branches, fallen from the modest willows and dogwoods that leaned out from the creek sides, swirled in the moving water, catching against one another and against the cattails and thin reeds that sprouted along the shores of slick red clay. Nimble water bugs skipped over the surface, darting from ripple to ripple, their small feet dimpling the skin of the water but not rupturing it. The stream was something of a curiosity, because most of the watercourses on the farm were dry or had been reduced by drought to slow trickles between banks of cracked, dried mud. This one flowed from the base of a shale bluff in the middle of the place, pouring undiminished from a narrow slot in the face of the rock.

Goody reasoned that the stream was one paltry tributary of a mighty underground river. It rushed through the network of limestone caves that underlay the farm and the entire county, coming near the surface here and spawning the creek. The river must be fed from a subterranean lake brimming in its domed basin, hidden in a vast cavern under the ridge of mountains to the east. And while the black lake continued full, the stream remained constant. But how was the lake itself fed? He could frame no answer.

When he drew abreast of the bluff from which the creek sprang, he thrashed his way through the thick growth around the headwaters. One of his feet slipped, and his leg plunged to mid-calf in the stream. His boot filled immediately with water; the saturated sock hung heavy around his ankle. His skin tingled where the frigid water parted to pass it. Water splashed from the gray rock surface as if from the spigot of a bath. Ignoring the muck that clung to his pants, he leaned forward and held first his face and next his hands against the spray. He scrubbed his hands together under the clear tide and then made a bowl of them. The vessel of his palms filled quickly, and he tilted his hands to his mouth and drank. The water was bitterly cold, and it grieved his teeth and gums. He raised his hands again, and a third time, and flicked the remaining droplets from his fingers.

He drew back from the streambed and watched the water pour out of the hillside. He considered putting his hand to the hole in the shale, putting his hand through the hole. It seemed wide enough to admit his fist, perhaps even his arm up to the shoulder, and he wondered what it would be like to explore with his fingers the place beyond the rock face, always dark except for the single weak shaft of sunlight blurred and filtered by running water. The light must not reach far into the hillside even on a very bright day. Would the walls of the pipe be rough, he wondered, or slick with calcite?

He knew that his hand would grow numb from the cold before long, and that the pressure would build against the arm and shoulder that stanched the current until it might push him out, like a cork popped from a bottle. He knew that afterward, even when they had grown warm again, the small, often broken, poorly mended bones of his fingers would pain him. In the end, it did not seem wise to him, sending his hand in like that to investigate a place that he himself could never see. Before long he rose and went back to the road.

Abruptly, the road ended. It came to a halt at the edge of a deep sinkhole in the center of an unplanted field. Goody was surprised to find himself at the sinkhole, which he had not seen before. He supposed that he had taken a wrong turn somewhere farther back, that he had missed the mouth of the dry wash somehow. To the west, a helicopter rose into the sky. Light flashed from the whirling blades of its rotor. The sun spilled over its various closely fitted parts: steel, plastic, glass. It looked like an insect. It proceeded northward, and Goody watched it, because air traffic was uncommon in the valley, and he was a man who enjoyed watching aircraft. He wondered what it was up to. Crop-dusting, maybe. The chopper soon vanished over a high breastwork of hills.

He turned back to the sinkhole before him. It was funnel-shaped, a hundred and fifty feet across its top, narrowing at the bottom, where the earth had collapsed into the caves below. The cavity was filled with greenery, jumbled thornbushes and shrubs and vines covered in lurid trumpet-shaped flowers, with here and there a stunted tree pushing its way up from the incline. Garbage lay scattered around the rim of the sinkhole, and down its sides: bundles of old newspapers, oil cans, plastic buckets with split sides, power mowers, discarded washing machines, refrigerators, a stove or two. At the very bottom of the pit, what looked like the bullet-holed trunk of an antique black Ford coupe poked out of the greenery.

A few yards below where he stood, on the near side of the slope, something the color of old ivory hung from the low branches of an oak sapling. Goody peered closely at it. It was a pelvis, the wide pelvis of a cow. He wondered how it had gotten into the branches of a tree, then decided that the oak had grown up beneath an old skeleton and that the bone had been taken up that way. The pelvis might, he thought, eventually wind up sixty or seventy feet in the air, to provide a puzzle, and perhaps shelter, for nesting birds.

Beneath the pelvis, shadowed by spreading burdock, lay a long jaw. Not far from that was a club-shaped bone, a leg bone. Now that he was looking for them, Goody saw bones everywhere, peeking out from the undergrowth, obscured by long grass and the reddish stalks of pokeweed, camouflaged by the enamel of old sinks and wrecked appliances. The bones thrust their rounded crumbling ends from the loose dirt. This was the pit, he reasoned, that the farm used to dispose of its dead cattle.

Here was a long segmented spinal column with the rib bones gone, a fossil anaconda winding among the brush; there a pair of melting hooves and a broken skull, through the eye sockets of which rose the hairy delicate stems and white wheels of Queen Anne's lace. Half of a rib cage, standing in the earth like the palings of a whited barricade, was draped with creeper. Sometimes the bones were single, and sometimes they formed whole limbs, or nearly whole, and sometimes they made sensible groups. Sometimes they were set in piles, tumbled cairns of yellowing skulls and horns and unknown parts, as though children had come here and played with them and stacked them for a game.

Some of the bones were clean, and others were matted with papery skin and roped with cured tendons that were like short cords of wicker. One of the skeletons lurked at the far edge of the pit, just under the rim, as though it had tried to creep away from the ossuary but had failed. It was atrophied and mummified so that it looked like an animal totem made out of some barbaric fabric stretched tight over a fragile framework of balsa wood. The tiny once-flexible bones of stillborn calves littered the earth. The foliage and the rubbish covered many of the skeletons but could not hide them all.

The smell that had driven Goody from his house was strong here.

It was not sharp, as it had been in the canebrake. It had soaked into the ground. He uprooted a handful of bright chicory and held the plants to his face, but the tiny blue flowers did not smell of chicory, and the feel of them in his hand repelled him. He pitched them down and walked stiffly across the field. He didn't look back at the pit but instead kept his eyes intent on the narrow farm road ahead, looking for the fork in the path that would lead him to the dry wash and home again.

3

The bright yellow Ryder truck was parked alone in the middle of a blazing, trackless alkali waste. The vehicle hunkered low on its rear axle, shock absorbers sagging under the too-heavy load in the van body. The engine putt-putted quietly to itself, and pale fingers of exhaust crept from the tailpipe. Dull crystals of salt clung to the grille and the front bumper and rimed the tires. A thick layer of the stuff filmed the windshield, clouding the glass into opacity. The windshield wipers flicked to life, thrashing at the salt deposits. There was no washer fluid in the reservoir, and the pump whined dryly on until it failed.

The door on the driver's side of the cab opened, and the driver stepped out of the truck. The white crust of salt on the earth crunched noisily under the thin soles of his elegant leather shoes. He stood peering around him, scanning the horizon, where the vault of heaven met the rim of the vast tectonic basin in which he alone moved. The sky was a faultless blue, as empty of life as the poisoned ground.

The other door opened a moment later, and the rental truck's passenger emerged. Though shorter and stockier, he bore a strong resemblance to the driver: same angular facial features; same narrow, sloping shoulders; same sallow, vaguely unhealthy complexion. Both men were foolishly dressed for the climate, in dark suits of some glossy expensive material. They wore thin ties, though the passenger had loosened his for comfort and the small knot of it hung well below his shirt collar.

"Well?" the passenger said. The driver ignored him, continuing his scan. "Nothing," the passenger said and climbed into the truck again.

"Not yet," the driver said. He too slipped back into the cab, where the rattling air conditioner was fighting a losing battle against the all-consuming heat of the day. They sat side by side on the truck's sticky vinyl bench seat, staring out through the shimmering haze that covered the land, the light painful to their sensitive eyes despite their identical Ray-Ban sunglasses.

After a while the passenger said, "We could die out here. Errand boys for this— What is his name?"

"Tannhauser." After a moment's consideration, the driver said, "Possibly."

"We don't have enough gasoline to return."

"They'll come."

A few minutes passed.

"Perhaps we should leave. Turn around and take the merchandise back."

"The gas. Not enough to return, as you just said."

A few minutes more.

"Are we in the right place? They might be elsewhere. Looking for us while we wait here."

"This is near enough. They'll find us."

And more.

"My God." Said in a tone of despair. The passenger licked his lips, but his tongue was dry and dragged painfully over the cracked skin.

"There." The driver jabbed a finger at the windshield. The passenger peered at the section of sky thus indicated but saw nothing. Just more of the empty depthless blue.

"Nothing there," the passenger said, throwing himself back against the seat in an attitude of resignation. The driver was already out of the truck, striding across the flat, his eyes shaded by his hand. Reluctantly, the passenger emerged to follow. Waves of heat warped the receding figure of the driver, making it seem as though just his coat flapped along, legless, headless, suspended a few feet off the ground, like some awkward carrion bird struggling to lift its bulk into the air.

"Come back," the passenger called, but it seemed to him that his voice lacked force, that it failed to carry for any appreciable distance in the desert atmosphere. His mouth was devoid of spit, and his head pounded.

Then, hanging above the dancing, indefinite figure of the driver: something, an illusion, surely, one of the famed mirages of this dangerous place. A flyspeck, a fly, an insect in a locale where there were no insects. The dark spot grew larger second by second, the distant throaty rumble of twin engines becoming audible to his straining ears. Pencil-shaped now, wavering but distinctly *present,* approaching head-on with amazing rapidity.

And it was there, directly overhead, only a couple of hundred feet off the ground, the lumbering airplane with its wide wings and cumbersome radial engines. Painted on the blunt nose, he saw, was the cartoon figure of a leering slat-sided wolf, slick tongue lolling from its gaping mouth; a svelte nude in silhouette, on whom the wolf's gaze was fixed; and the legend *Domini Canes:* the dogs of God. He had his suit coat off without knowing that he had removed it and was waving it frantically back and forth in amateur semaphore, shouting hoarsely. The plane passed between the sun and the man, and in its brief eclipse he felt something like the coolness of the stratosphere sweep over him. Then it roared past, leaving behind it the sharp distinctive smell of burned aviation fuel, and he stood exposed again in the harsh light.

His first thoughts were that the plane would not land, that having buzzed them it would roar on into the distance and leave them stranded there in the waterless crater. The driver was beside him now, breathless, excited, coatless as well. The pistol that he wore in a black nylon shoulder holster rested heavily against his ribs. "There," he said triumphantly. "There there there." The plane banked, the sun heliographing wildly off the lines of rivet-heads along its wings and fuselage. As it came around, its landing gear unfolded with magisterial slowness from beneath its wings.

It lit hard, bouncing a few times as it lost speed, throwing salt up against its belly in great chattering sprays. As the plane bounced along, it looked a couple of times as though it might take to the air again, pilot unable to keep it earthbound; but it did not. At last it settled to the ground and taxied over to the two men and the waiting truck.

"What kind of plane is that?" the passenger asked.

"I don't know," the driver said. He slipped his jacket back on, covering the holstered pistol, and the passenger did the same. "An old one."

It was in fact a Douglas DC-3 of 1930s vintage. It sat facing the pair, its engines at low throttle, propellers still turning, their silver disks throwing up small clouds of grit. In the cockpit, high above them, someone in a peaked cap waved a hand and rose from his seat, preparatory to leaving the plane and meeting his latest customers.

"Don't you worry about the Can," the pilot said. He was a young man dressed in navy blue shorts and an Atlanta Braves T-shirt. He had tucked his peaked cap, with its visor full of gold braid, under his arm. His copilot stood behind him, eyeing the men and their truck with a sardonic smile on his broad sweaty features.

"The Dakota is just about the best plane ever built," the pilot said. "She lands pretty stiff, but in the air she handles like a honey. Very forgiving. Carries a big load and takes a lot of punishment."

"It's only that," the driver said, smiling apologetically, "we were expecting something, well, newer. A bit more modern. We have many hundreds of miles to travel today. A continent to cross."

"A jet, maybe," the copilot said. "You thought a jumbo jet was going to drop down onto the salt flats and cart you and your precious cargo away."

"Perhaps," the driver said, pressing his lips together. The passenger made a noise in his throat, almost a growl.

The pilot appeared not to have heard the exchange. "In fact this plane—the Can, the very one behind me here—carried Queen Wilhelmina back to Norway when it was liberated from the Nazis in World War Two. So it's got what you might call a royal lineage."

"The Netherlands," the passenger said.

"What?"

"Wilhelmina was queen of the Netherlands."

The pilot looked perplexed.

"Never mind," the driver said. "If this is the plane, then this is the plane." He extended a hand to the pilot, who shook it. "We will introduce ourselves. I am Bodo." He gestured toward the passenger, who made a brief nod but did not offer his hand. "And that is Toma."

"Pretty funny," the copilot said. "Klaatu barada nikto."

Bodo inclined his head. "Pardon?" he said.

"Never mind him," the pilot said. "We weren't aware that we were going to use code names."

"Code names?" Bodo said.

At the same time, beaming, the copilot said, "Please call me Fubar. And that guy's name is Snafu, over there." The pilot laughed, looking a little embarrassed.

With every appearance of courtly seriousness, Bodo greeted them, bowing slightly from the waist as he did. "Hello, Fubar," he said to the copilot. To the pilot he said, "Hello, Snafu." The two of them dissolved in gales of laughter.

When they had finished, the pilot addressed the unsmiling Bodo. "So you're the boss of this outfit," he said.

"Yes," Bodo said. "I'm the boss." He looked at his companion, as though searching for a properly descriptive phrase. "Toma is my gunsel. My sidekick, as you might say."

"Okay," the pilot said. He took his cap, slightly crushed now, from his armpit and replaced it at a jaunty angle on his head. "Let's get to work loading this stuff on the Can." He gestured at the copilot, who followed him to the truck. They rolled the rear door up and regarded the wall of packing crates stacked within. The copilot positioned the loading ramp and located the truck's handcart. When Bodo and Toma stayed where they were, the pilot looked at them inquiringly. "You coming?" he asked.

"Oh no," Bodo said, holding up his hands in a gesture of helplessness. "We do not tote."

The pilot's mouth worked soundlessly for a moment. Then he found his voice. "There must be tons of stuff here!" he said.

"That's right," Toma said, speaking to him for the first time. Satisfaction was written on the features of his narrow face. "Tons."

While the loading proceeded, Bodo and Toma sat in the cab of the truck, sometimes watching the fliers as they struggled back and forth between truck and plane, sometimes just looking straight ahead, out over the featureless plain. As the copilot wheeled the last of the crates to the waiting Dakota, the pilot came to the closed window of the truck cab and rapped on it with his knuckles. He carried a yard-long green plastic tube under his arm. It looked like a section of PVC pipe, capped at both ends. When Bodo had rolled down the window glass, the pilot said, "I believe we've got it." He hefted the tube in his hands. "This here's the last." Sweat stained his shirt under his arms and in a wide streak down his back. It matted his hair.

"Very good," Bodo said. He motioned to Toma, and the two of them dismounted from the truck. Bodo took a slim gunmetal attaché case with him.

"Lot of cargo," the pilot said.

"Yes," Bodo said.

"It's a heavy load." The pilot examined the sagging suspension of the rental truck with a critical eye. It had not returned to the true. "I think it may of ruined your vehicle there," he said.

"No problem," Bodo said.

"Exactly," Toma said. In a smooth, practiced movement, he brushed back the lapel of his costly jacket with his right hand, swiftly extracted a gleaming Beretta pistol from a horizontal armpit holster with his left. He leveled the pistol without seeming to aim and emptied it into the truck. The nine-millimeter cartridges made a flat *crack crack crack*, report following report in the windless air. The Beretta seemed barely to move in Toma's hand. Spent casings jumped and spun away from the pistol, flashing sunlight from their small burnished cylinders, scattering in a wide semicircle around Toma's feet.

The truck's windshield fractured, tumbling inward, spilling into the cab; chunks of plastic molding jumped off the grille; the long driver's mirror shattered and tilted sharply downward, dangling askew from the truck's side. When he had finished his display, Toma ejected the used clip from the Beretta and replaced it with a fresh one that he retrieved from his pocket. The truck settled deeply onto its punctured front tires. A dark foaming pool formed beneath the truck: greenish radiator coolant, acid from the cracked battery, blood-colored transmission fluid, oil draining from the ruptured crankcase. The thirsty ground sucked the liquid down, leaving behind only an oval discoloration on its surface.

The copilot stared at them from the open cargo door of the Dakota. The pilot gave out a low whistle. "Some shooting," he said.

"It is simple," Bodo said, looking disapprovingly at Toma, "to shoot to death an automobile."

Toma laughed easily. He returned the pistol to its holster and buttoned his tailored jacket, patting at his sides to smooth away the bulge under his arm. He laid the palm of his hand softly against Bodo's cheek, crossed to the Dakota, and accepted the copilot's out-stretched arm. As the copilot helped him into the cargo section of the plane, Toma leaned close to him and said in clear, even tones, "You I will gladly kill."

The copilot looked from Toma to the bullet-riddled truck and back again. "Come again?" he said.

Toma sniffed, already moving toward the forward bulkhead, where seats had been prepared for him and for Bodo. "You understood me," he said. "I spoke perfectly plainly."

The pilot watched the copilot help Toma aboard, and then he turned back to Bodo, the green tube caught in the crook of his arm. "I believe I know what this here is," he said.

"Of course you do. An idiot could tell. It's an antitank weapon. What is referred to as, I believe, a LAW."

"Rocket launcher," the pilot said, his voice edged with awe. "Heavy shit. What are you doing with it?"

"It's a gift," Bodo said. "For a friend."

The pilot nodded. "Sure," he said. "And the rest of this. All gifts too, I bet. What's in these other crates here?" He and Bodo began to walk toward the plane.

"You've heard, I imagine," Bodo said slowly, "of the need-to-know doctrine of the Central Intelligence Agency?"

Again the pilot nodded confirmation. "I've worked for that bunch of spooks from time to time. Running weapons and personnel down to Cuba, Central America, that sort of thing. Don't tell me you guys are CIA."

Bodo smiled. "That," he said, "is one of the many things that you do not need to know."

Bodo and Toma sat belted tightly into their seats just behind the open door of the cockpit. The pilot turned and gave them the thumbs-up, his face smooth and boyish under the oversize braided cap. "Hope she'll fly," he called to them over the roar of the engines. "If we were carrying any more fuel, no way we'd get into the air." He turned to the front and ran the paired throttles to their maximum. The Dakota quivered like a racehorse and then surged forward as the pilot let off the brakes.

"What did he say?" Toma asked Bodo.

"Here we go," Bodo told Toma, almost joyfully. He took a cigarette for himself and offered the pack to Toma, who refused with a grimace. Bodo lit the cigarette, holding the flame of his silver Ronson lighter with some difficulty against its end as the plane thundered across the salt pan.

The plane caught the air finally and began to rise: half a wingspan off the earth, a full span; then it stopped ascending. Clearly unnerved that they weren't gaining altitude, Toma unfastened his seat belt and stood. Bodo put a restraining hand on him, but Toma shook it off and entered the cockpit. "What are you doing?" he shouted. The ground passed by beneath them with sickening speed, so close, too close. Toma glanced at the instrument panel, and his gaze fell on the altimeter, the hands of which hung trembling at just under one hundred feet. The plane faltered and he stumbled, steadying himself against the back of the copilot's seat. His fingers feathered the grip of the Beretta.

"Big load," the copilot said. "Hot day." His words came out in a rush. His face was white with strain, though whether it was something wrong with the plane or the threat of the pistol that frightened him Toma did not know. "Takes a while to climb out of ground effect." The pilot was hunched over the control yoke and did not bother to look around.

As if to prove the copilot right, the plane began to gain altitude. "See," he said, gesturing at the altimeter, which clocked their rapid ascent. "See there," he said, and Toma saw that the ground was falling swiftly away. Grumbling, he returned to his seat.

As he buckled himself in, Bodo touched him on the shoulder. "Let them fly the plane," he said. "You don't know how to fly a plane."

"Bucket of bolts," Toma said. "Bucket of shit." He palmed cool sweat off his forehead.

Bodo sat back in his seat, smiling serenely, listening to the steady turning of the Dakota's props and the rushing of the wind past the hull. He was pleased that the plane possessed a figurehead: the woman who had been airbrushed onto the prow. *Like the sailing ships of old*, he thought to himself approvingly. He closed his eyes, the cigarette dangling from the corner of his mouth. In a minute, he felt Toma's hands steal across the front of his jacket with the light tread of a scorpion, felt a finger and thumb fish in the breast pocket of his shirt. Furtive as the digits of a pickpocket, they withdrew the pack of cigarettes stashed there. Darting a hand upward, he caught Toma's wrist in his own strong grip. Toma gave a grunt of brief fury at being checked. "I thought you were asleep," he said.

"And I thought you didn't want one of these," Bodo said. He plucked the cigarette pack from Toma's unresisting fingers, replaced it in his pocket. Then he removed the half-smoked cigarette from his own mouth and placed it between Toma's pursed lips. He laughed at the expression of surprise on Toma's face, patted his breast where the pack of cigarettes rested, and closed his eyes, reclining once more into daydreams of long windy days spent before the mast.

4

Carmichael, the man from the Drug Enforcement Agency, forced himself to relax. He took a series of deep breaths, loosened his grip on the edges of his seat, and flexed his fingers to work the blood back into them. The topmost branches of the trees below whipped past with disorienting speed, the tallest threatening to slap against the hull of the little Defender airship, pull it from the sky, dash it to pieces on the hard-packed earth below. The vehicle rose abruptly, and then made a sickening nose-down descent as it crossed a wooded ridge, following the profile of the land. It was Carmichael's first ride through mountain country in a helicopter.

The voice of Loomis, the chopper pilot, came to him over the intercom, earsplittingly loud in his headphones. "Where we are now," Loomis said, "is known as the Dead Man Zone." Loomis's voice was almost mechanical, without noticeable accent or inflection. Mingled as it was with the slight static of the intercom line, it might have been the unemotional machine voice of the helicopter itself, Carmichael thought.

"What do you mean?" Carmichael said. He spoke carefully into the boom microphone that hung scant centimeters in front of his face, like a morsel of food out there just waiting for him to lip it into his mouth. He tried not to let the nausea that he felt, and the thin edge of terror that accompanied it, creep into his tone. He gestured before them, past the wide plexiglass windscreen at the green winding valley that unfolded beneath the Defender. The plastic of the canopy was scratched and milky in places, and the light of the setting sun caught and held in the abrasions, making orange pinwheels that obscured the horizon. "This here? This place?" Loomis was a native of the area, and he knew things that Carmichael wanted, even needed, to know.

"Not our map position," Loomis said, speaking in the slow, maddeningly deliberate way that he had. Carmichael wondered if Loomis considered him stupid or foolish, because he always talked to him in that punctilious, instructive manner. He wondered if Loomis was being deliberately patronizing. "What I mean by Dead Man Zone," Loomis said, continuing, "it's a function of our altitude and our velocity. Flying low and slow, your recovery rates in the event of engine failure—component loss, any kind of catastrophic equipment failure, really—are way down."

"A crash, you mean," Carmichael said.

"That's right," Loomis said. His tone did not at all reveal his attitude toward the eventuality; or perhaps it did: dispassion, pure nonpartisanship. "A crash."

Carmichael decided that to someone who spent a good part of his life like this, navigating winding ridges and heaped-up limestone ranges in search of contraband, suspended between earth and sky by the whirling disk of the helicopter's prop—to someone of that breed, the recognition of death might become a commonplace. Must become so. It was not a career for someone who overvalued his own hide. Carmichael was pleased to think that placed in dangerous circumstances (as he must be eventually, he reasoned, given the profession he'd chosen), he'd not fail to acquit himself honorably, nobly, even heroically. He was impressed with Loomis's professionalism and wondered if the lesson of it might be something he could take away from his assignment with the chopper pilot, his assignment to these mountains, where a stream shone like a silver thread at the bottom of nearly every obscure hollow.

"At this height, by the time you figure out what's wrong, you're already nothing but a big ball of flame on the ground." Loomis's eyes looked straight ahead through the clear lens of his helmet visor. His hands made slight continuous movements, as though he were restless in his seat, applying gentle pressure to the cyclic between his knees, the collective at his side; his feet massaged the torque pedals, urging the helicopter to follow in smooth rolling curves the harsh geography that revealed itself by degrees below them.

Carmichael wanted to tell him *Stop. Please just stop.* They reached the terminus of the stream they had been following and soared out over a broad stretch of river. A collection of shoals churned the fast water white. Finding that he was once again holding tight to the underside of his seat, Carmichael prized his fingers loose and laid his hands carefully in his lap. He listened to the constant gnashing of the main rotor overhead and to the whine of the powerful Allison turbine engine that kept it turning. He fixed his gaze on the ridge that they paralleled on their current course. Its rich foliage flickered by at a steady sixty knots, a dense mixture of hardwoods and evergreens, the underlying bracken thick and to his eyes totally undifferentiated. They were overflying one small corner of the national forest, which constituted about a fourth of the vast federal holdings in the state. The forest lay at the heart of the parcel of countryside that he was deputed to patrol.

"What exactly will they look like, these pot fields?" he asked. "From the air. I've seen pictures in the training literature, and videotape, but . . ." Carmichael let the trailing-off of his voice indicate the hopeless feeling with which he had regarded these photographic reproductions, unhelpful blurs of black and gray. He was nominally in charge of the operation, but the briefing he had received had been perfunctory and largely without substance.

"Any irregularity in the pattern of vegetation is what you're looking out for," Loomis said. "Likely it'll be nothing, or a homesteader's dahlias, or some old fellow culturing ginseng to keep his pecker shipshape. But sometimes—" Carmichael imagined that he heard something like wistfulness, or like anticipation, enter Loomis's tone, but dismissed the notion as fanciful. "Sometimes it's a buttload of contraband."

Prior to this assignment, Carmichael had briefly been stationed in Texas, patrolling the arid outback in a tan Ford Bronco, spending days at a time watching the brown sluggish flow of the Rio Grande. He had enjoyed jawing in the spirit of friendly rivalry with the stringy sunburned Rangers who worked the border down there, had enjoyed the enormity of the task of interdicting the flow of illegal drugs across the line from Mexico. An impossible job, but an important one apparently, given the effort and the funds expended on it. There, he had been part of an army, albeit a sprawling, poorly disciplined one. Here, as far as he could tell, it was just him. Him and Loomis, the Army pilot who had been hired by the agency to fly the helicopter. If he had enforcement needs, he had been instructed to contact the county sheriff's office for manpower. The high sheriff was a man named John Faktor; Carmichael had yet to meet him.

Marijuana's the chief cash crop up there, his superiors at DEA had told him before dispatching him to the mountains. Carmichael was not aware of any infraction he had committed, any offense, but still this assignment had the feeling of exile. *They're enjoying themselves too much, the yahoos, the growers, the new generation. Take some of the profit out of it. Some of the fun. Then we'll see about bringing you back to the big show along the Rio Bravo.*

The McDonnell-Douglas Defender had been a pleasant surprise: an agile four-seater helicopter configured for observation. "I flew a chopper pretty much like this model out of Danang," Loomis had said to him when they first met. "That version was named the Cayuse, but it was a hell of a lot like this whirlybird we have here." When Carmichael asked him what the unfamiliar word might mean, Loomis explained to him that a cayuse was a pony. A little Indian war pony. "But we called it a loach," he said. "Loach is a kind of a fish. Horse, fish. Strange, huh?" But his voice did not suggest that he thought it strange at all. He told Carmichael that he had flown psyops missions in Vietnam, flying hither and yon, wherever the enemy might be, a native speaker in the lefthand seat to shout propaganda messages into the helicopter's PA system. "Cac don vi chu y nghe," Loomis said. It was strange to hear the singsong stream of words coming from the normally taciturn chopper pilot. "Dau hong ngay tuc khac." When Carmichael said apologetically that once again he didn't know what the words meant, Loomis didn't offer to elucidate.

Usually DEA allocated to their agents helicopters that had been confiscated in drug raids, and Carmichael had been led to expect something clunkier, more elderly, something distinctively less rakish. To help keep him from getting his hopes up, one of his superiors at DEA had told him the story of an agent in the Florida Everglades who got assigned to an aging Army Iroquois air ambulance, early Vietnam War vintage. The big red medevac cross had still been painted on the side. According to legend, the pilot had been a balmy kid fresh out of flight school who blinked and stuttered and sang to himself as they roared along at head height over the marsh elders and swampy hummocks, and the crew chief had spent most of his time incommunicado in the cargo bay, his headphones and mike unplugged from the ICS, his sleeping form slung casually from the bulkhead in a mass of webbing, swinging loose-limbed, suspended. One day they had lifted from the helipad, turned the craft to the east as usual, and headed out, never to be heard from again. So Carmichael figured maybe he didn't have it so bad.

Now Carmichael and Loomis plied their way along the highlands, where the greenery-draped bluffs were shrouded in clinging mist morning and evening, mysterious to Carmichael, like some unfathomable optical illusion after the glaring plainness of the powdered-glass desert.

"Of course," Loomis said, "what gets most low-flying guys is wire strikes: running afoul of telephone lines, or electric." He laughed, a short bark so loud in the headphones that it made Carmichael wince. "But you don't have to worry about that kind of thing in most of these hills where we're looking. If a man doesn't have his own generator up here, he just sits in the dark and waits for the sun to come around again."

Carmichael longed to free his head from the bulky Buck Rogers helmet that bit pitilessly into his skull. There was sweat running from his temples and into his ears, and no possibility of getting at it to wipe it away.

Ahead of them on the flat expanse of river water, a rowboat drifted, anchorless, in the current. It bounded through a set of mild rapids and swapped ends gently, passing into calm water as they approached. Loomis pressed down on the collective, and the helicopter dipped toward the surface of the water. They were maybe a dozen feet off the deck, the wash from the main rotor whipping the river into a froth. The boat lay directly in their path, oars loose in the rowlocks and trailing in the water. As they bore down on it, a man sat up in the stern. Carmichael, thinking that the copter would decapitate the boatman, squeezed his eyes shut.

When he looked again, the boat lay in their wake. He craned his head around, thought he could make out the face of the man in the boat, eyes wide, mouth a taut O of surprise. He and his skiff swiftly vanished into the distance. Some poor damn fisherman, out for a quiet evening on the water.

"I believe that fellow's catch was over the legal limit," Loomis said, and though he listened for it Carmichael heard no hint of amusement in the stolid pilot's voice. "You want I should double back so we can pick him up?"

"What if he talks about that?" Carmichael said. "To his friends and family. To the media?" He masked his outrage at Loomis as best he could but was unable to conceal it entirely. "He's bound to, you know. You just advertised the fact that we're in the area and on the prod."

"People aren't like that up here," Loomis said. "He may tell his wife if he has one, but never a newspaper. Won't occur to him." He spaced his words evenly, and there was nothing in them of apology or placation. "No way he could know we're DEA, anyhow. No markings."

"Who else could we be?" Carmichael could feel his anger waning in the face of Loomis's imperturbability. "Who else runs helicopters in these parts?"

"Lots of folks," Loomis said. "Crop-dusters. Power company's got a seven-hundred-sixty-five-kilovolt transmission line that runs across the county not far from here, and they spray herbicides from choppers. Gas company checks their pipelines for leaks that way. Coal company birds here and there too."

Perhaps, Carmichael thought, Loomis spoke in the calculated way he did because of his injury, the true nature of which was not entirely clear to Carmichael. The pilot was pretty well concealed in his flight suit and heavy helmet, but it was obvious that Loomis had been badly wracked up at some point. The features of his countenance were a queerly asymmetrical jumble below the glossy eggshell armor of the helmet, at odds with one another as though the whole had been clumsily pieced together out of elements of other people's faces. The fine tentacles of a burn scar ascended from the collar of his nylon jumpsuit and climbed his muscular neck to his jaw. There was something unusual about the way Loomis smelled, too. Not malodorous, but distinctly mechanical, as though his skin had been impregnated with gasoline or maybe JP-4, jet fuel.

"Listen," Loomis said. "I'm sorry if I scared you back there. It's just I like to check out the reflexes sometimes."

"Yours?" Carmichael wanted to know. "Or the people on the ground."

"Both, I guess."

"We're supposed to go quietly," Carmichael reminded him.

"I'm a little tired of all this hedge-hopping we're doing. You want to take it up?" Loomis said. He maneuvered them around a tight bend in the river. "So you can see what this place looks like from a high vantage?"

"Mission parameters say we go nap of the earth," Carmichael told him. "NOE means we follow the natural contours of the landscape, as low as possible to avoid detection. Strictly sneak and peek, with no strobes, no anticollision lights. Complete radio silence."

"Detection?" Finally, a hint of exasperation in Loomis's voice. "By who? The hippies? The toking greengrocers?"

Carmichael shook his head. "Can't say. Latest intelligence at DEA has it the hippies around here got pushed out a little while ago. It's supposed to be hard guys up this way now. Mantraps in the woods. Dogs. Electric fence around the pot fields. Machine guns. I can't swear to you there isn't a Stinger missile or two lying around in there somewhere, come to that."

"Antiaircraft stuff. No," Loomis said. "I don't believe even the Mex—the really bad ones—have got that kind of heat. Maybe the Colombians. Maybe."

"I shit you not," Carmichael said. "The name DEA's got is Tannhauser. We hear he's a crazy man, real bad news. It's a whole new faction we're dealing with at present. New days, new ways."

Loomis considered. "You'll like it better up there in the sky. Not so claustrophobic."

The helicopter slowed its forward motion but did not rise. They hung over the river.

"Listen," Loomis said. "If there's no way to know we're DEA—that's what I'm telling you, and you can trust me on that point—why should anybody shoot at us?"

After a minute, Carmichael shrugged his acquiescence. "Take it up if you want," he said.

Loomis pulled up hard on the collective. The blades on the main rotor head bit savagely into the air, and Carmichael was forced back in his seat as the helicopter ascended. It shot upward like an express elevator. Loomis slowed the precipitous rate of their rise, and it was like riding in a soap bubble, something out of a pleasant but unsettling dream. Carmichael marveled at the way the golden evening light filled the air as they climbed free of the enclosing walls of the river valley. The shadow of the surrounding mountains already lay long in the depression, but up here—up here in the open sky it was day for a little while longer.

The helicopter gave a slight shudder as it passed through a thin, almost transparent layer of cloud. Its tear-shaped fuselage pendulumed under the rotor system. A few valleys at first, then a dozen, were revealed to Carmichael's gaze, in configurations that mimicked the river's route; and finally a hundred, hundreds. Roads, some darkly paved, others lustrous with salmon-colored dust, ran here and there among the hills, following the bottomland, rising oftentimes in lazy roaming switchbacks to the heights, where they lapsed and ended, futile among the vegetation.

"I rode in a hot-air balloon once," Carmichael said. "It was a lot like this. Hanging underneath something that was pulling you upward with it. A peculiar feeling." Loomis made no reply.

The land spread wide below them, mountains growing smaller and smaller: now the size of the green-gray barnacled backs of a school of whales riding companionably side by side; now waves lapping at the edge of the beach; now the crests of horny plate along an alligator's back; now the folds in the flesh of a man's hand. From altitude, the look of the land was uniform, minor patterns repeated and repeated until they became one large tapestry; order generating from chaos, ridge lines marching off into the distance, to the hazy curved rim of the earth.

"How high can we go?" Carmichael asked.

"High as you want," came the answer.

"This is fine," Carmichael said, and the helicopter ceased to climb. Even in a hover, Loomis's hands and feet shifted uneasily, responding to the arcane physics of air currents and thrust and gravity, flicking this way and that on the controls in a ballet of equilibrium too complex and too subtle for Carmichael to follow.

"Is this hard?" Carmichael asked.

"What?"

"This," he said. "Keeping us hovering."

"Like balancing a marble on top of a beach ball," Loomis said. "But you get used to it after you do it a while." He glanced down, casting his gaze around them. "You see a smoke trail, you sing out," he said.

"A smoke trail?"

"Smoke trail means incoming missile. You see a missile that's got us locked in, that's when I'll get excited."

"I'd like to see that," Carmichael said, half to himself.

"Yeah," Loomis said. "So would a lot of folks."

Carmichael continued to examine the expanse of the land below them, keeping half an eye out for Loomis's smoke trail. To the north, some light-colored things among the greenery caught his attention. As he examined the objects, they resolved themselves into a system of regular planes and perfect perpendicularities, a series of variously sized cubes that were strange to see in the jumbled landscape. He tried to gauge the size of the largest of the structures and came to the conclusion that because its features were visible to the naked eye from such a height and at such a distance, it was huge.

He reached out and tapped Loomis on the upper arm. He had to touch him twice to get his attention. "What's that out there?" he asked, indicating the buildings (for buildings they had to be; what else?) that he had seen.

Loomis barely had to look before he answered. "Little Hogback Mountain," he said, and returned to his job of keeping the chopper stable. "That's El Dorado."

Carmichael waited for Loomis to expand on that. At length, sensing the expectation on Carmichael's part, he said, "It was a big resort hotel a while back. Ran out of money and closed down in the sixties, and the dope farmers moved in not long after."

"Maybe we should check it out."

"Sure," Loomis said. "Swoop down there and give them a shout on the loudhailer. Throw the spotlight on them. Shake them up a little."

"Or maybe we should coordinate with the sheriff's office. See if there's anybody there and if they're cultivating. Set up some kind of a raid."

"Could be your hard guys you were talking about, I guess," Loomis said. "Good idea, in that case."

"Okay. We'll take it slow for a while. Get all our ducks in a row."

To the west, the last thin rind of the sun sank below the horizon, leaving in its wake a riot of colors. Those too soon began to fade. The meridian that demarcated the boundary between light and dark slipped swiftly away from them.

"Let's take it back to the barn," Carmichael said. "Call it a day.

We've been up here long enough to say we did our duty. We'll try a little night flying tomorrow, I think."

"Fine by me," Loomis said. "Daytime or night, I'm your man." He banked the helicopter, beginning their descent, wheeling through the night. Carmichael felt the acceleration in the pit of his belly but found that with the ground distant below and masked by darkness, the sensation was more exciting than it was frightening.

"You know what you ought to do, you DEA guys," Loomis said, "if you really want to clear out the dope?" His voice softened perceptibly, and Carmichael had to strain to hear it through his headphones, backed and almost overcome as it was by the thumping of the rotor blades. He listened as Loomis, navigating through the gloom, made his pitch. "Acquire a few squadrons of choppers, maybe a dozen heavy sections, and load us up with some kick-ass defoliant. Give us Agent Orange, or whatever new thing you might have, something even hotter. Let us loose to scald the hills with it. Just scald them and scrub them clean, like taking the bristles off a butchered hog. And then start everything—I mean everything—all over new again."

5

Dwight Pettigrew was leading his fifth tour of the day. He was head tour guide at Hidden World Caverns, and this shift, like most shifts, he had spent about half his time walking backward, talking. He was proud of the way he negotiated the slippery walkways that ran throughout the cave, one hand on the rough wood railing for balance, the other darting, gesticulating, jabbing to point out spectacular formations that hung sparkling from the wet cavern ceiling or rose up from its slick floor. And all the while that he talked, his sneakered feet trod steadily backward, feeling out the steps, confidently following the graveled downhill slopes, negotiating the steep winding passages between boulders.

"Here," he said, sweeping a hand behind him, "we have the War Club." A portable tape player at the base of the huge stalagmite poured out a series of percussive patterns played on huge hide drums. "The War Club," he said, "is forty-seven and one half feet in height. Its base is fifteen feet in circumference, and its top is thicker—thirty-three feet around, to be exact—thus giving the War Club its distinctive shape and name. Experts have estimated that the formation weighs well in excess of one hundred and twenty tons. That's as much as four fully loaded semidetached tractor-trailer rigs."

Dwight's group had already taken in the Diamond Room, with its dazzling deposits of quartz; the Egg Room and its broken geodes; the Giant Organ, with its ranks of colorful pipe-shaped stalactites; and the Sphinx, which looked more like a loaf of bread to Dwight than a mythical Egyptian god. They were a quarter of a mile in.

Someone in the crowd of tourists took a picture. Dwight squinted his eyes against the brief intensity of the flash, glad that the photo would set his small figure in dramatic relief against the stalagmite. He had been in hundreds of pictures by this time, probably, but he was nonetheless pleased to think that these people would be taking some image of him home with them.

There was a good-looking woman in the group, and he took note of her. She was older than Dwight, in her thirties maybe, but younger than the others, who looked mainly like retirees, pensioners, free to tour the cave because they were sucking at the tit of Social Security. This bunch wore yellow name tags with their names written on them in black Magic Marker, as though they were all together on an excursion. The young woman, who wore no tag, was dressed in light summer clothes, shorts and a brief halter top—much too light for the constant fifty-three degrees inside the cave. Dwight wondered what her name was and whether she was with the old people: their keeper, maybe. He admired her look but knew the brief outfit meant that it was another stinking hot day up top.

He had been down inside since just before dawn and planned to stay until after dark, if Mr. Askins would let him. Sometimes Mr. Askins, who owned the place, allowed him to stay after the cave closed. Dwight wondered if the woman was uncomfortable at all, standing there in her thin clothes. In his mind's eye he could picture the heat of the surface day rising in voluptuous waves off the pavement of the cavern's parking lot. He could picture the chrome and glass of the waiting cars glinting in the unrelenting sunlight. He pushed the image from his head and turned his thoughts back to the cave, with its cool tinkling rivulets of mineral-laden water and its refrigerated air.

"You've been here before, haven't you?" Dwight asked the woman.

"A time," she said. "Or two." She was certainly easy to look at, with thick dark hair and a muscular build. She smiled at him.

Dwight turned from her, finding his place in the patter again.

"Geologists believe that the War Club was formed over the course of millions upon millions of years. Drop by drop, and each drop leaving behind it a chunk of sediment too tiny for the naked eye to make out. It was a nub when the first of the multicelled animals crawled from the boiling sea onto the land, when the air was wet and smelled of rotten eggs." His voice rang against the stone. Mr. Askins had frequently praised him for his diction and his command of the language. Most of the other guides read from notes or through combinations of laziness and accident elided whole attractions from their routes, but not Dwight, not ever. He had this stuff down cold. "You can see shells preserved for eternity in the rock: the giant arthropods of the Paleozoic era. Year after year the trickling. The War Club was the size of a dogwood tree when the last of the dinosaurs lay down and quit his breath. The water never stopping. Not even for a minute."

He paused for effect. "One day, it's said, the accretion of material on the head of the War Club will grow to be too much; just that one final drop is all it will take to do it, the straw that broke the camel's back, to quote an ancient proverb; and the base will crack—" Here he brought his hands sharply together, and the sound was like the celebratory pop of a cork in that enclosed space. "—and the club will topple. It'll land like the hammer of the Norse thunder-god Thor, right where you're standing now."

The tourists shifted uneasily at this bit of intelligence, as they always did, imagining the fall of the club; perhaps momentarily conscious also of the unknowable weight and volume of earth overhead, just waiting to collapse into this unlikely vacuum, and they such small soft animals and easily pinched out of existence. Dwight delivered the punchline: "That is, in a hundred million years or so." The tourists giggled and sighed, relaxing, sounding like a bunch of sheep.

"It's not so much," said an old man who was labeled Frankl, the letters of his name scrawled on his tag in an uncertain looping hand. Dwight wondered if the peculiar name could be a spelling mistake.

Dwight himself had placed the lamps that lit the War Club, scuttling around on the cold, muddy, uneven cave floor for hours. He had hidden the power cords in the numberless fractures that threaded the floor, had snaked them around and under rocks to keep them hidden from the sight of the cavern's guests and out from under their careless feet. The lamps were placed to banish any shadows. When you got close, he knew, you could feel heat from their focused beams and see a thin vapor rising off the damp stone. He wondered sometimes what effect the lamps were having on the stalagmite's development.

Still, he was proud of the job he had done. Before he had come, the cavern's lighting had been sporadic, almost random, and it had been dangerous to traverse the paths without a flashlight. Lighting, he had discovered as he did the job, could be a kind of art. Beads of moisture like a delicate sweat slipped over the pearl-smooth surface of the War Club, refracting the brilliant glare, breaking it into tiny grids of color. Forgetting for a moment that he had a tour to conduct, he allowed his eyes to fasten on a single drop of water, watching as it disappeared into a slender crevice in the rock.

"This here," Dwight said, "is what we call the Veil of Tears." He ushered the group past him, maneuvering the old people so that they could get a good look at the cave's chief attraction. As the young woman came up to him, he reached out to take her by the elbow, to direct her to a good observation point within the grotto. She glanced at him as she went past, and he didn't dare to touch her. They stood all together on a balcony, a rock shelf bordered on its three open sides by a balustrade of rusty iron pipe. One of the old ladies—her name was Elinor—put a hand to the railing for support and drew it quickly back, grumbling and wiping her begrimed palm against her sweater.

The gallery they occupied projected out into a rock chimney. The chimney was dark and filled with mist. From somewhere overhead, water gushed, a huge volume of it. Dwight shivered, partly from the coolness of the air and partly from his sense of the open space around him. The senior citizens huddled together, and the young woman rubbed at her bare arms as though to settle the gooseflesh that had risen there.

"The Veil of Tears," he said again, his voice low, and he pressed a switch that he himself had concealed in a cavity in the chimney wall.

Spotlights blazed on. At the same time, the reels of a tape deck began to turn and the sound of a trumpet voluntary, grainy with distortion, roared from concealed speakers. Dwight stood back, taking in the effect that he had contrived.

The open shaft of the chimney extended away from them, upward into pitch black, downward the same, hundreds of feet in either direction. A foaming cataract poured from the darkness above and flowed down the opposite wall. The light from the spots danced and shimmered blindingly on the surface of the flow. When Dwight watched the downpour with his eyes half closed, his gaze unfocused, he felt that the water stood still and that he himself was rising, rising swiftly into the tube overhead, flying. He hummed along with the crying trumpets. Did they see it yet? They did not. All they saw was a waterfall; a spectacular underground waterfall, but still just a waterfall. He waited.

The oldsters backed away from the edge of the shelf. They opened their mouths, and Dwight could conceive the sound as a low moan, but he did not hear it through the music and the rumble of water. No one reached for a camera. They almost never did, and Dwight had seen them shake their heads and curse their foolishness as he herded them back toward the surface, wondering why they had allowed themselves to miss such a golden photo opportunity.

The young woman took a step toward the chasm, and then another, until her legs and torso were pressed tight against the iron railing, which gave slightly beneath the pressure of her body. The metal grated where it was bolted to the stone. She did not seem to mind the uncertainty of her perch, did not seem to mind that she was dirtying her clothes and her skin with grit from the railing. Her complexion was very pale in the wash of light, and strands of her hair stood out from her head as though she were caught in a strong current of electricity.

She sees it, Dwight thought. *She sees it but she'll not cry it out to these people.* Forgetting his duty to explicate the Veil of Tears—the length of its drop as great as the height of Niagara, the volume of its water so much per minute, on and on—Dwight took a breath, stepped forward, and stood beside the woman, his shoulder to hers, at the brink. He supposed that the railing could take their combined weight.

Behind them, Elinor peered nearsightedly into the waterfall. "Why, I do believe it's a face under there," she said.

"If it was a face, he'd of told us about it," Frankl replied. His voice rasped in his throat, and he breathed shallowly, like a blacklunger from the mines. Some of those guys, Dwight knew, got addicted to the depths and couldn't bear to stay away. He had a number of regulars like Frankl, who had probably spent half their lives underground. "He told us everything else. God, but he must adore to hear himself talk. Why would he miss this?"

"Still, it's a face," Elinor said. "A big face."

"She's right," another woman said. She was named Luona, to judge by her sticker. "The biggest face you ever saw."

"Where?" Frankl said, sounding belligerent, and he would not be shown, even when the women painstakingly pointed out to him every detail of the giant stone face behind the bright ribbon of water. The heavy beetled brow, easily six feet across. The dark, brooding eyes, deeply set. The hooked nose, the straight unsmiling slash of a mouth. The high, famished cheekbones and cleft chin. Dwight tested the pressure of his arm against the woman's, wondering if she was aware of it as he was, like a hot wire that passed through his living flesh, through the marrow of the long bones of his arm. He tried to time his breathing to hers.

"Why, it looks just like Kirk Douglas," Elinor said. A couple of the others chattered in agreement.

"Or maybe it's Jesus," Luona said. "Like that shroud that they have over in Italy."

"That's in Turkey," Elinor said. "On a mountaintop."

"You're thinking of the Ark," Luona replied. "The pope has Jesus' shroud, and the pope is located at the Vatican in Rome, Italy."

"I don't hold much with that pope," Frankl said. "He's got a shifty look on him that I never could take to. And a Polack to boot. They say he's a good fellow, but I don't know."

"Maybe it isn't a man's face at all," someone in the middle of the crowd said. "Could be it's a woman. I believe it's got a feminine cast to its features."

"So is it Jesus, or is it something else?" Elinor said, poking Dwight with a bony finger between his shoulder blades. He roused himself, with difficulty turning his back on the railing, the water, the young woman.

"Who can tell?" he said. "It's the face of the Veil of Tears. How long has it been here? Since long before you or me or probably all of humankind, that's for sure. And how long will it last? Till the flood of tears has washed its features from the surface of the wall, and it has passed particle by particle into the . . ." He struggled for the words, said, "The belly of the earth," knowing that *belly* wasn't what he had wanted at all. The trumpet chorus that he counted on for a background had ended moments before.

"Well, I believe it's a miracle," Luona said.

"Whose tears are they, then?" Frankl asked.

"Will you all be moving along soon, I hope? I got a bunch here that wants to see the waterfall." It was one of the other guides who spoke, a girl named Janina. She stood in the entrance to the chimney.

"The Veil of Tears," Dwight snapped. "Call it by its right name." He had a crush on Janina, who was vacantly pretty, with long teased hair that she said was wilted by the humidity of the cave. He continued fond of her despite the fact that she was an indifferently skilled guide and clearly didn't care much for Hidden World, or for Dwight himself, come to that.

"Whatever," she said, unfazed. "Can we get at it?" When he didn't stir to gather his people, she said, "Today? Please?"

Dwight knew that she was right, that it was past time for him to move on, but he was reluctant to give in to Janina in front of the tourists. He was after all the head guide, and Janina was only a high school student, hired for the summer break.

"It's a face in there," Elinor said. "He never told us about it, but we seen it for ourselves."

"Yes," Janina said. "I know. It's the face of the Veil of Tears." She looked impatiently over her shoulder at the spot where her tour group stood waiting.

"All right," Dwight said, shooing his people along. "Let's get to it." They had to shoulder their way past Janina's bunch to get out. Dwight heard Elinor and Luona tell the incoming tourists about the face that stared out from under the water, heard Frankl declare that he hadn't seen a thing and didn't know what all the fuss could be about.

"You're suppose to be out of here before another group comes along," Janina said to Dwight. She snapped the gum she was chewing. Her group straggled after her onto the balcony. These were more old people, and Dwight wondered if any of his had gotten turned around and mixed in with them. He thought that he probably wouldn't recognize them. He made for the light switch.

"Don't bother with that," Janina said. "And leave the music off too."

"You need the music," he said.

Janina bugged her eyes at him. "You slay me sometimes," she said. A few of the tourists were looking out over the precipice at the waterfall, but most were watching the confrontation between the guides. Saying nothing more, Dwight turned and left.

When he got back to his group, he did not see the young woman.

He very much wanted to see her again. He felt afraid he had lost her. He had never lost a tourist before. Soon he spotted her, standing in a cluster of shadows. She smiled at him and dropped one eyelid in a long, sly, private wink.

"This way," he said. "Follow me." And he led them quickly along the circuitous route that would take them through the rest of the cave and eventually back to the surface.

"We call this one the Ripper's Cloak," Dwight said. He flipped a peremptory hand at the formation as he passed by it, an ivory-colored outcropping that bulged into the path from the cave wall. It had vaguely the shape of a hunched man with a heavy mantle thrown over his back and head. The purity of the cloak was streaked with color, a dull ocher that seemed to be part of the grain of the stone. Music from other areas of the cave was audible here, the enginelike rhythm of drums from one place, the mournful shrilling of panpipes from another, but the cloak had no soundtrack of its own.

He moved backward along the trail as fast as he could go, continuing that way mainly for the pleasure of watching the young woman move. The muscles of her long legs moved like a slow heavy liquid under the skin. He noticed that she wore sandals. Her feet were long and slender. She had painted her toenails a bright shade of red.

"Wait up a second there," Elinor said as they swept past the cloak. She had been complaining for a time now, since the Veil of Tears, about Dwight's quick pace. She sounded out of breath. Some of the others seemed to be laboring along, too. Dwight slackened his stride. "What was that thing we passed just then? Ripper what?" Elinor asked.

"Yeah," Luona said. "Let's look at that one a minute."

"We ain't looked at anything since the big face back there," Elinor said. "We're just running past these rocks and not getting to hear about them. What about that Seal Rock, or the one before that, the Pig?"

"The Boar Beset by Dogs," Dwight said, stopping reluctantly. "What is it you would like to know?" He strove to keep his tone solicitous.

"Need to know nothing," Frankl said, hugging his arms tight against his skinny body. He was working hard to get his breath. "Ready to get on out. It's cold as a witch's tit."

"That thing there," Elinor said, ignoring Frankl and gesturing back along the path at the cloak. "Why is it painted like that? And what did you call it? Ripper something."

"That's not paint," Dwight explained. "The cloak's a formation of common calcspar, and the red streaks are iron oxides that have leached out of the water over the centuries. They're not just on the surface; they run all through the rock. We thought it looked like a man in a bloodstained cape, so we called it the Ripper's Cloak."

"After that fellow, what's his name. Jack the Ripper," Frankl said.

"Bloodstained," Luona said. "Not a very nice thing." The others in the group looked expectantly at Dwight.

"That's all I know," Dwight said. "We're almost back to the front room of the caverns now. I'll turn you over to Mr. Askins there, and you can put any other questions you have to him." He started along the path again, no longer walking backward.

"He cut up a bunch of whores in London," Frankl said. "Slit them open like cleaning a fish. Used their guts for his garters, hear tell."

"Hush," Elinor said to him, and he did. To the others she said, "He gets so excited sometimes."

The young woman caught up with Dwight as they moved toward the relative light and warmth of the front room, where the floor was of poured concrete and the walls showed the distinctive marks of pickax blades and dynamite. She tugged his sleeve. He glanced at her, expecting to find Elinor or some other senior pestering him. When he saw who it was, he stumbled, caught himself, walked on.

"I think you're doing a fine job," she said.

"Thanks," Dwight said. "We aim to please."

"You know a lot about this place. These caves and all the different rooms and such. More than the others that take the tours around."

Dwight took a deep breath. "Thanks," he said again.

"It's something, isn't it? This place. It's like we're inside a giant body here, laid down in the earth and hidden from sight through the ages. I thought of that the first time I saw the face in the water. The cave has a grim, handsome face, and we're crawling through its body now like we were bugs."

"Well, ma'am," Dwight said, and he coughed.

"Call me Dreama," she said. " 'Ma'am' makes me sound pretty old."

They were near the front room, and he could see Mr. Askins standing in the entrance, waiting for them. The seniors were strung out behind him on the path, Indian file. To them he said, "Keep together, folks. It's for safety's sake." Turning back, he said, "That's not exactly a real face back there, I have to tell you, Dreama. It's a trick of the light."

"Is that so?" she said.

"Sure. I set up the lights myself to make it look the way it does." He laughed. "The way they had it before I came, it looked like it was a duck or a swan or some other kind of a bird back there behind the water. I made it a face. I made the name up too."

"When you hold a flashlight just under your chin, you frighten people. You look like a monster," she said. "Only when the light hits your face in the right way does it look like you." She took Dwight's hand and squeezed it. Her long fingernails dug pleasingly into his skin. Her palm was warm and dry, her grip surprisingly strong. He stopped moving briefly, and Frankl, hurrying along with his head down, almost ran into him from behind.

"Watch your step there," Frankl said.

"You just got the light right. After all this time, it was you that found the right face of the giant." She released Dwight's hand, and he wished that she hadn't.

"Maybe—" Dwight said, but he didn't know what came after that, so he said it again. "Maybe."

Then they were at the front room, and Mr. Askins stepped forward, his arms flung wide in salutation. "Welcome back from your trip through the ancient past," he said. His voice was hearty. "Welcome back from the depths of the Hidden World." As the senior citizens made their way through the opening and into the front room, past Mr. Askins, he took in their downcast looks, their muttering, their shortness of breath. He threw a glance of inquiry at Dwight, who was too engrossed in the woman at his side to notice.

"This is the body of my older brother Floyd," Mr. Askins said to the assembled crowd. He stood atop the small plywood stage beside the bier, and the theater lights bolted to the ceiling threw a pink glow over his features and over those of the waxy corpse to which he referred. The coffin that contained the cadaver stood nearly upright against a limestone monolith; Dwight had seen something like it in pictures of Old West desperadoes who had been shot to death and then propped up in their caskets for the convenience of newspaper photographers.

A fence of black iron bars blocked the crowd's access to the body, and they milled about outside the barrier. Dwight's people had been joined by Janina's similar crew and another group made up of a couple of families with parents, grandparents, kids led by the hand, babies in strollers. A few people were taking pictures, leaning through the bars to get a clear shot of the dead man. Dreama stood in the midst of them.

"Some of you may find that shocking," Mr. Askins said. He reached out a hand and grabbed at one of the iron bars as though to steady himself, or to demonstrate the sturdiness of the barricade. "You may be asking yourselves, what variety of ghoulishness is this? Why doesn't he just bury the poor bastard and be done with it? Pardon my language." Dwight knew that he recited the same speech to every group that came through the cave. He believed that Mr. Askins secretly enjoyed calling his dead brother a bastard.

"And it's a good question. A proper question. So I'll tell you why. My brother Floyd rests in the only place that he would have found appropriate, the single place in which he might be able to find real peace. If I had buried him in a six-foot grave in the middle of some grassy green cemetery up above, it would never have been deep enough for him. He would have returned to the stone that he knew, to this very place. A remnant of him would have wandered these corridors, making itself manifest in the whisper of a subterranean breeze, in a drop of cool cave water on the skin, in the groans of the shifting strata of rock. This cave was the reason for Floyd's living, and it was the death of him. So I interred him here, in the Hidden World Caverns, the grandest sepulcher that man ever occupied!"

Askins paused as though overcome with emotion, and a number of people in the listening crowd spoke softly to one another, nodding. He continued. "In the fifties, my brother had a dream. I was just a kid then, a bony young kid like Dwight there." Here he gestured at Dwight, who colored, trying his best not to look self-conscious. "But Floyd was an ambitious young man, a man with a clear vision of going up in the world. He had this vision, and a plot of land, a couple hundred acres in the hills, arid stony land that everyone knew was worthless: the land above your head now. And I ask you, is it worthless?" No one replied.

"He found a vent in one of the cow pastures, a gash no more than a couple feet high at the bottom of a cliff. He came across it when he was looking for a calf one day in the spring of 1956. He heard the calf bawling but couldn't tell where it might be. Its noise sounded hollow to him where he stood in the pasture field, and far off. He searched for an hour, listening to the little baby calf, and finally he found the hole. The calf must have stumbled in somehow and not been able to squeeze back out.

"Floyd came and got me, and with nothing for light but one old carbide miner's lamp, we went into the cave. What we saw by the light of that flickering, hissing flame . . . well, you've seen it for yourselves. We never did find that calf. Never have, even to this day, not even so much as a bone of it. But it led us to our future, me and Floyd, and I'm grateful to it. Although it could also, I suppose, be considered somewhat at fault in the matter of Floyd's death.

"In any case, Floyd knew what we had here: something that was bigger, better, and grander by far than any other tourist cavern we knew of. He swore it would be more magnificent than Mammoth Cave, and he never, not for a single minute, stopped exploring it and expanding it toward that inspired goal, even after we opened for business and started taking tours through. The Hidden World was the center of his universe.

"And then one day in early '61, as Floyd lay on his belly in a cramped downward-sloping channel that passed through some loose limestone deposits, the roof gave way and came crashing in on him. He was trapped. His leg—his leg was caught by the rock fall, and he struggled manfully to free himself," Askins said. "I was just behind him in the passage, and I saw it happen. I was very nearly trapped myself."

"What happened then?" Frankl called out.

"I'll tell you, my friend," Askins said, and he commenced to speak of Floyd's ten-day struggle for freedom, and of the crowd of reporters and gawkers and would-be rescuers who had gathered at the mouth of the cave. He himself, he said, had reentered the crumbling shaft no fewer than thirty-one times, bearing with him on each trip some bit of food, cool clean water, a word of encouragement. He had prayed with Floyd until Floyd's voice gave out, and then he had prayed alone. In the end, an enterprising local doctor had shimmied down the tunnel and amputated Floyd's leg at the hip, to free him of the rock. The operation was performed without anesthetic, and Floyd died of shock on the way to surface.

Askins told of the embalmer's pains over the corpse, and its installation in the cherrywood coffin in the Hidden World. He told of a woman who, in 1970, moved to a kind of religious ecstasy, had brought a pair of garden shears to the cave so she could take a piece of Floyd away with her: some hair, a scrap of cloth, a finger—Mr. Askins didn't know what she had been after. And how, immediately following that incident, he had caused the iron barrier to be erected.

"And now," Mr. Askins said, concluding, "he lies here in state, martyr to his dream." He gestured at them all, a dismissal. "I hope you've enjoyed your time with us at the Hidden World as much as we've enjoyed entertaining you, and that you'll want to come back again real soon." He stepped down from the podium, and the crowd broke into its several components. Some of the people headed for the cavern exit, while others remained to chat with Mr. Askins. Eager photographers gathered around Floyd's body again, jostling one another for a clear angle. Dwight stayed where he was.

After a minute or two, someone approached him from behind. "There ain't no face," a man's voice said. When Dwight turned, he saw that Frankl stood there.

"Is that your real name, what it says there?" Dwight asked, indicating the name tag stuck to the old man's shirt. "Frankl?"

"Sure," Frankl said. "What's yours?"

"Dwight," Dwight said.

"Well, Dwight," Frankl said, "I got to tell you something. There ain't no face in yonder room."

"Not a real face," Dwight said. "Just a picture of a face. Shadows is all, made by the light and the rocks."

"Okay, Dwight," Frankl said. "I seen the shadows. And I seen the rocks. But you got no face in there. Maybe you think you do, but you don't." He laughed and sauntered away from Dwight to join the rest of his group, who were gathered near the exit. Dwight laughed too.

Dreama passed him on her way out of the room. Dwight watched her go. Before she went up the long steep ramp to the surface, she looked around the chamber and spotted him, crossed to him.

"Watch out down here," she said. "You don't want to end up like that poor baby calf."

"Baby calf?" he said.

"The giant drew it down for nourishment," she said. "Or did you think it just got lost?"

"Fell through a hole," Dwight said. "Washed down a river."

"Maybe so. Anyway, next time I come down, I'll be sure and get you for my guide."

Dwight brightened. "You'll come back?" he said.

"Most likely," she said. "If it stays hot up top. You all have got it nice and cool down here."

"Listen," Dwight said. "Maybe I could walk you out. See you to your car." He thought that he wouldn't take another tour around the cave. Just call it a day, punch the clock and go out. Suddenly the idea of the heat didn't seem so terrible to him.

"Thanks. You're sweet," she said. "But I'm okay. I'll make it just fine on my own." She turned and trotted in her clunky sandals up the steep slope of the exit ramp and on out, into the day.

6

Goody tried to keep his pace fast, but his thoughts kept straying back to the dead man he had found in the cane. He was doing his roadwork, and he had to concentrate. *The toothy open mouth.* Otherwise he slowed down, slowed down without noticing, and he ended up practically walking. *The twisted limbs.* Which did nothing for his endurance or for his strength. *The thick yellow fingernails packed with dirt.* So he tucked his chin in tight against his shoulder, like he would to protect himself in a fight, and picked up the cadence, ignoring the growing stitch in his side.

The day was another hot one, the air filled with the white glare of sunlight, and the rippling tunnel of heat that rose from the blacktop made the world seem to wander and stagger. Goody's head buzzed with the beating of the sun and his exertion, and he desperately wanted to stop, the painful churning of hunger and weariness in his belly made him want to stop, but he would not let himself give in to it. It was a weakness that he felt he could not afford. He pounded on down the road, his cheap tennis shoes slapping loudly against its gummy surface.

He passed houses every now and again, but they were mostly shuttered tight against the heat of the day: swaybacked frame places standing in the shadow of tall, frail-looking walnut trees, the acid roots of which had poisoned their yards and left them grassless. It was hot even in the shade beneath the trees. They were dying from the dry, but doing it slowly, over the course of seasons and years.

A few people were out on their porches. They uniformly nodded to Goody as he went by. One woman, tending her bedraggled vegetable garden, held up a sizable tomato, its overripe flesh parting to spill small tear-shaped seeds and juice down her arm. She was a stringy old woman with a grim set to her mouth, and for a moment Goody was afraid that she planned to pitch the tomato at him. He shied away from her, drawing his hands up in a protective gesture, but she merely smiled, offering him the tomato. By the time he realized that her intentions were friendly, his stride had carried him past her. He looked over his shoulder, but the old woman had gone back to her meager garden and her attention was all on the row of wax beans that she had begun weeding.

Farther on, he came to a tumbledown farmhouse whose entrance was flanked by a pair of man-high fieldstone pillars. One of the pillars had toppled, and it lay in a welter of crudely squared blocks and disintegrated mortar. The other column was whole, and Goody leaned against it for support, stretching his legs out behind him as he did so, first the right and then the left, loosening his hamstrings. His breath came fast, too fast, and he tried to control it, refusing to gasp for air.

When he had brought his breathing back into line, he prepared to go on with the roadwork. He stepped away from the pillar just as a cat dashed around its side. It was a narrow-shouldered cat, quick on its feet, with a thick, multihued coat. The cat dashed between his feet. It rounded the base of the pillar, out of sight, and then came back. After it had circled the pillar once more, it stopped and stood facing the stones, growling. He saw what it was after: a chipmunk clung to the stone, its tiny black claws clutching at the ledge on which it had found purchase. "You're in a hard place, boy," Goody said to the chipmunk, which pressed its body more tightly against the pillar at the sound of his voice. The cat did not know the exact whereabouts of the ground squirrel, and it continued to prowl the column's base, giving Goody's legs a wide berth when it had to pass them.

The chipmunk was a fat specimen of its kind, gaily striped red and brown down its back. The skin over its rib cage twitched with its rapid breathing. "A hard spot," Goody said. He considered plucking the chipmunk from its perch and tossing it onto the ground for the cat, which now sat a few feet away, regarding him coolly with its emerald-colored eyes. In the end he decided to allow the two of them to decide their own outcome, and he went back to his running.

He came to a store. It was housed in an old wooden building of moderate size, sitting not far off the road at the edge of a wide gravel lot. It had once had an island of gas pumps, but the pumps had been partly dismantled. The operation had taken place some time before, to judge from the dilapidated look of the things, the paint peeling in curling strips from their sides, the rust bleeding red down the cracked glass of their fronts. He trotted across the gravel and up onto the long wooden porch of the place, glad that he had thought to tuck a couple of dollar bills into the pocket of his shorts. He drew them out as he pushed the door open. The bills were crumpled and slightly damp from sweat, and warm with the heat of his body. He clasped them between his thumb and forefinger.

There were two men inside. One of them, the older one, leaned his weight against a long pushbroom, looking at Goody. The other stood behind the counter; he seemed to be the owner of the place. "Fellow won twenty-five hundred, Bill," he said to the older man. "Standing right there, over by the cooler."

"Twenty-five," Bill said, sounding wistful. "Twenty-five hundred dollars."

"Hey there," the counterman said to Goody. "Out for a run?"

"Just trying to keep in shape a little," Goody said. He scanned the dark interior of the store for a drink machine.

"You want to buy a scratch-off lottery ticket?" the counterman said. "A fellow not long ago won twenty-five hundred dollars on a ticket that he bought right here. That's a pretty big payout."

"I need to get something to drink first," Goody said. "You got Gatorade?"

The counterman appeared to consider. "No," he said. "No Gatorade. We got Tang, but it's just a dry mix, of course."

Goody grimaced. "How about pop?"

The counterman gestured toward the back of the store. "Cooler's back there," he said. "Get what you want."

Goody went back between the aisles. The sweat began to dry on his skin. It was an uncomfortable feeling. He found the drink cooler and extracted a bottle of root beer from it. After a minute he put that back and took a bottle of lime soda instead. The blast of cold air that issued from the cooler when he opened it chilled him, and he retreated with his drink. He twisted the top off the bottle and drank, glancing inside the bottle cap to see if he had won a sweepstakes. The cap wasn't a winner, and he set it down on a shelf filled with cereal boxes.

He walked the back aisle of the store, drinking. The place seemed to have some of everything: medicines, toothbrushes, bolts of cloth, packets of pins, bobbins of thread, handkerchiefs, carpentry tools, roofing tacks, fencing staples, fishing gear, cartridges, whistles, skillets, knives. He lingered a moment over the glass of the pistol display case, and he bent close to the rack of rifles and shotguns, but he touched nothing.

A bunch of half-derelict games and toys and such sat against the wall of the store. There was a puppet show in a box, little marionettes, women in long elaborate gowns and men in breeches and tricorn hats, and they danced and bowed and promenaded together when he turned the crank that ran them. A tinny, tinkling tune rattled out of the puppet theater's innards. He passed a nickelodeon that played "Streets of Laredo" from a metal disk with hundreds of small holes pierced in it. A short row of metal nickelodeon records, covered in yellow paper sleeves, occupied a shelf nearby. The nickelodeon sat next to a little half-size skeeball lane with five cracked wooden balls.

Bill said, "Twenty-five hundred dollars on one ticket. Imagine that."

Goody tapped the glass front of a tall, narrow game cabinet. Inside the housing, it looked like a set of Chutes and Ladders. There was a row of steel ball bearings sitting at the bottom, waiting to be kicked into play. "What's this one here?" he asked.

"Pachinko," the counterman said. "It's like pinball stood up on its hind end. They play a lot of that one in Japan, I hear."

"Huh," Goody said. "Pinball." He passed on to the next case. On its top sat the likeness of the head of a clown, cast from metal. The clown's mouth was open wide in a silent laugh, and its chipped red tongue protruded slightly from between its painted lips. There was a pistol grip fastened to the case in front of the clown, designed to test a man's hand strength. " 'I'm Tungo,' " Goody said, reading the lettering on the front of the case. " 'As your grip grows stronger my tongue grows longer.' "

"That one's busted," Bill said.

"Some strongman squeezed it too hard here a few years ago," the counterman said. "The clown's tongue stuck all the way out of its mouth and come loose at the rear and fell clear out of its head. I just set it back in the mouth so it'd look right, but it ain't attached to nothing."

Goody moved down one more place, to the last of the collection: a large glassed-in cabinet that stood next to the key-cutting machine. The cabinet contained the torso of a mechanical woman. Her name, according to the legend on the box, was La Zelda Fortuna. *Your Fortune Your Future Your Fate*, the front of the box said, the initial letter *F* in the three words outsized, rendered in golden rococo lettering. The fortune-teller was buxom, dressed in black lace and gauze, with a comb supporting a colorful mantilla stuck in the thick black wig on her head. The wig looked as though it might be made of real human hair. There were playing cards attached to the bodice of her outfit, all face cards. One of her glass eyes was cocked inward, toward her nose. She held her mannequin arms outstretched.

"She'll tell your future to you," Bill said.

"How much is it?" Goody asked. The counterman gestured at the coin receiver on the box, which was labeled 5 CENTS. "I saw that," Goody said. "I just didn't think a nickel worked anything anymore." He walked to the front of the store, and the counterman rang the cash drawer open and gave him change for one of his dollar bills. He returned to the automaton and dropped a nickel into the slot.

For a moment La Zelda Fortuna was still, and Goody turned toward the counter to demand the return of his nickel. As he opened his mouth, clockwork in the cabinet began to whir and crank. The figure's head wagged, and her mantilla seemed ready to pull loose from its uncertain foundation in the mass of her hair. Her left hand moved in a series of ragged circles over a cloudy crystal ball. Her right arm rotated, dipped, skimmed a slip of paper off the small stack that sat in front of her, forced it through an opening in the glass. The whirring stopped, and the arm sprang with inhuman swiftness back to its original position.

Goody picked up the card and looked at it. He read it through once, a second time, looked up. "What's this?" he said. "It's a card from a guy named Paulie Lewis. He sells insurance."

"Can't hurt," Bill said. He laughed.

"Turn it over," the counterman said. "Read the other side."

Goody flipped the card, inspected the reverse face, and read from it. "It says 'Walk softly but carry a stick.' That's no kind of a fortune. That's Teddy Roosevelt. Somebody just wrote that on here with a pencil." He held the card out to the counterman.

"I wrote it," the counterman said. "The factory-printed cards run out a while ago, so now I just make up the fortunes. I use the business cards I get. They fit perfect."

"They's all different kinds of fortunes he's got in there," Bill said. "This is your lucky day. You'll meet a red-haired woman. You're going to travel far. You'll get what's coming to you. Look behind you. You ain't got a dog's chance. Sell all you got and follow the path of Christ."

"That isn't worth a nickel," Goody said. "Just what you wrote on there yourself." He laid the card down.

"You thought it was," the counterman said. "You put your money in and you didn't have no idea what might come out. If you'd of asked me, I'd of told you. But you never did ask."

Goody's expression softened. He smiled. "Yeah, I guess," he said. "It's a pretty good joke."

"Sure it is," the counterman said. "I had a line one time on a similar machine that claimed to be able to play chess with you, but that fell through. Man that was peddling it said it could beat a person at the game, too. It was a robot built to look like a big fat Turk in a fez. Gears inside him turned and let him move the pieces, just like you or me."

"I never was much of one for chess," Goody admitted.

"Me neither," Bill said. "Too many rules, and I never bothered to learn them. I'm a checkers player myself."

"They've got them too, robots that will play you at checkers. Jump you, king you, everything. It's like playing a real man, they say." The counterman put his hands flat on the counter. "You want a scratch-off ticket?"

"How much?" Goody asked.

"A dollar. The game's called Hog Heaven." The counterman pointed to a rack of tickets that sat next to the cash register. Imprinted on each one was the picture of a smiling cartoon pig wearing a halo. The pig was marked in sections like a butcher's schematic. "You scratch off the gray patches, and if you uncover any three amounts that match, you win that much."

"Up to twenty-five hundred dollars," Bill said, "which is a nice chunk of change to stick in your pocket any day of the week."

"Okay," Goody said. He laid out his money. The counterman gave him a lottery ticket, and he pocketed it along with his change.

"You ain't going to do it here?" Bill asked. "You can scratch off the gray with the edge of a coin or with your fingernail, either one."

"No," Goody said. "Save it for later."

"Oh," Bill said. He sounded disappointed.

Goody drained the pop bottle. The soda burned a little going down, but it was sweet and tasted good. He set the bottle down on the counter. "Do I get a deposit back on that?" he asked.

"No deposit, no return," the counterman said. "That's the way it is anymore. You can take the bottle with you if you want, though."

"That's okay," Goody said. "You pitch it for me, will you?" He left the bottle sitting where it was and headed for the door of the place. The counterman plucked the bottle up and dropped it into a tall trash can that stood near the counter. It clinked against something else when it went in, some other glass object, and that seemed to Goody to be a cheery sound.

On the way home, he trotted slowly, the lime drink an unfortunate sloshing in his stomach. The change in his pocket set up a sluggish rhythm, clinking unmusically with every stride he took. As he passed the ruined house with the pillars, he saw the particolored cat lying in a patch of sun near the standing pillar. It looked up at him as he passed, blinking lazily. He stopped and went over to it, thinking to coax it into coming home with him. He liked the cat's lean looks and thought that it would make a fine pet.

When he saw the headless body of the chipmunk lying curled between its forefeet, he changed his mind. The cat stared at him defiantly, as though it would defend its catch. After a minute it rose, stretched luxuriously, and sauntered off into a dense patch of weeds and flowering vine. It carried the body of the chipmunk clamped in its jaws. Goody watched after it. Then he turned and went back to the road, running home through the blistering heat as fast as his leaden legs and straining heart would carry him forward.

7

The two Mingos were the first of the interlopers to rise. They climbed
from windows on either side of the caboose of the derelict train near
the wooded crest of Little Hogback Mountain, slim dark men who
might easily have been brothers, dressed alike in sharp tiger-stripe
fatigues and weathered Anzac hats, with the same straight dark hair
and high cheekbones. They pulled themselves with athletic ease out
of the canted windows of the ruined train car and checked their
weapons in the slanting gray light of morning. They carried short-
barreled scatter-guns and machetes socketed in leather scabbards
that swung from their belts. They turned and scanned the clearing
around them.

The anchorite crouched a hundred feet away, covert with shadow
in a stand of pines. He prepared to pull back from the field of their
vision. The two brindled hounds that usually accompanied him were
nowhere to be seen, off hunting mice to eat, probably, but they might
come back to him at any moment. That possibility concerned him,
because it would give him away to the sentinel Mingos. He had seen
them in action before, and they were not men to take it lightly, being
spied upon. They were capable of terrible violence. The anchorite
wanted very much to remain hidden. He forced himself to relax, to

breathe slowly, to hold his skittish hands, which strove to wander, immobile against his thighs. The searching gaze of the near Mingo passed without wavering over his hiding place.

As one, the Mingos moved off from the tilted caboose where they had spent the night and roused the others of their party, who had slept sheltered inside the two boxcars in the main body of the train. The train sat rusting at the eastern terminus of a short spur of abandoned narrow-gauge siding, stranded there decades earlier by some timbering company's bankruptcy. It was covered in swaths of creeper and flowering sumac and masked by rustling hedges of wild rhododendron. Already the insects of day clamored and swarmed on the vegetation, and the anchorite noted the bright hovering dart of a hummingbird, wings invisible with their frantic motion as it drank at the bell of a heavy crimson bloom. When the waking intruders began to stir from the boxcars, the hummingbird whirred off into the woods. The electric chirring of the locusts underlay all other sound.

The relict siding on Little Hogback's southern face was about three hundred feet long. There were six open cars in the line of the train, still bearing chained to their decks the crumbling, moldered remains of their final consignment of virgin hardwood logs, and the two closed cars where the crowd of interlopers had rested, and the tender and the undersize wood-burning locomotive which had hauled its cargo of wagons no farther than to that place. Women struggled in early morning confusion out of the two boxcars, and a number of men. They might almost have been passengers, stowaway tramps marooned there years ago with the failure of the minute engine that had strained to pull them, asleep at the time of their desertion and only now awake and emerging from the wreckage of their vehicle, so amazed they seemed by their surroundings.

"Pero es un trencito!" one of the women exclaimed when she saw where she had been sleeping. Though the anchorite could not understand her speech, her tone was clearly one of amazement. Her nearby companions nodded and laughed and made replies that failed to carry as distinct words to his haven.

The train did not resemble a train anymore so much as it did a series of long narrow shanties linked by frozen iron couplings. The boxcars, the engine, and the caboose had all been inhabited through the years by successive generations of hunters passing through on the trail of bear or deer or turkey, or tracking the singular breed of rangy, quarrelsome wild hog that lived at this altitude. Many of them had left their architectural mark on the train, patching leaky carriage roofs with tarpaper and sheets of cheap tin and slats of wood torn from the walls of the other cars, closing rodents' holes with tin cans beaten flat, adding makeshift awnings that collapsed soon thereafter. The anchorite had stayed in the train's second boxcar on more than one occasion as he traversed the mountain. He recalled the softness of the rotting wood floor under his bedroll, and the large clumsy beetles, apparently blind, that lived there: their small weight as they trundled over the skin of his hands and neck and face. He recalled the posters that hung in mildewed ribbons from the walls—movie posters, mainly.

One poster, the one most nearly complete, featured the figure of a plump doll-baby wearing a frilly christening dress. The doll was standing on its sturdy little legs, and its pudgy toes, complete with flesh-colored toenails, peeked from underneath the edge of the lacy outfit. It stood on an endless, featureless plane of white and seemed about to take a step forward, prepared to trade the limits of the horror movie poster for those of the boxcar. The doll's eye sockets were empty and hollow, filled with an impenetrable darkness. A dark tear, a drop of blood perhaps, ran down the doll's rounded plastic cheek; its tiny hands were empty and outstretched. The remaining text of the poster, from which a sizable fragment was missing, read

CAT OR WOM
or a thing too horr
Listen for the scre
Look into the eyes of
who rules the la

The anchorite had taken to reading the lines to himself when he stayed in the car, making of them a kind of prayer, a singsong mantra. He had memorized them. Along with a couple of half-remembered psalms and the Lord's Prayer, it was the whole of his religious repertoire. Like most prayers, it seemed to him, the words were impenetrable and full of portent. The anchorite had lain under the gaze of the gruesome manikin and speculated about where it had come from in that characterless dimension and where it considered it might be going. Even in the night he was conscious of that blank stare fixed on him. He hoped that the interlopers had not torn the poster down.

He was surprised to hear the bright voices of children among the people in the clearing. The brood of them spilled catcalling from the wide sliding doors of the boxcars as they rumbled stiffly open, and they climbed into the dark fetid space beneath the train, among the steel wheeltrucks that were frozen to the rails with a stiff, impenetrable rust. They played under the train cars, and dunged there, and shied sharp chunks of rock and clinkers from the roadbed at one another and at the trio of mongrel dogs that the group had brought with them.

The dogs wrestled with one another, snarling theatrically, and fled yelping before the fusillade of stones that came their way, only to come cringing back a few moments later, twining themselves around the legs of the adults, seeking food. The anchorite smiled to think that the interlopers had brought the dogs along with them for protection and that the dogs had failed to note his presence at all. He wondered whether the dogs were poor ones or whether he had lost entirely the scent of humanity in his long isolation and was thus beyond detection.

In the end it was the young women in the clearing down below, a clutch of perhaps a half-dozen of them, who caught the anchorite's attention and held it. He watched them with hungry eyes as the camp set about its morning. They seemed to be enjoying the sun that penetrated the thick green canopy sixty feet overhead and filtered down to the forest floor. Two of them took up a heavy bucket of water, sharing the wire bail between them and laughing and chattering together they went off to make their toilet in a nearby juniper thicket. As they left the clearing, one of them grasped the thick fall of her hair with her free hand and twisted it into a tight coil at the back of her neck, to hold it out of her way. The anchorite yearned toward her and nearly betrayed himself to the Mingos, who restlessly patrolled the perimeter of the camp, arms at the ready. They were watching the camp, though, and not the forest. It came to the anchorite that they were warders rather than pickets or sentries.

The anchorite gazed after the two young women who had disappeared into the undergrowth, and he believed that he could see them washing, vague tantalizing silhouettes at the edge of his perception, their poor shifts suspended from the branches of a bush and billowing in a light breeze. He considered circling the camp to a place above and nearer them, but he knew that he would have to cross open ground to improve his vantage, and he dared not make the approach.

The interlopers built a cookfire in a shallow rock-ringed circle that had plainly served the purpose any number of times. First they cleared from it the rubbish of other camps: scorched, splintered bones, soda cans, plastic wrappers, discarded tin mess-kit plates warped from heat. They pulled charred wood from the fire circle and replaced it with limbs they had found or torn from the trees themselves, as though they would not use what others had burned before them. With a lot of huffing and cursing and many matches, they got the fire drawing well. Orange flames rose between the lengths of oak, and a column of greasy smoke leaned away from the fire pit, drifting along the ground without rising.

One of the men of the camp started up the rise toward the anchorite's hiding place. He was a light-skinned man, the anchorite saw, as pallid as soap among the darker Mingos and the olive-skinned interlopers. He wore black military-style boots that were too large for him, and he had laced them only halfway. A large pistol was tucked into the waistband of his pants. He had crammed the legs of his jeans into his oversize footwear, and the boot tongues lolled from between the laces and flapped against his ankles as he walked. He approached at a leisurely pace, yawning a couple of times. The man's current course was one that would take him to one side of the anchorite's hiding place, perhaps enough to miss him altogether. The anchorite stayed where he was.

The man with the pistol was powerfully built, with a long torso and bandy legs. He whistled as he came on, no tune that the anchorite could recognize. When he reached the line of thick undergrowth at the edge of the clearing, he checked behind him to make sure that no one from the camp was watching him. Still whistling, he unfastened his pants. He paused for a moment, puzzling what to do with the pistol. Finally he hung it by its trigger guard from the bough of a nearby sapling. It was a heavy pistol, an Army .45, and it bent the branch under its weight.

The man dropped his pants around his ankles and squatted. He grunted, straining. His narrow shanks and hairless buttocks were milky pale, veined with blue as they hovered inches above the turf, and the anchorite imagined that he could almost see the individual blades of grass reflected on the flesh, upside down and distorted, as on the surface of a china bowl. He looked away, not wanting the man to feel eyes on him as he shat.

When the anchorite looked back, the man had selected a handful of dry leaves from the ground near him and was inspecting the bunch. He plucked a couple of twigs from among them and wiped himself before casting the clump away. The small dark mound of his stool steamed slightly in the morning air as he stood and rearranged his clothing. He retrieved his pistol, thrust it muzzle-first inside the waistband of his pants and, whistling once again, strode back to the camp with its bedlam of women and children and dogs.

The heady odor of manure drew close around the anchorite, and he thought he might swoon. His head was light from days of fasting, and though he was used to the dull gnawing of hunger and the knotting of his insides, this was too much, this meaty combustible smell when he could not move to escape it: the cloacal stench of man. The wind soon shifted the scent away from him, and he was glad of that. His forehead was lightly filmed with sweat.

In the camp, a couple of the older women sat hunched near the cookfire. They brazed meat and sliced up thick loaves of bread. As they prepared the food, wrapping the slabs of bread around the hot meat, the others of the camp formed a loose food line and received the sandwiches from them. The Mingos took their portion and, drawing apart from the others, began to eat with fierce concentration. Seeing them thus engaged, the anchorite relaxed. His eyes roved among the interlopers, many of whom reclined on the ground as they ate, and he granted himself leave to dwell on the features of the women, the women, the women.

When he had at last looked his fill, the anchorite took a small tough pear from a pocket and made his frugal breakfast, eating the fruit down to its slight, shriveled core. The saliva welled joyously in his mouth as he consumed the fruit, and the sugar seemed to sing in his blood. When he was through eating, he spat the hard seeds of the pear silently into the palm of his hand and then dropped them one by one onto the deep carpet of pine needles under him. Overhead in the lush blue boughs of the spruce, a squirrel chattered angrily at him for a moment and then went silent.

The camp had finished its repast as well and appeared ready to move on. The Mingos moved among the others as though they strolled through a drove of cattle they were herding to market. They spoke with no one, only motioning to each other from time to time, subtle signals: a sideward glance, a tilt of the head, a flick of the fingers. Soon they had the interlopers, who numbered twenty or more, gathered into a loose group near the small steam engine. The pale man stood beside the locomotive, thick arms akimbo, and the Mingos patrolled the outer edges of the crowd like stock dogs. One moment the interlopers were all speaking together, conversing in loud voices; the next they were silent, transfixed.

When the anchorite followed their collective lifted gaze, he saw for the first time a man seated on the roof of the locomotive's cab. He was large, and he slouched there easily, legs dangling over the edge, fingers drumming idly against the metal panel beneath him in impatient rhythm. The anchorite could not have said whether he had been watching the scene all along, through the activities of the morning, or had only this moment appeared. The line of his mouth curled into a tight smile. The anchorite held his breath.

The man stood, and his stern gaze swept the crowd below him. "I am Tannhauser," he said.

A man in the crowd called out in a tenor voice, "Es el Doctor Tannhauser."

Tannhauser's shoulders were broad and dense with muscle, and his body tapered nicely from them down to his supple waist and lean hips. He wore tight-fitting blue jeans and a chambray workshirt under a long linen duster, and his feet, shod in intricately tooled cowboy boots, boomed like hooves against the thin roof of the locomotive whenever he shifted his weight. His features were pleasant enough but unremarkable in their regularity. At the sound of his name, the crowd shifted nervously, muttering. Obviously this was a personage whose arrival they had been looking for, even if with some trepidation. A few of the men lifted children to their shoulders so that they could see. Tannhauser posed on top of the train engine, silhouetted against the dense background of trees, limned by a shaft of sunlight that caused his close-cropped blond hair to gleam. He said, "You know my name. You know who I am. I caused you all to be brought here, to this place."

The man in the crowd sang out again. "Ustedes lo han oído nombrar, y ahora lo ven. El es el que los ha llamado aquí."

A woman stood next to the translating man. A girl, really. The anchorite recognized her as one of the girls of the morning, the girls with the bucket. She was the one who had knotted her hair so carefully behind her neck. Her hair was braided now, one thick black plait that hung down the center of her back, in perfect alignment with her spine. Her dark eyes were fixed on the figure of Tannhauser.

He didn't return her gaze. He was looking at all of them and at none of them, his eyes seeming to take in the members of the crowd as though they had among them only one body, only one face, and that of no great consequence to him. He seemed weary, and angry.

Tannhauser continued. "I welcome you to this place," he said, "which is really noplace. It is only a place for me to find you, and for us all to continue together." The translator began to speak, but Tannhauser did not pause to let him finish. The translator said, "El les da la bienvenida, aunque no es el lugar apropiado. Es un lugar en el que . . ." He became flustered, unsure as to whether he should continue while Tannhauser was speaking, and after a minute his voice trailed off altogether. Tannhauser said, "You have slept on boats and in the backs of moving trucks and in sheds and sometimes under no roof at all to come here. This last night you slept on a wrecked train. But tonight—" He made a dramatic pause. "Tonight you will sleep at El Dorado."

When he said the name El Dorado, a sigh went up from the assembly. The translator carried on his high-pitched, halting antiphony. When he caught up to Tannhauser and said for the second time the words *El Dorado*, the interlopers shifted and sighed again, and a few of them talked excitedly to their neighbors. *El Dorado*, they said, *el hombre dorado*, until they were hushed by Tannhauser's fierce glance.

"You know the promise of El Dorado," Tannhauser said.

"Les he contado la leyenda de El Dorado," the translator said.

"In olden times," Tannhauser said, "it was a place so rich with gold that men mixed the stuff with their food. A place so rich that the king of El Dorado had himself anointed with oil each day, and his slaves blew gold dust onto his body through hollow tubes of cane until he was covered with a thick, even layer of it. It clung to him, and he became a golden king. When he touched a man here"— Tannhauser touched a fingertip to his forehead—"or here"—he touched his breast, over his heart—"that man was stained with the king's fine glaze of gold, and it made him special among his neighbors and all those that saw him. He would not wash the golden streak, but would instead allow it to dry and to crumble away. He tried to preserve it."

The translator struggled to keep up, fumbling, but even without his intercession the interlopers were entranced by Tannhauser's narrative. The Mingos looked on with interest, weapons held at port arms. The bandy-legged man alone paid no attention, staring out truculently at the crowd, his back to the train and to Tannhauser, arms crossed over his chest.

"And once a year, on their greatest festival day, all the people of El Dorado coated themselves with oil, just like the king, and covered themselves in a thin film of gold. And the rays of the sun ran and played over their bodies like fire. They became for that day a golden people." When the translator stopped speaking, saying "una gente dorada," the entire company muttered their approval, heads bobbing and nodding. Tannhauser's face darkened. "But El Dorado passed away from the earth, as a dream passes away when a sleeper awakes. Do you know why it did not last? That state so incredibly wealthy that all of its citizens could be clothed in gold, even if only for a single day?" Tannhauser waited for an answer.

The silence grew uncomfortably long, and finally the translator nudged the girl beside him. "Diga no," he instructed her. She was rapt on Tannhauser, who stood in his place, one foot thumping fretfully against the roof of the cab. More loudly, the translator said to those around him, "Digale que no." Soon his urging inspired a ragged cry of denial from the interlopers. They did not know what had brought the end upon El Dorado. They did not know. No sabemos.

"It ended," Tannhauser told them, "through the sheerest vanity of its population." He stood regarding them, and this time not even the translator could guess what response he might be looking for. "El pecado de la vanidad," the translator said. The pale man sighed heavily.

Tannhauser continued. "On one of those festival days—the last one, but they didn't know that at the time, of course—the golden king walked happily among his golden people, and some of those people thought that he was no different from them. They couldn't see a difference, because they and he and everyone they saw, all were painted with gold. They thought to themselves, *He's just the same as us*, and they said that to their friends, their families. They spread the word. And that was the end of El Dorado.

"When the king gave a command, no one listened to him or obeyed. Why should they? His subjects were no longer subjects. His slaves were no longer slaves. He was the same as they were. Let him do it. He was no longer the king. With no one to work the mines, the gold quickly ran out, and they were not a golden people.

"Soon after that, the Spaniards came, looking for the golden land of which they had heard such fantastic tales. When they found that there was no more gold, they refused to believe that they had found El Dorado, and they slaughtered everyone who lived there. Man, woman, child, all of them. They piled the corpses in the defunct mines and went on with their search.

"For centuries the Spaniards sought what they had already come upon and dismissed. They killed and died for it. The English did the same. And the Dutch, and all the civilized nations of the world. But no one could find El Dorado anymore, because it was gone." Tannhauser made a large motion in the air before him with his arms, as though to indicate how El Dorado had been swept away.

"Until the present day. We have rediscovered El Dorado, and it is a wondrous place, but far to go. You have come this far, and you will go farther. You think that you have worked before in your lives, and that you have worked to get to where you are now. But you have not really worked. You have not known me. I have not been with you, to make sure that you worked. But I am with you now." The girl stared at Tannhauser as though she were memorizing all the various details of him.

El Dorado, the anchorite thought. El Dorado. He knew where this crew was headed, then, and what they would find there. He had been skulking among the trees at the time of the burning at El Dorado. He had heard the screams and choked on the appalling stench. Later he had poked with a forked stick among the greasy ashes, stirring up bones. He thought of the girl, the slim girl, in that place, and his heart seemed to pause in its beating before it raced unevenly ahead.

"But in your former lives neither have you known such reward as you will find there," Tannhauser said. "I will make of you new men. New people. Wealthy people." He grinned broadly, and a number of the interlopers grinned back at him, though they could have understood little of what he had told them. Sitting on their fathers' numbing shoulders, a couple of the children laughed when they saw Tannhauser's merry expression. Even the anchorite in his uncomfortable hiding place among the trees felt momentarily warmed by the brilliance of the smile. It marked Tannhauser's precise physiognomy with a sudden unexpected beauty. As quickly as it had come, the smile was gone.

The translator struggled for a moment, buffaloed by Tannhauser's syntax. He began to speak, became stalled, started again. Finally he said simply, "Los va enriquecer," and shrugged apologetically at Tannhauser. At the words, the crowd broke into loud cheering, and the translator seemed relieved at the effect his words had elicited. Tannhauser's features stayed passive, his gaze remote. When the cheering had gone on long enough to suit him, he lifted a hand to still it.

One by one the interlopers went silent, nudged in the ribs by the Mingos, prodded with gun barrels if they failed to quiet quickly enough. The anchorite noted that Tannhauser's upraised right hand was strangely broad. It took him a moment to realize that an extra finger sprouted from the hand, a minor digit set somewhat apart from the others. He looked at the opposite hand, the left, which still rested on Tannhauser's hip, and it was confirmed: Tannhauser was a twelve-fingered man. The anchorite had known people in his life who were missing fingers, or toes, or even an eye, but as far as he could recall this was the first time he had seen a man with more than the usual number of any body part.

When the interlopers had calmed themselves, or been calmed, Tannhauser went on with his speech. "Remember carefully," he said. "You are on the mountain now. And there is no law on the mountain. None," he said, "but me, and Yukon here," indicating the pale man in front of him, "and the Mingos there beside you. They are Indians, and they know this land like no other men on earth. They are my right hand, and my left." He gestured at each of the Mingos with the appropriate extremity, and holding their guns out before them they crowded the interlopers even closer against one another in their already compact circle. Though there was plenty of room in the clearing for them to spread out comfortably, the adults did not resist the further packing. A child squealed, caught in a tightening forest of legs, and was silenced.

"Hagan exactmente lo que el les dice," the translator said, and his voice shook a little. "O ellos los matan, los indios pequeños, alli y alla. Y el terrible tipo palido." He gestured at the Mingos as Tannhauser had done, and at Yukon. The people surrounding him drew back into themselves to allow him to spread his hands. Tannhauser nodded at him with apparent satisfaction, and the translator dropped his arms back to his sides.

"You are dismissed," Tannhauser said.

"Retirensen," the translator said. The Mingos backed off and the crowd broke apart, murmuring their relief. They were sweating with the rising heat of the day and the close contact with other overwarm bodies, and their clothes clung to them. The anchorite found himself distracted by first one young woman and then another as they left the group, but always his attention was drawn back to the slim girl, who had not moved.

Tannhauser levered himself easily from the roof of the engine, gripping its edge with his six-fingered hands. His loose duster caught for a moment on some metal projection, and he paused long enough to tug it free. Then he clambered down the rungs of the short ladder set into the side of the cab, grimacing when he reached the bottom, rubbing his hands roughly one against the other to rid them of the dark rust that had accumulated on them. He stood next to the glowering Yukon.

The Mingos approached him and stood waiting at his side. Without looking at either of them, he said, "One of you scout ahead, make a good path. The other one rides shotgun on this bunch here, with me and Yukon. We get there tonight. Understand?" The Mingos reached a silent agreement between them, and one of them trotted out of the clearing, headed east. He drew his machete from its sheath as he went and, swinging it at the encroaching underbrush, was lost to sight.

East, to El Dorado. The anchorite calculated and, though he knew that it would be a tough trek for the women and children, decided that with Tannhauser pushing them, this bunch would probably make it before night fell.

The interlopers broke camp. Tannhauser moved among them, giving out a word here and there, issuing an occasional curt command, not seeming to notice whether or not his instruction was understood or undertaken. The translator trailed after him, saying nothing. When Tannhauser came to the girl, he paused, examining her. After a minute of this close appraisal, he said, "What is your name?" She made him no reply, and he gestured irritably to the translator, who moved closer.

"What are you called?" Tannhauser said to the girl. He snapped his fingers at the translator. The anchorite observed that he used the same fingers that normal ten-fingered men used to snap, the thumb and the second. No reason that such a thing should be different. The sound popped loudly in the quiet forest, and the translator licked his lips.

"Digale su nombre," the translator said. The girl looked up at

Tannhauser, but still she said nothing. The muscles in her elegant throat worked as though she were trying to find her voice but could not.

"She's scared of me," Tannhauser said, to no one in particular. "Why in hell should she be scared of me?"

"Por Dios, digale su nombre," the translator hissed at her. He held his round, sweat-shiny face only inches from hers, in the manner of an interrogator. "Usted es tonta, muda?"

"Doesn't she want to be here? Doesn't she want to be going with us?" Tannhauser asked. A few of the others had stopped their activity and were gathered around to watch the exchange. The women were sniggering. "She sure oughtn't to be here if she doesn't want to be," Tannhauser said. He straightened. "None of them ought to be here if they don't want. They should know that."

"Diga," the translator told the girl, and he stretched back his hand as though to slap her. Tannhauser grabbed the man's thin wrist in his own large hand to forestall the action, and the translator grunted. His face blanched with pain.

"No," Tannhauser said.

At the same time, the girl blurted out in a small voice, "Paloma."

Tannhauser released his grip on the translator, who rubbed at the skin of his wrist. "What's that?" Tannhauser asked the girl. The expression on his face was jolly.

"Paloma," the girl said, more loudly this time. She looked Tannhauser full in the face.

"Paloma," Tannhauser said thoughtfully. "That means pigeon, doesn't it?" The translator said nothing. Tannhauser lingered on the girl's name, saying it again. "Dove, I mean," he said, and he brought his face very near the girl's, as though in the midst of that crowd they might share a private conversation between them, never minding that they had no language in common.

The anchorite was concentrating on the tableau in the clearing— Tannhauser taking the girl Paloma's slight hand into his broad one, the girl not resisting; Tannhauser wrapping her hand in the unnatural number of his fingers—when his hounds returned. The bitch came first, a light-boned dog that appeared out of the brush and trotted daintily to the anchorite where he crouched. It snuffed at him, wet snout touching his jawline just below the ear, where his long matted hair fell against his collarbone. The kiss sent a spasm through him. His imagination conjured a danger (the yawning muzzle of a scatter-gun) where there was none, and he made a clumsy, frogging leap to the side. Even as he jumped, he saw it was his own dog that had frightened him and his shout of fear was stillborn in his throat. He gave out a strangled *yark* and came to rest on his back in a wet drift of leaves. The hound regarded him with calm, mild eyes, wondering what the rules of this new game might be.

The anchorite shoved the bitch down to hide it. It thrashed over onto its back, tail curled into a tight loop between its legs, the whites of its eyes showing. The anchorite kept a hand on its narrow chest, silencing it, waiting to see if they had been discovered. The interlopers continued busily to pack up.

A few minutes later, the anchorite's male hound wandered back, mouth working over something that it had caught—a mouse or a vole that it had trapped in the roots of a tree, most likely, the anchorite knew. The bitch leaped up to greet the male, snapping playfully at its muzzle, trying to dislodge the prey from its grip. The dog snorted and turned away, flopping down to enjoy its meal in peace.

When the anchorite gave his attention back to the clearing, he saw that the camp was in full motion, following the hastily struck trail of the Mingo. Rank by rank, the interlopers entered the woods and were swallowed from sight, the adults silent, intent on carrying their burdens. The children's shrill voices carried to the anchorite after they had disappeared from sight. Musclebound Yukon slapped at mosquitoes, cursing volubly. At first the anchorite thought that Tannhauser was not among them, had vanished back into the brush the way he had come. Then he saw the tall man walking behind the others. He was in animated conversation with Paloma, who nodded her glossy head from time to time. Tannhauser placed one of his hands on the girl's back and motioned before them with the other, ushering her into the forest.

Silence held the clearing. The anchorite waited a few moments, to see if someone might nip back to the camp to retrieve some forgotten item or if one of the Mingos might sweep through on some final reconnaissance. No one came, so he rose, shaking his legs vigorously to combat the stinging of his flesh as blood came back into it. He entered the clearing, his hounds following a few paces behind, still tussling over the male dog's prize.

When he came to the center of the opening, the anchorite looked around him, marveling at the efficiency with which the camp had been cleared away. The fire had been thoroughly quenched, and when he put a hand to the soaked mass of ashes, it was cold. Moving to the train, he pulled himself into the second boxcar. The funk of close-packed bodies washed over him, but he did not feel lightheaded as he had earlier, when Yukon with the bandy legs had relieved himself. He breathed this scent in, this musk of the tide of human-kind, reminded by it of much. Much that was bad, and much that was good too. The scents of hair and skin and sweat, effort and kinship and the tang of sex. Much that he had renounced years be-fore. Much and much and much. Time was the only thing required to disperse it all, and not a lot of that.

He was pleased to find that the poster of the walking baby-doll was intact, still in its accustomed place on the wall. In dark grease pencil across one corner of the white plain, someone had scrawled the words *A El Dorado*. Elsewhere, against the dark border of the poster, where it was difficult to make out, a different hand had written in a crabbed, slashing script *Tannhauser come mierda*.

Dropping from the train car, he whistled up his dogs, who came swiftly to him. He thought of the interlopers, of their impassive faces as they were marched off into the woods. He thought of the girl Paloma, and of the hand that Tannhauser had laid on her back, his whole attitude frighteningly proprietary. He thought of El Dorado, which Tannhauser had called a place of great wealth, and of the place he knew as El Dorado, with its dark crumbling buildings, its windows like empty eyes, its razor wire and thick walls topped with broken bottles.

"Come on," he said to the dogs. "We'll follow them in a little ways, anyhow." They cocked their heads as though they would un-derstand the words. He made for the path cut by the lone Mingo and trampled down by those who followed behind. Divining his intention, the hounds raced across the clearing ahead of him, whip tails curled over their backs, mouths open. They crossed with their sure swinging canine stride the broad fairy ring of the interlopers' footprints and were immediately received into the green estate of the trees.

8

Peanut had been unsuccessfully trying to hitch a ride for several hours, so he was grateful when a car, a big new Lincoln Continental, pulled to the side of the road in a cloud of fine gray dust. He trotted up to the Connie where it sat idling on the highway berm. The driver powered down the tinted passenger-side window and sat there, grinning vacantly. Peanut worked the door handle but the door refused to open for him. He thought it might be some kind of a trick, and he waited for the Continental to roar off and leave him behind.

When it did not, he bent to peer into the car. The man had opened the window to about the span of a hand, and Peanut looked at the leather interior through the slot. Refrigerated air gusted out at him. The breeze felt good on the hot skin of his face. "You want to unlock the door for me?" Peanut said. The man turned the vacuous grin on Peanut but made no move toward the electric door locks. The Continental's mill turned over sluggishly. Peanut could feel its vibrations in the hand that he rested on the car's roof.

"Unlock?" Peanut said again. "The door?"

"Oh, sure," the man said, as though just now noticing that Peanut was waiting for something. The man's voice was deep and well modulated. Peanut thought he might be a radio personality or something. One of his hands left the wheel to reach out and touch a button. A mechanism inside the passenger door thumped, and Peanut swung it open. He climbed in and sank gratefully down onto the thickly cushioned passenger seat.

"I was getting pretty tired, out there walking," he said.

"Where you headed to?" the man asked. His voice was pleasant to listen to, Peanut decided, even if he sounded a little affected.

"Just up yon way," Peanut said, gesturing faintly in front of him. "You're going in the right direction."

"Anyplace this direction in particular?"

"I'm not exactly sure of how far it might be."

"Got a name, does it? This place?" There was no real curiosity in the man's voice.

"I'll let you know if it looks like you're going past it," Peanut said.

"Okay," he said. "Do that thing."

"Thanks," Peanut said. "Thanks for the ride."

The man waved a dismissive hand. He punched the Connie's accelerator and the large car slewed out onto the road, spraying gravel in a hissing roostertail behind it. The wide Michelin tires chirped when they hit the hardtop. The road unreeled emptily toward them, broken white center lines blurring by. It fatigued Peanut to watch their constant passage, and he felt his eyelids begin to draw down. Steeling himself, he fought his way back to wakefulness. He yawned hugely, and the man, though he had not been watching Peanut, gapped and yawned a minute later.

It was rolling country through which they rode, and the heat lay on the land like a mirror. Low places in the highway were filled with a liquid haze. The man was not distracted and plowed through the mirages with equanimity. He squinted his eyes at the horizon like a person who is nearsighted but won't wear glasses. His hair was fashionably long and uncombed, and it had the color and texture of straw as it lay on his shoulders and across the headrest of his seat. He was heavy, not fat but prosperously solid, and his meaty hands gripped the steering wheel tightly.

"Where are you headed to yourself?" Peanut asked.

The man looked him over, suspicion in his gaze. "Who wants to know?"

"Just me," Peanut said.

Apparently finding that answer satisfactory, the man said, "South

Carolina. I'm going to Hilton Head Island. I'm going to take some vacation time down there. R and R. Been getting a little ragged around the edges is the problem."

Peanut stretched his arms over his head, ran his hands along the seams at the edge of his seat. Looking at the man's profile, he said, "Hey, this is what I call nice. All leather interior."

The man continued staring straight ahead. He said, "None of that Corinthian leather stuff for me, that goddamn Naugahyde. They skinned a real cow to get this. They roll the seams under when they sew them so they'll never come unstitched."

Peanut said, "How did you manage to come by such a sharp ride as this?"

The man shot him a look. "You don't think I could have a car like this one here?"

"No, it's nothing like that," Peanut assured him. "It's just I never knew anybody with a car like this, and I'd like to know the secret of how you get one. If there is a secret."

"Tell you the truth, it's a company car. I've got a good job."

"I guess so."

"Perks aplenty, and this is one of them that you're riding in right now."

"Perks?"

"Perquisites. A privilege that you get with a certain level of professional attainment. And it's not just the car, either," the man said. His lower jaw jutted out in a bellicose way. "I've got some pretty hellacious credit cards too. Gold card this, platinum card that. I bet I've got cards a person like you hasn't even heard of yet."

Peanut shook his head. "I might have a credit card," he said. He wasn't insulted. He knew how he looked. He'd been sleeping outdoors, and he hadn't had a shave in a while. He looked pretty rough.

"No," the man said. "I don't think so. Fellow that carries nothing with him and hitchhikes down the road." He glanced up at the rearview mirror, and something that he saw there riveted his attention for a moment. After a few seconds he relaxed. He looked over at Peanut and shrugged, gave a brief laugh, and went back to his driving. "Nobody there," he said. "I knew there wasn't, but sometimes you see something that fools you."

Peanut craned his head around to check. The road behind them was as clear as the road ahead. A sign proclaimed in sloppily arranged letters two feet high NOAH'S ARK BEING REBUILT HERE, but Peanut could see no sign of any boat at all, let alone the Ark. He let out a long breath, settling more deeply into his seat. They rode on in silence for a while, the hiss of air rushing over the hood and past the windows the only sound in the car's dark interior. The highway they followed had been cut through the hills, and the land rose steeply away from the lanes on either side of them. The truncated slopes were terraced, and lean saplings and tough scrubby grass were finding a paltry foothold on the narrow stairlike flats. Peanut thought that there would be fossils revealed in the rock faces that whipped past, tiny leaves or ancient calcified insects. He shivered. "You keep it pretty cool in here," he said.

"The air conditioner's got a compressor on it like a refrigerator. I like a car where you can make it really cold. Nothing I hate worse than the heat."

"I don't know," Peanut said. "You get used to heat after a while. It comes to seem natural."

"Not for me. All I do is sweat when it gets too hot, and pretty soon I come down with the asthma. Which is not a sissy thing as you might think." He made a cautioning gesture at Peanut. "It's in the blood. My father's got it too, and he just passed it on to me. He can't go a hundred yards without carrying his inhaler along with him."

"Lots of people have that," Peanut said. "It's nothing big."

"Do you?"

"No," Peanut said. "That's one thing I have not got."

"People without it can't understand people with it. They think we're making it up or something. But I've got to keep the heat off of me or I pitch a fit. Have to spray that mist down my throat, and it makes me sick. You should taste it. Like sucking a mothball."

"I think you're safe from overheating, long as you stay in the car. It's like a meat locker in here."

"That's all I do is sit in the car," the man said. "It gets pretty dull sometimes. Pretty lonely. Stop to get gas, and I use full serve if they give it. If I sleep in a motel room, they've got to have good air conditioning or I won't stay there."

"Sounds smart."

"You may not think so, but you wouldn't like to see me throw one of my fits. I get red in the face and the veins in my forehead stand out. That's why I got this car."

"It's a good car," Peanut said.

"I just got it a couple of days ago," the man said. "But I'm pretty well used to it already." He studied the steering wheel between his hands for a short while. While he was absorbed in whatever he saw there, the Connie drifted steadily to the right. The wheels on that side dropped off the pavement onto the low shoulder, and gravel spurted up from under the wheels and hammered noisily at the floor panels. Peanut could feel the small concussions in the soles of his feet. The guardrail flashed by, uncomfortably close to the passenger door.

"Hey," Peanut said. "Hey, guy."

The man looked up and, seeing where they were, steered the car back onto the pavement. "I've got it, I've got it," he said. "Under control." When they once again traveled the solid surface, he asked, "Did you call me *guy*? When you were yelling at me just now."

"I don't believe I was yelling. I just wanted to get your attention."

"People call me Chilly."

"The way you keep this car," Peanut said, "I imagine they do."

"Oh, it's not because of that," Chilly said. "Or at least not mainly. It's really because I don't get hot in certain situations. Business situations. I react well to pressure."

"You stay chilly," Peanut said.

"That's it," Chilly said. He seemed relieved to have been understood. They drove on for a while.

"You want to know my name?" Peanut said.

Chilly looked surprised. "I never thought about it," he said.

"It's Peanut." He waited to be asked where he had come by such a moniker.

Chilly plucked at the safety belt that stretched over his solid chest. It pulled from its rollers with a quiet zipping sound. He extended it as far as it would go and then allowed it to snap back into place. He said, "You've got a shoulder harness there behind you, Peanut. Put that on, would you? It'll hold you down in case of unforeseen circumstances."

Peanut looked around him until he located the three-point belt. He tugged it across him and locked it down. Its narrow width chafed against his flesh, and he struggled mutely for a time beneath it. Then he said, "These things always catch me wrong." He unfastened his belt, and it slipped back behind him.

Chilly clucked disapprovingly. "I wouldn't do that if I were you," he said.

Peanut was not listening. He settled back in his seat to grab a nap. He turned his head away from Chilly, toward the window. After watching the swiftly changing landscape for a time, he closed his eyes. Speaking to the back of his head, Chilly said, "Well, okay. But I guess you must not know what can happen to a person when they don't wear their seat belt. I know it. I've seen."

Without turning his head, Peanut said, "What is it you've seen?"

At first Peanut thought that Chilly wasn't going to answer. Finally, though, he did. "In a driver reeducation class one time," he said. "They showed us a film about drunk drivers. A cameraman went out on the job with an ambulance crew. He followed them for about a day or so and filmed everything they did. I don't know how they could take it, all the things that they saw. Truck smashes, car wrecks. People that were pitched into culverts and over bluffs. There was even a schoolbus full of kids that had smacked a bridge abutment." He sounded a little breathless.

Peanut rolled his head back to the left so that he could see Chilly, who drove with one hand. With the other he brushed the long hair back from his face. A silver post set in his pale earlobe winked in the light. In a moment his hair spilled forward again and covered the earring. Peanut said, "What were you doing in a class like that?"

Chilly said, "I was arrested for DUI. It was my second offense, and the judge said I had to attend these classes. The whole course took about six weeks. It really made a convert out of me, I'll tell you."

Peanut turned his face back toward the window. He stretched his legs out and tried to ignore the cold.

"Yo there," Chilly said. He struggled with the name for a moment, and finally came up with it. "Yo, Peanut. Are you going to sleep?" When Peanut failed to reply, Chilly reached out and put a hand on his shoulder. The touch startled Peanut and he convulsed. Chilly's palm was dry and warmer than the air in the car, and the contact was light. He said, "How will I know to let you off if we get to your place?"

"I'll tell you when it comes up," Peanut said. "It's a good long way off. I'll be awake by then." He felt lassitude coming toward him like a great wave that he could neither duck nor overleap. He closed his eyes, and his hearing was filled with the sibilance of the car's steady progress.

Chilly poked him with a pointed forefinger and said, "I need you to pump some gas for me."

Peanut jerked upright when Chilly spoke. He didn't remember their having pulled into a gas station. He'd been asleep. It was eight o'clock, according to the digital clock set into the dash. He had to think, to force his muzzy brain into gear, in order to decide that it was eight at night and not eight in the morning. The car was suffused with a weird amber light from the lamps attached to the service station's canopy. The tinted glass all around gave to Chilly's skin and to Peanut's a bruised, undersea quality, as though the car were submerged with them trapped in it, flesh pulpy from drowning.

Chilly poked him again. "Got to earn your keep," he said. "Can't ride for nothing."

"Stop sticking me like that," Peanut said. "You've got some long pointy damn fingernails."

"No I don't." Chilly held up his hands and waggled his fingers at Peanut. "I've just got hard fingers. How about getting us some high-test?"

Peanut worked his cramped limbs and briefly massaged the stiffness in his neck. "Slept on it wrong," he said to Chilly with a grin. Chilly looked at him without amusement. A car pulled up to the other side of the pump island, a green Chevrolet Caprice. Peanut stepped out of the Connie onto the station's concrete apron. A humid wind blew out of the west, bringing heat with it. He closed his eyes and laced his hands behind his head, relishing the warmth. He bowed his back until the vertebrae crackled. After he had stretched, it took him a little while to find the gas cap. Chilly had pulled up the wrong way to the line of pumps, and the cap was on the far side of the car from them. As he reached for the nozzle of the 93-octane pump, so did the driver of the Caprice.

Looking up, Peanut noticed the hat first. The Chevy driver was wearing a wide-brimmed, high-crowned campaign hat. Then Peanut saw the green military-style uniform and slanting Sam Browne belt of a sheriff's deputy. The patch on the deputy's shoulder said *Dwyer County*. Peanut glanced at the Caprice again and saw that it was unmarked but carrying county plates. "You go ahead," he said to the deputy, standing aside.

"Well, strictly, you got here before me," the deputy said. He was a thick-necked young man who wore his Smith & Wesson .38 Special low on his hip, like a gunfighter.

"No, you," Peanut said, and they stood on their respective sides of the pump, looking at each other. Finally, to break the deadlock,

Peanut reached out his hand. The deputy did too. Just before their hands met, though, the deputy drew back again, frowning. Peanut forced himself to complete the motion. His hand closed on the nozzle, lifted it from the pump. He had to drag the gasoline hose around the rear end of the car to reach the mouth of the gas tank. The hose caught under the rear bumper, and when he bent to clear it, he saw that the Continental bore no license tags. He felt a moment's panic and fought it down. His mind worked frantically as he labored to unkink the hose. Chilly had not bought the car; he had stolen it. He felt the deputy's stare on him. His mouth went dry. He could not bear to look up, but instead fixed his gaze on the whorls of gasoline that patterned the pavement beneath the Continental.

He managed to unhook the tangle of hose from the bumper. Rounding the car, still crouching, he crammed the pump nozzle into the throat of the tank and started the flow of gas. The metal of the nozzle grew cold in his grip as the gasoline rushed through it. His gaze fell on the temporary license, lettered in Magic Marker, that was taped in the bottom left corner of the rear glass. It was a thirty-day tag, dated two days earlier.

He laughed to himself and looked around for the deputy. He wanted to say something, to demonstrate his blamelessness. He wanted to say, "Is this a nice car here, or what?" Or maybe, "What kind of engine have you got in that Chevy? I bet it's not any little old four-banger. I bet it's supercharged." The deputy was not in his expected place. Peanut saw him silhouetted in the window of the station, paying the cashier for something that he held in his hand: gum perhaps, or breath mints.

For one reason or another the pump's automatic shutoff didn't work, and gasoline poured from the tank opening, down the side of the Lincoln, and onto Peanut's shoes before he stopped pumping. He cursed. The deputy came from the station as Peanut was returning the nozzle to the pump. He stamped his feet to get the gas off. "Your go," he said, and the deputy made a quick nod in his direction.

Peanut went to the driver's window of the car and tapped on it. Chilly slid the window down a little way. "Twenty-two dollars and thirty-seven cents," Peanut told him.

"Is it that much?" Chilly asked. "That seems like a lot."

"Gas is expensive," Peanut said. "And you got a big car with a big gas tank."

"I guess," Chilly said resentfully, as though he suspected Peanut of trying to bilk him. He reached into his back pocket and pulled out a thick wallet. He leafed through the cash in the billfold, selected a twenty and a five, and handed the money to Peanut, who trotted into the gas station to pay. He emerged shortly.

As he was climbing back into the Lincoln, the deputy, still pumping gas into his cruiser, called over to him. "Hey," he said, and Peanut's head snapped around as he realized that he was being addressed. He knew it was the way convicts and parolees responded to the authority in a policeman's voice, and he hated himself for it. He looked deliberately away from the deputy, who was squinting at him in the peculiar light of the gas station lamps, and took his time about facing around again.

"What?" he said.

"Don't I know you?" the deputy asked. "From somewhere."

"I couldn't tell you," Peanut said. He felt reckless. "Do you? Do you know me from somewhere?"

The deputy continued to inspect him for a moment. "No," he said at last. "I guess that I don't."

"Well, I don't know you either, nor much care to," Peanut said, climbing into the car.

Behind him, as if in apology, the deputy said, "It's just you looked familiar to me there for a second. In this light."

Peanut pulled the Connie's door closed behind him and fastened his seat belt, recalling too late that he had meant to get something to drink. The car was already in motion out of the gas station's lot.

Chilly wrinkled his nose at Peanut. "You smell like gas," he said. "You smell to high heaven."

"It spilled. I got some on me."

"What did the trooper want with you back there?" Chilly asked.

"The who?"

"The state trooper. At the gas station. You were talking, and then you yelled at him as you got into the car."

"That's no trooper," Peanut said. "That's just a county mountie." When he saw Chilly's look of incomprehension, he said, "Sheriff's deputy." He dug into his pocket and came up with two dollar bills and some coins. He held them out to Chilly, who did not reach for them.

"Keep it," Chilly said.

"Thanks," Peanut said, "I will." He heard Chilly chuckle when he pocketed the cash. He said, "That may seem like a joke to someone like you, but it isn't to me. I'll take your money. I'm not proud."

Chilly patted him placatingly on the leg. His hand was large and square, and his nails were neatly trimmed. "I know," he said. "I know that about you." When he had finished speaking, he did not withdraw his hand, but left it where it rested on Peanut's thigh. They drove on, and silence, a new energetic kind of silence, grew up between them.

9

Goody had the Pontiac up near its top speed, and the telephone poles along the berm flickered past like fence posts. Insects collided continuously with the windshield—bugs that swarmed frantically in the air above the road, drawn there by the heat that rose from the blacktop; blood-filled mosquitoes—or they flew in through one window and whirred around the interior of the car until they blundered back out through the same window or its opposite and were sucked away into the car's hot slipstream.

Goody slapped at a sweat bee that lighted on the back of his neck, failing to crush it but not missing by much, and the small bee lifted from his skin and cruised away. The car rocked as it hustled through a dip and then climbed a hillock. The road passed under a length of aqueduct. The death mask of a Shawnee chieftain, carved lifesize in the stone at the pinnacle of one of the aqueduct's several arches, watched the car's approach with opaque eyes. Beneath the vault of the aqueduct, the roar of the car's dual glasspack mufflers was briefly magnified. Then the Le Mans was in the clear again, racing across the big level toward the mountains at the north end of the valley.

Entering a hard righthand curve, Goody braked, downshifting. The pitch of the bridled engine rose. At the curve's end, the road crossed a stream, and the Pontiac's wheels burred noisily against the steel honeycomb surface of the single-lane bridge that spanned it. As he crossed the bridge, Goody thought he spotted a dog's head poking out from the underbrush along the banks of the creek. He could not be sure what he had seen. He craned his head around to check whether the animal might stick its head out again.

When he looked back, a deer blocked his lane. It was a big white-tail doe, and it stood spraddle-legged, squarely between the lines on his side of the road as he bore down on it. Its nostrils flared. Goody mashed the brake pedal to the floor, not pumping it as he knew he should do but trying for an all-out panic stop. For a horrifying moment the pedal sank loosely under his foot, no resistance to it, and then the wheels locked up. The tires wailed and the big car slewed sideways. The steering wheel seesawed madly against Goody's grip, and he tried to turn it in the direction of his skid. Rubber stripped off the tires in sections of ever-increasing size, like parings from an orange rind. The two right tires, front and back, blew out simultaneously, the hubcaps on that side skipping and rolling down the road, preceding the car. The locked wheels traced looping black streaks on the hardtop, and smoke rose from the skid marks.

The deer left the road in a great stiff-limbed leap, clearing the front fender of the Pontiac by inches, the delicate hoof of one of its back legs nicking the paint and knocking loose a long narrow piece of chrome molding that clattered to the road and lay among the marks of the car's passing. The deer bounded awkwardly up the earth bank on the side of the road, its damaged leg held tight against its body. Still the car spun. Goody had ceased to fight the steering wheel.

A tight knot of dogs in full cry shot from the woods by the side of the road, hot on the trail of the deer. Less agile than the whitetail, or less savvy, they bounded into the path of the oncoming Pontiac, which rode over several of them and scattered the bodies. Other dogs emerged from the line of trees along the road and watched with unsurprised eyes as the car plowed through the animals and careened onward. One of the injured dogs hauled itself back toward the woods by its front legs, screaming.

The Pontiac lurched from the road, caromed off an aluminum guardrail, and slid partway up a dirt slope, where it came to rest on its side. The horn tooted weakly, once. The engine howled, chattered, and went silent. A choking cloud of red soil bloomed around the car, settling on it, on the glass of its windows and its chrome fittings. The dust lit on the heat-wilted leaves and branches of nearby trees. It drifted into the passenger compartment, coating the seat covers and the faces of the instruments and Goody's prostrate form.

He lay cramped in the angle of the driver's side door and the floor and waited for the car to roll from its side over onto its top, crushing him. He imagined that the roll would begin slowly when it started, gathering speed as the car turned turtle, and that he would be conscious through the whole process. When the Pontiac didn't spill onto its roof, he stirred, felt over his body and limbs for injuries, and raised his head.

A dog stared with black pop eyes through the windshield at him. It was a happy-looking dog, low to the ground, a dachshund bitch with a double row of black teats along its sagging belly. When it saw Goody looking back at it, it yipped excitedly. It trotted closer to the windshield, barking, and stood with its front feet on the glass. The pads of its paws splayed out before Goody, shaped like dark clovers, and its wet questing nose marked the glass. Then it backed away again, squatting on its fat haunches, observing him.

Goody pulled himself up, holding onto the driver's seat. He froze when the car shifted slightly beneath him. The driver's side door was wedged against the dirt of the bank, its window only inches off the ground, so he hauled himself gingerly upward toward the passenger door, pausing each time he felt the car move.

The dachshund abandoned its place. It paraded on the ground above the Pontiac, barking in a high, agitated voice. Other members of the pack trotted back and forth across the road, sniffing at the scattered corpses of the posse of dogs. A soprano keening rose from a culvert at the edge of the woods, where the injured dog had gone.

A handsome, savage-looking malamute sat behind the car. When Goody pulled at the handle of the passenger door, the malamute's ears flickered forward. Although it was a solidly built dog with a well-shaped head, its coat was matted with burrs and mud. The hair was missing in places. Goody pushed the car door open. He had to lean up and across the seat to do it. One of his feet rested on the transmission hump, and the other found an uncomfortable roost on the steering column. The malamute left its place and circled the car, its jaws slightly open, tongue out. As Goody drew himself upward, the big dog barked. "Hey there," Goody said. He was amazed to find that he was unhurt. He chinned himself with difficulty, got an arm out into the open. He could see the malamute just over the lip of the door, sitting and watching, its head cocked to one side.

"Hey," Goody said again. "Hey boy." The dog half rose from its seated position, sank back. "That's great," Goody said. "That's a good dog." He prepared to boost himself out of the car. He was sweating with the effort of climbing, and he wanted very badly to be free of the unstable vehicle. As he began the final pull, the malamute darted forward and nipped at his fingers. He shouted and pulled his hand back, losing his grip on the door's edge in the process. He fell back, banging his hip against the steering wheel as he went. The car listed alarmingly. Lying against the driver's side door again, he examined his bitten fingers. The skin was reddened, but it had not been broken. He clutched the hand to his chest.

Over him, the malamute loomed in the open door. The sky behind it was a hot blue, and the dog's features were obscured against the bright background. It looked like a shadow, standing up there. It crouched with its paws just at the open door's edge, as though it were contemplating jumping down. Goody hoped with all his heart that it would not. It stood and barked, its long snout inside the car. The sound was deafening in the enclosed space. The bark seemed more encouraging than threatening.

"Go away," Goody said.

The dog lay down, making itself comfortable where it could keep an eye on him. It licked its front paws and then reached around so that it could wash its hindquarters. Afterward, it seemed to doze. Goody rearranged his body, trying to hold himself off the door handle beneath him and the projecting knob of the window crank, which dug cruelly into his back. He finally found the position that caused him the least distress, one in which he could look up and watch the sky while seeing very little, just the hairy outline, of the dog that guarded him.

He listened for cars coming along the stretch of road, but none did. The birds were loud in the trees, a huge flock of grackles that screeched at one another in raucous voices. From the sound of them he guessed that they must fill the trees around the car, bending the tree limbs under their massed weight. Their screaming conversation went on and on, and after a while the sound took on the droning, calming quality of fast water over rocks.

Suddenly the birds went silent. Together they lifted into the air. The sound of their wings came to him like a stiff, storm-bearing wind. The flock passed over the Pontiac, and Goody could see their darting shapes above him as they went. It was like watching the passage of a school of long-finned, darkly iridescent fish. The malamute cast its eyes skyward, making small nervous movements of its head. It stared after the birds when, minutes later it seemed, they had all gone. In the quiet that followed them, Goody could hear the injured hound whining in the culvert. Its voice echoed weirdly in the concrete basin.

A vehicle stopped beside the road. One of its doors opened and closed. The dachshund yelped, and the other dogs scattered, their claws skittering among the rocks and loose shale. The malamute stayed where it was, ears pricked forward.

"Hey," a man said. "Somebody inside there, or are you all dead?"

"I'm in here," Goody said. His voice was hoarse with dust, and he cleared his throat. "I'm here, but I can't get out." His voice was stronger this time. The malamute's gaze shifted down to him and then back to the man on the road.

"Okay," the man said. "When I didn't see nobody, I thought maybe you had died in the wreck. How many is it?"

"Just me," Goody said. The dog's eyes narrowed. "Listen," he said, "you might want to be careful of that dog there."

"What?" the man said.

"The dog!" Goody shouted to make himself understood.

"That your dog?" the man asked. The malamute laid its ears back against its skull and sprinted toward the voice.

"Look out!" Goody shouted. At the same time the man cried, "Jesus!" The malamute made no noise at all. Goody stood upright and was pulling himself toward the open car door when he heard the sharp crack of a pistol shot. The round whined off a rock or some other hard surface near him. It made a low humming sound as it passed overhead, the bullet flattened and tumbling. Goody ducked, and the car swayed dangerously under him. Determined, he drew himself up and out of the car, ignoring the pistol when it popped again, and a third time.

"Goddamn," the man said. Goody slid from the car to the ground. He scrambled on all fours away from it. "Can't you hit nothing, Dreama?" the man said. "Shoot it again." He gestured furiously toward the dog, which was climbing the bank on the far side of the road. A woman leaned from the passenger window of the Bronco that sat there, a blunt pistol in her right hand. She squinted along the short barrel, drawing down on the malamute as it loped toward the woods. It disappeared from sight into the underbrush, and she relaxed, let the pistol hang loose from her trigger finger.

"It was moving pretty fast," she said. "And I didn't want to hit you, but you wouldn't get out of my way."

"Safest place in the entire world to be," the man said. "Where you're aiming." He was a heavyset older man, with a head of thick wavy silver-white hair.

"Rescued your sorry butt, didn't I?" she said. She was young and good-looking, with long dark hair and bangs cut straight across her smooth brow. Her eyes when she shifted her gaze to Goody were a piercing green. "Didn't I?" she said, to Goody this time.

"If you say it," he replied. Gesturing at the Pontiac where it lay against the hillside, he said, "I was down inside, so I didn't get to see." To the man he said, "It sure sounded like that dog was going for you."

"It was," the man said. He fingered a long tear in the sleeve of his shirt. "Them dogs had you holed up inside of there?" he asked. Goody nodded. "I thought it was your dog setting near the car is why I come up the way I did. I'd of brought the pistol myself if I knew."

"There was a bunch of them, but really only one that was giving me trouble," Goody said. "It wouldn't let me climb out."

"Most of them run off when they heard us come up," the man said. "They lit for the woods with their tails down, but that one looked like he meant business. He stayed right where he was."

"I heard a story like that once," the woman said. "About a guy that got trapped all night in a deep hole by a pack of dogs. Turns out it was a grave, and when they found him the next morning, he was laying in a puddle of cold water at the bottom of the hole and he was raving. He never did care for a dog after that."

"I never cared much about dogs in the first place," Goody said.

The man went to the woman and took the pistol from her. He walked to the wounded dog where it thrashed in the culvert and shot it. He put the bullet into its spine, right behind the head. A small spray of dust gouted from beneath the dog's head, and it quivered and went still. The man handed the pistol back to the woman. He eyed the tilted Pontiac. "I don't believe there's a whole lot we can do for your car," he said. "Give you a ride if you want. We're heading south."

"As far down as Titan?"

"That far and a little farther," the man said. "We can drop you off if that's where you're going."

"I wasn't going anyplace in particular," Goody told him. "Just joyriding."

"You're done with that for a while," the man said. "In that car at least. Nobody else in there, you say?"

"Just me is all." Goody turned a critical eye on the Le Mans. "Do you think it'll stay the way it is?" he said. "I don't want it to come down the hill and get in the road."

Goody and the man both studied the car for a minute. Finally the man spoke. "Hard to tell," he said. "What exactly have you got planned to do if you think it won't stay?"

"I don't know," Goody said.

The man turned and headed for the Bronco with his quick stride, and Goody followed him. Dreama slid over to the middle of the truck's front seat to make room. The man climbed in behind the steering wheel, and Goody got in on the passenger side. The man cranked the Bronco up, and they headed back along the road, crossing the Pontiac's skid marks, tracks that wove crazily in all directions across the pavement. Curled strips of tire rubber lay strewn like confetti for a hundred yards. The remains of the pack of dogs were there as well, their bodies in various stiffening attitudes beside the road and on it.

"Looks like you got you some," the man said.

"Nothing I meant to do," Goody said. "They were in the way of the car."

"You went all over the place. Bore down pretty hard on the brakes, didn't you?"

"I was trying to stop."

The man coughed a derisive little cough, but he didn't say anything more.

Dreama had secreted the gun somewhere, and she was smoking a cigarette. Goody considered asking her for one but decided against it. She looked at him with her sharp green eyes. Her gaze was level, and frankly appraising. "How long were you in there?" she wanted to know. Her voice was low. Jammed against her in the Bronco's narrow cab, Goody could smell the cigarettes on her, and a sweet smell. He decided that it was the smell of her shampoo or some other chemical she used on herself. He tried unobtrusively to sniff her hair, and she smiled at him like she knew what he was doing.

"Not too long," he said. "About fifteen minutes before you showed up. I didn't want to chance climbing out of there with that dog getting in my face like it was."

"Big damn dog," the man said. Goody noticed his hair again. It was startling, white with a sheen to it like polished steel, as though he were wearing a helmet on his large head. It gave him the air of a warrior.

"It sure was," Goody said.

"I wish you'd of shot it," the man said to Dreama. "It must of gone ninety pounds or more."

"You shut up, Wallace," she said. "If I'd put a bullet through your leg it might of hit the dog. Would that be better? Should I of done that?"

"Too many of them fuckers running around up here," Wallace said. "They get loose from their doghouse in town somewhere and they go wild and breed and breed. They tear up the livestock like you wouldn't believe. You can't throw a rock without you'll hit a dog."

"They were chasing a deer," Goody said. "It came out in the road in front of my car, and I tried not to hit it. You saw what happened."

Wallace nodded. "Too many of them too. They're starved, and they get in your corn and crops and eat them down to the ground. We'll have a hell of a winter, when there's a million of them starving bastards and nothing for them to eat. They come down out of the hills and you'll be hitting them with your car then, by God, see if you don't. You'll have to push them out of the way with a plow blade."

To Goody, Dreama said, "He hates a deer as much as he hates a wild dog."

"More," Wallace said. "I didn't see no deer back there. You said you hit one?"

"I missed it. It went up over my hood like a rocket and came down running. I never knew anything could jump so high."

"Like grasshoppers," Wallace said. "Like locusts."

Dreama leaned her head against the high seat back and blew a long stream of smoke toward the truck's ceiling. The smoke eddied there, dissipating, and finally disappeared altogether. They passed under the aqueduct with the Indian's face carved on it. The road traced the contour of the valley bottom, following the course of a narrow river that wound its way southward. The shallow water just covered the smooth gray stones of the riverbed, sliding over them in a bright sheet. The Bronco jolted along on its bad shocks. When they had ridden that way for a while, Dreama sat up abruptly. She pointed past Goody, and he noted the solid muscles of her forearm and the light dusting of freckles on her skin. "Look there," she said. She pointed to a sign that sprouted from the side of the road. Goody had not noticed it on his way north. It was a large wooden arrow, seven feet long, tacked to a telephone pole at the height of a man's head. Painted on the arrow in foot-high letters, in a kind of Gothic script, were the words THE HIDDEN WORLD.

"What is it?" Goody asked. They sped by the sign, which pointed the way up a narrow gravel road that climbed unevenly over the crown of a knoll and out of sight. Wallace didn't acknowledge that Dreama had spoken, and they sped past the place without slackening their speed.

"It's somewhere," Dreama said. She turned an accusing look on Wallace. "Somewhere I want to go to, but that he won't never go with me."

"I went," Wallace said.

"Once."

"That's all the more I needed to go. I saw what there was to see and I don't care to see it again. Anyhow, you go without me when you want to. How many times you been there?"

"A couple," Dreama said. "A few."

"Is it an Indian village or something?" Goody asked.

"It's a tourist trap," Wallace said.

Dreama pursed her lips. "It's a cave," she said. "It's a whole series of caves that goes back in under the hills. You never saw nothing like it. They've got colored lights all through the whole thing, and a taped musical soundtrack that plays. They've got guides that will tell you the story of the place as they walk you all around inside it. It's the premier attraction in the valley."

"It costs six bucks every time you go," Wallace said. He drummed his fingers against the steering wheel.

Dreama said, "A man died exploring it. They've got his body preserved for all time in a casket down there. His name was Floyd Askins."

"They've got a body?" Goody asked. He looked to Wallace, who nodded resignedly.

"Just like goddamn Lenin in his tomb," he said.

"There's caves under this whole area," Dreama said. "Miles and miles of tunnels. They're cool all the time. You never get hot in the caves."

Goody said, "There's a cave under the farm where I'm living. There's a stream of water that comes from a sheer rock wall. It just pours out like a fountain."

"Those caves are all connected under there," Dreama said. "Miles and miles of them. The chance is, your cave is part of the whole network. You're drinking the same water that runs through the Hidden World. You're bathing in it."

"What about that," Goody said.

Wallace said, "Coming up on Titan. You want out here, or farther along?"

They were in a place that Goody recognized as being not far from Mr. Inchcape's farm, a couple or three miles at most if he cut through a few hayfields instead of going by the road. "I can walk it," he said. "Just let me out anywhere along here."

Dreama said to him, "We're not in no hurry." To Wallace she said, "We're not. You take him on wherever it is he might want to go."

Wallace shrugged his shoulders. "I guess that's right," he said.

Goody pointed out the turn that Wallace had to take, a quarter-mile or so up the road. A few minutes later they drew up in front of the house. Wallace threw on the hand brake, and the Bronco rocked to a stop. "Well," Goody said, reaching for the door handle, "many thanks for the ride, and for getting those dogs off of me. I don't know how long I'd have had to lie there if you hadn't come along."

"It might of decided to come in there after you," Wallace said. "If it got hungry enough. You can't never tell with these ones that have gone wild. They act pretty crazy sometimes."

"Maybe we can go up there to that cave after a while," Dreama said. "Up to the Hidden World. The three of us."

"Count me out," Wallace said.

Dreama turned her smile on Goody, who slipped out of the cab.
"Us two, then," she said.

"Maybe," he told her. "Probably I won't be going much of anywhere for a while."

"We'll go after you get the car fixed," she said.

"Sure," Goody said. He started for the door of the house.

Wallace backed the Bronco around. On his way out of the yard,
he called after Goody. "Hey," he said, and Goody turned. "We heard
somebody died around here not too long ago."

"A man died in the canefield here. I found him."

"What did he look like? It might be somebody we know. We
know pretty much everybody around here."

"You couldn't really tell what he might have looked like. He'd
been dead a while." Goody considered. "He was skinny. That's about
what I can tell you. I hope he wasn't anybody you knew because it
didn't look like he enjoyed the way he died."

Dreama had not moved from her place in the middle of the
truck's front seat, near Wallace. She looked at him, but he couldn't
read the expression on her face.

Wallace said, "You know, a man killed his wife with a pickax here
a couple of decades ago. He really tore her up. My brother was a
deputy sheriff then and he came out and saw it. He said he couldn't
imagine such a thing, one person doing that to another person."

"I heard it was a ballpeen hammer."

"Hammer, pick, shovel, whatever it was. He killed her. My
brother told me he took his time with it too, like it was some kind of a
project, and he didn't care a thing about what he had done afterward. No remorse. Why do you imagine he would do a thing like
that?"

Goody made a gesture of uncertainty.

"I don't know either," Wallace said. "People like us, that are
normal people, can't imagine committing a terrible crime like that.
But some people, it's how they do things. They just pick up something heavy and let somebody else have it. To some people it's just all
in a day's business."

"I guess that's so," Goody said.

"He'd be getting out of prison about now, the husband, if he was
going to get out," Wallace said. "But he got killed himself in a riot
upstate. He wasn't in the riot, but some state trooper nailed him after

it was over anyhow. Put a rifle bullet through him. He lived a couple of days and then he died. They say he was a model prisoner the whole time that he was in. Never touched a fly." The sun was lowering, and for the first time since Goody had lived in the house, a cool breeze sprang up. "I thought it might be a comfort to you, knowing he was dead," Wallace said. "In case you were worried about him coming back or something. He won't be coming back."

"I never worried about it. I never even thought about it."

"Oh," Wallace said. He seemed disappointed. "I would of thought about it, if it was me living out here. So I thought you might like to know."

"Thanks for telling me."

Dreama and Wallace sat in their Bronco in front of Goody's house for a little while longer. Maybe seeing how it had happened, here in this place, the woman plunging through the loose screen door, carrying it with her. No voice to scream with. Momentum carrying her out into the yard, bare feet moving slowly now, shuffling through the blood-spattered dirt, toed-in like the feet of a clumsy dreamy child. Dropping to the gray grassless yard while something, someone, stood framed in the doorway, just out of the reach of the light, watching with uncaring eyes.

Dreama called out pleasantly, "You get that car fixed, now," and then they were gone, the Bronco bottoming out on the rutted lane that led back to the road. Low-hanging branches lashed the truck's finish. By the time it had gone from sight, Goody was inside the house, opening the windows to catch as much of the breeze as possible. The wind had freshened, grown stronger and cooler as it bore down on the valley from the west, and it seemed to Goody that it promised rain.

10

The buttons. The translucent plastic buttons of her blouse. They slipped so easily through the buttonholes, came undone so simply. The bra unhooked in front. Ingenious. She pointed that out to him, he would never have thought of it on his own, and he expected to be clumsy with the closure, but it imitated the buttons, snicked neatly and easily open. She snuggled into him, murmuring, and he murmured back, about bodies, the only bodies he knew. His. Hers. The cave's.

"I don't believe you," Janina said. She stood, snatching her blouse out from beneath Dwight. She put on the rumpled cotton shirt without buttoning it, brushed her hair back over her shoulders, and stood, hands on her hips, regarding him. Her breathing was slow and even. Dwight kept his gaze on the narrow opening—a finger's breadth, perhaps, or two—of the shirt front and the band of skin that it revealed. "This cave is a what?" she said.

"A body," Dwight said. "The body of a buried giant." He was immensely sorry to have brought the whole thing up. He sat on the ratty sprung sofa in Mr. Askins's office. He wiped his damp palms against the legs of his blue jeans and tried to slow his own rapid respiration, to seem less flustered. "It's nothing. A dumb idea," he said. "Forget it." He patted the seat of the sofa next to him, composing the features of his face into what he hoped was an inviting smile. The expression felt frozen. Holding it became quickly excruciating. Beneath his hand, he could feel the heat of Janina's body radiating away from the sofa cushions. Soon they would be room temperature again, cave temperature. "Sit on down," he said.

"It's got a face, and the outside is what?" Janina said, her brow furrowed, her mouth pursed in disgust. "Its ass? A giant's ass? My God. We walk around out there. We *live* out there. What does that make us?" Her tone became patient, as though she were speaking to someone feebleminded. "What kind of way is that to talk, when you're getting it on with me?"

"You're right," he said, grimacing. He kneaded his hands together in his lap, in an agony to know whether she would return to the sofa. He thought that he had never known anything as sweet as her warm breath on his face, the touch of her nimble tongue. "It was a stupid thing to bring up. I won't talk about it anymore."

"Glad to hear it," Janina said. She continued to adjust her clothing, rebuttoning her blouse, deftly knotting it below the fourth button to show off her flat, tanned belly. She brushed at the wrinkles in the cotton, smoothing them. As she did, she took a step back away from the sofa, and a sour kind of excitement washed through Dwight when he saw how the shadows cast by Mr. Askins's desk lamp patterned her body and legs but hid her face from him. A harsh diagonal spear of light crossed her stomach, illuminating the neat pucker of her navel.

"We're alone here, you know," he said. His voice was strange to him, grating and loud. It seemed to come from somewhere inside him that he did not know, a hollow empty ringing place. He had never heard a voice quite like it. "Everybody else went home when the cave closed."

"So?" Her tone was flat and utterly devoid of curiosity.

That voice came rumbling out of him again. "So I might not let you leave." The rotten springs of the sofa gave a screech as he rose. He took a step toward Janina and was both delighted and frightened when she retreated a step farther. The broken sheet of light from the desk lamp revealed only her slender legs. Darkness covered the rest of her, but her legs seemed to glow, vividly golden. Dwight thought of the other woman's legs, Dreama's legs. These limbs were slimmer, less muscular, the skin slightly pebbled. Dwight remembered the pleasantly grainy feel of it against his fingertips.

"Not let me leave?" she said. "That's brilliant. You can just keep me a prisoner here forever." No hint of sarcasm or anger carried to him in her words.

"Not forever." He took another step forward, and still maintaining the distance between them, she moved away, out of the light altogether. Her back and shoulders were set flat against the thin door of the office. Her breathing had quickened perceptibly.

Dwight's lungs seemed overinflated. His own breath rushed in and out of him without giving him strength or refreshing his blood. It stank in his nostrils like diesel exhaust. They were both free of the lamp's illumination, and as the pupils of his eyes dilated he could see the stricken expression on Janina's face, her wire-taut posture. Her eyes were slitted, her hands crooked into claws. He took another step, reached a hand toward her. She tried to shrink from his touch but had no place to go. The pads of his fingers brushed her hair, the collar of her blouse, her breast. She was trembling.

"Please," she said, her voice expressive of no strong emotion. She sounded as though she might have been requesting a dollar's worth of change.

He pressed himself to her. He was not large, but she was smaller still, and he pinned her arms at her sides without difficulty. The door gave slightly beneath their combined weight. He speculated that it might easily burst open and spill them onto the floor of the room outside, leave them struggling and thrashing together before the dead and mummified gaze of Floyd Askins.

"You wanted to earlier," he said. With a boldness that he could barely believe, he socketed his pelvis to hers, ground himself obscenely against her. "You let me touch your tits on the couch," he said. He kissed her, and the skin of her face was hot to the touch of his lips. He tried to lure her away from the door, back to the sofa, but she would not go.

"Please," she said again.

As quickly as it had rushed through him, Dwight's lust drained away. His face, absurdly squashed against Janina's, grew hot with shame. His groping hand fell away from the unyielding fabric of her shirt. His erection, which felt monstrous to him, was lodged painfully against the zipper of his jeans. He reached down to arrange himself.

Janina pushed him away, slapped at him. "You bastard," she said. "You prick."

"Well," Dwight said, helpless in the face of her fury. "You did." His voice was his own again, and he found himself shrinking from her. As he had advanced on her, so Janina advanced on him, her hands lashing the air. A sharp fingernail raked a shallow groove across his left cheek, and Dwight raised his hands in front of his face, to protect his eyes. She clawed their backs, drawing blood.

One of his hips bumped the edge of Mr. Askins's desk, spilling a container of pencils and pens onto the floor. A sheaf of papers slid off the desktop as well, the pages fluttering through the air with a lazy seesaw motion. Some loose dollar bills followed. A mug overturned, pouring tepid coffee across the papers that remained. The desk lamp toppled, flickering briefly, but it was not extinguished. Its metal shade became detached and rolled along the edge of the desk, finally landing with a clatter on the floor among the cascade of pencils and papers. The exposed bulb cast a bright light over the room, and for the first time Dwight saw the tears on Janina's cheeks. Mascara trailed down her face, from her eyes to the corners of her mouth. A dark droplet of the stuff hung quivering from her chin. Dwight half sat, half fell on the couch. The drop of mascara-tinged water fell from Janina's chin and another immediately gathered to replace it. "What is wrong with you?" she said. She spat the words.

"Nothing," Dwight said. Even as he spoke he was humiliated by his excuses. "You got me excited. I was mad. We . . ." His voice was made puny by his confusion. Janina wasn't listening. She hustled across the room, threw the door open, and passed through it. By the time Dwight summoned the energy to rise and pursue her, she was ascending the concrete ramp toward the cave entrance.

"Hey," he called after her. He wanted her to come back, to come back into the office, where he could explain. Tell her of the weight of his desire, for the woman Dreama, for her. For anyone. He knew that she would not come back. "Hey," he shouted again.

Far above him on the slope of the ramp, Janina turned to face him, and he thought for an insane moment that she *was* coming back down, that he would be able to make everything all right. He thought of the old sofa in the office and of their moist embraces earlier, and for that instant he imagined, he believed, he knew that it could be made to happen again. He could will it to happen.

"You're a rapist!" she screamed at him, and the word sent a thrill of terror through him. She continued, looking over her shoulder from time to time as though to gauge the distance to the surface, to assure herself that she could outrace him if the need arose. "I see you sitting in the office and for five minutes I'm dumb enough to think you're cute. I try to make you feel a little good. Five minutes! I give you a break, let you kiss me, and what? You try to rape me." She closed her eyes, as though to collect herself. When she opened them again, she called down the corridor, "I guess not all the shit's up there, is it?" She hooked a thumb behind her, toward the surface. "Huh, Dwight? Huh?" He made no reply, and she whirled, dashed away from him, toward the surface, toward the open sky of evening.

Stunned and miserable, Dwight sat on Mr. Askins's sofa. He rocked slowly back and forth but could find no comfort in the motion. He did not know the time, did not know how long he had been alone underground. He knew that he should clean up the mess in the office. He wondered if Janina would tell anyone about what they had done. What he had done. He wondered who she would tell. He wondered who she would tell first.

    She had come to him while he was totting up the day's receipts in Mr. Askins's office. He had not know she was there, had not known anyone else was inside the cavern system, until she had come between him and the money, between him and the light, setting herself lightly on the edge of the desk, facing him. Laughing excitedly. Her face flushed. He had considered whether she might be drunk, might have been drunk on the job, wandering that way through the caverns at the head of a column of vulnerable tourists. The duty fell to him, as head guide, to report such behavior. Then she began to touch him, not just to touch but to caress him, his hair, his face, his chest, and he knew that drunk or not, he did not care.

    She drew him over to the couch, and he had time to calculate that her behavior might constitute a joke of some sort. Maybe they had put her up to it, the other guides, the ones who laughed at him behind his back. Always borderline insubordinate, smarting off, and she chief among them. They knew how he felt about her. They had to. He was not practiced at hiding his emotions. Then she pulled him down, beside her, atop her, and these considerations were lost to him. She was still laughing, and when she kissed him she seemed also to be drinking him somehow. His hands had trailed down the line of her throat, the collar of the blouse, and they had encountered the buttons.

Dwight sat alone, listening to the coffee as it dripped from the edge of the desk and landed on the sodden papers in uneven rhythm. He sat among the scattered pencils and the uncounted receipts, bathed in the severe light of the uncovered bulb, waiting for the morning that he would not see, and for Mr. Askins, or whoever else might come along.

11

Trailing his two brindled hounds, the anchorite walked eastward through the forest, the sinking orange bulb of the sun behind him. Finding himself confronted with a grass-covered bank ten or twelve feet high, he scaled it with ease, hounds scrabbling for footholds behind him. It seemed to the anchorite that he had come upon a brief section of raised highway half-hidden in the mountain's undergrowth. The dirt along the top of the rise was loose and moist and thickly furred with spears of tough sedge and other low foliage.

The dogs passed by him, one to a side, and trotted purposefully ahead along the spine of the mound, long noses down and working. As they breasted their way through the grass, the rustling carpet of it opened for them, closing swiftly behind their twitching rumps without the mark of their passage. They moved along with a rolling motion like dolphins through water, only their narrow backs revealed, disappearing occasionally from sight and then resurfacing a moment later, farther on.

Fleshy elephant-ear grasped at the legs of the anchorite's trousers and deposited its bristling seedpods in his pants cuffs. Trees grew along the pathway, but not many, and those slim-trunked and easily bent aside or skirted to make a passage. When he put his hand to a young ash that was in his way, it pulled itself from the earth with weird silent ease and tilted away from him to fall lengthwise on the ground, as though it had only been temporarily propped upright in its place, waiting for him to drop it with his touch. Black dirt spilled from its sparse roots. He searched along the ground for signs that Tannhauser and his press-gang had come this way, but there were none to be found. In his effort to follow them without being discovered, he had lost their track. Ahead of him somewhere, he knew, was the place called El Dorado, but he could not be sure how far it was, or exactly in what direction.

He passed the first crossroads of the mound without much noting it, a brief north-south routing that measured itself in equal lengths on either side of the barrow. When he came to the second one, ten yards farther on, he paused at the junction, calculating. He pictured in his mind's eye the path he was walking as though he were not traveling it but hung suspended well above and was able to observe it: a hundred yards' length of upright and a pair of transverses three-quarters of the way along it, the westernmost one somewhat longer than its partner. He knew it then for a great two-armed patriarchal cross raised in low relief against the forest floor. He paused briefly, struck by the knowledge that this was sanctified ground.

He imagined that the barrow on which he walked must be a mass grave, earth covering the heaped bones of the unnamed dead. It was plainly not an Indian mound, though those were plentiful on Little Hogback. He whistled up his dogs, which had disappeared from his sight altogether, and slipped on his rump down the northward side of the mound, between the transverses. A hemlock bush had taken root in the cul-de-sac, and it spread its greens wide so that he had to sidle between its branches and the face of the mound. As he rounded the bush, his foot strayed on a slick tilted surface hidden among the twisted grasses and he went sprawling. The hemlock's branches crackled as he clawed at them on his way down, and its small compound leaves came away in his hands like emerald confetti.

His downside shoulder struck stone and went numb beneath him; likewise the ball and socket of his nether hip. A slender picket of iron entered the palm of his outstretched and flailing hand, skewering it. The hand went immediately numb, and he knew without being aware of its exact nature that he had done himself a grievous injury. He stayed still a moment, aware of the strange new weight of his impaled hand and of a fierce cold that seemed to emanate from the ground beneath him, that seeped into his stricken joints. The hounds peered down at him over the rounded shoulder of the mound. Then they went away.

He lay where he had fallen, half under the hemlock bush, gasping a long curse as he made out with blurred vision the pencil-width stake that had pushed itself through his hand. It protruded from his flesh just behind and between the third and fourth knuckles. It looked as though it had grown there, the metal from his flesh. He held the injured arm still and probed the offending rod with the index finger of the other hand. It quivered with his touch, and a dark bead of blood slid down its lower length. The anchorite's face went slack with pain.

It was a miniature iron flagstaff that transfixed his hand, flagless now with decades of exposure and weathered a dull uniform no-color. A child might brandish a baton like this one in a parade. The staff's pointed finial projected an inch or more from the gathering of the welt and fixed the shaft in him as solidly as though it had been the barbs on a hunting arrow. The metal seemed to be humming with electricity. He listened to the sound for a while before realizing that it was only the grinding song of the locusts.

He whined like an animal and sat, bracing his back against the mound. The butt end of the two-foot flagstaff dragged in the dirt as he drew it toward him, and the vibrations of the movement caused him to suck his breath shallowly between clenched teeth. He settled the wounded hand in his lap, supporting both it and the stake against his quaking thighs, and contemplated the mess. The hand was growing hot and he could feel the meat of it swelling against the flagstaff. He remembered a time his mother had held a dying pigeon gently before her just so.

Its gray-feathered head was bulbous on its limp neck, its eyes closed, blood staining its breast and the linen skirt that she wore. The pigeon's body was crawling with lice, but she didn't seem to notice.

He had shot the bird. It had fluttered brokenly down to him from its perch on a rafter at the top of the haymow, pirouetting lightly to the rough board floor of the loft, and he had taken it to her. "See this?" she said to him, and stretched one of the pigeon's flaccid wings out from its body. She ran a finger along the small feathers that lined the trailing edge of the wing, riffling them to show how fine and delicate they were, and how important an aid to controlled flight. To her, the bird's corpse was a lesson in functional anatomy.

When she released the wing, it did not slip tidily back into place against the bird's body as he had expected it would, but instead lay loose against the light cloth of her skirt. As with the lice, she failed to notice, and laid the bird on its back to show him how neatly its claws were made for precise landing on narrow purchases. She turned the body over, and its other wing unfolded in her lap like the first, exposing the pink skin of the pigeon's thinly feathered sides. He was fascinated and nauseated by the utter relaxation of those wings and missed the rest of her discourse.

The male hound was back on the barrow above him now, panting loudly. Dirt crumbled from under its nervously shifting paws and trickled down the side of the mound. Some of the dust drifted into his shirt collar. The dog on the ledge above him whipped its head around and bit at its offside shoulder, at some itch embedded in its hide. It stood poised on the verge of the mound, hunched as though it would descend. It appeared to change its mind, a moment too late, and battled to stay where it was while gravity dragged at it. Soon it gave up the struggle and came to ground level. It stood off from the anchorite, regarding him, and then approached, tail up and batting enthusiastically from side to side.

"Get away," the anchorite said. There was panic in his voice. He imagined the dog jostling his damaged hand, licking it. He imagined it grasping the slender flagstaff between its jaws. The last six inches of the staff were grimed with moist dirt where it had been planted in the earth, and he imagined it grabbing that part of the stake and tugging on it in mistaken play. The dog took another tentative step toward him, and he made frantic hand gestures at it. "Get back, you bastard," he said. The dog was warned, and it took a seat facing him. Soon it turned away and dragged itself by its forelegs a short distance through the grass, scrubbing its bottom, casting worms. Then it trotted the length of the transverse and went again out of sight.

The anchorite's hand had begun to throb, and his hip, and his shoulder where it had jarred against the ground. He sat near the loose footing that had turned his ankle. Investigating the treacherous place, he drew the curtain of grass back from an object there, the one that had caught him, and found an inscription. In worn letters carved into the face of a chunk of granite it said LOVIS HVNTER. There was a set of dates below that, both antique. Searching with his free hand, he found a smaller stone nearby, similarly covered by grass. On it were carved a levitating cherub and a single date: no name.

The anchorite surveyed the narrow sward between the two transverses. Dockweed stood in ranks, leaves the shape and size of shovel blades rocking with a light breeze that bore their vegetable scent to him. The shadows stood long in the waning light, though he knew that the top of the barrow was still warm from the sun. He imagined himself home, or not home yet but headed toward it, within sight of the glen where he lived. Or among the interlopers, sharing their food and the human company that he had shunned for so long. Shaking his head, he looked out over the grassy cove again and pictured it as he had the immense cross, from above and without its dense cloak of fodder.

The lumps and masses out there were, then, headstones like the one that had pitched him down in this spot. Variously angled, they held themselves up from the fertile ground. There were humble rounded gravestones and obelisks toppled from their broken bases and low bronze markers that hardly showed themselves through the grass at all, cenotaphs of a race that had absented itself or died out utterly. His gaze fell on a slim slope-shouldered seraph, wings hiding eyes, wings folded over feet, the third pair of its wings outstretched for flight, all of it overhung with vivid green vines. Farther on, a fluted Grecian column thrust itself up through the bracken, surprisingly straight and whole. Though it must once have been surmounted by some memorial entablature, the pillar's capital was bare. A willow flourished on the broken roof of a low stone vault, its roots thrust insistently into the dank interior.

At the center of the defile was the marble figure of a woman, prone along the top of a high tomb. She lay in an attitude of weeping, one stone hand thrown across her eyes to conceal her tears, or to ward off the sight of some terrible thing: her dead self, perhaps. Tendrils of ivy encircled her delicate wrists and ankles, her graceful neck. She was lovely.

The graveyard with its massed dirt and shaded stones had begun to cool. Deciding that he had rested long enough, the anchorite gathered his legs under him and pushed himself up, using the bank of dirt behind him as a buttress. He raised himself several degrees, and then a few more, but he was weak with shock and couldn't straighten.

Droplets of sweat stood on his upper lip. Blood ran in a stream down the back of his hand, parting at his wrist and braceleting it. His vision began to fail and he groaned, biting at the soft inside of his cheek to keep his concentration sharp. He strained a few moments longer and then subsided, dropping back to his hard seat on the ground. He leaned his head forward and fought the nausea that rose in him.

He breathed deeply, and after a time he was able to raise his head again. The prospect that he had of the cemetery did not swim away from him. He grinned weakly in the deepening gloom, and addressing the miniature flagpole or the wreck of his hand, he said, "Well, I fucked up this time okay."

Then he stretched out his traitorous legs in front of him and arranged a nearly comfortable seat against the barrow, reciting to himself the bits of the Twenty-third Psalm that he recalled and awaiting as serenely as possible the coming of dark to this isolated necropolis.

Sometime in the night, the anchorite fell asleep. His dreams were uneasy, red-tinted visions of the vengeful dead rising up from the earth of their graves to claim him, of the nixes and wights that had populated the terror-filled landscape of his childhood. He whimpered and from time to time called out a name, but there was no one to hear him. The air grew cold, and he gathered his limbs close about himself, nearly waking once when his injured hand pulled painfully against the awkward iron that pierced it.

The dogs returned to him while he slept, coming from the same direction, trotting shoulder to shoulder, panting. They capered gleefully together among the graves, playing a shifting game of tag, leaping out from behind the gravestones and mausoleums at each other in mock attack. Their frolic finished, the bitch leaped up onto the tomb that bore the statue of the weeping woman and licked at the gleaming marble, seeking moisture on its surface. She licked the woman's face, and after a time the male hound joined her and they licked the statue from head to foot as they slaked their thirst, working toward each other, dislodging the clinging vines as they did so.

Then they leaped down from the tomb and approached the sleeping anchorite. They approached him slowly, bellies low to the ground, tails tucked obsequiously under. They sniffed around him, sniffed at his feet and pants legs and at the small trail of his blood that lay crusting on the ground. They frequently came upon him lying insensate in the grove near the buried dome where he lived, his back dappled with blood blisters, when he had been reaving himself; his shirt crumpled on the ground nearby; near his open outstretched hand the slim sheaf of branches that he used as a scourge.

The male hound gingerly picked its way over the anchorite's legs, finding a spot for itself beneath the hemlock bush. It lay there, gently washing its hindquarters, the female watching. Finally, desiring the heat and the closeness of the pack, the male dog picked itself up, crossed the short distance to the prostrate anchorite, and laid itself over his lower body. The anchorite stirred and shifted but did not wake. Shortly the bitch joined them. The three of them rested that way, one of them slumbering, the other two conscious and watchful.

A great noise awakened the anchorite, and he opened his eyes to find himself bathed in light. When his eyes had adjusted to the glare, the first thing to meet his befuddled gaze was the male hound. The dog's front paws and muzzle were clotted with dirt, and it held between its teeth a long yellow bone. It chewed the bone hungrily, and the grating of its strong teeth seemed to the anchorite to be the source of the unbearable din that assailed his ears. In his waking confusion, still immersed in dreams, he believed that the hound had drawn out one of the bones from his injured hand to make a meal. He lashed out at the dog, kicking it away from him with both feet, pounding at its rib cage. It cowered and slunk off, darting blame-filled looks back at him, the bone caught in the corner of its mouth like an oversized cigar. The bitch dashed away as well.

Fully alert, the anchorite knew his mistake: the cacophony came from overhead, directly overhead. A violent wind flattened the lush grass around the barrow, battering the trees, stripping leaves from their branches. The anchorite was pelted by twigs and bits of bark driven by the ferocity of the blast.

The light above him, which was not the natural light of day, moved as though it flitted from perch to perch among the tops of the trees, and the shadows of the objects in the defile shifted, clockwise, counterclockwise. The weeping woman was picked out in perfect detail, shimmering whitely where she had been scoured by the dogs. Though the light was blindingly bright, it carried no heat. The anchorite bowed his head and screamed, but the shrill sound of his voice did not carry over the roar.

Then a thundering voice. "Who is it?" the voice seemed to say, again and again. The anchorite could not be sure of the words. "Who is it?" or something similar, again and again until the anchorite thought that he could bear it no more.

"It is I," he said quietly, his gaze still directed downward. The voice, the Voice, made its repeated request.

"Come into the open where we can see you," it called. And again, "Who is it?"

Mustering all of his failing strength and courage, the anchorite bellowed in reply, "It is I!" At the same time, he turned his pale face heavenward, forcing his eyes wide open, daring to look for a single moment into what he knew to be the beautiful burning face of the Angel of the Lord.

12

Again Carmichael spoke into the mike and heard his voice eerily amplified through the boomer. "I repeat, come out into the open where you may be identified," he said. His words pealed from the bullhorn mounted on the helicopter's belly. He could hear the bass tones of them, even feel them in the soles of his feet. He wondered if the meaning would be intelligible over the thumping of the chopper's blades to the person or persons that he suspected on the ground. "Who is there?" he said for the third or fourth time, straining to keep his voice steady, his enunciation crisp.

The tight beam of the spotlight lanced downward from the helicopter, seeming in contrast to the darkness a physical thing, a tether binding them to the earth. Motes of dust winked, bright as stars, in the brilliant pillar. Even here, forty feet off the forest canopy, insects dashed themselves against the lens that covered the lamp's blazing element. They swam up the swath of light, throwing vast dancing shadows across the expanse of greenery below. Carmichael found it astonishing that they could climb so high against the dense wash of the copter's rotor.

"I make it two possibles," Loomis said. Carmichael peered through the windscreen at the circle of light on the ground beneath them. "One back in under the brush a ways and the other . . ." Loomis paused. "Looks like the other one is lying down." He jock-eyed the helicopter around in a tight circle, keeping the nose pointed at the figure below. Carmichael made it out now too. Small. A child? A woman?

"We may have a shooting," Carmichael said. "Two unmoving subjects, unresponsive to query, one definitely prone. How long before the sheriff can get his people up here?"

"Stand by," Loomis said, working the torque pedals, battling the capricious air currents that threatened to push them away from this place and their quarry. "There may be enough room for me to get us in. I believe I could put it down there if you wanted." The tip of his tongue had crept out from between his thin lips. The moist pink of it against the general colorlessness of his face was shocking, almost lewd.

Carmichael reached around to the small of his back and un-hooked the restraining strap that lay across the butt of his service revolver. It was a short-barreled .357 magnum, a Colt Python. "Okay," he said, pleased with the calm tone of the words. "Let's go in." He barely had time to wonder whether Loomis had shut down the loudhailer before the conversation, whether their words and his decision might have been broadcast to whatever, whoever, was wait-ing below. As soon as he finished speaking, the copter began its abrupt descent.

Ten feet down, twenty, near the level of the treetops now. He kept his eyes open for Loomis's second possible, the one back in the brush, while trying not to lose sight of his prone subject. He slipped the revolver from its holster and held it ready in his right hand, put his left on the door handle preparatory to flinging it open. "The LZ might be hot," he heard himself say, "so as soon as I'm out, you take it back up. Maintain visual contact unless you're picking up fire."

"Affirmative," Loomis said in his toneless voice. And then, just as the skids were about to touch down, he said, "Wait a second. Wait just a damn second." Then he laughed and held the shuddering heli-copter in its place, neither rising nor falling. They were among the trees, and rotor wash caused the carpet of grass beneath them to thrash and dance.

Carmichael paused. His door was open, his hands to his helmet, already lifting the carapace from his head. "What?" he asked. "What did you say?"

"I know this place," Loomis said, his voice restored to its former neutrality. He pivoted the copter, one complete clockwise rotation in its own length, so that the beam of the spotlight fell on everything around them. Carmichael had the impression as the landscape swung by of a place of stones placed at regular intervals, of thick overgrowth, a mound of earth nearby. "There's nobody here," Loomis said. He turned the helicopter again, counterclockwise this time.

"Nobody?" Carmichael closed his eyes. The spinning was making him distinctly uncomfortable.

"Nobody but a mess of dead corpses," Loomis replied. "And statues. It's an old boneyard is what it is." Carmichael shoved the snub-nosed Smith & Wesson back into its holster, replaced the restraining strap with a feeling of letdown, of real regret. Loomis went on. "Your prone subject is a stone angel-lady."

Carmichael looked ahead of them, to the place where Loomis directed the light, and saw that it was true. What he had spotted from the air, what had brought them down here, was nothing but the nicely carved figure of a lissome girl sprawled in an attitude of grief across the marble slab of a burial vault. "Yikes," he said. "A graveyard." He motioned overhead with his hand, and Loomis took them smoothly skyward.

"A big graveyard," Carmichael said presently, when the size of the place was revealed to them. A great barrow in the shape of a double-armed cross, surrounded on all sides by graves, deeply overgrown with brush and low bracken through long years of neglect. The trees were small and thinly spread over much of the ground, and Loomis took Carmichael on a slow low-flying tour of the place.

"Old Civil War cemetery," he said by way of explanation. "The Federals brought a bunch of their prisoners here: Confederate regulars, captured spies, saboteurs, horse thieves, profiteers. Executed them all. Slaughtered them. Union commander said they tried to make a break for it and he had to shoot them. Well over a hundred and fifty men." They were passing over the greatest length of the barrow now, and Carmichael wondered at the shape of it, with its pair of arms. He thought that the Egyptians had a cross like that. He had heard of an Egyptian group called Coptic and thought maybe this was what their cross looked like. He wondered if there had been any Coptics among the prisoners.

Loomis said, "Union paid some families reparation, other families not. After the war, people who thought they had family here put up monuments." They completed their circuit of the cemetery, and Carmichael indicated that they were done for the night. The Defender lifted and gained speed, banking across the mound as they wended their way back to the makeshift base at the country airport.

"Used to be a road up in there," Loomis said. "Dirt road. Memorial Day when I was a kid, the school classes would come up and clean off the graves, leave flags and pots of flowers and whatnot. Then again later, on Veterans' Day. I remember us boys all used to like that woman's statue pretty well. She appeared to have clawed her dress open, and her tits showed pretty good. Plus we thought she had a nice ass."

Carmichael said, "Nobody's cleaning off the graves these days."

"No. It's got real grown up is why it took me a while to recognize it," Loomis said. "People seem to have fell behind pretty badly in that respect."

"Well, I'll make an effort not to alert you to statues in the future," Carmichael said.

"Don't let it bother you," Loomis said to him. They were crossing the dull gleaming stripe of the river now, and the bulk of El Dorado lay not far to the west of their flight path, though they could not see it. "It was a break in the pattern of vegetation, all right. You saw that."

Carmichael sat back, trying to relax. The checkered grip of the revolver had felt so *good* in his hand. He had hated to let it go.

"You know what you need," Loomis said, and Carmichael thought that he did know, and thought that probably Loomis did not. Loomis went on. "You need you one of those Sikorsky Blackhawk assault choppers. Those bastards have got what they call FLIR, that's forward-looking infrared. Lets you fly NOE at night without lights. Reads the heat signature from the marrow of plants, if you can believe it."

"Maybe," Carmichael said. "If we're successful up here, maybe I'll put in a request."

Loomis warmed to his subject. "Got two pilots up front, and a cabin where you can sit in the back. Crew chief to help you in and out like some kind of a potentate. Drop you and your SWAT team into the woods with a forest penetrator on the winch. Pull you back out again too. That's the way to handle this type of an operation."

"Like I say. We prove our worth, DEA may want to come through

with something like that. But until then, it's you, me, and the Defender."

"Sure," Loomis said, sounding neither resigned nor disappointed.
"Sure." He corrected their heading slightly, easing down on the collective. And as they came in to the home field on their final approach,
neither of them gave any thought to the forgotten problem of their
second sighted possible.

13

The anchorite scuttled through the undergrowth, the hooks and needles of barbed shrubs grabbing at his clothes, tearing the skin of his face, his hands. He did not notice the pain of the gashes, even when the thorns of a wild multiflora rosebush laid open his right eyebrow, split it as neatly as scalpel work. He looked in the brush around him for his dogs, but the high-pitched whine of the helicopter's turbine had caused them to abandon him for the security of the deep woods. He was intent on escaping the descending horror behind him, with its crown of whirling blades, its harsh barking voice and single lidless eye. No angel that, no indeed, no, that idea had been an error, a mistaken vision, the residue of a dream. This was a stinking machine, come to search him out, to kill him or to pluck him from his solitude and return him to the snakepit, and he wanted no part of it.

He ran from the clearing with his back hunched, his legs bent at the knees and scissoring awkwardly beneath him. He dragged his injured hand behind him like a convict lugging the burden of heavy shackles. Pain had left the impaled member; sensation of every sort seemed to have drained out of it, and the anchorite was left with an extremity that felt to him like a length of stovewood, or like a clumsy portmanteau that he had no choice but to haul along with him. He would have left it behind if he could, disengaged it from himself entirely. The hand and the iron rod did not matter to him at all as he hurried across the graveyard.

Fleeing, he staggered over a number of the grave markers that surrounded the burial mound. He barked his shins on granite memorials, stumbled over broken blocks of masonry, felt the raised lettering of inscriptions on brass plaques through the thin soles of the moccasins that he wore. The helicopter wheeled in its place behind him, the shaft of light radiating powerfully from it like the beacon of some inland lighthouse, and he ducked behind a nearby vault. He waited in the concealment that it offered for the light to pass over him and move on.

The light did pick out the vault, as he had known it would, but rather than sliding swiftly over and past, it paused, lingered, as though suspicious that he had hidden himself in just the place that he now occupied. It shifted away, came back, shifted slightly again, returned to irradiate the tomb a third time. The anchorite had seen hunting dogs hesitate in just that way over shallow rabbit warrens: move off a little, shivering with excitement; return; move off, only to return again, always return. He stiffened, flattened himself against the stone wall behind him, wondering what the revealing clue was, how he had managed to betray himself.

He listened for the approach of the helicopter's occupants, prepared himself, if the need arose, to dash out into the light. When he stood revealed to them, what would their reaction be? He speculated about their orders: would they gun him down, or had they contracted to capture him? Who were they, that they should pursue him in this abandoned place? He had imagined himself long forgotten by everyone living in the world of men. He straightened, and something poked him painfully on the top of his skull.

Looking up, he saw a pair of feet, unshod human feet. They projected slightly over the edge of the vault, toes downward, the left crossed over the right. It was the big toe of the right foot on which he had bumped his head. He rubbed at the sore spot with his good hand.

They were slender feet, delicate and fine, with high arches and long narrow toes. They were made of stone, and the helicopter's searchlight made them seem to glow, as though the figure lying on the tomb were lit from within. The weeping woman, he thought. He had chosen to hide behind her monument. She was shielding him.

The ribbon of light passed on then, finally, and illuminated another stretch of clearing that shaded into forest, and the anchorite was left alone with her in darkness.

Hours later, when the morning sun began its long process of burning the fog off Little Hogback, the anchorite awoke again. He lay at full length on the slab that covered the vault, though he had no idea how he had come to be there. Climbed up, he imagined, sometime after the helicopter had lifted and reeled away into the night. Had the helicopter, the searchers, been a real thing or just another nightmare vision brought on by fasting? The flattened whorls of grass across the graveyard confirmed their reality. He felt lightheaded and weak. His uninjured arm was thrown across the statue of the weeping woman, his legs against her legs, his chest to her back. He held her close in the attitude of a lover.

He ran his hands over the smooth slopes of her shoulders, admiring the sheen of the marble. She was carved out of rock imported from the Carrara quarries in Italy, and the stone was as white as soap, and cold. He clasped her again, admiring the unyielding feel of her against him, the way the stiff folds of her vestments cut into him. Below, his dogs barked. The male braced its front feet against the upper edge of the vault and peered over the side at the anchorite and the stone maiden, dark eyes unblinking. It watched them for a while, and then it went away.

Before long, the anchorite released his hold on the statue and began the slow climb down from the top of the tomb. The bruises he had from his fall among the graves pained him sorely. The cold of night on the mountain had sunk into his bones, and something else: a nauseous heat in the muscles and vertebrae of his upper back that he knew was generated by the iron on which he had spitted his hand. The heat, he suspected, would spread unless he took some action, would become an uncontrollable conflagration along his nerves and blood vessels that, in burning itself out, would leave him dead.

He groaned as he levered his aching form to the ground. His legs threatened not to carry him, but he rested against the tomb and in the end they took his weight, if ungratefully. The dogs danced around him, threatening to knock him down, giving out with little yips and squeals. His wounded arm refused all instructions, lifeless from elbow to fingertips, and he had to support it with his good hand. The flesh was unexpectedly hot and felt rubbery to the touch, though it looked sound.

The anchorite knew what he was looking for—a place to fix the flagstaff so that he might pull his hand off it—and after casting around for a time among the stones and figures of the graveyard, he found it close to the place from which he had come. The weeping woman's left hand covered her eyes and could be of no use to him, but the right was held open near her breast, the fingers splayed wide. Raising his own ruined hand, he slid the barbed finial of the metal stake between the weeping woman's first and second fingers, slipping it deeply into the narrow opening, working it until it held solid in the manner of a grapnel. The female hound wandered off after some scent that intrigued it; the male stayed and watched interestedly, head cocked to one side. With the intruding flag stick anchored and immobile, the anchorite was able to take his pinned hand in his free one and begin, with a series of sharp upward tugs, to slide it free.

The hand came stubbornly at first, moving toward him a quarter of an inch, a half-inch at a time. The dark crust that had formed around the wound broke open and he bled copiously, the blood dripping onto the ground or sliding down the iron bar and dribbling darkly across the fingers of the statue. Frustrated, the anchorite spat on the iron and rubbed the spit into the metal with his good hand, hoping to lubricate it and ease his injured hand's passage.

Then he began to tug again, and his hand came toward him more quickly now, one inch, two, with every fresh pull. The bones of the hand grated loudly but painlessly along the metal rod. The head of the flagstaff rasped against the weeping woman's fingers, digging shallow grooves in the stone, and minuscule particles of white grit pattered down. The anchorite breathed a quick prayer that became an imprecation as a wild arrangement of lights and colors without name filled his vision. He swooned and dropped.

His hand came free of the stake, and he fell without obstruction. The statue's fore and middle fingers gave way with a brittle crunching sound and fell also, along with the bloody iron shaft, which plunged point down into the soft earth like an arrow. The anchorite lay wheezing softly on the ground.

The male dog trotted to him and began to lick his face. It washed the grayish skin there for a while, then moved down his arm to his damaged hand. It worked its rough tongue over the split flesh roughly and sloppily, and the anchorite drew the hand back. The dog came after it again, friendly but eager for the salty taste of the blood. The bitch wandered up to him as well, breath hot and rank in his face, and to keep his injury out of the mouths of the dogs he was forced to rise and hobble back to the tomb of the weeping woman. He managed to clamber up next to her, and the atmosphere of icy cool that surrounded her was a balm to him. He breathed deeply, using the small of her back and the swell of her buttocks to pillow his head. Relishing the new feather lightness of his hand, he brought it up and revolved it before his eyes. He was shocked by the lifeless hue of it, by the livid gash that disfigured both its palm and its back, by the clawed look of the fingers, and he put it away from him. Overhead, warmed by the growing warmth of the sun, birds twittered in the trees.

He lay like that for several hours, until the early afternoon. He knew that he could not survive another night in the open. Finally, gauging the time of day and the distance to be traveled against his own depleted condition, he roused himself and began the long walk back to his homestead. The dogs knew the direction in which they were heading and seemed glad. He turned around before the weeping woman was lost to sight. He went back to her and, bending, took up the iron stake.

Hefting it, he marveled at its insignificance. It was no thicker or sharper than a knitting needle. He pitched it away from him, and it flew end over end to disappear in the brush, where it landed with a muted rattle as though it had struck against rock. Then he took up the statue's two fingers with their blunted, broken ends. He fitted them futilely, sorrowfully, against their stumps, and pocketed them. Accompanied by his hounds, he left the clearing again and at his new feeble pace began to make his lonely way homeward.

14

John Faktor, high sheriff of Dwyer County, sat at the battered desk in the center of his office, staring at the telephone. It was hot in the little windowless box of a room, and the slow-turning ceiling fan seemed to have little effect on the temperature. Sweat ran in rivulets over the sheriff's broad bald scalp, trickling down behind his ears and into the collar of his uniform blouse. From time to time he unlaced his hands from in front of his belly, pulled out a yellowing handkerchief, and ran the damp cloth over his skull. He did not take his eyes off the telephone, even as he extracted a cigarette from the crushed pack on the desktop and tucked it between his thick lips.

A tall skinny deputy sitting in a corner of the office started forward as though to light the cigarette, digging in his pocket for the plastic Zippo that he carried. Sheriff Faktor waved him back into his seat. The sheriff sat the way he was for a minute before he plucked the cigarette from his mouth, looked at it with an expression of disgust, and pitched it into the metal wastebasket beside the desk.

"Trying to quit," Sheriff Faktor said.

"You bet," the deputy replied.

"Vile habit." Sheriff Faktor took another cigarette from the pack, put it to his lips.

"You bet," the deputy said again.

The sheriff patted himself all over until he found a book of cardboard matches in a pants pocket. Pulling one from the book, he struck it and held the flame to the tip of the cigarette, drawing until the tobacco glowed a fierce orange. He coughed and expelled a cloud of smoke into the air, shaking the match to extinguish it and tossing it into the trash. "Trying," he told the deputy. "Not succeeding." He offered the cigarettes to the deputy, who took one.

"This DEA guy," the deputy said, beginning a thought that he plainly hoped the sheriff would complete.

"Yeah," Sheriff Faktor said. "This DEA guy." He continued to keep his attention on the phone. "It's a pisser, ain't it? Him and his little helicopter."

Some county prisoners were playing basketball on the fenced court behind the jail building, and the slapping of the underinflated ball against the blacktop was clearly audible, as were the prisoners' running footsteps and, from time to time, their angry voices as they contested some point or call. One prisoner bodychecked another into the cinderblock wall of the building, and the sound of the contact was surprisingly loud. The deputy shifted uneasily in his seat.

"Pretty physical game today," Sheriff Faktor said. Sustained shouting came to him and to the deputy, a number of voices all together, and the whistles of the corrections officers breaking up the fracas.

"They been watching the NBA playoffs," the deputy said. "When it gets violent on the TV screen, it turns mean out there too."

"Maybe we ought to shut down the television privileges for a while," Sheriff Faktor said.

"They'll riot if you do that. Burn up everything in the cells."

"Fuck them if they do," the sheriff said. "Let them sleep on the ashes. Wipe their butts with the ashes."

"Naw. Then they'll write the newspaper and get everybody down on our necks."

"With what?" Sheriff Faktor asked. "They'll use all their paper to light the fires."

The deputy shrugged.

"I guess you got a point," Sheriff Faktor said in the tones of resignation. The basketball game seemed to have returned again to its normal pounding rhythms, and conversation in the room flagged.

When the phone rang at last, the sheriff did not answer it immediately. He stubbed his cigarette out in a glass ashtray that sat on the
desk and spread his hands on the desktop to either side of the black
instrument, leaning over it. Finally he picked up the receiver, very
deliberately, and spoke into it. "Dwyer County sheriff's office," he
said. "High Sheriff John Faktor speaking." Then, "Yeah. Hello there,
Agent Carmichael. I was just sitting here waiting on you, wondering
when you might be calling." He listened. "Sure, I know about El
Dorado. It used to be some hippies growing dope up there, but that's
all finished far as I know. There was a fire up there and they moved
on. So no need to worry about—" He broke off and his face twisted
into a mask of displeasure. "Tannhauser," he said.

The deputy coughed. The sheriff shot him a look, listening to the
voice on the line. "No," he said. "No sir, I don't believe I've heard of
anyone by that name."

Carmichael talked for a while.

"Well, it'll take me some time to put together the manpower for
any kind of a raid. When were you thinking of?"

Another pause.

"Listen, you want to go up there, we're there with you. Nothing I
hate worse than when some drug-smuggling, gun-running son of a
bitch sets himself up in my county. You bet. We're happy to cooper-
ate with the federal government." Before he finished speaking, Carmichael had hung up, and the closed line hummed in the sheriff's
ear. He set the receiver down in its cradle, and the phone bell chimed
softly, once. The deputy was looking at him.

"You heard that, I guess," Sheriff Faktor said. He lit another
cigarette but did not offer the pack this time. The deputy leaned
forward as though to pick it up but reconsidered. The sheriff blew a
stream of smoke into the air.

"Your part of it, anyway," the deputy told him.

"Don't let this get any further than you and me and these walls
here," Sheriff Faktor said. "But we're going to pay a visit to Mr.
Tannhauser's establishment up on Little Hogback. An official visit,
which is going to cost us all a sight of money. And which is going to
cost Mr. Tannhauser his life."

The deputy whistled. "That's a tall order," he said. "Them boys
pack some very potent iron. I'll hate to tangle with the Mingos."

"Potent, yes," the sheriff said. "But some things have got to be done. And we have at least got a little time to plan the action." He shoved the phone out of his way on the desk and planted his elbows firmly in its place. Then he motioned to the deputy to haul his chair over close, so that they could talk face to face about what was to come.

15

Inchcape drove the length of the dry wash from his own place to Goody's. When he shut his pickup's engine off, he could hear a sound, a repeated slapping sound, coming to him across the yard. A few drops of tepid rain spattered against the skin of his face and hands, and he peered up at the slate-colored sky, examining its potential. Satisfied that a hard rain was imminent, Inchcape moved to the open living room window of the small house and stood outside it, observing Goody through the tattered screen.

Stripped to the waist, wearing only a pair of loose cotton shorts, Goody was jumping rope. He skipped the rope a dozen times on one foot and a dozen more on the other, then alternated his feet, running swiftly in place. His chest was sheened with perspiration, and he tossed his head from side to side to fling the sweat from his face. The heavy rope struck the board floor with the regularity of a metronome. The soles of Goody's bare feet whispered against the wood.

Goody increased the pace of his exercise. The rope blurred, and it made a low hissing sound as it passed in its cycle around him. Goody's upper body was stiff and tense; only his legs moved, and his wrists, which turned with remarkable regularity, like pivots in a machine. Perspiration ran down his legs and flew in a fine spray from his arms and body. His skin reddened with exertion, and blood vessels stood out under it like the map of a complicated river system. His breath came in short choking gasps. Inchcape might have been looking at the same thirty frames of film played over and over before him, so precise was the repetition of what he saw: Goody with his wrists up, Goody with his wrists down; the rope overhead, the rope underfoot. Goody's eyes were closed, and he made a little grunt every time one of his feet hit the ground. Inchcape was mesmerized.

Still Goody went on, until Inchcape felt his own breath quicken and catch in his throat. Goody increased his speed again, and now the rope whined as it cut the air. Each time he brought the rope around, he crossed his wrists so that it described a neat figure eight. He turned his face up to the ceiling, his teeth gritted and bared. Straining tendons stood out in startling relief on the flesh of his neck, and veins pulsed at his temples. Inchcape waited for him to falter in his furious pace, and before many more moments went by, he did. The rope snagged around his left ankle. He stumbled forward. The jumprope tore itself from his hands and whipped across the floor, wooden handles clattering. It gathered into a loose tangle in one corner. Inchcape felt briefly guilty at having imagined the misstep before it happened.

Goody began to fall forward but caught his balance before he went down. He straightened and on his way to retrieve the jumprope spotted Inchcape standing at the window. He started, and Inchcape recoiled at having been discovered. Then they both laughed, and Goody, wiping sweat from his eyes with one hand, breathing hard, gestured for Inchcape to come inside.

Inchcape circled the house to its front and pushed open the door. He walked down the long entry hall of the house, toward the kitchen, and as he went he put his fingertips to the walls again and again, touching the several shoulder-high patches of mismatched paint there. The hue of them was uniformly a few shades darker than the surrounding pigment, and it had a gloss to it that the rest of the walls lacked. He thought uneasily of the marks hidden under the paint: the smeared impressions left by those fluttering, frantic hands as the murdered woman had dashed brokenly down her front hallway toward the door. Most of them had been little more than dried streaks and blots on the walls. The blood had darkened and seeped into the plaster until those blemishes might have been anything—

water stains, almost any kind of stain—and Inchcape hadn't looked closely at them as he ran his paint-covered roller over them.

He had managed to ignore all but one of the handprints as he repainted the hallway. That one was perfect, and as deliberate as a painting. It was hard to believe the thing had been done hastily, let alone in terror, in the midst of homicide. The hand seemed to have been laid carefully against the surface of the wall, the pressure of its application equal in all its portions, the resulting stamp of the hand's palm and of the fingers and the thumb scientifically precise. It was the left hand; the featureless band of a ring rode just at the base of the third finger.

The fingerprints had been sketched on the wall, inked in dried blood: all the tiny ridges and whorls of them; and the neatly aligned crevices of the finger joints; and the deeper intersecting furrows of the hand itself: love line, health line, life line, without meaning in that dark simulacrum. The hand that had made the stamp was a narrow one, slim-knuckled, its fingers long and slender and daintily tapered. Inchcape had thought that he could make out in the print the line of a scar that ran nearly the length of the middle digit. From the look of it, the gash that left such a scar must nearly have split the finger. But perhaps it hadn't been a very deep wound.

He had covered up all the other residue first, the beads and dribbles, the grouped dots of fingertips, the wide splashes, the splayed clawing fingermarks, leaving that single almost elegant image for the last. After he had stood before it and studied it a while, half ashamed, he had covered it with paint, its camouflage as imperfect as the rest.

When Inchcape entered the kitchen, Goody was standing at the sink. He turned the cold water tap and watched water purl from the spigot. He let it flow until the stream ran clear, and then he filled a glass and drank it dry. There were colorful cartoon characters drawn on the sides of the glass, and the paint of them was chipped. Inchcape couldn't tell who they were meant to be. Goody filled the glass again, and again drained it. He still had not looked at Inchcape.

"Hey," Inchcape said.

"Hey, Mr. Inchcape," Goody said. He was trying to catch his breath after drinking, and his words came out in a rush. He filled the glass a third time, inspected it for floating things, and drank about half of the water. He wiped his chin with his forearm.

"That's good water," Inchcape said. "It comes out of a three-hundred-and-fifty-foot well. Did I tell you about that when you moved in? Pipe goes down through a layer of limestone and then through a layer of nonporous shale and into another layer of water-bearing limestone. It's a lot better than the well over at my place."

"Sure," Goody said. "But sometimes the water's got stuff in it."

"That's just sediment," Inchcape said. "It'll settle out, if you let it stand a minute. Anyway, it's good for you. Minerals." He thumped his shallow chest. "You won't get water like that in town. In town there's chlorine and fluoride and I don't know what all. You watch. Here after a while everybody in town will have bone cancer, or some worse thing."

"But excellent teeth," Goody said. He set his glass down on the white kitchen counter. The glass clicked against the porcelain.

Inchcape shrugged. "It's good and cold, too. Fifty-three degrees, in summer and in winter. Like it's been refrigerated. There's an advantage you don't get with city water." Goody said nothing. Inchcape went on. "You keep in pretty good shape, I see," he said, gesturing at the jumprope, which Goody still carried with him. Goody laid it on the kitchen table. The blond wood of the handles was stained dark with use, shadowed where Goody's hands had gripped it, and the shadows were edged with dried white lines of salt.

"I like to try," he said. "When I get the chance." He took up a T-shirt that hung over the back of one of the kitchen chairs and pulled it on. With the palms of his hands he smoothed the shirt over his torso.

"I never could do that rope-jumping," Inchcape said. "Too much coordination. Everybody else seemed like they could do it—my baby sister could do it—but it was like a complicated dance to me. I'd get all caught up in the line and couldn't keep going."

"You have a baby sister?" Goody asked.

Inchcape grimaced. "Not a baby now, of course," he said. "She'd have to be . . ." He thought for a minute. "Hell, fifty-six or -seven. I don't see a whole lot of her anymore."

"Anyway, skipping rope's just a rhythm," Goody said. "That's all it is. You find a groove and keep in it."

Inchcape sat heavily in one of the chairs that bordered the kitchen table. Its torn plastic cushion sighed under his weight. He leaned his elbows against the table's edge and sat that way, looking out one of the windows in the north wall of the house. The dry wash led off in that direction, and his truck was visible from where he sat. "I'm an old man," he said. "I don't feel much like I have to worry about all that stuff at this point. If I ever did."

"I guess I don't either, really," Goody said. "But I was a fighter once, and I never got over the habit."

"Say you were a what?"

"A fighter. A boxer. It was a while ago."

Inchcape's gaze had shifted back to Goody, and he kept it there until the attention began to make Goody uneasy. He picked up the half-full glass, dumped the contents out into the sink, rinsed the glass, and set it to dry in the plastic dish rack by the basin. When he turned back, Inchcape was looking out the window again. "So you don't fight much now," he said.

"I don't fight any," Goody said.

"Would you take a fight if you could get one?"

Goody considered. "Well. It would depend on what it paid."

"Pays good. Pays real good, if you win."

"Then it would depend who I'm supposed to fight. I'm getting pretty elderly to be climbing into the ring, and I don't care to get my lights punched out by some muscular child."

"Elderly?" Inchcape sounded amazed. "Hell, you're not old. You're just a kid. You're in the pink. You could do anything, a man with stamina like you got. I seen you."

They were silent for a little while. Then Inchcape said, "Anyway, that's a good thing to know. If I hear about anything, you want me to tell you?"

Goody hesitated, then nodded. "If it pays," he said.

"I'll do her," Inchcape said. He snapped his fingers. "Shoot," he said. "I almost forgot why I come over here. I wanted to tell you something."

Goody laughed. "I was wondering," he said. "What you came over for. I thought maybe the rent was due again or something. I worried a little when I saw you outside my window."

"No," Inchcape said. "That's not until the last of the month, and this isn't but the twenty-third. You got a while on that. This is something else." He stood. "You recall that fellow out in the cane?"

"The dead guy?"

"The very one."

Goody laughed. "Of course I remember. I don't imagine I'll ever forget about him."

"Well, they found out who it was. His name was Billy Rugg."

"Did you know him?"

Inchcape shook his head. "Not to talk to. I'd see him on the street in town from time to time, but not lately. He got into a fight with some drunk and the fellow swore out a warrant on him. People said he'd gone to live up on Little Hogback until they quit looking for him."

"I guess they've stopped now."

"I guess they have. Man I talked to said all the bones in Billy Rugg's legs and feet were broken. Said Billy Rugg didn't walk out into the middle of the canefield to die. Said he must of crawled there."

"Or been dragged."

Inchcape nodded. "They'll get whoever did it. Probably it was the fellow he had the fight with. You hear about that sort of thing all the time."

Goody said, "I've been meaning to ask you something. Did you get my call the other morning? I got somebody on the other end but I never knew whether it was you."

Inchcape shook his head. "I don't know. Sometimes I get calls on the phone and I can't tell who's at the other end. The voice doesn't sound just right, or it isn't a voice I recognize. That's what you got to hate about a phone, not knowing. I hear they got a machine now that will call you and talk to you just like it was another man. Sell you things you don't even want, over the phone. Now there's a thought. What did you say to me when you called?"

"I just told you about the man that had died out there."

"And what did I say to you?"

"You asked if it had been somebody's people. I couldn't tell exactly what you meant."

Inchcape's brow furrowed. "I can't recall it if it was me or not," he said. "Ain't that the damnedest thing, though? I can remember when I was a little boy and my mother listened to the party-line telephone. She liked it better than radio, because she said the radio wasn't real. I can remember my mother sitting there listening all night long, and my father trying to get her off, but I can't remember who I talked with yesterday or the day before that. Hell of a note." He made his way toward the door, shaking his head.

"I hear it's that way for a lot of older people," Goody said. He followed Inchcape through the hall and out into the yard. "You shouldn't feel too bad about it." He patted Inchcape on the shoulder, but Inchcape took no notice of the touch. Instead, he stood in the yard, looking up at the darkening sky with weak, blinking eyes.

16

Toma gasped as the Dakota took a jarring midair bounce. His seat leaped beneath him and then dropped away, and his stomach rebelled at the momentary feeling of weightlessness. The crates in the cargo space thumped solidly against one another, but they had been expertly secured and none came loose. Bodo laughed softly and stretched out a hand to touch Toma on the shoulder. "A little bad weather," he said. Rain pattered like gravel against the fuselage of the plane, and water streaked the glass of the small oval portholes.

Toma turned a stricken face to Bodo. "Do you think we'll go down?" he asked.

"This plane has been flying for better than fifty years. It carried the dignified queen of the Netherlands, perhaps. It has surely been through much worse than this. Why should it crash now, only in order to kill you?" Off the starboard wing of the plane, lightning leaped from cloud to cloud, and it was momentarily as bright as noon in the DC-3's cabin. The sound of the thunderclap was overmastered by the droning of the twin Pratt & Whitney engines.

Toma said, "One rivet out of place. One bolt not quite tightened, or tightened one quarter of a turn too far, and then? Down we go."

"That's right," Bodo said. "Down we go. And after that what? Does the world end?"

"For me it does," Toma told him, and turned to the contemplation of his own thoughts.

Bodo became aware that the pilot was watching them, standing in the open cockpit hatch, his hands gripping the doorframe. Beyond him, Bodo could see the copilot, his thick hands on the yoke, his eyes scanning the instrument panel and then flicking up to peer out past the windscreen at the gray roiling clouds through which they rode. "Shouldn't you be flying the aircraft?" he asked the pilot. "That is what you do."

"He's fine," the pilot said, indicating the copilot with a negligent wave of his hand. He had removed his peaked hat, and his thick hair was damp and flattened against the crown of his head. "He needs me, he'll be sure to give a shout."

"I see."

"I just wanted to tell you that we're now cruising at speed and altitude, on the heading you indicated. This storm system's moving the same direction we are, so we're getting a little help that way. Solid forty-knot tailwind. Get you where you're going a little ahead of schedule."

"No," Bodo said. "Not ahead of schedule. Not behind schedule. We will arrive on schedule."

The pilot looked briefly nonplussed. "Okay," he said. "Okay. We'll drive off that bridge when we come to it, as the senator told the young lady. Anyway, I came back to ask you for the charts. You do have some charts for me? So I know where we're going and how to get there."

"I have them." Bodo began to unfasten his seat belt, looked up questioningly at the pilot.

"It's okay," the pilot said. "Get up and walk around back here if you want to. Just watch out and grab hold of something when we hit an air pocket or you'll fly around like a pool ball." As though to illustrate his point, the plane dropped sharply, rose, dropped, rose again. The cargo shuddered and Toma moaned. Bodo's teeth clicked sharply together, pinching his tongue cruelly.

"I understand," he said, and spat a bright red jewel of blood onto the metal deck underfoot. The pilot watched the drop of spittle as it ran along the pitching floorplates, leaving behind it an unpleasant discoloration, and finally dissipated. Without unfastening his belt,

Bodo reached beneath his seat and retrieved the gunmetal briefcase. He placed it across his knees, fiddled with an apparently complex pair of locks, and popped it open. He extracted a handful of leaflet-size aviation charts and closed the briefcase's lid. In the instant before it closed, the pilot thought that he saw greenbacks in there, a lot of them, stacks of cash. His eyes widened.

"Here," Bodo said, extending the hand with the charts in it. "For navigational purposes. A carefully laid route, you'll find." His speech was slightly slurred by the swelling of his lacerated tongue.

The pilot went to him and took the charts. Unsupported, he moved through the body of the plane with the seasoned walk of a train conductor, clumsy-looking but efficient on such unpredictable ground. Papers in hand, he retreated to the doorway, where he wedged himself while he read through them.

"Jesus," he said, looking up when he had finished perusing the charts. He shook them at Bodo. "That's a hell of a long haul, all the way across the country. Do you really expect me to put down in this place?"

Toma stiffened in his seat at the pilot's indignant tone, but Bodo merely replaced the attaché case under his seat and sat back up. He nodded, smiling. "Yes," he said. "I really do."

"I've landed in some pretty tough places, but this takes the cake. Are you sure there's even a strip there?"

"I am told that there is."

"And it's wide enough and long enough for me to land."

"I am told that it is."

"And get off the ground again afterward? This thing takes up some runway."

"I am confident the facilities will meet your needs."

"You're confident." The pilot stared at the two of them, his eyes moving from Bodo to Toma and back again. They returned his level look. "Be like finding a needle in a haystack," he said.

"You will accomplish it," Bodo said.

"You're confident about that too, I guess," the pilot said. Bodo nodded assent, and the pilot laughed. "What am I going to do with such a confident guy like you?" He looked at Toma, who was openly hostile, his eyes narrowed. "With such a confident pair of guys?"

"Take us to our destination," Bodo said. "It's all that we require of you. Such a simple thing, after all."

"A simple thing." Shaking his head, the pilot returned to the cockpit. As he slipped into the lefthand seat, he bopped the copilot playfully on the shoulder with his closed fist. The two of them conversed for a moment, their heads close together, and when they finished the copilot shook his head too, and they both laughed mirthlessly.

Well ahead of the plane, miles ahead or leagues as far as Bodo was able to tell, a patch of golden sunlight revealed itself between two piled masses of cloud and then disappeared from sight as swiftly as it had come. The pilot planted his overlarge cap on his head, adjusted the bill to a jaunty angle, and settled down to the job of guiding them all in safety through the storm.

17

Peanut emerged from Room 156 of the Peerless Motel just before
dawn and pulled the door softly closed behind him, shutting off the
gust of freezing air. He was carrying a small hard-sided suitcase and
a bundle of clothes. He glanced around him, but the motel's gravel
parking lot was empty of other people. There were a couple of cars
parked in front of the long row of rooms. He ran his hands through
his freshly washed hair. At least, he thought, he had been able to take
time for a shower and a shave, using Chilly's razor, Chilly's shave
cream. A man never feels more like himself than when he has stood
under a good hot stream of water for fifteen minutes or so. A soaking
really took the edge off.

    He moved to a green garbage dumpster that stood in the middle
of the lot. Raising the metal lid, he pitched in the small suitcase. It
landed among the litter and busted glass with a smash. He tossed the
rolled bundle of Chilly's clothes after it and closed the dumpster. He
crossed to the parked Continental, picking through a heavily populated ring of keys until he found the one that he believed would work
the door. It did, and he slipped behind the Connie's wheel. The door
closed solidly behind him. Another brief search, and he inserted a
key in the ignition, twisted it. The sedan's engine came to life with a

roar. He powered down the driver's side window and sat, savoring the early morning air, letting the engine warm.

To his chagrin, the door of Room 156 swung slowly open. Beyond it, he could see the wreckage of the room's furnishings: the chair with the snapped cabriole leg, the broken lamp, the television on its back on the thin nap of the cheap red motel carpet. The TV still worked, the picture flickering, rolling upward across the tube. He could hear the voices of the TV people as they squawked and jabbered from the speaker, but he could not tell what they were saying. Chilly emerged from the room, a wet washcloth pressed to the knot of swollen discolored flesh on his forehead. Pink splotches of blood were seeping into the white material of the cloth. He was naked but for a bath towel clutched around his waist. The towel was too small to fit all the way around his generous middle, and it gapped obscenely. Peanut managed a giggle.

Chilly blinked when he glimpsed Peanut behind the wheel of his car, but his right eye, the one below the lump, did not close fully, so it looked as though he winked at Peanut: a long, slow, lascivious wink. He started across the parking lot toward the Continental, taking large lurching steps, the bottoms of his bare feet tender on the gravel. The pink-skinned barrel of his chest hitched and heaved.

Peanut drew the Connie's gearshift into reverse and began to pull away. He backed out of the parking space that the car occupied, banging into the dumpster as he did so, pushing it backward a foot or two. Before he was able to drive off, Chilly had reached the car. He stood in front of it, weaving slightly, holding the washcloth and the towel. He stared in through the windshield. Peanut was trapped between the dumpster and the man.

"You bastard," Chilly said. His lips twitched spasmodically. He spat and wheezed, barely able to choke the words out. His face was red, and thumb-size veins stood out from the flesh of his neck. "You son of a bitch." His breath caught in his throat, and his good eye seemed ready to bug out of his head before he was able to inhale again. He patted his naked body with the hand that held the washcloth as though he were searching for something, as though he were wearing clothes and there might be something he wanted in one of his pockets. His asthma inhaler, Peanut guessed. Good luck finding that. It was in the suitcase, in the dumpster.

Peanut stuck his head through the open window. "Get out of the way," he said. Chilly shook his head. He could not speak. "I thought you reacted well to pressure. That's why they call you Chilly. This isn't so good," Peanut told him.

Chilly gasped and gasped. He tried to speak. He would have fallen if he had not braced himself against the hood of the car.

"What?" Peanut asked. "What are you trying to say?"

"Business," Chilly managed to get out. "I said business pressure."

"Fine," Peanut said. "So maybe you're still Chilly. Now get your asthmatic ass out of my way, or I'll have to go over you. Never doubt that I will."

"Wallet," Chilly said. He tried to breathe through his nose, but that was no better. "Please."

Peanut considered the request. He pulled the thick billfold from his pants pocket, extracted the money from it (not as much as he had hoped; just over three hundred dollars. A lot of the bills were fives and tens; only one C-note), and pitched the wallet onto the gravel beside the car. The credit cards were no good to him anyway, or wouldn't be as soon as Chilly collected himself enough to get to a phone. "There," he said. "Now out of the way, fat boy." Still Chilly wouldn't move from his place in front of the car.

"Move your ass," Peanut said. His voice was loud. Chilly did not remove himself from the car's hood. "Okay," Peanut said. "However you want it." He trod the accelerator. Still in reverse gear, the Connie leaped backward, bashing into the dumpster again. The force of the impact demolished the turn indicators, the back-up lights and brake signals. Peanut's head snapped back and then forward again. The dumpster tipped over, spilling its noxious contents. Chilly's clothes and suitcase were buried in the rush of trash. Chilly stood where he had been, staring in mute disbelief.

"Well shoot," Peanut said. He had meant to run Chilly down. The rush of adrenaline that he had felt when he climbed into the car had begun to ebb. He felt the pain of his whiplash. He thought that probably he hadn't handled this whole deal as well as he might have. A few people emerged from their rooms to watch the fracas in the parking lot, rubbing sleep from their eyes. One of them darted into the motel office. Chilly had found his breath somehow, and he was shouting at the top of his lungs. "My car!" he shrieked. "My car!" *Faker*, Peanut thought. *Where's that asthma now?*

Chilly took a stumbling step toward the door of the Continental. Peanut put the car into drive and mashed the accelerator to the floorboards. Gravel shot out from under the spinning rear wheels, and the Connie hurtled forward. Chilly yelped and threw himself out of the way at the last moment before the car struck him, sprawling at full length in the parking lot. He lost his grip on the concealing towel.

Peanut twisted the wheel, and the big car slewed around in a wide, sloppy half-circle that ended when it was pointed toward the highway. It made a terrible thunking noise as it plunged ahead, and Peanut realized that he must have done some grievous damage to the rear end. Still, the car was moving, moving rapidly, and that was a blessing. Now to leave the fairy-boy and the podunk fleabag motel behind. Far, far behind.

The spectators had gathered in a loose group around Chilly, but they didn't touch him or try to help him in any way. Stark naked, on his knees in the gravel, Chilly pawed at the loose pile of trash that had spilled from the dumpster. Objects flew over his shoulders as he pitched them away from him: a limp banana skin, some soft drink cups, old newspapers. At length, he came up with his trousers, and while the crowd looked on, he struggled into them, his face streaked with tears of fury.

Peanut believed that his heart might stop when he saw the flashing blue lights behind the Continental and heard the brief howl of the siren. He had been traveling the back roads all day, and he had gotten badly lost. He was on some single-lane track that looked like its surface was made of oiled dirt, and he hadn't seen a town or a house or any sign of habitation at all for the last forty-five minutes. An hour, maybe. The damaged car had begun to run choppily, ugly smoke pouring from the exhaust, and he thought that probably it wouldn't last much longer. He had been trying to think his way out of the situation and had failed entirely to notice the sheriff's car.

He slowed and pulled to the side of the road. He stopped and sat with the motor idling, his foot on the brake pedal. Behind him, he could see the driver of the police car, ramrod straight in his seat, tall hat planted firmly on his head. Was it the deputy from the gas station? No way to tell.

A voice from the county car's bullhorn cut the air. "Shut off the engine. Get out of the vehicle. Keep your hands high." Peanut's immediate impulse was to obey. He reached out for the keys to turn the car off. When his fingers touched the metal of the key ring, swiftly, irrevocably, he changed his mind.

There were no working back-up lights on the Continental to indicate that it was in reverse, so the deputy was mightily surprised when the big car came rocketing backward along the berm of the unpaved road and plowed into the front of his cruiser. He had expected a routine stop for vehicle warning-light violations. A caution, maybe a citation if the driver got shirty. The bullhorn mike flew from the fingers of his left hand, and his right slipped off the riot gun that was clipped to the dashboard. The steering column collided sharply with his breastbone, fracturing three of his ribs and knocking the breath out of him. His round hat fell off his head and rolled on the floor of the car.

The cruiser's engine died immediately, damaged beyond repair. When the deputy looked up through the cracked windshield, dazed from the impact, he saw the Continental in motion again, this time away from him, heading slowly down the road, leaving behind a trail of milky floating smoke as it went.

It was six hours later, well after dark, when the hastily arranged dragnet from the Dwyer County sheriff's office found the stolen Continental, only a few miles from the scene of the ramming. It had been driven up a desolate logging road, as far up the deeply rutted trail as it could go, and abandoned. The engine was still turning, unsteadily, when the county officers, revolvers drawn, flashlights held high, approached the car from all sides. The gas gauge stood just above empty. The driver's door hung open; the interior dome light glowed brightly.

18

Inchcape gestured at the woven wire fence that bordered the field behind Goody's house. "I built that fence by hand in a dry summer, like this one. Dug post holes thirty-six inches deep, and every one of them was dry at the bottom. It was like setting posts in talcum powder. They never were solid enough to be worth a damn." The square posts of the fence, colorless with age and overgrown by brush, leaned drunkenly one way and the other in their uneven line. The fence gapped and sagged between them. Inchcape headed toward his truck. Tonto lay in the back, huge woolly head clearing by several inches the siderail of the truck's bed. The dog stared at them with his weird blue eyes. As Inchcape was climbing into the cab, he turned back to Goody. "Where's your car at?" he called. "I always like to look at that hot-rod Pontiac of yours when I come over here."

"I had an accident," Goody told him. "Up the road a ways."

"Ouch," Inchcape said. "Joyriding, I guess."

"I didn't hit anybody," Goody said. "Just some dogs is all. They chased a deer out in my way and I got in amongst them."

"It can happen like that, I know," Inchcape said. "What did you do with the car?"

"Left it where it sat."

"How far are you?" Inchcape asked.

"I don't know. Pretty good distance. That way." Goody pointed north. "I caught a ride with some people to get back here."

"Well, why didn't you tell me about it earlier?" Inchcape said. "Get on in. I'll give you a tow."

"Do you think so?" Goody said. "It's got a couple of flat tires, and I've only got one spare."

"I can give you a wheel and a tire to use a while," Inchcape said. "I don't care about that. As long as it ain't got a busted axle, you're in good shape. We'll just throw a towing strap around the front bumper and haul you back here. Save you a pile of money."

"I can't pay you," Goody said. "Not anything like what it would be worth."

"We'll worry about that some other time," Inchcape said. "It ain't like I don't know where to find you if I want you."

"That would be great," Goody said.

"Sure it would," Inchcape said. "But we better get going if we plan to beat the rain."

"Give me a chance to change my clothes," Goody said, indicating the shorts and T-shirt that he wore. Inchcape nodded and sat waiting in the truck as Goody went back into the house.

When he emerged, dressed in jeans and a workshirt, the two of them drove back up the wash to Inchcape's place, the Ford's tires bobbling unevenly over the flat stones of the old creekbed. Inchcape parked the pickup next to the dump truck and disappeared into the shed that stood next to his house. He emerged a minute later, carrying gathered in his arms and looped about his neck a long towing strap with heavy metal buckles at its ends. He explained to Goody, who had remained sitting in the pickup, that they would be taking the ten-wheeler.

"That old Ford runs okay, but you don't want to try and pull nothing with it," Inchcape said. "The frame's about eat up with rust, and you might jerk the truck into two pieces if you didn't do it just right." After collecting a couple of tires from the shed, ones that Inchcape thought might fit the Pontiac, and tossing them into the dump bed, they climbed into the high cab of the Mack truck. Inchcape dropped the towing strap in a coiled heap onto the floor at

Goody's feet. The strap looked like a length of canvas fire hose, and it smelled strongly of mildew. With his toes, Goody shuffled it away from him, as far forward in the leg space as it would go.

Inchcape primed the dump truck's big diesel motor and started it, and it idled noisily, warming. The single exhaust stack was mounted against the cab behind Goody, and he could feel its vibrations in the bones of his spine. The cap at the top of the stack clinked and jingled as the jet of hot exhaust gases made it dance.

At the sound of the truck's engine, Tonto rose up from his place in the bed of the Ford and leaped over the side. He stretched elaborately, then came to the driver's side of the dump truck and placed his great front paws against Inchcape's door. "Get down," Inchcape said. "Get away from there, you idiot." He opened his door an inch or two—Goody could see a swatch of Tonto's shaggy coat, and then an eye and a strip of tongue as the dog tried to force his head into the narrow gap—and slammed it again, but Tonto wasn't discouraged. Goody could hear the dog's claws scrabbling against the metal door panel. "You ain't coming!" Inchcape shouted.

He tugged at the lanyard that triggered the truck's air horn. The three trumpets bolted to the cab's roof blatted. He pulled the lanyard again, a sustained blast of the horn this time, and the panes in the windows of his house rippled like water. "That took care of him," Inchcape said with satisfaction. Tonto crossed the dirt yard to the porch. He threw himself down, his wide hairy back to them.

"Look at him. Now he's going to ignore us like we aren't even here. He likes to go for a ride when he can," Inchcape said, throwing the truck into low gear and easing it out of the yard, "but he's got to learn he can't go with me each and every time." Inchcape pointed to Goody's seat. "He usually sits right there where you're sitting. He sticks his head out the window and squints his eyes closed against the wind and sucks down the bugs as they come along. It's like he's more a bat than a dog, the way he nabs them out of the air as they come past him. I don't know how he does it. He'll eat his weight in insects if you don't stop him."

"Some dogs have a talent," Goody said. "I knew a guy once who had a dog that would catch a Frisbee. You didn't even have to throw right to it. You could throw over it or even in the opposite direction entirely, or into a mess of bushes and brush, and that dog would never goldbrick on you. It would play with you long after a person might have tired out or given up."

"Tonto wouldn't catch a Frisbee," Inchcape said. They came to the state road and headed north. Goody marveled at how Inchcape handled the truck, such a small dried-up old man and such a big rig. "He won't catch a ball or play fetch or anything else either, like you'd think a dog ought to," Inchcape went on. "You can toss a ball if you want, but he'll just look at you like you're a fool for doing it. Let it bounce right off of his face. I tried to teach him once, but after a while it got to seem pretty silly, me standing there pelting this dog with various objects, so I stopped." He bore down on the accelerator, and the truck rocketed along the road.

"Along in here?" he asked when they had gone a few miles.

"Further on," Goody said, pointing north. "You'll see it when you come up on it. I left tracks for about a mile, it seems like. And the dogs I creamed."

"I hate that, when a dog gets hit," Inchcape said. "They don't know what's happened to them, and there's no way you can explain it. I've lost more dogs that way." He hunkered over the wide steering wheel of the truck. The wheel turned unhurriedly from side to side, loose on its column.

"I don't believe these belonged to anybody," Goody said. "The man who gave me a ride said they run wild all through the valley. I've heard them going up and down the gully behind my house."

"Sure they do," Inchcape said. "I don't mind that you hit them, but I do hate it like hell when somebody hits mine." He said nothing for a few moments. Then he asked, "Who was it gave you a ride? Anybody I know?"

Goody struggled to remember the man's name. He remembered Dreama well enough: the scent of her, and the way she had pressed herself against him in the front seat of the Bronco. Or perhaps it was he who had pressed himself against her. He squirmed to think he might have humiliated her by touching her, and she simply too polite or too embarrassed to pull away from him. "Wallace somebody," he came up with at last. "I don't know if I got his last name or not. Or maybe Wallace is his last name. He drives a Bronco."

"Oh sure," Inchcape said. "That's most likely Wallace Clay-maker. Did he have a woman with him?"

"Yes."

"Big jugs and long red fingernails?"

Goody considered. "I don't recall her fingernails."

Inchcape gave a long, low whistle. "I bet you don't," he said. "That's Dreama Claymaker."

"His daughter?" Goody asked.

"Don't you wish," Inchcape said. "Dreama's his wife, and woe betide the fellow who should mistake her for something else. He's a hard man is our friend Claymaker."

"He put a bullet through a dog with no qualm, that's for sure. It was hurt and lying in a ditch, and he just shot it in the back of the head with a pistol. He did it clean, and he never mentioned it afterward."

"I believe you," Inchcape said, nodding. "He's got a little place, sixty or seventy acres up in the foothills where he farms dope. Them fellows are usually pretty damn tough or they don't last too long."

"Dope? You mean he grows pot?"

"Sure he does. A lot of those boys out that way do, on federal land, in the national forest. I did it myself for a while, around the edges of my mountain pastures and back in the woods, but I didn't have the stomach for but one or two seasons of growing. There's a lot of money in it."

Inchcape spun the dump truck's wheel to the left to pass a slow-moving cattle van and then guided the truck back into its lane. "Claymaker, though, he keeps a sizable plot out in the clear. I've seen it myself. He plants a field with about half a dozen rows of corn around the edges, and then he sows the inside of the square with marijuana. Takes balls to do it that way. Unless of course you've got the law in your pocket, which Claymaker happens to have. Wallace and this new fellow, Tannhauser. Crazy son of a bitch with too many fingers. They grow the pot and the sheriff's deputies peddle it."

"I just thought he was a farmer of the regular sort," Goody said, "or a man with a job."

"Would you of figured me for a pot farmer?"

"No sir," Goody said. "I wouldn't."

"But I was," Inchcape said. "So there you go. Did he have any dope in the Bronco when he picked you up?"

"Not that I saw, he didn't. I never looked too close."

Inchcape laughed. "Just as well for you that you didn't. I bet he had six or seven garbage bags full of the stuff in the back, or under the seats. He operates that way. He trundles around his product like it was old clothes or something. Reckless."

"He didn't seem so bad to me."

"He'd of shot you if it had occurred to him that there was advantage in it." Inchcape lifted his right hand from the steering wheel, made a pistol of his thumb and forefinger, and placed it lightly against Goody's temple. "Pow," he said, drawing the hand swiftly back and up, as though from the recoil of a pistol shot. "Like that. And took your body up into the mountains and dumped it into a ravine or a lime pit and forgot about you for all time. Never mentioned you, just like that dog."

"So why did he stop, if he's as bad as you say?"

Inchcape shrugged. "Who can tell? Maybe he was bored. A wrecked car can be an interesting thing."

They drove on in silence. Ahead of them, a blue Volkswagen Beetle with one yellow door labored along at a pace well below their own, emanating a choking cloud of dark smoke. Inchcape eased off the throttle as they came up to it, slowing enough to match its speed only when the dump truck's heavy steel grille was within inches of its back end. He blew the truck's horn. The road wound through a series of curves, and there was no long straight stretch where he might pass. He stayed right on the VW as though he were glued to it.

Goody saw a male passenger's face framed in the rear window of the small bowl-shaped car. The Volkswagen's driver, a young woman, nervously checked her rearview mirror every few seconds. "Yes, honey, I'm still here," Inchcape said to her when she looked a fifth time, and a sixth. He played the accelerator, lying back for a little while and then gunning it to close the gap again. The Volkswagen continued on at its solemn pace. Goody felt sure that it could go no faster.

He said, "Why don't you slow up a little?"

Inchcape threw him a sidelong glance, and in the instant that his attention was turned from the road, the Beetle slowed, its brake lights flashing. The dump truck advanced on the car, and though he could not be sure, Goody thought he felt a slight shudder communicate itself through the massive frame of the truck as the two vehicles touched. Inchcape shouted and threw his weight on the brake pedal. The truck's air brakes hissed, and Goody put the flats of his hands against the dashboard to avoid being spilled from his seat.

As the truck decelerated, the Beetle shot away from it down the road. A few hundred yards farther on, it pulled off the highway onto the gravel berm at a slant, and the passenger door opened. The passenger, a lanky boy in tan pants and a sweatshirt, emerged and shook his fist at them when they passed. Inchcape grinned. The driver was hunched over the steering wheel, and she appeared to be crying. The passenger trotted gamely alongside the truck for a few steps, still waving his fist, but he quickly fell behind and soon after that stopped running. Goody watched in the large mirror on his side of the truck as the little car and the gesticulating figure dwindled with distance.

"A little excitement," Inchcape said.

"I used to drive a truck for a while," Goody said. "I was working for the Solid Waste Authority. It was a garbage truck, and I slammed into a row of parked cars. Just wasn't looking. I totaled four of them, but I barely put a scratch on the truck. Cost me my job in the end."

"You think that's something?" Inchcape said.

"I don't think it's anything," Goody said. "Just an event that happened, is all."

"I saw a wreck not too long ago that was really something," Inchcape said. He seemed excited; his voice had grown uncomfortably loud. "It'll make any smashup you been involved in seem pale by comparison."

"I believe you," Goody said.

"You better," Inchcape said, "because it's the Lord's truth."

19

Inchcape told it this way:

"We're going down the long slope on Little Allegheny Mountain. Three of us have got our trucks in a line: Looney Martin in the front, then me, and Asa Boggs bringing up the back door. It's eight, nine miles long, the stretch of mountain highway we're on, and better than an eight percent grade for most of its length, with a steep drop-off on either side, so it's got a pretty wicked reputation. A lot of guys have gone over on that grade, burned out their brakes, rolled their rigs. It's a killer.

"Most all of the trucking companies won't even let their haulers use it anymore, because so many people have pitched over the edge and took their trucks with them. That gets to be expensive after a while. You have to go the long way if you don't use it, though, around by the Henderson Gap, so there's some of us that still take the old route. You can carry a lot more loads in a day that way, if you don't screw it up.

"So we're going down the slope, and Asa's on the radio telling us about some guy who fell asleep and ran his rig full tilt into a bridge stanchion. *Did you hear about that, Inchworm?* he asks me. Inchworm is my handle. Asa says it was a Transtar eighteen-wheeler semi, going like the hammers of hell, and the trailer snapped like a whip, flipped up over the top of the cab. He says it looked just like some kind of a giant metal scorpion, waving its tail up over its back.

"While Asa's going on, I smell a terrible smell. Looking, I see Looney's got smoke boiling out from his brakes. He's got a real load on, probably seventy thousand pounds gross or more, loaded with twenty-five tons of gravel anyway, and he's pulling away from us down the hill. I've got the same load, and Asa the same as me, but I've got it in the low range, just creeping down the hill. I get on the radio and tell Looney to let up on the brakes or he'll burn them out. Maybe he don't know the smoke he's laying down. He can't hear me, though, because Asa's still talking, and I imagine he's walking on my signal pretty good, and me on his, so Looney's probably just getting noise.

"*Clear the channel*, I tell Asa, and he says, *Come again?* and goes right on back into his story. He hasn't smelled Looney's cooking brakes yet, and he can't see Looney because my truck's in the way. *Get off the radio, goddamnit*, I say, and this time he does it. I listen to see if Looney's broadcasting anything, though if he is I don't know what I can do. He's as far beyond my help as if he was on the moon, and all I can do is watch whatever's going to happen. Still, it seems to me like it would be good to hear his voice. There's nothing on the CB but static, and way back in the background some voices that you can hear but you can't tell at all what they're saying, like they might be in the next county over or the next state and their signal just getting to you by taking a freak bounce off the clouds.

"Finally I say, *Looney. Breaker, Looney-tune. How about you?* His truck's way out ahead now, rolling down the slope, getting faster, and I wonder if his brakes could be gone already. If so, there's nothing holding him back. His truck's older and badly outfitted, so he's got no jake brake on the engine to shut him down if he gets in trouble. Asa's on the air again, wanting to know what's wrong. Finally I get him to clear, and I give Looney another shout. *Looney, Looney, you got your ears on?* I say, but I'm starting to think he must of shut the radio off so he wouldn't have to listen to Asa tell his story.

"By this time he's losing control, but he rolls right on by the first runaway truck ramp like he hasn't seen it. I don't blame him, because if I was in trouble but figured I could hold out for the second one a few miles on down, I'd do it that way too. The second ramp is a kind of upward corkscrew, a dirt track; up and up it goes, and you're losing speed all the time until you're stopped right there at the top. But the first one—the first one's just a straight single lane that leads off the highway at an angle, runs for a couple hundred yards, and drops sheer into the ravine. Nothing to stop you at the end but a mound of crushed limestone. It's got a carpet of deep gravel covering it that's supposed to wear away your speed, but if I've got to trust my life to gravel stopping me, thirty-five tons of truck haring along at eighty or ninety miles an hour, I'll take another choice, thank you very much.

"So Looney skips the first ramp and heads on down the mountain. I pick up my speed a little to keep him in sight, but I don't want to end up where it looks like he's going, so I keep my eye on my velocity, just using the brakes as much as I need them, testing the pedal to make sure they don't fade. Asa's crowding me, because he wants to see what's up, and because he hasn't got much in the way of brains. And all I can think is *How did you let it get away from you, Loon? Weren't you watching?*

"It surprises me to hear him on the citizen's band. He's shouting. *Hey, hey, hey,* he yells, and then there's a sound like he's banging the mike against the dashboard. Hammering it. Then he's yelling, *Hey, hey,* again. He's keeping the mike keyed, so it's no use to try to talk to him. He won't hear anything through his own transmission. His truck's just screaming along the grade now, brakes gone for sure, and it sounds through the radio like a plane that's on its way down. This awful rising rattling pitch that you know has got to end in a smash. He goes around a curve, out of my sight for a few seconds until I round the turn myself. He's still on the CB, talking now, and I try to pay attention to what he's saying. It may be all that he gets to say. He's shouting, but still it's hard to hear him over the noise of his truck. *Maketh me to lie down,* he says. *Valley of the shadow,* he says, and *death.*

"We're still a couple of miles above the second truck ramp, which is near the bottom of the grade, and he's starting to weave with the speed; the truck's sloshing back and forth over the center line, and the few cars that are coming the other way, up the grade, have scattered off to the edges of the road one side and the other. He sideswipes one of them and it spins in place and winds up sitting on the guardrail. The impact doesn't slow him down a bit. Over the radio I hear him hit the car. It sounds like he has crushed a tin can in his fist. *You're killing people, Looney,* I shout, but into the air, into the windshield, not into the radio. A couple of seconds later I'm going past the car he hit, a big Buick, its front end and driver's side crushed, and nobody's getting out of it or even moving so far as I can tell.

"My head with oil, he says, his voice over the radio as clear as though he is sitting next to me in the cab of my own truck. He begins to say something else, but his voice is cut off by a loud cracking noise. It sounds like he has been shot. His voice, and the sounds from his truck, are gone from the radio. It's just static again. It takes me a second to recognize that popping sound: one of his front tires has blown out.

"You don't try to steer or brake when that happens; you just ride it on down. We're nearly to the second truck ramp now, the better one, but he won't make it. The tire has gone, and he's rolling on the rim, throwing up a trail of bright sparks like it's some kind of a light show under his truck, like he's an electric trolley following along a high-tension wire. The other front tire goes pretty soon after, and the fuel tanks rip loose from under the tractor's running boards. The tanks carry back into the rear wheels, the wheels under the load, and all eight of them go at once. It's like watching a drunk stagger down the street though traffic, seeing Looney's truck with all its tires gone, wandering over the road. It swerves and then it tips over onto its side. The load of gravel washes out onto the road, a little rock slide right there on the highway.

"I'm into the junk trail that Looney's truck is leaving behind it as it dies, and I'm spending all my time trying not to hit nothing, dodging axle parts and bouncing fuel tanks and riding over all the rocks and pieces of scrap that I couldn't tell you what they are. It scares me to think I might lose a tire and go down myself, and I think that's the first time I've been scared during this whole experience. I throttle back, looking to pull over onto the berm, hoping Asa's giving me enough room that he won't smash into the back of my truck.

"By the time I look up, Looney's about six feet from hitting a milk tanker that has just started the climb up Little Allegheny, and still sliding. The tanker's got a blue tractor with a big sleeping compartment behind the cab, and I can't help but wonder if there's anyone napping back there. Then I close my eyes, even though my truck is still under way, because those two vehicles colliding is something that I simply do not want to see.

"The sound of it—the sound of it I'm unable to describe. A giant man digging his thumbs deep into your ears, way back in where it is waxy and dark and it is so sensitive that you can't bear anyone to touch. Or that same place, if a bug were in there, a big black beetle, and its wings were beating against your eardrum a hundred times a second, and there was no way to get it out but to go in after it with something long and thin and pointed, something sharp made out of steel. It's a sound I can hear in my head perfectly, but one I cannot imitate and wouldn't like to. Right at the last, I hear Looney's mike key on, and I hear him screaming, and then stop screaming. But there is no way that could happen, and no way I could hear his voice over the sound of the grinding metal and busting glass."

Inchcape took a breath.

"Afterward, there's a lot of cleaning up to do. Asa and I are the first men on the spot, and then some people from cars that have stopped on both sides of the road. Twenty-five tons of gravel seems like a lot when it is riding just back of you in the dump bed of your truck, but when it is all on the road it don't seem like so much. Just a thin covering is all, and our feet are crunching through it all the rest of that afternoon.

"The milk is everywhere too, and I'm sure it was a lot of money's worth of milk, thin blue-looking stuff, but before long it has streamed down the hill and ran into the culverts, mixed with the diesel that is draining from both trucks, and down the drains with it and it is gone. It has been a dry season, and whatever liquid leaves the hardtop road is sucked down into the dirt in no time at all. Flies collect on the shredded metal of the milk tanker's container.

"The results are pretty much what you might expect of such a thing. The folks in the Buick have been injured but not killed, although one of them dies in the hospital later that night. Looney is dead as a mackerel, we can see that right away; it takes a rescue squad a couple of hours to cut his body out with acetylene torches and power saws and the Jaws of Life gadget that they got.

"In the end, the wrecker crew that comes to pick up the two trucks can't get them apart. They have hit so hard they are practically welded together at their cabs. I heard later that they took both of them down to the salvage yard in one piece, dragging them behind a couple of their heaviest wreckers. At the yard, they got a couple of those big Komatsu crawlers to come in and cut the trucks apart from each other. It was the only way they could do it.

"One surprising thing: the driver of the tanker is alive. A long breaker bar slid out from a toolbox behind the seat and cracked him on the leg, and he's got a knot there the size of a football. But overall he's pretty happy when we drag him out of the wreck and set him by the side of the road. We tell him to take it easy, sit quiet and wait for the ambulance because the leg might be busted, or he could have other injuries that we can't see, and he just doesn't feel it because he is jazzed up. But he won't listen, goes gimping around the wreck, marveling at the whole thing with this silly grin on his face. He even grins when he looks into the dump truck's cab and sees what's left of Looney.

"Asa goes over to him. I go over there too, because I don't like the way Asa's walking, got his shoulders hunched and his arms held tight against his sides like he wants a fight. Asa puts a hand on this guy's shoulder—he's still staring in there at Looney—and spins him around so the guy nearly folds up on his bad leg. The seam of his trouser leg is splitting over the swelling, and I can see the skin in there's a bad color, got to be a fracture of some kind. I saw guys that got injuries like that when they were playing football and they never knew it for hours, high on winning and the game. This guy's just like that.

"Asa says to him, *Get that look off your damn face. A man has died here.*

"And the guy says, *Look?*

"Asa says, *You're smiling. Why the hell would you be smiling?* Other people are drifting over to watch what's happening, but nobody interferes. They've had enough excitement for a while, maybe. I'll step in if it gets any worse than it is, but I'm holding off for the minute.

"The guy holds up his hands and says, *I'm not smiling.* At the same time there's this big grin on his face. When he says that about not smiling, the grin gets even wider. He's showing all his teeth, and he has nice white even teeth. From drinking a lot of milk, maybe. His teeth are beginning to chatter together a little, and his lips are going blue, but altogether he looks very merry.

"*You're looking in there at my dead friend's corpse and you're smiling,* Asa says. I can tell he's about to go in swinging, so I take him by the arm. He doesn't want to come at first, but I manage to lead him away. Behind us, the other folks are gathered around the tanker driver, and I can hear his voice. He's saying, *I'm not smiling, I'm not smiling,* over and over again. Asa and I go over to my truck, and we get up into the cab, and we tune in an FM station to listen to a few songs, and we smoke a couple of cigarettes, waiting for the police and the ambulance to show up.

"*He was smiling*, Asa says. He's got a cigarette in his hand, but he's not smoking it. He's just letting it burn down toward his fingers. *I didn't like to see that.*

"*I know it, Asa*, I say. *I know exactly what you mean. But listen: I think the guy is in shock.*

"He looks over at me, and I wonder for a second if he's going to take a swing at me. Then he laughs, and he says to me in this angry voice, *Shock, hell. That man's as happy as a clam.*

"The guy has gotten away from the people who were trying to tend him, and he's hobbling around, really moving like a cripple, twisting on that busted leg. He's going from place to place on the road around the two wrecked trucks, pointing at the mashed pieces that are laying everywhere on the ground, telling their names in this big loud voice that carries to us even in the closed cab. *Looney's dead*, is all I can think, and this injured guy's climbing on his truck, sounding glad and excited and calling out the details of his survival to anybody in the crowd around him that'll listen."

20

Peanut had been walking along the power company right-of-way for a while and he was winded, wandering up a steep slate-strewn grade. At the top of the ridge he paused. The power company cut stretched ahead of him like an empty rolling highway. He saw nothing but the unbroken reach of it, its series of gantrylike steel pylons spaced at regular intervals, disappearing over one hillcrest, reappearing at the zenith of the next. A dozen high-tension cables strung their shallow curves from the arms of the pylons. The brush and trees were cut well back from the path of the power lines.

The pylons put him in mind of pictures, black-and-white photographs his father had shown him of gateways they had in Japan. Great tall structures made of glossy lacquered wood. His father had told him that there were huge doors in the gates through which a person could walk. His father had been in most of the pictures, dressed in Army fatigues; thin, forty pounds thinner than the man Peanut knew; decades younger, standing in the gateway openings; wearing glasses with chunky plastic frames, his hair cropped short, his arm usually around a serious-looking Japanese girl dressed in a patterned bathrobe. *Kimono,* his father had taught him to say. Many of the pictures were fuzzy and out of focus, and Peanut had never

known if it was one girl over and over again or a number of different
ones. He had never asked. He didn't know who had taken them,
either. Someone who frequently got his forefinger and thumb in front
of the lens.

The high-tension wires hummed and crackled. Peanut looked
back the way he had come, and that view was the same as the one
before him. He squinted, thinking that he had perhaps turned a full
three hundred and sixty degrees rather than the half-circle he had
intended. He looked first one way and then the other, and there was
no good way to tell the two directions apart. The brutal sun stood
directly overhead. His shadow was pooled across his shoes and provided him no compass. The light seemed to dance, and a thousand
bits of dust floated in the air. He shook his head to clear it.

One way or the other. What difference did it make? The power
lines had to go somewhere. Electricity always ended up somewhere.
He wiped sweat from his forehead and from around his stinging eyes,
wishing for a pair of sunglasses, and began again to walk.

An hour or so later he came on a prospect that overlooked the jumbled expanse of a landfill project. Peanut stood at the top of a short
bluff whose face was made of brittle red clay. The air over the landfill
was hazy with smoke, and piles of debris smoldered on the ashy flats
below him. His head buzzed, and he couldn't tell if the cause was the
heat of the day or the stink of burning rubbish, or if it might be the
magnetic influence of the high-voltage wires suspended above him. A
lone Caterpillar dozer crawled over the mounded garbage, pushing at
the stuff with its high slotted blade. From his vantage point, Peanut
thought the bulldozer looked like a yellow hard-shelled insect. In
place of treads, the dozer had cruelly spiked steel wheels, and it rode
up and over the discarded tires and appliances and furniture, grinding them down with its weight.

The driver of the bulldozer, who wore helmet and goggles and
pig-snout particle mask, looked around as though he felt Peanut's
gaze. Peanut decided that he needed to ask the man for help. He
breathed deep and took a tentative step onto the slope that led down
to the landfill. The dry clay crumbled under his feet, and he
pinwheeled his arms, fighting for balance before sliding halfway
down the rotten bank. Broken clay and pebbles cascaded past him.
He sat abruptly, and a small wash of dirt piled up behind him. He
dug the heels of his hands into the ground.

Below him, the dozer reversed direction. The spikes on its wheels dug great divots in the dirt and garbage as it moved sedately away, threading its course between piles of waste. Disturbed by its passing, a trio of turkey buzzards abandoned a sprawled donkey's carcass. They stroked laboriously up into the air, circling higher and higher, then stiffened their wings as they caught and rode the thermals that rose from the dump. Traversing the angry red ball of the sun, they sailplaned, still rising, over the spot where Peanut squatted uncomfortably on his hams.

He held his precarious perch. Greasy smoke poured from the bulldozer's exhaust stack as it left him. "Hey," Peanut called after it, without much hope. The crawler moved off, and the deserted landfill became quiet. Peanut watched the donkey's cadaver, wondering if the buzzards were likely to return and finish their meal. Soon his thighs began to cramp, and he knew that he had to reverse his slide and gain the top of the bank, or else allow himself to pitch forward and skid the rest of the way down to the fill. After a moment's consideration, he pushed himself backward with all the force his tired haunches could muster.

The earth beneath him gave way, and he slipped down another ten feet, cursing. His shirttail pulled loose from his pants and rucked up, wedging under his armpits. The skin of his back stung, and dirt adhered to the flayed places where loose rocks had caught him. He lay spread-eagled on the slope, and the sun was in his eyes. He blinked, then rolled over onto his stomach, losing a little more ground in the process.

Arms outstretched, he began a slow crawl back toward the power company cut, now twenty yards or so above him. At first he moved like a measuring worm, humping along on his belly and thighs and elbows, losing an inch for every two he gained, the ground shifting and breaking away under him until he came to feel that it was not earth there at all, but some less substantial stuff into which he might at any moment plunge and be lost. He dug his fingers into the dirt, which gave itself up to him in hand-size batches, leaving behind it loose cavities that afforded him no hold at all.

He toiled meanly up the fractured slope, varying his climbing method by slow degrees, until a dozen yards from his goal he discovered a kind of swimming motion that allowed him reasonable progress. He continued upward so, sweeping his arms out and back, kicking froglike with his legs, obliged continually to spit and blow to keep his mouth clear of the fine red dust that rose up and enveloped him. And as he went, he left carved deep into the bank behind him the queer ideogram of his thrashing passage.

Just before nightfall, he heard the sound of running water from somewhere in the growth beside the right of way. He stopped, turning his head this way and that, trying to locate the exact source of the sound. Finally the pressure of his thirst caused him to give up on his effort at triangulation, and he plunged into the underbrush, flailing blindly. He fought his way through brambles in one direction, veering off in another when he came upon the papery bolus of a wasp's nest, as big as his head and crawling with venomous insects. When he stopped to check his progress, he could still hear the water, but it sounded no nearer than it had before. His thirst was terrible now, and he closed his eyes. He moaned, swaying in his tracks. He heard the grating, terrified sound of his voice, and the strangeness of it shocked him into quiet. The dark grew deeper around him. He forced himself to move on.

He discovered the house first, a little bungalow pleasantly situated in a grassy glen. Behind the house there ran a clear stream, still high despite the lack of summer rains. He went to it and knelt and cupped his hands in the cool water, drinking from his raised palms. The red dust on his hands was carried away down the stream in smoky swirls as he drank. When that first method proved too slow to slake his craving, he went on all fours, bent his head to the surface, and sucked the water straight into his mouth. His narrow belly strained against the waistband of his trousers with the weight of it.

He stopped after drinking for a while, turned his head to the side, and in a liquid rush vomited up what he had drunk. He went immediately back to the stream and drank again without pause. This time the water stayed down.

After he had drunk all he wanted, he made his way up the glen to the house, feeling half drowned and agreeably logy. He burped loudly, put a hand to his mouth, gave forth with a rustling giggle. There was a clothesline strung between two man-high wooden posts in the back yard of the bungalow. When he put his hand to the line, it parted noiselessly, and the halves fell back toward their respective poles. A single clothespin, clasped to the line for some unknown length of time, broke with a musical clatter when it hit the ground.

The house itself was abandoned, had been abandoned for any

number of years. The paint had peeled from its sides. Most of the glass was gone from the windows, and Peanut amused himself as darkness gathered by finding stones in the yard and pitching them through the few remaining panes. The sound of their brittle bursting filled the glen.

When there was no more glass to break, Peanut ventured inside the house. The door stood open, swollen and warped until it was impossible to close. The interior of the house smelled heavily of mildew, rodent droppings, and dust. Cobwebs floated in the corners. There were four good-size downstairs rooms. The staircase to the second story leaned heavily to one side. It was very steep, more of a ladder than a set of stairs, really. A number of the treads were broken, so he did not try to climb it.

In the kitchen, he was delighted to find six dust-covered cans of Vienna sausages sitting on the counter beside the sink. They were stacked in a neat pyramid. He grabbed the top can, prized off the lid, and extracted the sausages in a clump. He ate them quickly, greedily, sucking at the salty jelly in which they had been packed. He started to open a second can but stopped. Who knew when he might come across more food?

The place was devoid of furniture, except for a couple of thin sleeping pallets. These he stacked one atop the other near a window at the rear of the house, which gave him a view of the stream. He set the Vienna sausage cans next to the makeshift bed. At this remove, the babbling of the creek sounded like the distant barking of dogs. The moon had risen, nearly full, and its bright light glittered on the ripples of the water.

As he sat and watched the flow, Peanut gave in to his hunger. He opened another can of sausages and consumed them in a rush. Though by the look of the cans they had been in the house for a long time, they were perfectly preserved. He ate a third can, slowly this time, working the sausages, churning them into a thick, savory paste between his moving jaws. When he had finished eating, Peanut leaned back against the wall. A feeling of well-being such as he had not known for some time filled him.

The house showed signs of having been a hunters' camp. Turkey hunters, by the kind and number of feathers that were scattered across the floors of all of the rooms, and by the pile of empty shotgun shells in the filthy kitchen sink. Lying back on his pallet, he took up a large multicolored feather and brushed its soft edge against the skin of his forearm. As he ran the feather back and forth, the ticklish sensation of it pleased him, and he kept on, shedding his shirt and his pants, moving the feather over his body and pretending that someone else held the hollow shaft of the feather, that the feather was some-one's hand; lulling himself finally, with thoughts of amiable company, to sleep.

He woke in the late hours of the night, thirsty again. He passed a hand across his mouth, smacking his lips in an effort to work up some spit. His tongue cleaved, as fat as a thumb, to the roof of his mouth. He discovered that he needed urgently to urinate.

He rose and left the house. The air was cool on his skin, and he shivered as he made his way down to the creek. Once there, he pissed into the brook, aiming carefully downstream, enjoying the sound of his water meeting the world's. Overhead, heat lightning flickered fitfully, producing no thunder and promising no rain. When he had finished relieving himself, he knelt beside the creek and scooped several handfuls of water to his mouth. As before, he continued to drink even after he had killed his thirst, pouring the water into himself, chewing the mineral-rich stuff almost like food as it went down. When he had finished, his shrunken belly was as tight as a drum.

He returned to the house, and cradling his painful stomach in his folded arms, groaning softly, he fell quickly and deeply asleep.

An hour before dawn, the DEA helicopter flew past the house, heading northward along the power company cut just as Peanut himself had done the day before. The rising thump of its main rotor shook the thin walls of the house, and the glow of its spotlight, weakened by the intervening screen of tightly woven underbrush, painted the walls with faint color. It was making sixty or seventy knots, and it had come and gone before its noise penetrated Peanut's consciousness and roused him.

His dreams just before waking again were vivid ones, filled with shouting apelike creatures that unfurled their bat wings against the night. When they moved, the wings made machine sounds, train sounds, the sounds of the railroad, passenger trains that traveled always in the dark. And those trains: their long silver cars were filled with the white grubby bodies of the dead, twined together, their puffy limbs overlapped, pressing against the doors, their faces squashed pitifully against the glass, flattened, staring. And one face above all commanded his attention.

Peanut woke with the image of that face before him. He woke just as the helicopter passed out of hearing. He tried to slow his rapid breathing, tried not to see that face as the howling train bore it away from the station, away down the water-filled tunnels through which it traveled, away. He shook his head and listened for the sound that had awakened him, and heard nothing out of the ordinary: night sounds, lapping water. Listened again, and heard the booming voice of a great horned owl, once, not repeated. Listened longer, and heard grunting, and a queer snuffling noise.

He stayed by the window and began pulling on his clothes, suddenly afraid. The grunting grew louder, more distinct, and it was accompanied by the clatter of hooves. Little of the moon's light reached him, and he had to identify the different articles of his clothing by touch. He shoved his arm down the twisted sleeve of his jacket, tried to button his trousers and pinched a wide fold of skin instead. He could see the vague humped shapes of the creatures now. They were the size of dogs, moving swiftly toward the house, continuing their unearthly noise.

Heat lightning flashed again, a hot sheet of it that spanned the sky, and Peanut saw that the yard was filled with wild hogs. The lightning stroke threw them into a panic: eyes rolling white, jaws foaming, kicking, slashing one another with razor tusks. They fought out in the yard, the dozens of them screaming, their voices as shrill as trumpets. Peanut stopped up his ears with his index fingers. They were massive hogs with high dark-bristled backs, narrow muscular flanks, and bullet-shaped heads. Their legs were short, their hooves slender and cruelly sharp. A number of them fell dying under the onslaught of some loose confederation of neighbors, and the whole shivering mass of them wheeled with surprising speed toward the open doorway of the house.

Peanut was barely ahead of them as they entered. They cut at his legs, snorting and woofing as they pursued him through the rooms, more of them pouring into the house all the time. One hog heaved itself through a window, spilled onto Peanut's pallet, picked itself up, and joined the others. Another followed by the same route. A couple of the hogs slipped and fell as they came on, hooves awkward on the slick uncarpeted wood of the floor, and the hogs behind the fallen ones simply rode over them, dispatched them with a clean thrust of paired tusks, and moved on. The dim light in the house reflected redly in their tiny sunken eyes.

Peanut found himself trapped. As he rounded the corner from one room to another, hopping along one-legged in his snarled pants, several screaming hogs hard behind him, another group entered the same room through a different door, headed in the opposite direction. One of them slammed against him, almost knocking him down, and its bristled hide scraped over his flesh like sandpaper. Knowing himself in mortal danger, he did not hesitate, but leaped immediately for his only possible salvation.

He hit the listing staircase on its fourth stair and continued up, kicking out the rotted risers behind him as he went. A hog tried to climb after him, slipped, failed, trundled upward again. The whole tottering contraption went over with a crash as Peanut gained the upper story, pinning a huge bad-tempered boar beneath its weight. The boar struggled and screamed, and soon his compatriots set gleefully to work on him with their jaws and tusks and hard pointed feet.

Peanut crouched above them, listening to them as they slaughtered their brother and, that finished, turned on some other vulnerable member of the group. From time to time, strokes of heat lightning revealed to his unbelieving eyes the horrors they wreaked on one another. The house shuddered with the blows of their bulky bodies against its walls. He thought they might tear the whole house apart, board from board, joist from joist, and bring it crashing down around them. The sharp metallic odor of pig manure rose to his nostrils. He retreated from the stairwell but was unable to find anyplace in the small upstairs that was not inundated with the smells and the sounds of the wild hogs.

At last he brushed a mound of broken plaster out of a corner of one room and reclined there, wedging himself into its confines in an effort to find a comfortable sitting position. He rested his head on his hands. An image rose unbidden into his weary mind: not the dream picture of his own twisted face, borne away under the earth in a trainload of corpses, but a picture of the canned sausages, abandoned alongside the rough pallet on which he had slept. He cried out, but his words were lost among the high-pitched shrieking of the hogs. And nothing at all, no lost treasure, not a single thing in the world, could induce him to lower himself into the stinking, milling brawl below.

21

Bodo's first impression of El Dorado, glimpsed through one of the Dakota's misted ports, was that it resembled a permanent encampment for the training of paramilitary insurgents that he had once visited in South America: a large central building, no doubt for command and control, surrounded by a number of smaller buildings to house personnel. He recognized the rolls of razor-studded concertina wire and the squat watchtowers set at regular intervals along the compound's perimeter. Broken glass atop the high stone walls gleamed with the brittle reflected light of late evening. Very picturesque.

Nothing on the ground moved, but Bodo knew that there must be many pairs of eyes fixed on them, watching their passage overhead. He signaled forward that the pilot should waggle the wings as a greeting, and he did, the Dakota wallowing briefly in the air. Then they were past the cluster of buildings, and unbroken forest covered the landscape beneath them.

"I don't see a landing strip," the pilot called back. There was exasperation in his voice. "This is the place, according to the charts. You told me there would be a strip."

Bodo consulted his watch. "We're somewhat early," he said, shouting to make himself heard. "We were to arrive under cover of darkness. Fly on until dusk, and then return."

The pilot shook his head in disbelief but did as he was told, pointing the nose of the plane eastward. The DC-3 bumped and wobbled over the air currents that lifted off the mountain ridges. Behind them, the lower edge of the sun's disk touched the horizon.

Toma leaned toward Bodo. "So," he said, "they'll build a runway for us in the next few minutes, will they?"

"O ye of little faith," Bodo said. "This magnificent airship is called *Domini Canes.* Will the forest not open to admit the dogs of the Lord?"

"You're mad," Toma told him.

"Quite," Bodo said. Leaning forward in his seat, he asked through the open cockpit door, "Are you religious men?"

The copilot and the pilot exchanged glances. The copilot shook his head. The pilot answered, "My father was. He was a monk for a while, or training to be one, if you can believe that. Novice monk, a Dominican monastery in Vermont. But he met my mother and they booted him out of the order. He told me it was all right because he'd rather not be part of that bunch of Inquisitors anyhow. I guess a little of his sense of things might have rubbed off on me."

Bodo nodded approval. "So transcendent events are not out of the question for you? It seems possible to you that the forest will clear a way for us. That it will smooth itself and allow us to land. Yes?"

The pilot considered. "I've never seen a miracle, that I know of," he said. "But that doesn't mean they can't happen somewhere along the line."

Bodo appeared satisfied. "That's good," he said. "Very good." He began to speak more softly. "In this place that we're going to—I've not been there before, but I have an idea—to be a religious man might be a good thing. I suspect that quite a nasty piece of work awaits us."

Judging that it was time, the pilot turned the plane back on its course and began to lose altitude. The last slender crescent of the sun slipped below the rim of the planet, leaving behind it a bruised-looking western sky and impenetrable darkness to the east.

Shortly, the copilot gave a shout. "There it is!" he cried. On the ground, two parallel rows of flickering lights marked a short airstrip where previously there had been only greenery. The strip appeared to have been hacked out of the forest; the stumps of recently shorn trees gleamed whitely at its edges, and the surface was rough and uneven, made of packed dirt. Toma looked at Bodo in astonishment.

"Are you surprised?" Bodo said. And then, fondly, "Doubting Toma."

They passed low over the runway, and through the near porthole Bodo could see people on the ground, moving busily in the uneven red light of the marker flares. They worked feverishly to draw in the last of the giant camouflage nets they had used to obscure the opening. Those stooped figures, grotesquely foreshortened as seen from above, toiling amid the choking clouds of pink flare smoke: they looked like wicked scuttling gnomes to Bodo, underworld creatures from a child's fable. *They are beings of the earth*, he thought, *and I am, for the present at least, a being of the air.* The rising smoke whirled in the vortices that rolled off the wingtips of the Dakota.

The pilot shook his head. "No way," he called out.

Bodo started from his reverie. "What?" His face darkened.

"Can't put it down," the pilot said. "Too short. Your people should have made it longer."

"Land," Bodo said. His tone brooked no argument. A green star shell arced through the air, throwing its glow over the forest as it drifted slowly down. Another, this one orange, followed; it came perilously close to striking the airplane. "This is the time," he said.

"No sir," the pilot said. He had turned in his seat to face his two passengers; the copilot handled the plane. "No can do."

"Land," Bodo said again. He motioned to Toma, who extracted his Beretta from its holster.

"What?" the pilot said. "You going to shoot us? You'll end up in the trees down there if you do."

"No," Bodo said. "Not both of you. Just him." He pointed to the copilot, and Toma moved the muzzle of the pistol to cover him. "In the legs first, starting at the ankles and working gradually upward." The copilot shifted in his seat but kept his attention forward. "You we save until the plane lands elsewhere."

"Jesus," the pilot said. "You guys are cold. Next to you the Company spooks are a bunch of teddy bears."

"They labor under constraints that do not apply to us," Bodo said.

The pilot spoke to the copilot, who brought the plane back around and put it on final approach to the airfield. The guttering flares were pinpoints, just barely visible in the distance. He switched on the Dakota's powerful landing lights, and the forest before them bloomed into vivid color. The wheels came down, locking into place with a thump that jarred passengers and cargo. Toma put away the Beretta.

"Even if we do make it down in one piece," the pilot said, "we'll never get the Can into the air again."

"That," Bodo said, tightening his seat belt in anticipation of a rough landing, "is a problem that we'll save for another day entirely."

The *Domini Canes* rolled to a stop just short of the screen of trees at the end of the runway. Even as the pilot and copilot went about shutting down the engines and securing the cockpit, the crew of the airfield were drawing the great sheets of camouflage netting back over the gash in the forest, calling encouragement to one another as they worked. One of their number, a child, darted along the landing strip gathering up the marker flares. Quickly, to avoid being burned, he tossed the hissing flares into a canvas bucket full of water that he toted along with him. As he crossed the runway, he paused to marvel at the patterned tire tracks of the Dakota's landing gear and at the furrow dragged into the hard-packed soil by the tail wheel. Some member of the camouflage crew shouted at him ("Rapido!") and he went back to his duty, finishing and dashing away just as Bodo and Toma emerged from the rear hatch of the airplane.

Bodo carried his briefcase at his side. He looked around him, and even Toma, who knew him well, could not read the expression on his face. The pall of pastel smoke had begun to drift off, driven by a light breeze, but there was enough of it left to cause Bodo to sneeze. He fished a crisp handkerchief from a pocket, blew his nose into it, refolded and replaced it. His gaze fastened on a pair of dark-haired figures at the far end of the runway. They seemed to be watching over the men with the camouflage nets. The watchers held scatter-guns braced against their hips, muzzles pointed nonchalantly at the sky. "Twins," Bodo said. The two were in fact, Toma noted, very much alike.

Behind them, the pilot and copilot left the airplane. The pilot strode over to Bodo. "I hope you're happy," he said, gesturing toward the plane. "This *airstrip*—" he spat the word—"isn't half big enough to get us in the air again. We're grounded."

"I am indeed happy," Bodo told him. "Very happy. You've done a fine job. You're both to be commended, and you'll be amply rewarded."

"Did you hear me?" the pilot asked. Toma took a step toward him, but Bodo held out a restraining hand. "I'm telling you that we can't take off. There's not enough room. We're stuck here."

"Because the runway is too short," Bodo said.

"Damn straight," the pilot said, and the copilot nodded in agreement.

"Then we'll have them extend it to the proper length," Bodo said. "They appear to have a sufficiency of laborers here, and the price of their work will not be high. That should solve your problem."

The pilot shut his mouth. Several men bearing camouflage net approached the Dakota and began to spread the mesh over it, starting with the wings. "Hey," the pilot called to them. They ignored him. "Don't do that!" he shouted, and when they still failed to respond, he went to argue with them. "You'll tear something up if you don't watch what you're doing." The copilot went as well.

From the direction of the settlement's buildings, a man approached Bodo and Toma. He was big through the shoulders, powerful-looking, and he carried in his right hand a thick-barreled Very pistol, no doubt used to fire the star shells that they had seen. Short words were tattooed in blue ink across the backs of his hands. As he approached, he switched the flare gun to his left hand and held out his right to Bodo.

"Mr. Tannhauser," Bodo said. After a moment's hesitation, he extended his hand as well, and the approaching man took it, pumped it vigorously. His grip was painfully strong.

"No," the fellow said. "I'm Yukon. You might call me Mr. Tannhauser's lieutenant." He wore his hair to his shoulders, very unkempt. He was long-waisted, with uncommonly short legs. Bodo was relieved to hear that this strange musclebound vision was not the man in charge, but disturbed that Tannhauser had not come to meet the arriving plane himself, as protocol dictated. He withdrew his hand from Yukon's.

"I am Bodo," he said. He indicated Toma at his side. "And this is *my* lieutenant, Mr. Yukon. His name is Toma." Toma did not offer to shake hands.

Yukon waved a large hand affably in Bodo's face. "Not Mr. Yukon," he said. "Just call me Yukon, Bodo. We don't stand a lot on ceremony here at El Dorado."

"I see," Bodo said. "Certainly. As it should be." They stood together a few moments longer, Bodo and Toma growing steadily more uncomfortable. The pilot had lost his argument, and the Dakota was now thickly covered in camouflage netting. The pilot and copilot chocked the plane's wheels with large stones dragged from the runway's pitted surface and came to join the group.

"Neat nose art," Yukon said to the pilot, pointing at the wolf and the woman painted on the fuselage. "Especially the tootsie. Makes me think of those nudie pictures by that Spaniard what's-his-name. Vargas. He painted them on bombers, didn't he?"

The pilot said, "She's supposed to represent my mother."

Yukon inspected the painting again. "Some mom," he said.

"Yeah," the pilot said.

"So," Yukon said, clapping his hands together and turning his attention back to Bodo, "did you bring the stuff we ordered?"

Bodo shifted. "I'd really much prefer to have that discussion with Mr. Tannhauser in person, Yukon. If you don't mind."

"Mr. Tannhauser isn't here. It may be a while before he arrives. Hard to tell about him, his comings and goings out."

"Very well," Bodo said. "Would you be good enough to show us to our accommodations? We've had a long and difficult passage, and it would be pleasant to freshen up while we await his arrival."

The request seemed to take Yukon by surprise. "I don't know," he said. "I'm supposed to find out if you brought everything. I was told . . ."

"Oh, all right," Bodo said. He handed the briefcase to Toma, who held it up so that Bodo could get at the dual locks in the lid. After he had fiddled with them for a few seconds, the lid popped open, and the pilot was pleased to have his earlier impression confirmed: the case was filled with money in neat stacks. Bodo pulled a typed invoice from the briefcase, which Toma then shut and locked. Bodo peered at the sheet of paper in the dim light, and then at Yukon. "Would you like to take notes?" he said.

"No," Yukon said. "I just want to hear."

Bodo began to read in a clipped, even voice. "Listing of ord-nance," he said. "Fifty M16A2 Colt assault rifles, .223 caliber, ten thousand rounds of ammunition apiece. Banana clips to fit same. Bayonets to fit same. Silencers to fit same. TacStar T4 laser sights to fit same, with mounts. Twenty-five forty-millimeter M203 grenade launchers, for installation on M16s. Five hundred rounds of antiper-sonnel ammunition each." He took a breath before continuing. "Five 7.62 millimeter belt-fed M60 machine guns, twenty thousand rounds of linked ammunition apiece. One thousand M18A1 Claymore mines. One thousand of each of the following: M67 fragmentation grenades, M34 white phosphorus grenades, ANM14 TH3 incendiary grenades, M72A2 riot control canister grenades. One hundred one-pound bricks of Semtex plastic explosive."

He was prepared to go on reading from the list, but Yukon stopped him. "Wait," Yukon said. "Hang on just a second."

"That's what we were carrying?" the copilot said. "We're lucky we didn't end up hanging from the trees in pieces. One big bump while we're landing and *boom.* Hamburger."

"Did you think it was tissue paper that we hired you to haul?" Toma asked him. "Cast-off clothing for the needy, perhaps?"

Bodo looked up from the invoice. "I thought that you wanted to hear this." He rattled the paper in his hand. "To be certain that everything is in order."

A voice boomed out of the encroaching darkness. "You can stop reading that now. We're sure." A huge man, bigger even than Yukon, made his way to them. Yukon stood aside for him. "No need to say anything more." He was a jovial fellow, by the sound of his voice. It was difficult without more light to make anything of the features of his face. "You must be Bodo," he said.

"I am. And you are—?"

"Tannhauser. Sorry not to have been here sooner, but I was de-layed elsewhere."

"Ah." Bodo observed him a moment longer. "Not that I doubt you, sir," he said. "But would you mind . . ." The unspoken end of his question hung in the air.

"Of course," the man said. "Happy to oblige." He held his hands up. Bodo motioned to Toma, who fished a pen-size flashlight from the inside pocket of his jacket. He snapped the tiny beam of the penlight on and passed it over the outstretched hands. Six fingers on each, twelve in all. The extra fingers were tiny; they sprouted from the sides of the hands at a peculiar angle, just to the outside of the smallest normal finger. Toma put the light on Tannhauser's face. It was a strong, good-looking face, square and well proportioned. The lips were thin and pressed tightly together.

"You want to get that out of my eyes," Tannhauser said.

"Certainly," Toma said, stashing the flashlight in his jacket again.

"I'm glad to meet you, Mr. Tannhauser," Bodo said. Tannhauser didn't supply a first name. Bodo held out his hand in greeting, and Tannhauser clasped it. Bodo's pinkie intertwined unexpectedly with the extra finger on Tannhauser's hand, bending it back and pinching it. The finger felt boneless. Tannhauser drew his hand back hurriedly.

"My apologies," Bodo said.

"Not a problem," Tannhauser replied, but the faintly resentful tone of his voice suggested that it was indeed a problem. An inauspicious beginning, Bodo thought. He marked the note of ill temper in his memory for future reference. Tannhauser covered his right hand with his left.

"Retrieve our gift to Mr. Tannhauser, would you please?" Bodo asked Toma. Toma nodded and went to the airplane. He had to brush aside drapings of camouflage mesh to enter it.

Tannhauser appeared to regain his equanimity. "You saw the facility that we have here?" he asked. There was pride of ownership in his voice. "From the air?"

"We saw something of what it has to offer," Bodo said. Then, shading his voice with careful disapproval, he added, "I was surprised to see that the razor wire on your perimeter is exposed to aerial inspection."

Tannhauser laughed. "This was a prison for a while before we took it over. Federal women's prison, maximum security. El Dorado's had quite a varied history. So most of that stuff was here well before we came to it. Nobody's shocked if they see a little barbwire laying around. Probably they'd worry about it if they didn't. Ironic, huh?"

"Yes. Ironic," Bodo said. "Your work with the camouflage seems to have been flawless. We detected nothing to indicate your presence on our initial flyover." Toma returned from the plane, bearing the olive-drab tube of the LAW with him. He handed it to Bodo, who in turn held it out to Tannhauser. "This comes with our compliments.

Something that you did not ask for but that we thought you might appreciate."

Tannhauser took the package and examined it. He turned it this way and that. "Man," he said at last. "You guys really travel first-class."

"There are twelve more like those in a crate in the airplane's cargo hold, to make a baker's dozen," Bodo told him. "As a measure of our gratitude for your custom, our confidence in your undertaking here, and our personal affection for you."

"How does it work?" Tannhauser asked. He tugged at the ends of the rocket launcher, trying fruitlessly to extend it to its full operational length.

Toma stepped forward. He had to shoulder his way past Yukon to get close to Tannhauser. "You pull this pin here," he said, indicating the rear cover of the LAW, "and you open it. The sights snap up. Set it on your shoulder, arm it"—here he touched a finger to the safety handle on the top of the tube—"point it, and shoot." He shrugged. "It could hardly be simpler."

Tannhauser had located the pin that enabled the launcher, but he refrained from pulling it. Instead, he set the thing on his right shoulder and peered down its length as though at an armored target. "Just like a bazooka," he said. He looked around at the members of the little group. "Thanks, you guys," he said. He pulled the LAW to his chest as though he were hugging it. "Thanks a lot." He passed it to Yukon, who tucked it under his arm. "Get a crew together to unload the plane," Tannhauser said.

Yukon grunted assent and called across to the camouflage crew. "Ernesto!" he shouted. A small man detached himself from the group and drifted over to confer with Yukon, who gave instructions in a loud voice, waving his hands to indicate what he wanted done. The man to whom he spoke stood listening impassively, fingering the nightstick that hung from his belt. He had heavy workboots on his feet; the rest of his crew wore leather sandals or shabby sneakers. They stood quietly together and watched the progress of the conference.

"That's Ernesto," Tannhauser told Bodo. "He's the kapo of the nonindigenous workforce here. Our translator, and a good man. I like to promote from within the ranks."

"A good policy," Bodo said. "Sensible."

Yukon rejoined them, and Ernesto began giving instructions to his people, who scurried to follow them. "Now let's get this show on the road," Tannhauser said. "I've got to show you fellows around, right?"

Without waiting for agreement, he turned and headed toward the buildings of the compound. The six of them—Tannhauser and Yukon leading, then Bodo and Toma, with the pilot and copilot bringing up the rear of the procession—left the airfield to enter the grounds of the defunct hotel, passing as they did beneath a high arch of disintegrating wrought iron. The elements of the decorative entryway had been forged to resemble trees, climbing vines, branches, buds, the bells of flowers; and across the top of the arch stretched the proclamation, in metal leaf-covered letters better than two feet high, EL DOR DO WE COMES YO.

They toured the compound. They inspected the defenses on the periphery, the wire, the thick woods that Tannhauser said were already full of punji stakes and steel leghold devices and other booby traps; that, with the arrival of the weapons shipment, would soon be mined with Claymores and studded with tripflares. "Just like a firebase in Nam," Tannhauser told them. They visited the thick-walled springhouse, its sulfurous waters congealed into a thick jelly, which would serve as the magazine when the Dakota's explosive cargo had been off-loaded. They saw the armory, with its pitiful collection of antiquated bolt-action Springfields and shotguns, where Yukon moved to stash the rocket launcher. Tannhauser stopped him, saying, "No. That one I'll have in my quarters with me. The others can go in here, but that one in particular is a special gift from our special friends, so I think I'll just keep it." Yukon took up the LAW again.

They ate a quick and unappetizing meal of cold military MREs: ready-to-eat dinners of turkey, spaghetti, chopped steak, sealed in envelopes of thick brown plastic. There was a small square of toilet paper in each meal pouch (Bodo saved his, tucking it into a pocket, while the others discarded theirs; the ground was littered with the thin stuff), along with a treat. Toma got sugarless chewing gum, the pilot some flavored toothpicks; Yukon came up with a small spool of dental floss. They drank bottled water. The cistern, Tannhauser told them, had been inexplicably fouled. It was contaminated, the water undrinkable. The sanitary facilities consisted of a rank, fly-haunted slit trench behind the main building.

The compound's few inhabitants, when they came across any,

moved quickly to get out of the way, eyes fixed on the ground. They resembled the men in Ernesto's work crew: dark-eyed and dark-complected, underfed, poorly shod and dressed. A stringy dog encountered the group as it trotted out from between two of the cottages. When it saw them, the cur sank to the ground, baring its teeth, its tail curled tightly under its belly. It seemed to be caught between fury and abject fear. Eventually fear won out, and the dog crawled away, cringing, throwing nervous looks at them over its shoulder as it went.

They were not allowed to inspect the marijuana crop that they had come to buy, but Tannhauser described it to them in glowing terms: its prodigious height, the spread of its leaves, its expected potency. Really, he said, just the damn *beauty* of the stuff. He had a hundred sizable marijuana plots spread throughout the woods surrounding the resort, stretching out in every direction for miles, all artfully camouflaged, assiduously monitored, diligently guarded.

They took in the barracks, the hulls of what had once been a dozen luxurious guest cottages, had once been painted white and surrounded by borders of picket fence. Now the walls were patched with sheets of peeling tarpaper, the genteel porches had collapsed and the wreckage been pulled away. The clapboard walls bulged and gapped. The pickets had been broken and used for firewood. Most of the cottages appeared to be uninhabited. A couple of them had burned, and beneath the charred skeletal tracery of roofbeams their stone foundations lay exposed.

Tannhauser pointed out to them the stockade: one of the dilapidated cottages with its windows boarded shut, its outside walls wrapped in shimmering coils of razor wire that jangled with the passing breeze. It was larger than the others and set a little apart from them. At one time it had been, Tannhauser explained, the presidential cottage. The place stank of offal.

An arm projected from one of the windows of the stockade, from a spot where a board had been wrenched loose. It was a thin arm, and the wrinkled skin hung loose on its bones. The arm waved and the hand clawed at them as they went past. A voice croaked from behind the boards, "Nos estan matando." *They are killing us.* That much Spanish Bodo had. The group continued on, Tannhauser pointing out this aspect of the compound and that. Bodo caught the liquid gleam of eyes—how many pairs of eyes?—peering from within the stockade. The voice said, in weak but matter-of-fact tones, "Pronto no quedara nadie. No hay nadie quien nos ayude?"

Ahead of Bodo, Tannhauser said, "A couple of crawlers, some first-rate construction materials, some design talent, and there you go."

Behind him, the arm was withdrawn from the opening. The voice said, "Nos estan matando a todos."

They stood in the center of a room of lofty proportions. The long windows in the room, floor to ceiling and with barely a pane of glass left to them, admitted little light, though the moon had risen and was only slightly past full. Tannhauser walked across the trash-strewn floor with confidence, but the rest of them had to pick their way carefully among the pieces of cast-off furniture that lay there.

Toma took the penlight from his pocket and flashed its weak beam before himself and Bodo, and they were able to avoid foundering on the sprung couches, ruined chairs, cocktail tables, banquet tables, steam tables, bedsteads, mattresses, refrigerators, freezers, and serving carts that lay in the room, heaped up, scattered about in no particular order. Behind them, the pilot cursed as he blundered into some obstacle, which crashed noisily against its neighbor junk.

"This," Tannhauser said, turning in place when he had reached the center of the room, "will be the main storage site. Good ventilation, to be augmented by the installation of fans, dehumidifiers, automated environmental control systems, what have you. The silo, heart of the whole place." Over his head, a length of chain depended from the ceiling, and a sheaf of truncated wires. Bodo imagined that a chandelier had once hung from the chain, ablaze with a thousand lights while richly dressed couples wheeled across the dance floor beneath it.

He knelt, and taking the penlight from Toma's hand, he cast its illumination around him until he came across what he was looking for: a lead crystal pendant in the shape of a teardrop, lying unbroken amid the splinters of wood and scatterings of straw, the animal droppings and loose feathers. The small light ran like water across its faces. He took it up, pleased with its density, its weight, and slipped it into his pocket. He returned the penlight to Toma, who searched the area for a similar piece but failed to find one.

"That'll wear a hole in your pocket pretty quick," the pilot said. "Sharp edges. Probably started to eat through already."

"No doubt," Bodo said.

"This used to be the grand ballroom of El Dorado," Tannhauser said, his voice raised so that it rang in the empty space. Birds, pigeons to judge from their cooing, stirred and rustled nervously in the dark spaces overhead. "When William Howard Taft danced here, the whole place shook, he was such a fat bastard." Tannhauser laughed, and Yukon laughed with him. The pilot and copilot managed a couple of weak guffaws.

"This place is like Hisarlik or something," Tannhauser said. "Incarnation covering incarnation. Its history goes back in layers through time." The facility, he explained, had been opened as a hotel in the 1840s. It had flourished because of the cold mineral springs that welled to the surface nearby. The waters were rumored to have restorative properties, and according to Tannhauser's account had made the place (then called the Old Tavern) one of the most popular spas in the eastern United States.

In the initial phase of the Civil War, Tannhauser told them during his rambling disquisition, the resort had been commandeered by the Confederacy and used as a military hospital. "This very room here," he said, stamping a foot against the buckled parquet of the ballroom dance floor, "served as an operating theater. Think of it: all those guys, limbs shattered by minié balls, guts laid open by steel bayonets and grapeshot, screaming and crying, lying in cots and on pallets, cheek by jowl, the living nearly on top of the dead—and how to tell the difference, when you come down to it? So the living tried not to sleep too soundly lest some butcher of a doctor, looking to clear a space in the mess of them, should have them hauled away to the burial ground. The shriek of the bone saws cutting away all the time. Arms and legs in piles. Makes you shudder, doesn't it?" He seemed pleased.

In 1863, the Old Tavern had been captured by Union forces after a bitter struggle in which the main building, the one that contained the operating theater, had been cannonaded for a day and a night and a further day. When the roof gave way, its thundering fall killed nearly everyone huddled inside: surgeons, orderlies, patients. The crushed bodies had been extracted from the rubble and unceremoniously buried in a mass grave in the surrounding countryside. The cemetery had been huge, shaped like a great cross, but its location had been forgotten in subsequent generations. The walls of the hotel were thick and sturdy, and reroofed, the Old Tavern had been used by federal forces to quarter captured Rebel officers. The men who had run the place for the Confederacy found themselves interned in it.

After the conflict ended, the Old Tavern was renamed Lone Springs. People resumed coming to it for the water, which was bitingly cold and loaded with acrid sulfur, though they did not perhaps throng to the springs in numbers as great as those before the war. They drank the sulfurous stuff to ease their bowels; they bathed in it to thicken their blood. They reveled in its stench; they punished themselves with it. For seventy years they came, the crowds dwindling, always dwindling, until in 1935 Lone Springs was bankrupt. The hotel closed; it and the land around it were sold to the federal government.

With the advent of the Second World War, the Army came again. They opened up the bracken-choked road that led to the summit of Little Hogback. They added the airfield. They replaced rotting fixtures, rewired, replumbed, refurnished, reglazed, recarpeted. They painted the walls a gleaming white. And finally, when everything was in readiness, they brought the prisoners: high-ranking Wehrmacht officers, pivotal Luftwaffe strategists, the occasional Nazi rocket scientist whose advanced notions might prove useful after the Allied victory.

The Army hired whores, brought them to the hotel by the truckload. Some of them had serviced Lone Springs before the war, and they were glad to be back. They said that the hotel had never looked so good, all bright and shiny and new. The captive Germans and the prostitutes staged lavish dances in the grand ballroom. The place resounded with music and laughter. It shone with light. Glenn Miller and his orchestra played there: "String of Pearls" and "In the Mood" and "Chattanooga Choo-Choo." First they danced, the lonely men and the inexpensive women, under the light of the sparkling three-ton French chandelier; then, sweating and happy, they went to the guest cottages and they fucked. Some of the whores fell in love with their dashing officers, and some of the officers had favorites among the women, or even fell in love with them in return, though nothing much ever came of it. The days were easy; the beds were soft.

After that war, the Germans were repatriated or hired by the American government, and the whores were forced to hustle again to make a living. The hotel reopened under new management, briefly, as El Dorado. Sulfur spas were no longer the rage, and the place was in operation for less than a decade. In the fifties it had a new embodiment as a women's federal correctional institution, maximum security. Watchtowers went up along the perimeter, equipped with powerful searchlights. Razor wire and broken glass topped the walls. Inside, the place was little changed. A couple of the whores from the era of the Germans did time there; maybe they had been there before the Germans, back in the Lone Springs days. In the sixties, a consolidation of the federal prison system shut the place down for good.

"So where are the whores?" the pilot asked Tannhauser. The copilot laughed.

"Who knows? No whores here now," Tannhauser said, and then, quietly, "The time for whores is in the past, and not yet come around again. But we've got girls for you, if you want them. Strong, good-looking girls. No harm in that."

The pilot didn't reply, either to say that he wanted girls or to say that he did not.

After the prison ceased operation, El Dorado was dormant. Occasionally kids drove their parents' four-wheel-drives up the deteriorating road, now deeply rutted and overgrown, that led to it. They broke windows and climbed into the cottages and the main building, scaring themselves with the shadows that hung over the place, jumping out at one another, amazed at their bravado, amazed to find themselves inhabiting, even for a short period, this gigantic ruin. They brought bottles with them, and drank. They built fires in the buildings, even in the grand ballroom, and sat around them singing. The couples retreated to the smaller rooms, dragging derelict mattresses, and mated. In time the passage to the hotel became too difficult even for the off-road vehicles to follow, and then only hikers came, and then only the hardiest of those, and then no one.

Until the hippies. How they first came upon it, which of them first came upon it, that wrecked oasis on the mountain, no one could say. They came hoping to evade the draft, evade taxes, evade spousal support, child support, subpoenas, warrants, all the oppressions of society. A loose aggregation of them at first, ragged souls not having much to do with one another, tending their individual plots of vegetables among the buildings, groves of mild pot farther out, raising goats in the cottages where they lived. Soon they made a community, working the dope plots in concert, and the trade in marijuana became profitable. They sent legations into the valley. They profited, in their small way. More goats. Better gardening tools. Drinking water brought from the valley in jugs, untainted by sulfur. Chemical toilets. Their needs were simple.

It went on in that gentle manner for some time. And one day Tannhauser heard about them. And on a day soon after that, he came to see El Dorado for himself.

"And the hippies?" Toma wanted to know. In the dark beside him, Bodo smiled. He knew the question, and he believed he knew the answer to the question. "When you came in and took things over, where did they go?"

"Go?" It was difficult to tell, without being able to see him, where Tannhauser's voice was coming from. It echoed in the vast empty space of the ballroom, took strange bounces off the piles of junk scattered about. It seemed to come from everywhere. He had talked for a long time, and the moon had vanished from the sky, taking its dim light with it. "They didn't *go* anyplace. Exactly."

"So they're still here somewhere." The copilot this time.

"In a manner of speaking."

"Stop the riddles." The pilot.

"It's not a riddle." That was Yukon, his voice not possessing the same ringing omnipresent quality as Tannhauser's. Bodo found him easily enough, his bulky silhouette, seated on a broken chair before one of the long windows. "We burned them."

"Burned their stuff." The copilot again. "Their belongings, their crops. Their goats."

"We burned them," Yukon said again. "We tried for a while at first to get them to do things our way. Modernize. They were growing ditch weed, and they thought they had a product. We knew different."

"Ditch weed?" the copilot said.

Tannhauser explained. "Back in the thirties, the CCC planted cannabis all through these mountains. They cultivated the hemp to make into rope, and it spread like wildfire. It grows on its own all over the place now, in ditches and on hillsides and everywhere you look. Pretty low-powered stuff, but the locals seem like they've developed a taste for it."

Yukon took up the thread of the narrative. "Some of them kept beehives. They counted on the bees to pollinate the pot crop. So after a while we went and took some of the honey from the hives. I got stung pretty bad when we did it, and I swell up when I'm beestung. Like to suffocated to death; my neck got big as an inner tube. We mixed the honey in jugs with gasoline." His silhouette gave a shrug. "Jellied gasoline makes pretty good napalm. Sticks like glue while it burns."

"My God," Toma said.

"We only did the ringleaders. Gathered just a few of the trouble-makers and marched them at gunpoint out there in front of the presidential cottage. Some of those guys were pure Luddites. They wanted to stop every single advance we made. They opposed the idea we had for a mechanical irrigation system. Cultivators, fertilizers, automation. Opposed our bringing in a satellite dish for communications, computers, telephones, fax machines, photocopiers. All that good Sears & Roebuck shit. Said they'd tear it apart with their bare hands. We drove posts into the ground, tied them to the posts real good with wire, covered them in honeyed gasoline, and set them afire. They melted like candles."

"The posts," the copilot said. His voice was strong with emotion, but the nature of the emotion was hard to judge. "I saw them when we were walking around. I wondered why they were charred like that."

"Now you know," Tannhauser said.

Yukon continued. "The rest of the hippies freaked out when they saw what we did. They still wouldn't do what we told them—they tried to escape and that sort of shenanigans—so we penned them in one of the cottages with no water for a few days. Then one night we lit fire to the building and sat around outside, waiting. Me and Tannhauser and the Mingos. We were ready to shoot anybody that came running out, but nobody did."

"Jesus." That was the pilot or the copilot. Bodo couldn't be sure.

"They would have hated your airplane," Tannhauser said. "They'd have wrecked it if they could. They ruined the first generator we brought up here. And after all the effort of lugging it up the mountain, too. It was a disappointment to me, the way they acted. They showed me their true nature. They revealed themselves as unreal. They were synthetic men, and synthetic men must not be suffered."

"They poured honey in the generator's gas tank," Yukon said. He sounded amused. "Froze the engine up solid. That's what gave us our idea."

Bodo interrupted. "That's all very interesting information, Mr.

Tannhauser," he said. "But it's very late, and we've had a long, difficult trip."

"Of course," Tannhauser said. His voice was definite now, coming from close at hand. Something clanked as he moved, a falling piece of angle iron, and Bodo flinched as though he feared being hit. "I'm being thoughtless."

"And I have to say, Mr. Tannhauser, that I'm a little surprised by what I saw on the tour you gave us." Bodo knew that he was on dangerous ground, but his fatigue and his contempt for these people, for the way they were willing to live, made him brave. He went on. "We were given to understand that your operation was somewhat— no, not somewhat. That your operation was *distinctly* more advanced than what I've seen today. We were told that you were on a major production footing here, but I've seen nothing to merit such a supposition."

He waited. The silence grew long, and Bodo became convinced that Tannhauser was not going to reply. He wondered how long he could bear to stand in the dark of the grand ballroom, listening to the others breathe shallowly around him.

At last Tannhauser spoke. "There have been setbacks," he said. "Unavoidable setbacks, utterly beyond our control. And for those I will not apologize."

"Apologies are not what I seek, Mr. Tannhauser." Beside him, Toma's indrawn breath hissed between his teeth, an apprehensive sound. Bodo reached out a hand and, finding Toma, touched him to make him be still.

"Assurances, then." Tannhauser was questioning, unsure of himself. That was good to hear.

"We've had assurances from you. Assurances in gracious plenty. We came here with a planeload of goods, based on your assurances, and found that the airstrip was too short. Its insufficient length endangered our safe arrival here. We will not be able to achieve the air, with the runway at its present size."

"The runway? I didn't know. I thought it was long enough. We'll get a crew, make it longer. Right away."

"And the weapons. We brought you hardware enough to equip an army, but you've only got a handful of able-bodied men here."

"Recruits," Tannhauser said. "That's what we need. We'll get them, too. You watch. The people are just waiting for the chance to rise up. The revolution is coming around, and then you'll be glad that you invested in us as you have."

"And the camp? These Stone Age conditions? We came here in good faith."

"You'll get your product," Tannhauser said, his voice betraying anger but also steely control. "In spades. Just wait until the harvest. I'll make rich men of all of us. We're working on such a scale here, I can hardly convey it to you. A magnificent future is within our grasp."

Bodo was weary of discussion. He was exhausted. Words. It was all words, and who was to say which words were true and which were not? They ran past him, over him like water. Perhaps he had pushed Tannhauser as far as he could push him tonight. Perhaps that was far enough. "Very well," he said. He felt Toma relax, and he withdrew his hand. "Very well," he said again.

"To bed, then," Tannhauser replied, and he began to make for the double doors of the ballroom, the others groping their way along in his wake. "You're in one of the restored cottages. Next to mine."

Outside the main building, the pilot asked Yukon, "What do you all do up here? To entertain yourselves."

Yukon grinned at him. "Besides the girls, I guess you mean," he said. The pilot nodded. Yukon thought for a few moments. "Your options are pretty limited, come to that," he said finally. "We used to fight chickens, but then we ran out of chickens so we had to quit that. Sometimes we'll fight a couple of dogs, but the hounds that we've got don't fight worth a damn. Sometimes we hook up the movie projector to the generator and show a film or two. On clear nights we can do it outside. Most of what we've got is porno."

Tannhauser overheard. He slackened his stride. "We hunt," he said. "You ever hunt a wild hog? I mean a really big ferocious one, a boar? Nothing like it in the world, the way a boar will turn on you and fight, even if it could get away. A Bengal tiger will run if it can, but not a feral pig." The pilot said that he had not hunted hogs before. The copilot allowed that he had not either.

Toma spoke up. "I have," he said. "Years ago, when I was just a boy."

Bodo looked at him. "Really?" he said. He had never heard Toma speak about it.

"We used spears. Pikes with long points and crosspieces welded to them just behind the blade. They were sharp and extremely clumsy. You must have the crosspiece on your spear, because without it an impaled boar will simply climb the shaft of the lance to get at the hunter. Shove the spear right on through its own body. You use the crosspiece to fight the boar off until it dies."

"Sounds like some excitement," the copilot said.

"We hunted them from mountain ponies. One of our party had his pony cut out from under him, and he was badly wounded in the stomach. We lost several of our dogs too, as I recall."

They had come to their cottages, and Bodo was relieved to see that these houses were in better shape than the majority of the residences. They had been recently painted, and the walls stood true. Light shone in the windows, too steady for flame. Electric, then. Faint, but it glowed. Somewhere behind the cottages, a small generator roared.

"We won't use spears," Tannhauser told them. He had ascended the porch of his cottage and stood as though addressing a large crowd. "We'll use guns." Yukon handed him the rocket launcher and he propped it against his shoulder as though it were a fishing rod. "Hell, maybe we'll use rockets."

"I'd like to give that a try," the pilot said. "Count me in."

"Me too," the copilot said.

Toma and Bodo were silent. Tannhauser said, "We'll have a safari, then." He turned and entered his cottage.

Yukon gestured toward the cottage beside Tannhauser's and said, "Well, I guess we're all bunking in here together." They filed into the cottage. The rooms of the cottage were spacious and, though sparsely furnished, reasonably comfortable. Bodo and Toma chose a corner room, one with two windows. The room held a pair of narrow sagging rope beds with thin mattresses, a washstand with a plastic bottle of commercial spring water on it, and little else. A cartoon penguin cavorted on the label of the water bottle. Bodo was pleased to find an electric lamp, bulb burning hotly, on a small table in the corner of the room. He felt as though he had been moving through the dark for years, centuries. He had an almost irresistible impulse to reach out and touch the lamp, to switch it off and then on again, simply for the pleasure of making the light so easily. He did not give in to the urge, and within minutes the dynamo out back shut down, ending the flow of current.

He undressed without being able to see. He laid his pants across the back of the only chair in the room, inseam against inseam to preserve the creases, and the crystal from the ballroom chandelier dropped out of the pocket where he had put it. It fell heavily to the floor and bounced but did not break. He retrieved it and placed it carefully on the seat of the chair.

When he had stripped, he stood at the western window, savoring the crosscurrent that ran through the room. He leaned on the sill while Toma moved cautiously behind him, stumbling from time to time against the spartan furnishings. Bodo listened to the sounds of the camp: a dog barking close by, answered by another somewhat farther off; the hushed babble of voices that came from the row of workers' dwellings; feet on a gravel path, walking slowly. Unexpectedly peaceful. Under all of it lay the low-grade humming of the cicadas.

"Something is wrong, Toma," he said.

Toma snorted, climbing into one of the creaking rope beds. "With this place? Everything."

"With the crop, Toma. Something is wrong with the crop, and he isn't telling us."

He turned, ready to sleep. Hearing something else, he paused to identify it. It was the muffled sound of Tannhauser's voice, coming from the cottage next door, the volume of his words rising steadily. Bodo returned to the window and, despite the heat, drew it closed. He could still hear Tannhauser, so he crossed the room and closed the second window, but that did not bring quiet either. Tannhauser was shouting, howling in anger, a string of curses punctuated as though by blows, and against them like the cries of a waterbird against the unanswerable roaring of the ocean came the high thin wailing of a woman.

22

"There were these three guys with long steel poles, and they were walking the grounds just inside the perimeter," the copilot told the pilot. "And every few yards they would stop and stick the poles into the ground, really jam them in, sometimes three or four feet in, as far as they could get them to go. The poles were sharp on one end. They would all do this in an area maybe ten feet square, jabbing it full of holes, and then go on, further around the edge of the compound, to another place they thought for some reason might be likely. I watched them for a while. One time, one of the poles didn't go very far in. It hit something, and I heard it ring, *ting!* like that."

It was their fifth day at the encampment. They were relaxing in their quarters, reclining on the rickety bunk beds there. The beds had been built for children, apparently. The pilot, who had the top bunk, lay with his feet hanging over the edge. In fact, much of his leg, from midcalf on down, wasn't accommodated by the short mattress. The copilot, being smaller, was marginally more comfortable, though he detested being low to the ground. He constantly had to battle the beetles, the earwigs, and strange horned caterpillars that made their way into his bed. He pinched a biting ant between his thumb and forefinger, flicked it away, crushed another. There was no end of insect life in the place.

"They got real excited. They jabbed around for a while, talking a mile a minute in that palaver they've got among them—I can't understand but about half of what they say—and the thing under the ground looked to be pretty sizable. One of them took off and grabbed some shovels and they went to digging. The dirt was really flying, I'll tell you that. When they had got down a couple of feet, I went over to see what it was they were after. I thought maybe buried bullion or something. You never can tell.

"By the time I got to them, they had stopped digging and were just looking at their feet. It was a boulder down there, a big damn slab of granite that you couldn't see the edges of. They'd marked it up with their shovels some but there wasn't any way they were going to shift that thing. They looked up at me and back down again real quick. I said, *What are you guys up to?*

"Nothing. Not a word. One of them scraped his shovel over the boulder real slow, and some sparks jumped off the blade. Then they climbed up out of the hole they'd dug, laid down the shovels, and took up poking holes in the sod again. I looked back along the line they'd been following and I saw five, maybe six of these pits where they'd been at work. I couldn't figure it.

"So then Tannhauser came up to me. He gave me a pretty bad scare, because I never heard him coming. I'll never know how as big a man as he is he moves so quietly. He tapped me on the shoulder and said, *I bet you wonder what in the world they're doing.*

"I allowed I did. He said they might be looking for a fallen object. I said what object and he told me, *Some alien technology from an unknown place and time. It crashed into the earth here long ago.* I told him that was sheer bullshit and he assured me it was not. He assured me! I laughed in his face, which seemed to piss him off.

"I said, *Ship from outer space? Why aren't you using a metal detector to find it, then?*

"He said, *Because it's not metal. It's not metal of a kind that we have here on Earth. It landed here eons ago, and it's poisoned this spot since that time, but if we can find it, then the power we can unleash is . . .* He didn't say what it was. His face started getting all shiny, like the skin was too tight on his bones."

"He was yanking your chain," the pilot said. He rolled over, trying to find an attitude in which he could sleep a little while. The small bed, top-heavy with his weight, rocked dangerously, and he desisted.

The copilot took up his story again. "I said, *You're yanking my chain. Poison spaceship.* He looked at me a long time after I said that, and his face relaxed, and he relaxed. He laughed and put his hand on my shoulder, which I don't much care for. He told me I was right. He said he was joking, that he was glad he'd found a man who knew when he was only joking. *Everybody here*, he said, *takes me too seriously. Hell, sometimes even I take myself too seriously.*"

"I don't take him seriously at all," the pilot said. "I think he's some kind of a fruitcake. He asked me the other day if I saw anything strange when we were on approach here. I said, *Strange? Stranger than this place?*"

"So anyway," the copilot said, "Tannhauser told me what they were really looking for." He went silent.

Finally, the pilot asked, "What? What are they looking for, stabbing poles into the earth?"

"They're looking for the entrance to a top-secret underground bomb shelter. It's sealed with a concrete plug, he told me, ten feet across. The Army Corps of Engineers built it back in the late fifties, when this was a prison. It was big enough to hold the President and all the Cabinet officers and the Congress too, in the case of a nuclear attack. They figured a prison, hell, Khrushchev or whoever will never think to plant an ICBM on top of something like that."

"What do you imagine they want to save the President and Congress for, anyway?" the pilot asked. "If they got us involved in a nuclear war, it seems like time they took a look at retiring anyhow. Don't you think?"

The copilot said, "There's food in that place for a hundred men for a hundred years. Dehydrated rations. Bottled water. Generators. Communications gear. Everything you could want. Tannhauser plans to find it because he figures he could use the supplies. Plus he said maybe he could transfer his whole operation below ground and that way never get found out or caught. They looked in the caves around here first, but he gave up on that when he lost a couple of his people in them."

The pilot laughed. His laughter shook the bed. "I can't believe that would bother him very much, somebody disappearing down a hole in the ground. Man that burns people at the stake."

"He said it wasn't the men so much. He was just afraid they were escaping him some way. Going in one entrance and coming out at another, hoofing it down the mountain. Anyway, I told him I had read a story one time. It was a science fiction story about some important group of guys that had managed to survive a nuclear holocaust in a bunker deep in the earth. The very smartest men. They had it all: the water, the food, the purified air, plus a VCR and every movie ever made, practically. The thousand best books, too, if I recall correctly.

"So they were getting settled, pretty comfy, and everything up above had gotten turned into molten slag or what have you. Everybody was dead but them. And one man went into the galley to get a snack, and when he opened a packet of the dried food he found out that it was full of little fat white grubs. The little white grubs had eaten up the food. They broke open all the supplies, and the stuff had been down there so long in storage there were little white grubs in every bit of it. So they had a choice. They could eat the grubs or they could starve. And these were very sophisticated, very rich men, mind you."

The pilot had rolled onto his stomach, and he hung his head over the railing of the bunk bed so that he could look at the copilot. "What did they choose?"

The copilot shrugged. "Some went one way, some the other. But Mr. Tannhauser, he had another solution to the dilemma."

"Which was?"

"He said he was surprised, a collection of the so-called finest minds, that they hadn't thought of it themselves. He said it was his feeling, his considered opinion, that the strongest ones among them should just have turned immediately to cannibalism."

23

Metal groaned, a long, almost human sound of complaint. The Pontiac jolted slightly, and small streams of soil sifted down the bank from beneath it. Goody held his breath. The car moved a few inches; stopped; moved again. Goody could hear rocks scraping against the chassis. The towing strap, strung from the dump truck's massive bow-shaped leafsprings to one of the Pontiac's engine mounts, went taut. Dust spurted from beneath the driving wheels of the dump truck as they slipped, churning furiously. Then they found new traction, and the pulling went on. Goody closed his eyes, but unable to bear the continuous grinding noise without watching, he opened them again. Inchcape played the truck's throttle and clutch carefully, and the Pontiac began to ease forward and down the slope. An ominous popping noise issued from beneath the hood, and Goody waited to see if the motor would be dragged out through the radiator.

The car slipped down the bank. It seemed briefly that it had tipped too far the wrong way, seemed inevitable that it would slam down on its roof and lie there, beyond salvage or repair. Then the moment passed, and the Pontiac came to rest on its wheels beside the road. It sat unevenly, the right side slumped lower than the

left. Behind it a small rock slide ensued, and the rush of earth
piled up against the right rear tire, reaching the height of the quarter
panel.

Inchcape emerged from the truck cab, grinning. He gestured ex-
pansively at the car. "There you go," he said. At the sound of his
voice, a dog raised its head from the shelter of the culvert and looked
at him. Goody recognized the malamute. Its muzzle and face were
slathered with red as far back as its ears, and its deep chest as well,
the hair slicked down and matted. Its eyes were crusted half-shut
with gore. Goody thought at first from its terrible aspect that one of
Dreama's shots must have struck home, wounding it, but he soon
decided that it had been eating the hound that lay dead in the pipe. It
craned its neck to watch them, laying its ears back against its coated
skull. Then it lurched from the culvert and ambled past the Pontiac
and the rest of the way up the slope. At the top, it turned, cast a
glance back at Inchcape and Goody and its interrupted meal, perhaps marking them in its savage memory, and vanished into the
scrub pines.

With its dust-covered finish, the Pontiac might have been sitting
abandoned by the side of the road for months, maybe years. It looked
oddly out of date, its sharklike lines almost comical in their immobility. The chrome of the split grille was clotted with hair. A fine rain
drizzled down, the raindrops hissing faintly against the blacktop. A
stream of oil escaped from the underside of the car, cutting its way
through the red dirt and oozing onto the berm, where it pooled. The
mix of water and oil made small rainbows that washed over the
surface of the spill and soon lost their luster. Goody was surprised to
note that the car's windshield just in front of the steering wheel was
starred, shot through with thin powdery cracks that radiated out, like
the strands of a spiderweb, from a central point of impact. He
couldn't remember his forehead striking the glass, but it seemed to
him that it must have. He had no pain there, no contusion that he
could find.

"Really tore yourself up," Inchcape said, laying a hand on the
broken glass. "You'll have a heck of a bruise tomorrow. Probably a
pair of shiners too."

"It doesn't hurt," Goody said. "Maybe it was something else that
hit the windshield besides my head."

Inchcape looked at him doubtfully. "Maybe so. You'll know it
here after a while, one way or the other. Do you feel sleepy?"

Goody shrugged. "No," he said. "No more than usual."

"That's good. If you feel sleepy, that can be a concussion. Go to sleep and your heart can stop on you. Just stop like a busted clock." He went on calculating the car's disorders. Goody circled the car himself, counterclockwise, his motion the opposite of Inchcape's. From time to time he reached out and touched it, drawing back fingertips cloaked in dust. A couple of cars passed them, headed south. They slowed as they approached, and Inchcape waved them on, gesturing down the road, pointing toward Titan as if they had asked him for directions.

The light rain pattered against Goody's shoulders and hair and ran down the back of his neck. He leaned against the high tailgate of the dump truck. Stenciled there in foot-high white letters, the paint scratched and fading, were the words DO NOT PUSH. Under that, in the thick layer of grime that coated the truck, someone, some kid most likely, had scrawled "Help Me Wash Me," using his finger for the blunt stylus.

Inchcape got Goody to boost him up into the high dump bed, where he retrieved the tires they had brought with them. One of the tires fit the pattern of the Pontiac's wheel lugs. They made quick work of changing the flat right tires, Goody's spare on the front, Inchcape's on the rear. They tossed the shredded tires into the trunk. The trunk's lid wouldn't latch; when Goody slammed it down, it rose again, slowly, as though on invisible strings. After several tries, he left it that way.

Almost reluctantly, he climbed into the driver's seat of the Pontiac. For a moment he sat there, marveling at the different feel of the car. The steering wheel was gritty with dust, and grains of dirt crunched between his teeth. The seat beneath him seemed to have a different give, as though its springs had softened, its stuffing shifted. He had left his keys in the ignition, and he flicked at the keychain with a finger. The fractured windshield had a prismatic effect on the dull sunlight that passed through it, and bars of color streaked the car's interior. The tinted light flashed from the keychain as it swung unevenly back and forth, a syncopated pendulum.

"I could try to start it, I guess," he said through the window to Inchcape, who stood by the door. "The damage isn't as bad as I thought it was. It might drive."

"Don't," Inchcape said. "You're losing oil. You'd just seize up the engine, and then you're really up a creek."

"I imagine that's right," Goody said. "We better see if you can pull it."

"I can pull it," Inchcape said. "The question is, can you follow? I'll go slow, but you got to keep it right on my line. Stay with me. And you got to watch for my brake lights, or you'll slam into the back of me. The edge of the dump bed'll cut your head right off." He laughed. "Don't want that," he said.

"No," Goody said. "We don't."

Inchcape climbed into the cab of the dump truck, and the two of them, the car tethered behind the truck, began to roll along the side of the road. The two strap snapped tight. As they gathered speed, Goody tested the steering and found it looser than it had been. Still, the car responded when he twisted the wheel from side to side, and that was something. He applied the brakes lightly and the pedal ground noisily under his foot. The car braked, if not well. He followed along that way, wondering how fast they might be going. The countryside with its wealth of trees and creeper seemed to pass with an appalling slowness. He rocked the steering wheel from side to side, testing the new play in it. The day had grown cool, and he tried to roll up the windows. The passenger side glass rose without a problem, but the driver's window refused to crank. When he forced the handle, he heard a splintering sound within the door, the noise of glass falling to the bottom of the door cavity. After that, the crank turned effortlessly in his hand, without result.

Briefly, he thought he saw the malamute keeping stride with them in the brush that grew along the side of the road. A bounding shape, darker than the surrounding bracken. It moved with astonishing ease and grace, in great parabolic leaps. He wondered at its strength; they had to be making thirty or forty miles an hour, faster than any dog could go. At last he decided that the movement must be an illusion, an optical trick of some sort. He turned his head from it, and when he turned back to look again, it was gone.

The pace of the rain increased, and water beaded on the cracked glass. Evening was falling, and the headlights of the few cars that passed became dazzling mosaics of white light through which he could barely see. He spotted the Volkswagen that Inchcape had harassed, heading north as before, the driver's face a livid oval. He did not see the passenger.

He watched the unblinking red eye of the dump truck's single working taillight, waiting for it to brighten with the application of the air brakes. He watched it also for clues as to direction, steering the car with difficulty, following the truck's path as precisely as he was able. When he deviated from it, the tow strap tightened and dragged the Pontiac, tires wailing, back into line. He stared into the light, fixing it as the beacon by which he traveled.

When it did flash finally, he had been entranced for some time, staring with wide unseeing eyes. He stood hard on the Pontiac's brake pedal. The twenty-foot tow strap looped and doubled on the damp surface of the road, gathering itself into a quick pile between the two vehicles. The space that separated them vanished rapidly. As suddenly as it had slowed, the truck accelerated again, and the tow strap straightened itself above the road, swift as a snake striking. Goody was thrown back in his seat as the Pontiac surged forward. He struck the horn ring with the heel of his hand, but the horn made no sound. The battery had been cracked and drained of its juices, or the horn torn loose, or both.

Goody put his head out the window in order to see better. He blinked the stinging rain from his eyes, swabbed at them with a dusty handkerchief that soon ran with thin mud. He kept one hand on the wheel and one hand to his face, shielding his eyes like the pilot of a sailing ship in a gale. The two linked vehicles plowed slowly south, over the new steel bridge, beneath the aqueduct with its stone Indian head, past the tourist caverns, moving along at their sober speed toward Titan through the gray rain that sizzled down.

Inchcape pulled the Pontiac into the yard of Goody's house. The two men went about the work of unhitching the car from the dump truck without speaking. Goody thrust the unwieldy pile of the two strap onto Inchcape, who took it from him and mounted after their nodded goodbyes into the truck cab. The dump truck's engine wound up, and Inchcape headed off to his own house.

Goody's face felt raw. The skin of his cheeks and brow tingled as though it had been scrubbed, and his eyes smarted. Sighing, he pulled open the door of the Pontiac and slumped once more behind the wheel. No lights burned in his house, and he hesitated to go inside. He sat in the car as evening darkened into night, fiddling with the defunct knobs and controls on the dash: headlights, windshield washer, wipers, turn signals, hazard flashers. He tapped his finger on the glass face that covered the speedometer; the needle was frozen evenly between sixty and seventy miles an hour.

"I'm lucky," he said to himself, "that I am not dead. I am a lucky man."

The peepers began their nightly serenade from the treetops, little frogs filling their pale round bellies with air, clinging to the branches with the suckerpads of their long splayed toes. They chirruped like birds, but they had only a one-note song, and that they repeated, over and over. From time to time their bright voices were drowned out by the drilling of the cicadas, which seemed to come from everywhere, from the trees, the house, from inside the stationary car itself. The rain increased its drumming tempo against the car roof, but the tree frogs and the insects continued through it. A trickle of soapy water ran down the wash behind Goody's house. It was the first moisture that he had seen there.

He gripped the steering wheel, clenching his fists hard enough against its grained plastic surface that the blood drained out of them. The ivory nails of his fingers, reflected in the flawed windshield, gleamed like a curving line of small moons. The weave of cracks in the fractured windshield floated before his eyes in the darkness, as though the breaches were things themselves and not just ruptures in the glass. He could make out nothing of the canebrake in which Billy Rugg had died.

Soon he got out of the car, which stood in a shallow puddle. Inchcape had left it in a low place on the lawn. Moving at an unhurried pace through the soaking rain, Goody crossed the yard and entered the unlighted house. He stood in the long front hall, waiting for his eyes to adjust, smelling the wetness of his hair and clothes and, overlaying those odors, the scent of mildew that the rain had brought out. He ran his hand blindly over the wall near the door, but not finding the light switch immediately, he went farther into the house, shuffling his feet before him so that he would not crash into anything, any stray piece of furniture whose placement he had forgotten. He stretched his hands tentatively out before him.

When he reached the kitchen, he hesitated. Someone was there. He felt the presence of another person in the room with him. He looked to the window, expecting to see a figure framed against its lighter rectangle, but he was disappointed. The person must be sitting at the table, he decided, in the chair that faced him. Or perhaps leaning against the propane stove across the way. He listened for any small sound that might betray the intruder. He thought he knew who it was, and sudden pleasure prickled in him, low in his belly.

"Dreama?" he said. And knew that it was not Dreama, and that he had made a terrible mistake in speaking. Nameless dread washed over him, a sickening wave of it. He was afraid that he wouldn't be able to bring himself to move at all, but his hand flew out from his side as if by its own volition, scrabbling over the smooth surface of the wall, seeking the light switch. He could not find it.

It isn't, it *isn't*, he told himself, that inner voice bizarrely calm as it informed him at the same time that the murdered woman had rounded the kitchen table, her dead naked feet jostling numbly against each other as she tottered across the slick linoleum of the kitchen floor toward him, her dented ravaged skull bobbing loose on her neck, her raddled face held out to him in desperate longing.

He began to search with his other hand, starting low on the opposite wall and moving rapidly upward. Straining away from the advancing thing, he squeezed his eyes shut, opening them only when his fingers had encountered the small plastic toggle of the light switch and flipped it, flooding the kitchen with light from the bare hundred-watt bulb in the ceiling. He was alone in the room.

He pulled a chair out from the kitchen table—not the one that he had believed occupied—and sat in it, cradling his face against his palms. His heart pounded. He wanted to sob but was afraid to make a noise. The muscles in his neck and shoulders and arms twitched, and every spasm felt as though a cool unseen hand had brushed lightly over him. His spit tasted odd and disagreeable in his mouth.

He sat that way until his breathing slowed. Then he stood, and glancing into the dark recesses of the rest of the house and cursing himself for his fear, he retrieved a flashlight from the pantry. It was a cop's flashlight, a heavy one that took six D cells, with a long barrel and shatterproof lens. The weight of it felt good in his hand and he hefted it with genuine pleasure, but when he turned it on, the beam that it cast was a dull yellow. He tried to picture someplace where he might have stowed a new set of batteries for it, but he could imagine none.

Holding the flashlight extended, he left the kitchen and went through the house, room to room, switching on the overhead lights, bare bulbs in their ceramic sockets or etched glass fixtures filled to overflowing with the shadow-bodies of insects. The house seemed uncomfortably large as he moved among its rooms, the pale beam of the flashlight picking out his scant possessions. When he had managed to fill the house with light, he pulled off his clothes and lay naked on the mattress in his bedroom. Thunder growled to the north, but he had as yet seen no lightning.

He tried to think of Dreama, but his imaginings were not of her, and he couldn't force his mind in that direction. He tried, but her form refused to replace that of the terrible murdered thing wallowing on the far side of the kitchen. In the end, he found it better not to contemplate Dreama at all. With the flashlight beside his bed within easy reach of his hand, he drowsed, thinking of little, thinking of nothing.

He could not have said how long he had been asleep when a bolt of lightning struck a power transformer mounted on a nearby utility pole. The noise of the exploding transformer startled him awake. He opened his eyes fractionally. Violent incandescence blossomed, limning the confines of the room and the objects within it and Goody himself in brilliant detail. In the glare, he thought that he could see the chalky armature of his bones. Thunder followed hard on the heels of the lightning. The darkened house shook with the force of it, and he covered his ears with his hands. It echoed up and down the narrow valley, bounding and rebounding from the hillsides all around without seeming to diminish. When it ceased at last, there was quiet and the steady fall of rain. The acrid smell of burning wire drifted to the house.

Goody unclasped the sides of his head and found that he heard not only the pattering of rain outside but inside, seemingly close at hand, the tolling of miniature chimes. He thought at first that it was some trick of the downpour, droplets pelting a metal surface—the tin of the roof, the steel of his car—or that his hearing had been deranged by the lightning. Finally recognizing the sound for what it was, he reached out and clicked the switch of his bedside lamp, which did not light. He took up the waiting flashlight. Guiding himself by its weak beam, he went to the living room. The ghost image of his bedroom walls, imprinted on his retinas by the lightning stroke, still drifted across his vision.

He stood beside the telephone. Its ringing seemed smaller than usual, discreet. Lightning flashed outside, less intensely this time, and shortly thunder boomed. Four seconds between the two events. The storm was four miles off. Another flash, and the phone gave a louder, more insistent ring. Goody did not count from lightning to thunder this time, confident that the storm center was moving away from him.

The phone continued ringing. He took up the receiver, annoyed but reluctant to ignore the summons. He said hello a couple of times, experimentally, but got no answer. "Mr. Inchcape?" he said into the mouthpiece. A crash of static greeted him. He listened but heard nothing else. "Mr. Inchcape," he said again, the irritation clear in his voice now. "I think we ought not to be talking on the phone in an electric storm. I knew a guy who got shocked to death by the tele-phone. The lightning ran right up the line and entered his brain."

On the other end of the phone, someone whispered Goody's name against the soughing hum of random noise. Or did not.

"The power's off here, Mr. Inchcape," he said. "Is it off there too?" Lightning flickered outside, painting the tree-covered crest of Little Hogback Mountain with light. The fillings in Goody's teeth seemed momentarily charged with current; his gums and the soft tissues of his mouth scintillated. No answering voice came over the phone. "I got a flashlight," he said, "but it's not much." He realized that the phone was still ringing, had been ringing constantly but with that same understated volume, even after he picked up the handset. When lightning flashed, the buzzing sound of the small bell increased in intensity. In the moments between lightning strokes, its amplitude decreased until the sound almost disappeared.

"Hello, hello," he said, without hope of success. Then he pushed the phone away from him without hanging up and crept back to his mattress, where he lay watching the fretful play of light through the window, trying once again to estimate the distance of the storm from him. It was difficult to guess, though, because the shape of the valley distorted the sound, and the lightning came so frequently that it was impossible to tell what lightning stroke generated what thunderclap.

Lying restless in his bed, the droning of the phone forming an almost musical background to his thoughts, Goody chuckled, swear-ing softly at Inchcape. His final thoughts before sliding into sleep for a second and last time were framed as speculation: it occurred to him to wonder whether Mr. Inchcape had perhaps been trying to call to say that he had set up a fight somewhere, sometime, for Goody, and if he had, to tell him who he would be fighting, and how much the contest might pay.

24

The anchorite dragged the statue of the weeping woman along the leaf-strewn ground, stopping from time to time to catch his breath and to wipe the streaming sweat from his forehead. He had underestimated the sheer mass of her, and he found the going to be very hard. His heart strained and pounded in his chest, even as he rested. The muscles of his shoulders and upper back were rigid and alive with pain.

He had fashioned a travois from two stout ashwood poles, with a sling between them made of plaited strips of raw leather, cloth, and bits of rope and wire to support the statue and hold it in place. He had equipped the travois with leather straps for dragging purposes, and the unpadded straps dug wickedly into the flesh of his hands and his chest where they crossed it. His injured hand, still numb and swollen, had begun to bleed again. He had tried to lash his hounds into the traces so that they could assist him in hauling the thing, but they were silly dogs and darted purposelessly this way and that, yowling in a stricken way and fighting against the harness that he had put on them. When, exasperated, he finally turned them loose, they scampered into the deep brush, not even looking back at him.

Now he was concerned that the travois might not hold together until he reached his home. To look back at it, he had to twist his head awkwardly over his shoulder, because he dared not let himself out of the cumbersome halter, dared not let down the weight of the statue, lest he not be able or willing to take it up again. The sling sagged dangerously beneath the carved figure, its haphazard parts fraying and loosening under the constant pressure of travel. The anchorite could not tell when the hastily assembled materials would split and spill the weeping woman to the ground, but it looked to be soon. Soon. Because there was nothing else for him to do, he threw himself against the traces again, dragging the statue forward another few feet.

He had used a long steel pry bar and a rock hammer to break her loose from the slab of which she had been a part, and now the surface of her belly, her elbows, her slim upper thighs were ragged with broken stone. As he had levered her onto the travois, she had slipped, the cool stone slick beneath his hands, her great weight a surprise to him, for she had seemed so small, so sylphlike on the crypt; and the toes of her right foot had been clipped neatly off by the vault's upper edge. One of her hollow, beautifully famished cheeks had fractured. The tip of her nose lost itself among the burdocks. She lay on the travois, face up as she had never lain, and she rocked gently from side to side on her slow passage through the forest.

None of this damage mattered in the slightest to the anchorite, who burned with secret delight at his ownership of her. In the dimly lit recesses of his home in the days after his injury, he had thought of her constantly. He had spent many hours prostrate with the fever generated by his mangled hand, crying and vomiting, but the image of her had stayed before him. He became convinced that he had survived to make her his odalisque.

He knew that she was made of stone. He knew that she was not alive. He had not fooled himself into that mental error, oh no, and he never would; he could never begin to think that she stirred and breathed, that she might return his affection. That sort of self-delusion was not in him. In point of fact, the main attraction of her was her lifeless quality: lifeless but not dead. Never to speak, to complain, to berate, never to grow mad, old, to sicken, to die. He could never find another woman suited so perfectly to him, to the life of isolation that he had chosen, to the place in which he had chosen to live it.

(He thought briefly of his mother, alone in the house that his father had built for her for them for the three of them with his own hands. Alone, but for the seventeen dogs—or was the number of them greater? Had there been, at the end, more?—that she kept there with her, all barking, barking, shitting, breeding constantly, dying and lying unburied on the rotting cherrywood floorboards. She never let them out, and they did not seem to notice or to care. They might be stolen if she did; they might be hit by a carelessly speeding car or truck; they might die as she was convinced she herself would die if she ventured into the world again. His mother, once so beautiful, so practical, so intelligent: a genius, he had thought her, many of her acquaintances had thought her. He had been unable, unwilling to recognize the raving stick-thin *thing*, the hairless creature bound to the mechanical hospital bed by leather manacles, bedsheets knotted around her legs, holding her tight against the rails. Had they called him home from the Army to see *this*? This which he did not know at all. His father had died in the Chevy pickup that was parked in the yard, died in the camper bed of the truck where he had slept for the last several years. She would not have him in the house and he would not leave. A blood clot had moved from one of his swollen legs to his head, his brain, and he had died peacefully, quickly, quietly in his sleep, dead for two weeks before somebody found him, dead among the stacks and piles of clothes, boxes and racks of pretty clothes with which he had tried, unsuccessfully, always unsuccessfully, to tempt her out of her self-imposed imprisonment, always to try again with some new colorful swatch of cloth. The county authorities had come to the house, had covered their mouths with oxygen masks to combat the stench, had used clubs and the chemical exhalations of fire extinguishers to stand off the snarling pack of dogs while they dragged his screeching mother into the light.)

The anchorite lived below ground, in one of a dozen concrete domes that had been used for the storage of trinitrotoluene before and during the Second World War. They had been emptied and abandoned soon after. The walls and ceiling of the dome in which he lived were ten feet thick, steel reinforced, and they shut out everything: noise, light, air; the atmosphere inside grew thick with carbon dioxide and difficult to breathe if he left the massive door sealed for more than a few hours at a time. It would be easy to stifle and suffocate in the dome, by design or by accident, he knew, easy and perhaps not entirely unpleasant. Inscribed on the wall of his dome, seemingly cut or molded into the surface of the concrete in large letters, was the chemical notation $C_7H_5N_3O_6$.

The roofs of the domes had been carpeted with dirt and sod at the time of their construction; seen from the surface they appeared as grassy, gently rolling mounds, tiny hills in the midst of the landscape of greater hills. At one time all of the storage spaces had been connected by a series of tunnels, but the majority of the passages had collapsed, whether through some accident with the TNT or simply through subsidence of the soil over time the anchorite did not know. He had managed to clear the tunnel that led from his dome, and so had access to one other. Until recently he had stored his food there, at twenty yards' remove from his dwelling, so that he might not be tempted by the sight or the smell of it when he was fasting.

In the last couple of days, though, he had moved the food out of the adjoining space and into his own. He had emptied the second dome of everything but a thin bed of burlap sacking, on which he planned to set the statue of the weeping woman. He imagined her lying on her stomach, head toward the opening from which he would emerge when he came to visit her. And though the statue's left hand covered her eyes and the upper portion of her face, he imagined the hand open in greeting, leaving the delicate features revealed, laid bare for him alone to see: the brow high and smooth and unwrinkled; the eyes wide and smiling, seemingly not blind, not empty at all.

He continued to struggle forward, and one of the poles of the travois gave way with a resounding crack. He stumbled, and the statue pitched to the side. She slid from the sling and thumped heavily to the ground, and the remaining splayed fingers of her right hand shattered, leaving only the thumb. Her head struck the anchorite on the ankle, peeling loose a section of skin, and he skipped back to avoid having his foot trapped. She rolled over onto her stomach and lay there on the forest path.

The anchorite stood regarding her. He made a choked sobbing noise. Soon he began to shuck off the harness that he had constructed. When he was done with that, he cast it and the broken travois away from him, into the brush. The rock hammer and the pry bar, lashed to the travois with raveling bootlaces, clattered musically when the contraption hit the ground. Unexpectedly, a voice spoke from nearby. It said, "This fellow appears to need our help."

Another voice, much like the first but higher, breathier, said, "No, I don't believe he does. I don't believe he wants to have anything to do with us at all."

The first voice replied, "He tried to avoid us the other day at the train, that's for sure. Thought we couldn't see him. But maybe to-day's different. Maybe he's planning on being sociable today."

Tannhauser's men. The ones called Mingos. Though he had never heard them speak, the conviction was immediate in him that these voices could belong to no one else. He thought fleetingly of the dis-carded hammer with its blunt heavy head, dismissing the idea of fighting them as soon as it came to him. He took a running step, but his way was blocked by a figure dressed in tiger-stripe fatigues. The man seemed to coalesce into being, to materialize out of the wall of forest.

The Mingo struck out with his rifle, and its hard plastic stock caught the anchorite on the shoulder. He shouted in pain and spun, keeping his feet with difficulty, intent on running in the opposite direction; but the other Mingo was there. This second one swung his rifle upward in a neat arc, and the buttplate of the M16 caught the anchorite just above the eyes, reopening the deep thorn scratch there. He fell at their feet, black lozenges swimming in and out of his vision like fish in a cloudy tank, and curled himself into a ball, expecting more blows.

"Look at that," the first Mingo said. The anchorite was scrawny, half-dressed, thickly haired, a mess of dirt, burrs, scabs. He covered his face with his hands. He could not stand their eyes on him.

"He smells like a mountain lion," the second Mingo said. He prodded the anchorite with the barrel of his slick new rifle. "He smells like that damn renegade Billy Rugg is what he smells like."

"That," the first said, "was one hardy son of a bitch. Took a licking but went on ticking. I heard he made it all the way down off the mountain before he snuffed it."

The second Mingo grunted. "It's a long way to go with your legs broken."

The first turned his attention back to the anchorite. "You guys give me a pain in the ass," he said, "sneaking around, blundering into our operation. You and Billy Rugg. Do you know we've been hunting you the better part of a week?" The anchorite made no reply.

The second said, "We better take him back to the compound."

"Okay," the first said. He leaned down and helped the anchorite to his feet, gave him a strong arm to lean on while he got his bearings back. The anchorite's breath came in ragged gasps, and he looked

wildly from one of them to the other. The first Mingo indicated the
weeping woman. "What about his cargo?" he asked.

"Leave it," the second Mingo said. "What would we want with
it?" He poked the anchorite with the muzzle of his rifle again, indicating that he should precede them. He began a stumbling progress
through the forest ahead of the two armed men, making his way
toward El Dorado. He held a hand to his forehead, trying to stanch
the flow of blood from the cut there. His head rang, and his vision
seemed to have darkened, had narrowed to a dim gray band that
floated queasily before him. Still, it was good to be out of the traces
of the travois, no matter what the future held, and he rolled his
shoulders and straightened his back, stretching the overused muscles.

"I wonder what Mr. Tannhauser will say when we bring this into
camp finally," the first Mingo said.

"What he always says. *Death to spies.*"

"I hope we don't have to burn this one," the first said. "I really
hate that shit."

"I don't know," the second replied. The anchorite was unable to
tell whether or not his tone held a joke of some sort. "The way I
figure it, once you've burned one hippy, you might just as well go
ahead and put the torch to them all."

25

"Back in the early seventies," Loomis said, "the Army brought a couple squadrons of Hueys up here to try an experiment with the fog." They were in the foothills now, rocking their way over the slopes and rises as though they were on rails. Carmichael had begun to enjoy riding in the helicopter, the way the terrain skipped by underneath with such incredible speed that while he managed to see pretty much everything, he saw none of it in detail. He had given up on trying to remember where they went mission after mission, what ground they covered and what was left to them to scrutinize and patrol, delegating management of those details to Loomis. He was a tourist, along for the spectacle. Loomis, for his part, seemed perfectly content to fly all day, or all night, whatever was required of him.

This was one of their day missions. They were varying randomly between day and night flights so that there could be no predictable pattern to their inspections, and the peculiar schedule was beginning to tell on Carmichael. He felt weary all the time, heavy, his limbs not his own, as though his body were a poorly made suit of clothes, one that did not fit him well. The insides of his eyelids had roughened. He had taken to moistening his eyes with saline drops several times a day. He watched Loomis for some similar signs of exhaustion—lapses in attention, loss of motor coordination—but found none.

"Apparently the fog here has exactly the same consistency, same density, as what you encounter on the Mekong Delta. That was the finding of the Army meteorologists, anyhow," Loomis said.

They had skimmed through banks and billows of fog early that morning. It boiled off the rivers and the creeks and the marshes; it rose out of the hollows. The thick mist gave to the landscape a ghostly quality, for the most part obscuring it but breaking occasionally in such a way as to frame a particular feature—a tree, for instance—and by singling it out bring it sharply though only momentarily into focus: the pattern of the bark on the trunk, the branches, the creeper along the branches, even the rough serrated edges of the leaves. Then it all vanished as though a curtain had been pulled in front of it; just fog again.

Now, in the afternoon, the sky was as clear as glass. The rays of the sun, refined by the glareshield, were hot where they lay on Carmichael's skin.

"So they brought in these chopper teams and had them simulate combat landings," Loomis said. "They flew all around the place in different formations to see if they could clear the fog for one another, cut holes in it with their rotors."

"Did it work?"

"Not so that you'd notice. Dumbest thing I ever heard of, fighting the fog. They tried cloud-seeding experiments too, and spraying the ground with this plastic resin sealer to dry out the soil, maybe prevent the fog altogether. That stuff poisoned the livestock and ruined the crops. But no matter what they did, those guys were still flying around blind. They had a few midair collisions. In the end one of their helicopters hit a house and killed the family that was sleeping inside. That got the locals pretty riled up. They'd put up with the noise and the fuss and the plastic goop from the sky pretty well, seeing it was asked of them in the service of their country, but the accident put another face on it. They got to thinking, *Sure, we've got the right kind of fog that they're looking for, but do we have to die for it?*"

He paused, swiveling his head as they moved past something of interest on the ground below. Carmichael could not see beyond him to whatever it was. Loomis said, "Lookee lookee," and smacked his lips as he brought the Defender around in an unexpected tight righthand bank, dumping altitude until the skids were practically in the branches of the trees. The slurping sound that he made with his mouth was loud in Carmichael's headphones.

"What is it?" Carmichael asked. His pulse began to race. He reached behind him and checked his revolver. It was snug in its holster. "What is it?"

"All right all right all right," Loomis called. He seemed to be pursuing something that fled along a deer path below. He banked to the left, affording Carmichael a look. The DEA man glimpsed flesh: long pale legs flashing, narrow back, someone, some girl, bare feet kicking up dirt from the track as she ran among the trees. Then the helicopter pivoted, slewed sideways, hung hovering over the path. "Damn," Loomis said. "Lost her." He kicked the right torque pedal and spun the helicopter on the axis of its main rotor, surveying the land below.

"Was that a woman?" Carmichael asked. He was breathless with outrage. "Were you chasing a woman?"

"Sir yes sir, a woman," Loomis said, still scanning for her. "She was taking a sunbath in the altogether. Hell of a woman, I'd say, from first impressions."

"I don't believe it."

"Where are you, honey?" Loomis asked. His voice had lost its monotonous cadences, had taken on a wheedling quality. "Come out come out wherever you are." Thinking that he saw her, some hint of her among the brush, Loomis shifted the cyclic forward. The Defender's nose dipped and they closed in.

"Desist, Mr. Loomis!" Carmichael barked. Even as he shouted at Loomis, he kept an eye out for the woman. Had she been the vision of beauty and grace that she had seemed as she darted away from them, or was that only adrenaline and boredom talking, making the incident into something that it was not, into a story, an anecdote for the Rangers in Texas? He had caught the suggestion of a fall of dark hair, the sheen of tan skin, muscled limbs, a luminous backside, a pair of arms pumping in a flat-out run.

The deer path opened into a flat place, a field that had been cleared for crops, a few precious unobstructed acres in this rocky mountainous place, planted in corn, and a small house beyond. The woman's house. She would have to cross the clearing to reach it. The wash from the helicopter's prop ruffled the corn, moved it in waves like water. Loomis nudged them closer, and the rotor's vortex threatened to flatten the crop, uproot and ruin it. A few stunted stalks had already toppled, torn from the dry dirt of the plot.

"The ways of the Lord are mysterious indeed," Loomis said. His voice had assumed its normal dry tenor.

"I told you to desist, mister," Carmichael said. "Now let's scram, hear me?"

"Seek and you shall find," Loomis said. "Knock and it shall be opened to you." He laughed.

Carmichael cast about them for the woman but did not see her. "I don't know what you're talking about," he said. He decided that he had been slack, too easy on Loomis, who was, after all, at least nominally his subordinate. It was a mistake he should not have made, would not make in future. He jerked a thumb upward. "Motivate!" he said.

"I think you're missing the point," Loomis said. Carmichael was flabbergasted at the impertinence of the man. Loomis went on. "You've made your first bust."

"I've done what?"

"Look around you, at all the riches of the earth," Loomis said. He hovered the helicopter effortlessly forty feet off the ground at the edge of the clearing.

Carmichael glanced at the clearing again, forgetting about the woman for the moment. He examined the patch of corn. Around the edges, yes, three rows, four, half a dozen deep. But further in the plants were not corn. They were slender, dark green, without visible ears, many-leafed. Marijuana, maybe a thousand burgeoning plants. The shield of corn rendered them invisible from ground level, made it look like just another oversize garden patch. "Hot damn," he said.

"That's right," Loomis said. "Hot damn."

A man stepped from the door of the house. He had a headful of white hair, striking even at this distance. In his hands, at waist level, he carried something gray and boxy. A camera?

"Whoops," Loomis said. He pulled up on the collective and pushed the cyclic over.

The object in the man's hands began to buck and chatter. His mouth was open; he was shouting, but it was impossible that his words should reach them. "Watch out!" Carmichael shouted in disbelief as flame leaped from the barrel of the submachine gun. He had forgotten all about the snub-nosed Python at the small of his back. "Watch out!"

"I am," Loomis said. They gathered altitude and speed, the turbine whining angrily overhead. They had not so far been hit, Carmichael thought, realizing at the same time that he did not know what it might be like to be hit. He hoped that they had not been hit.

Spent cartridges spilled from the ejection port at the side of the machine pistol. They fell in a loose scattering around the man's feet, bounced off his steel-toed boots. He twitched the gun back and forth in front of him, as though he held a garden hose, as though he were watering his plants and wanted each one of them to get a good drink. Its bolt worked forward and back like a piston as he squeezed off burst after burst. Then, suddenly, it ceased to work. The gun went dead, its clip expended. While the man struggled to extract the empty magazine and insert a full one, the Defender roared off, leaving him looking after it and shouting.

"Are we hit? Are we hit?" Carmichael asked. They continued on their way.

Finally, Loomis answered him. "I don't believe so. Nothing vital if we are."

"Wow," Carmichael said. Despite Loomis's reassurance, he continued listening carefully for any wrong note in the beat of the helicopter's rotor. He blinked in fear with every bump and shudder.

"I wish we had a Vulcan gun on this thing," Loomis said. "I'd have burned him down plenty fast if we did. Him, his house, his contraband, everything. He wouldn't have gotten a round off."

"We'll have to get the high sheriff's people to nab him before he gets away," Carmichael said. "They can hold him for us."

"Sure." Loomis reached out a hand toward the radio. "You just tell them they're looking for a fellow named Wallace Claymaker. Armed and dangerous. They'll understand who you're talking about."

"You know him?"

"I know of him. That white head of hair gives him away. When I was a little boy, he was the major moonshiner in these parts. Brewed his own liquor from peaches, potatoes, corn, whatever he could get his hands on, and brought bottled stuff into the county without a tax stamp. This was a dry county for years, so if you wanted a drink you got it off of Wallace. My father talked about him like he was really something special, like he was Al Capone or somebody. I guess he's nailed now."

"Yes," Carmichael said. "He's nailed now." His hands had begun to shake: delayed reaction to stress. Except for a certain dour energy in his words and actions, Loomis did not seem to have been affected by the encounter with Claymaker.

"That must of been his wife Dreama back there," Loomis said. "She was a friend of my younger sister's. I guess I always did want to see her in the nude."

"You shouldn't have chased her like that, no matter how it came out in the end. It isn't . . ." Carmichael searched for a word. "It isn't seemly."

Loomis did not appear to have heard the reprimand. "We used to chase water buffalo every now and then for a change of pace, when I was in country," he said. "Spot them from the air and swoop down. They'd take off running, but they never looked up to see what was after them. They didn't know to look up. We'd chase them until they dropped dead from heart failure."

"Still," Carmichael said. "A woman."

"The gook girls," Loomis said, "they'd strip down to take a bath in the river." He sniffed. "They looked just like fish, like schools of fish when you saw them from above. Legs kicking and kicking. You felt like a hawk or something hovering over them and looking down, like you could go right on into the river, under the water after them, and come up with one of them caught in your claws. And when you rushed at them, dropping down out of the sun for all they knew, they'd climb out of the water and run. They'd scamper up those rocky beaches and try to hide under the trees. They'd stand there, clinging to the trunks of the trees, these shining wet girls, like you maybe couldn't see them if they just stayed still enough. You know it had to be cold. And you could circle them and look as much as you liked." He paused.

"This one South Vietnamese translator I carried for a while—he was the guy that yelled the psy-ops messages to the zipperheads—he carried a Japanese camera with this big lens on it. He was a handsome guy with a beautiful wide smile. Always had that camera strap around his neck. He liked it when we buzzed the girls, because he could take pictures of them, closeups through that telephoto scope of his. He offered to give me money, and he offered me some of the pictures. I said no. I didn't care to get paid for it, and I didn't want any pictures of those little naked peasant girls." He laughed ruefully. "I was young at the time. I wasn't a whole lot more than just a boy myself, I guess. Hell, I wish I had those things now. That's growing up, isn't it. I'd take them in a minute, if somebody was to make the offer today. Take the money and the pictures both."

26

Late the next morning, when he was sure the last of the wild hogs had departed from the place, Peanut lowered himself carefully down to the first floor of the house. There, he picked his way among the gashed bodies, hunting for his sausages. The house was stripped of the little that had been inside it, and a slick layer of mud and excrement coated the floor. Blowflies crawled thickly on the dead hogs, their black insect shapes hard to make out against the hairy dark hides. A few of the flies buzzed Peanut, lighting on his lips and at the corners of his eyes, but he waved them away and continued his search.

He found nothing in the house, and left it to look in the yard. When he did not come across any cans there either, he went to the stream to get a drink, hoping the cool water would help to clear his head. The hogs had carried on their battle there, too, as the thousand hoofmarks on the muddy banks of the creek attested. Taking his first gulp of water, Peanut spotted something coming toward him, borne along on the stream's strong current. He raised his head and watched its advance, thinking it at first a tree stump, a floating garbage bag, one of the straw-filled pallets that he had slept on. He strained to make it out.

It came abreast of him, rolling loosely over the stony shallows, and he saw that it was another of the hogs. Its mouth gaped open; its throat was torn. It caught an eddy and spun neatly in place, displaying to him its glossy hooves, curved spine, tail, stubborn head. Then it beached itself on a gravel spit not far downstream. The water sucked at it, moving its little trotters in a parody of running, but it would not budge from its landing. Peanut turned away, still thirsty but no longer willing to drink.

He reentered the glen, prepared to make his way empty-handed back out to the power company right-of-way, and there he came across a single can, its label gone. It lay at the edge of the yard. It had been trampled into the dirt. He picked it up, expecting to find it open and empty, and was surprised that it was whole. The aluminum had been dented and marked by the hooves of the hogs, but it had not given way. He shook the can and it made a reassuring sloshing noise.

Can in hand, he headed for the cut, happily battering his way through the undergrowth. Halfway there, he heard overhead a loud avian screech. He looked up and beheld, for the first time in his life, a peacock. The turkey-size bird sat on the thickest branch of a big silver maple tree, twenty-five feet off the ground. The feathers of its blue-green throat gleamed like the gorget of an iridescent suit of armor. Light shimmered on its back and the six-foot train of its tail, both marked with the design of a hundred eyes, one staring eye to each broad feather. The bird fashioned its serpentine neck into a tight *S* and gave its choking cry again.

Peanut imitated it as best he was able. The bird immediately swung its head toward him and as quickly away. One of its eyes, Peanut saw, was covered with the thick white film of a cataract. It was half-blind. It called another time, its voice surprisingly harsh for such a decorative bird. Watching it as it perched there above him, its yellow claws gripping the tree branch, he thought of a story his father had told him, about a place in China where these birds gathered, their flocks in the thousands and hundreds of thousands. They darkened the sky when they flew over, deafening the populace with their voices, and picked the fields as clean as any locust swarm. He tried to imagine this peacock multiplied by a thousand, its numbers jostling against one another for space in the branches of the silver maple, and the same tumult in the next tree over, and the tree beyond that, and all the hundreds of trees around him. The entire forest would look as though it had leafed out in green and blue and silver and gold, all ablaze with the light of the rising sun.

And the sound! he thought. The glorious raucous sound of it!

27

Set about on all sides by snarling dogs, the old boar fought its way to its feet, eyes rolling wildly, and bowled over the loudest of the hounds with a short sidewise swipe of its curved tusks. The wounded dog squealed and thrashed on its side in a drift of leaves, the fur of its belly wet with blood where the flesh had been laid open. The other dogs fell back a couple of paces, still baying like mad but watching their quarry warily, standing respectfully off from it. The hog darted through the gap in the skirmish line of dogs and out of the matted bed that it had made for itself in the lush undergrowth, making straight for Yukon. The big man shouted, backpedaling as fast as his short legs could carry him. He stumbled into the trunk of a tree and caromed off it, dropping his rifle, his arms flailing for balance. The boar came on, streamers of leafy vine trailing from its tusks and mouth, wrapped around its legs, draped over its high narrow shoulders. Yukon went down.

The boar did not pause when it came to Yukon but simply over-ran him, its hooves striking him like hammer blows. Heat boiled off the hog's body as it clambered past, and with the heat a bitter odor that made Yukon gag. Tears sprang to his eyes. He was not cognizant of his own screaming, but when a flying rear hoof caught him in the solar plexus he became aware that he couldn't scream any longer. He lay where he was, writhing and choking. Not far from him, a voice, Tannhauser's, said, "I heard something. The dogs. This way."

The gored dog had gone quiet, its skinny rib cage rising and falling, more swiftly with every second. The other dogs recollected their mission, and in a body they plunged after the hog, still in full cry. Yukon stretched out a hand to the last of them, a strong-boned brindled hound, and caught it by the left rear leg as it went by. It whirled, snarling, and snapped at the hand that held it, toothy jaws closing against each other scant millimeters from his fingers. Yukon turned the hound loose, and it ran on.

The hog blundered headlong into the group of hunters, slashed Ernesto's legs out from under him, reeled broadside against a shocked Bodo and impelled him into a spreading thicket of wild roses, and passed beyond them, the caravan of wailing dogs in pursuit. Only Toma unlimbered his weapon, bringing the Beretta out of its holster, leveling it, and firing before any of the others had time to react. The pistol twitched, and a bullet splintered the boar's left tusk; another punctured a leathery ear; a third buried itself deep in the muscle of the hog's left flank. None found a vital target. The fusillade that followed, issuing from the automatic weapons of Tannhauser, the pilot and copilot, and the seated, moaning Ernesto, knocked limbs from trees, stripped the foliage from the limbs, shredded the stripped foliage. A couple of the dogs screeched and folded. The hog pounded onward.

The members of the hunting party gazed at one another. "Holy shit," the pilot said. "Man alive," the copilot said. Toma worked to free Bodo from the entangling rosebush, oblivious to the wickedly curved thorns that tore at his hands and face. Bodo swore.

Ernesto sat on the ground, rocking gently as he cradled his gashed thigh. He bound his upper leg with his belt, wound the belt tight by thrusting a stick through it and turning the stick like a handle. His entire concentration rested on that belt and that stick, and on the project of preventing his life from leaking away through the torn artery.

"Did I tell you?" Tannhauser said. "Did I tell you these hogs were something up here? Zoom, like a hot knife through butter, and that sucker's out of here. I'm glad I was here to get a closeup view of that." He slid a fresh clip into the M16 that he carried and ran a cartridge into the breech.

Bodo stepped away from the thornbush, freed by Toma's efforts. He brushed at his clothing, straightened the collar of his shirt. "Very exciting," he said.

"Hey," the copilot said, noticing for the first time that their company was one short. "Anybody seen Yukon?"

Exhausted, the hog spun to face the trailing hounds. There were five of them, and the boar killed the first outright, tossed its limp body to one side, and stood facing the others, who hesitated. The boar's head buzzed with pain: the pain of its broken tusk, its torn ear, its damaged hip. It blinked its red-rimmed eyes and advanced on the small pack of trembling dogs, which would not attack but which dared not turn their backs in order to flee.

The boar rushed the dogs and, a bare yard from the foremost of the survivors, began to sink. It scrabbled its feet against the receding ground, bellowing in outrage. It sank as though caught in a tarpit, or quicksand, slowly at first but faster and faster as it struggled against the shifting earth that trapped it. The dogs watched as the hog, their ordained death, melted into the earth. Its fury was boundless. First its legs were gone, and next its hairy humped back, and its shoulders, until only its huge grizzled head was left aboveground, moist nostrils flaring, gaze darting from dog to dog to dog. With a final crumbling of limestone rock, the boar was gone.

The dogs gathered in a ring at the lip of the hole that had borne the hog down. It was a straight shaft for the first few feet of its length; after that it opened out into a vault of unknowable size. The sunlight that came through the forest canopy did not plumb its depths. Hearing something, the hounds pricked their ears. One of them thrust its muzzle down and yapped into the hole, and the sound of the bark returned to them as an echo, distorted and unrecognizable, from the dark below. Frightened by the sound, they turned from the hole and, after briefly snuffling at the body of the hog-killed dog, commenced finding their way back to the men.

The Mingos came upon Tannhauser's group where they were gathered around Yukon. The pilot and copilot supported Ernesto, one to either side, and counseled him on how best to deal with his leg wound. "You want to let the tourniquet a little bit loose every few minutes or so," the copilot said. "Otherwise, you cut off the flow of blood, and you lose the leg after a while."

"But not too loose," the pilot cautioned. "Or you'll bleed to death. Better to lose the leg than to bleed to death."

"You don't have to do either, if you time it right between tight and loose," the copilot said, giving the pilot an angry look, to make him be quiet. "Just don't worry." Ernesto's pants were soaked with blood; his face was dewy with sweat and empty of all emotion. He tried to nod his head, to indicate that he took in everything that they were telling him. He tried to tell them that he appreciated their assistance with what was, after all, his problem.

Tannhauser helped Yukon to sit up. Yukon was gasping and bruised but he seemed otherwise unhurt. "Get over here and give me a hand," Tannhauser said to Toma and Bodo. They did not make a move toward him. Then he caught sight of the Mingos, who stood a few yards away from him, their rifles held at port arms.

"It fell down a hole," one of them said. "The hog," the other said. "Into the caves," the first one said.

"Where the hell were you?" Tannhauser asked. "Great trackers. Great goddamn hunters. And you weren't even anywhere around."

"We were following a different trail," the first said. "About thirty hogs," the second said.

"Thirty," the pilot said. "Can you imagine thirty of those bastards at one time? I mean, I've seen pumas and leopards and cheetahs, I've seen bears and lions and rhinos, but nothing like these pigs you've got." He released his hold on Ernesto to gesture, and had to grab him again when he slumped toward the ground. "If those things got organized in any kind of significant numbers, they could rule the world," he concluded.

Yukon stood up and ran his hands over his limbs to make sure that nothing was broken. He spat. "Terrible taste in my mouth," he said.

Tannhauser turned a keen look on the Mingos. "A hole?" he said. "What kind of a hole?"

"Sinkhole," the first Mingo said.

"And it just opened up underneath the hog and swallowed it?"

The Mingos looked at him, saying neither yes nor no. The remaining dogs had found the men again and danced joyously around them, making little yips of victory and welcome and excitement. The men ignored them.

"Well," Tannhauser said, "I guess we better go see this magical hole of yours." As one, the Mingos shrugged and turned to lead.

*   *   *

At the hole, Tannhauser asked if anyone in the party happened to
have a flashlight. No one spoke. The dogs refused to approach too
close to the opening. After a moment, Tannhauser turned to Toma
and said, "You've got that little bitty thing, don't you? I bet you do.
The flash you stuck in my face the other night."

Toma nodded, and though he could not imagine that it would be
any good to Tannhauser, he handed over the penlight that he always
carried. Tannhauser took it from him and, with a little coaching,
managed to switch the beam on. "All right," he said. "Let's see what
we can see." On his belly, he crawled to the hole, keeping the weight
of his body well away from the crumbling edges. He peered into the
chasm, held out the penlight, and let it fall. The others could not see,
but Tannhauser's gaze followed it down as it went, end over end, into
the dark. "It's water down there," he said finally, when the light had
winked out. "I heard it splash. Long way down to it, and who knows
how deep that water is?"

The pilot said, "I can't believe the pig is still alive." The others
looked at him, except for Ernesto, who stared ahead at the trees, or at
nothing. The pilot and copilot held him braced between them, and
the copilot had taken to loosening and tightening the tourniquet on a
schedule of his own devising, as Ernesto no longer appeared capable.

The copilot said, "Wait a second. I hear it too." They all stood,
listening. And heard it, like a shortwave station badly tuned and
drifting, a signal from the other side of the world: the hog's shrill
shrieking. It was thin and high, wavering, and it seemed to come to
them on the wind. Sometimes they could hear it, and sometimes they
couldn't.

"That's a whole other hog," Yukon said. "That's coming from
the bunch that the Mingos were following. The hog in the hole is
dead."

"It's no hog at all," Tannhauser said. "It's a trick of your ears.
You don't really hear anything. You just think you do."

"It is a hog," Toma insisted. "And it is coming up from the hole."

They began to argue, Tannhauser that it wasn't a hog, Toma that
it was. Yukon immediately took Tannhauser's part, and soon the
pilot was convinced as well. He stepped away from Ernesto and the
copilot in order to engage in the controversy. Bodo and the Mingos
said nothing. The men shouted at each other, called each other
names. When they had exhausted their stock of arguments and in-

vective, there was quiet. They strained their ears for traces of the sound, hog or not. It did not come again.

"You see?" Yukon said. "There was nothing to hear."

"There *was* something," Toma insisted, "even if there is nothing now."

"No," Tannhauser said, "the hog died on impact. No way it could have lived through the fall."

"I thought there was water down below," Toma said hotly. "You threw my penlight into it, and you told us that you saw water. I'm sure the hog could have survived a fall into water."

"And hogs can swim," the pilot said, making a gloomy admission. "I saw it on a television program. This farmer in Iowa had taught his pigs to play water polo."

"Falling into water, from far enough up," Yukon reminded him, speaking as though he were addressing a child, "is just like falling onto concrete." Tannhauser opened his mouth to say something further, but he was interrupted.

"There's something I think you'll all be interested to know," the copilot said. The strangeness in his voice, its pitch and cadence, silenced them. He took a firmer grip on Ernesto, whose head lolled loosely on his neck. The tourniquet had fallen away from his leg, lost among the grass and brambles, and blood filled his boot. The copilot hoisted him higher, holding him by his arm and by one of the belt loops on his pants. "While you were arguing, this man here? Well, I believe while you fellows were having it out about the hogs and all, this man that I'm holding, he decided to die."

28

Goody stood gazing through the barrier of iron bars at the preserved corpse of Floyd Askins. It hurt him, in a not entirely unpleasant way, to look too closely at Dreama, who stood beside him. She seemed so young and so pleased to be with him. With *him.* So he looked at the dead body instead. He had gotten in the habit of thinking about Dreama when he ran, keeping her image always before him, always just down the road so that he was moving toward her but never reached her. It kept him motivated.

He regarded Floyd Askins laid out in his fancy casket and tried to decide whether the body was real, preserved by a chemical process that he could not name, or whether it might be some sort of a facsimile, made out of wax or another substance. It had been skillfully made, if it was. Its face was narrow, the expression pinched, the eyes close together; the nose was prominent, the nostrils large and filled with hair. Fine hairs sprouted from the skin of the arms as well, and from the face, he thought, peering closely. Would a wax statue have body hair? He tried to imagine how such a thing might be done, and what kind of expense would likely be involved.

"He looks like he might just open his eyes and stare out at you, don't he?" someone said. "Looks like he might just sit up and gap a yawn, stretch his arms out over his head, and say, *Damn, I had a night of peculiar dreams.*" Goody turned to find himself face to face with a man who bore an unnerving resemblance to the body in the coffin. Same large nose, same wide pores, same close-set eyes. His color was no healthier. This version was older, though, the skin of his face loose and sagging away from the underlying bones of the skull, his hair going gray and beginning to thin at the temples.

"The name's Askins," the man said, extending a hand. "Melton Askins."

Goody shook the hand and was relieved to find the flesh warm, the grip firm. He grinned and said, "I would have known who it was anyway." He gestured vaguely at the bier, suddenly unsure whether that might be an insulting comparison.

Apparently Askins didn't think so. He laughed. "Strong family resemblance, ain't there? After all this time." He stood staring at his dead brother, propped against the wall of the cave. "Not very fair, I think to myself sometimes. He just lays in there day after day. Never a hair out of place, never a pound heavier, never a day older. It's a kind of immortality for him that the common run of men will never know. All I have to do is dust him off from time to time. And me? Well, I go on getting older and after a while no one will even want to think about preserving me when I'm dead." He slapped his hands against his body, against his chest, his belly, his thighs, as though to show how soft he was getting, how decrepit.

Dreama laid a hand on Askins's arm, and Goody felt his solid right biceps jump as though it were him she was touching instead of the old man, her painted fingernails just dimpling the skin, her fingers long and supple and strong. "How you talk, Mr. Askins," she said. "Comparing yourself to a dead body. It's not right."

Askins colored and seemed to be struggling for an answer. Dreama giggled at his discomfiture and released him. He quickly found his voice again. He said, "I'll bet you young people didn't come down here to stand in front of a corpse and jaw with some old man, did you? You came to see the glories of Hidden World Caverns. I'll see if I can find you a guide. It's a slow day, so you can have one of them to yourself, if you want." He began to move off.

"I'd like that boy to show us around, if he's here," Dreama said.

"Boy?"

"The little one. Young, and real pale. He knows a lot about the place, about the formations and all. I don't remember his name. He told it to me, and it was on the tip of my tongue a minute ago, but it's gone now."

Askins's mouth formed a word, stopped, moved again. "Dwight," he said.

Dreama clapped her hands. "That's it!" she said. "Dwight. I'd like Dwight to show us around, if he's on the job today."

"He's on the job, all right. I can't hardly keep him away if I wanted to. It'd take a stick. It's just he's not giving the tours anymore. I took him off that duty. I got him doing maintenance: setting up lights, tape recorders, sweeping up, that kind of thing. It's what he used to do, before I let him take the tours around."

"Could he lead us through? Just one tour. I really liked him." Dreama looked at him, and Goody felt called upon to say something.

"We'd sure appreciate it if you could see your way clear, Mr. Askins," he said. "Dreama's told me about this Dwight, and he really sounds like he knows his stuff."

"Melton," he said, "call me Melton. My daddy was Mr. Askins." The request was not a friendly one, particularly.

"We'd appreciate it, Melton," Goody said.

"Tell you the truth, I think I'm going to have to let Dwight go before much longer," Askins said. "We've had some problems on the job." He paused, licked his lips, looked around him to make sure that no one was listening. "Trifling with the other guides."

"Trifling?" Dreama asked the question.

"Trifling with the *girl* guides," Askins said, as though that explained all. "A number of them have approached me about it, about his unwelcome advances. After hours, when there's nobody supposed to be here." He nodded sagely. "I haven't told him yet, haven't given him his official notice, but I think he knows. Dwight may be a troublemaker, but one thing he's not is dumb."

"I know he's not," Dreama said. "He knew everything about this cave the time he took me through."

"Everything," Askins said. "Front to back, back to front. Dwight memorized it all. I'll never know what gets into people sometimes. I swear to God I thought that boy was my heir, even though we were no relation at all. I thought that I must of bred him myself by accident or miracle, the manner in which he took to this cave. And then he starts tearing it up. Ruins it all. You never know with some people."

Goody and Dreama offered no reply.

"So, Dwight," Askins said. "Dwight gets to pull one last tour of duty." He sighed. "I believe he's in the back of the system, changing the arrangement of some lights. It'll take me a minute to go get him. You can wait, or you can have one of the other guides right away. That's the course of action I'd advise, if you were to ask me."

"We'll wait," Goody said pleasantly. Dreama took his hand and squeezed it to show her approval. Grumbling, Askins turned and shuffled off in the direction of the deep cavern.

"He seems like a pretty sour old man," Goody said when Askins had moved out of earshot. "I believe he was about to tell us he wished he was dead and it was his brother who had to run this place. He wishes it was him lying over there in that casket, looking like some kind of a plastic dummy."

"Wouldn't you feel like that?" Dreama said. "After all, he watched his own brother die."

Goody wondered how long it would take for this boy Dwight to appear. He was cold, standing underground in his summer clothes. He wished that Dreama had told him to wear something warmer, or that he had thought of it himself. He hadn't been thinking of much when she pulled into his yard in the Bronco. The T-shirt she wore had a happy face printed across its front. He'd been working on the Le Mans, had it precariously balanced on a pair of jackstands so that he could get underneath. It was a mess. *Come to the caves with me,* she'd said, and he hadn't even paused to take a breath. Into the truck and away they'd gone. On the way to the Hidden World, she'd told him about Wallace's arrest, and he'd felt a wave of excitement and anticipation sweep through him. Now here they were, in the caverns. He had to admit that it was good to get a break from the heat.

"Wallace knows this Sheriff Faktor who picked him up, huh," he said. "I met Faktor once myself."

"When Billy Rugg died over at your place," Dreama said.

Goody was surprised. "You knew Billy Rugg?"

She shrugged. "Knew him, yeah. Everybody knew Billy Rugg. He was hiding on the mountain, to stay out of some trouble. Everybody knows everybody around here. Wallace hated like hell what happened to Billy. It was nothing he wanted to happen. See, there's a man named Mr. Tannhauser up on Little Hogback. And sometimes Wallace works for him. And sometimes Sheriff Faktor works for him."

"So Wallace probably isn't in too much trouble."

"Well, I don't know," Dreama said. "He never shot at a Fed before. But I don't think he is."

Someone approached them, trudging across the room with eyes lowered. He wore coveralls that were caked with mud, and his hair was disheveled and dirty. The skin of his face was pale, and there were dark patches under his eyes, almost like old fight bruises. Been a while since this guy slept well, he thought. When Dwight's washed-out eyes lit on Dreama, they widened momentarily. Goody nearly laughed. She had that effect.

"You asked for me?" the kid said.

"Dwight," she said. "You gave me a tour the other day, and I liked it so much I brought back a friend with me to see it all again."

"I remember," Dwight said. He was almost surly. Goody wasn't surprised that this kid was about to lose his job. He had a thing or two to learn about how to treat customers. "I remember real well."

"I'm glad," Dreama said, and she sounded genuinely pleased. They stood that way a while, Dwight looking at them out of his hooded eyes.

"I'll give you your tour if you want it," he said. He spoke directly to Dreama. It was as though Goody weren't there in the room for him to see, as though if he put a hand into the space where Goody stood, it would just pass through his skin and hair and blood as if they were composed of air, or something thinner and less valuable than air. Goody wondered how much time the skinny boy spent underground, that he had become so unlike other people.

"Awful good of you, Dwight," Goody said. He made no effort to disguise the distaste he felt for this runt. He could not understand what Dreama had been doing, asking after him so particularly.

Dwight ignored him. "They got me reconfiguring the lights now, that kind of thing," he said. "I was just back there at the Veil of Tears. He's got me working to lose the face. He got too many complaints, people getting scared, having religious fits, calling him an idolater. Now he wants it to look like a bird again. Big swan." From the quality of Dwight's voice, its crystalline contempt, it was clear who *he* was, and what Dwight thought of *him* and his swan idea.

"But we'll know," Dreama said. Her words puzzled Goody. What secret might these two share, this beautiful woman and the dirty boy? "The two of us will know that in back of the bird and under it lies the face."

Dwight shrugged again, apparently a trademark gesture with him. "I don't know," he said. "Maybe it is a bird, if it looks like a bird. Maybe it is exactly what it looks like, whatever it looks like. Maybe it's nothing."

"You know that isn't so, Dwight," Dreama said. She sounded perfectly assured.

"Well, come on," Dwight said, gracelessly waving them into the downward-sloping passage that led to the Egg Room. "You'll be the last people who get to see the Veil of Tears." And he took them on a guided tour of the cave, a tour that took the full regulation forty-five minutes, that passed by all of the required sights; but he didn't talk much, and he didn't bother to walk backward.

"Well, what did you think of it?" Askins wanted to know. He stood in the front room as though he had been waiting for the three of them to return.

"It's quite a place," Goody said. "Large."

"Spooky," Dreama said.

"Spooky?" Askins said. He blinked at them. "Spooky. Damn right. I'm glad you liked it, anyway. A man died to bring you all this. A good man."

They moved past him onto the exit ramp. Behind them as they ascended Goody heard Askins laugh. "Hah. Spooky," he said, and laughed again. "What do you think of that?" And Goody could not decide whether Askins spoke to himself, or to Dwight, or to the corpse of his long-dead brother Floyd.

"Oh, too rough," Dreama said, twisting free of Goody's embrace. They were back at his house. She had taken him home from the caverns after their tour. They had driven along without speaking, Goody sitting closer to her on the bench seat than was strictly necessary. It hadn't taken a whole lot of coaxing to get her to come inside. She moved away from him, out of his arm's reach. "I don't know what you're doing," she said. "You're making some pretty far-fetched assumptions about me, I believe. I never meant for it to be this way with you and me. I want us to be friends." They were in the kitchen, and she had gone to the other side of the table from him. He thought she was teasing him.

Unbidden, his thoughts moved to the old murder. Had it begun here? Had she maybe tried to keep the kitchen table between them, circling, moving left when the killer-husband shifted to his left, right when he made a move to the right, like some nasty version of a kid's game? The kitchen table with its chipped Formica top the only refuge, the only shield that she could think of? Had he fooled her, head-faked one way and then gone fast the other, catching her as she strove to elude him? Had she tried to make a sudden break for the door, and he had caught her? The image of the raised hammer, hovering in the air, frozen as though it had been flash-photographed in the moment before it descended, came to him. He could imagine it, sixteen ounces exactly, the dull play of light over the metal of its head, the grain of the varnished wooden handle; and the hand that gripped the hammer, the wrist and forearm thick with muscle, dense with hair; but nothing more of the man who had wielded it.

"Good friends, but still just friends," Dreama said. She smiled broadly, and Goody took that as a sign that she meant more than she said. He came around the table toward her, and she didn't try to dodge. He snaked an arm around her waist and drew her irresistibly to him. She made a weak sound of protest as he pushed his mouth against hers. He dug a hand deep into her thick hair. The wall of her teeth parried his avidly questing tongue for a few seconds, then parted for him, and he could taste her. She tasted medicinally sweet, a flavor that he couldn't identify, and it took him a second to decide whether it was pleasant or not. Deciding that it was, he pressed harder against her. Her hips bumped the table, and its legs scraped backward over the linoleum floor.

When he came up for air, she gasped and said, "I don't kiss very well. I never really learned how."

"You kiss fine," he said.

"Wallace married me pretty young," she said. "And he never was much of a one for French kissing and that kind of thing."

Goody laid his mouth over hers to make her quiet. They bumped foreheads painfully, and she squeaked, but he kept on. He felt like a dentist, as he always did at such times, learning the pattern of her teeth. They were small teeth, ridged and sharp. She bit him, lightly, and he drew back, but only for a moment. He dragged the tail of her T-shirt out of the waistband of her shorts and ran his hands over her strong torso. Her skin was warm, so warm.

She tore her mouth from his, gasped for breath. Her exhalations were hot against his neck. "All right," she said, and there was as much resignation in her voice as excitement. "But only above the waist. You got to promise me you'll stay above the waist." She wanted to bargain with him. He promised nothing. She went on. "Remember, won't you," she said, "that I'm a happily married woman."

29

A great horned owl perched, perfectly motionless, on one of the defunct light stanchions near the ceiling of the grand ballroom. The stanchion had the form of a little naked fat boy who held a torch up and out in one pudgy dimpled hand. A light bulb shaped like a flame, long unlit, crowned the torch. There were thirty-nine others like it at regular intervals along the wall, and the owl gripped the head of this fortieth one with its hard horny claws. The owl was approximately the same size as the cherub: two and a half feet tall. It was a magnificent specimen, with a considerable spread of wing and coin-size iridescent yellow eyes and a great baritone voice that could be heard throughout the compound. A spreading mound of guano, bird bones, and indigestible feathers lay directly beneath the owl and the bronze boy, and it was added to each day.

The owl's keen expressionless eyes were fixed on a young possum that cruised the littered floor of the ballroom. Although the possum was on the far side of the vast room from the owl and the predawn light was dim, the owl had no difficulty in tracing the course that the possum followed, or in making out the features of the possum itself. It was fat and sleek, and its pink hide showed through its thin patchy hair. Its claws made a slight scratching sound against the wood of the

floor; its nose twitched, a far more sensitive and useful organ than its
weak pop eyes.

The owl swiveled its head in a slow smooth revolution, watching
the possum as it cast about among the junked furniture for some
morsel to eat. When the possum disappeared behind a heap of trash,
the owl waited, quiet, patient, imperturbable, until it came back into
view on the other side. The marsupial moved placidly, slowly, covering the ground thoroughly, unaware of the owl's pitiless, covetous
surveillance.

The possum was making for a short tin can that lay on its side in
a small pile of straw. The can was in the center of the room, not far
from a large overturned paisley couch. The owl ruffled its feathers
slightly, blinked, fixed on the possum again. Nearer and nearer it
came, slaloming from one side of the room to the other but always
drawn further on by the smell of that can. Vienna sausages. The rich
smell of them came to the owl also; but that was foreign stuff, unknown, and not much of it. The possum was more interesting by far.
The owl's gaze never wavered. When the possum stuck first its nose
into the can, and then its whole head, the owl knew that the time had
come. With a loud rustling of feathers, it spread its prodigious wings
and launched itself into the air, gliding swiftly down to take the
unwary animal.

Before the owl hit it, the possum squealed. The drift of straw
around the can and beneath the possum seemed inexplicably to shift
and ripple as though alive. The possum rolled over onto its back, feet
waving helplessly above it, scrabbling at nothing. The can clattered
away over the ruined parquet floor.

The owl landed on the possum's belly and sank its talons deep
into the soft flesh there. Beating its wings violently, it surged into the
air, taking the struggling possum with it. Dust and straw billowed in
a choking cloud, propelled by the thrashing of the owl's pinions, and
the floor beneath it was swept clean. Two feet, three, four feet it rose,
the possum battling to free itself from the cruel hooks of its claws.
The possum was healthy and strong, and it bowed its body and
thrashed and bit at the owl's legs. It made a grunting, growling sound
as it fought. When the owl had attained the height of five feet, it
stopped climbing as though it had struck a solid obstacle. Its wings
continued to belabor the air as before, even harder than before, but it
could not gain lift. It refused to release its hold on the possum, always
straining upward.

A thin steel wire of light gauge led from one of the possum's rear legs to the overturned couch nearby. A tight slipknot held it in place, just behind the small splayed foot. Peanut was attached to the other end of the snare line by a loop around his wrist. He emerged from his blind beneath the couch. He shouted at the owl while digging frantically at the length of wire, which, drawn unexpectedly tight by the phenomenal strength of the bird, had buried itself in the skin of his forearm. Peanut looked as though he were flying an elaborate, wildly vibrating kite.

"You son of a bitch!" Peanut screamed at the owl, taking a step toward it with his fist raised to strike. The owl receded. Every time he moved toward it, it moved farther back, holding the now-slack body of the possum, keeping the wire taut between them. Threads of blood began to run down Peanut's tortured arm. "Jesus Christ!" Peanut shrieked, following the owl, which continued to back off and seemed resolved never to let go of the possum and of Peanut. Perhaps it thought that it had caught him, and had visions of killing him and dining off his body for weeks and months to come.

With a sound like the chiming of a small bell, the wire parted. The greater length of it curled back on itself, whipping viciously through the air and cutting Peanut across the face. He cried out and fell. The owl, unexpectedly released, whirled backward as though it had been shot out of a cannon. It thumped with a bone-rattling jar against the wall of the ballroom and, fluttering weakly to the dance floor, dropped the possum. The possum opened its eyes when it struck the ground, rolled onto its feet, and scampered away.

The owl lay against the wood, dazed, wings outstretched, watching the possum cross the room again. The possum paused frequently to lick at the gashes on its bulging stomach. It made poor time in reaching the shelter of a pile of broken boards, but there was nothing the owl could do to arrest its progress. Beneath the boards the possum located a hole that led to a place of safety in the foundations of the building, where it stayed, panting as it rested and recovered.

Soon enough, the owl stood and waddled several steps away from the wall, blinking its startling yellow eyes. It tried its wings, flapping them experimentally a few times. Finding nothing damaged, its hollow bones intact, it took to the air and circled the ballroom a couple of times as it ascended again to its hunting perch.

The first time that it passed over Peanut, he had just finished picking the wire from the groove that it had cut in his flesh. The second time, he held the Vienna sausage can in his hand. He had found it empty, his bait gone, and with it his only hope of supper. He pitched the can at the owl, but it missed its target, sailing past the bird in a lazy parabola that carried it across the width of the room to the far wall, where it disappeared through one of the broken windows. The owl returned to its cherub, settling there and closing its eyes as if in sleep, ignoring the imprecations that Peanut called up at it.

Peanut shouted a few more names. His voice echoed eerily in the empty hall. When its last reverberations had faded, he took up the search for the half of a Vienna sausage that had disappeared from the can. He searched for five minutes, ten, refusing to give up, and finally found it where it had rolled beneath the sprung seat of a broken dining chair. He picked it up and debated between trying his luck with trapping another scavenger and eating it himself. Finally he brushed the dust from it, picked off a piece of lint, and tucked the sausage end into his mouth. Then he sat on the upended couch and surveyed his surroundings again, looking for clues as to how he might survive. The last of his rations was gone. He had made the can last, drinking the clear liquor that sat in the bottom, sucking the jelly off the sausages, savoring each sausage, each single sausage, each one a meal. The salt in them had made him thirsty.

He had come upon the grand ballroom in the night, after stumbling through what he took to be some insane trapper's ward. Every few steps, it seemed, he had come upon a steel leghold trap or a shallow pit filled with sharp stakes. It was only by the sheerest luck that he had seen a number of them and had managed not to be caught and mangled by those that he failed to see. Twice he had stumbled across tripwires, feeling them only after he had snagged his foot on them, never knowing exactly what they were attached to. Both times, nothing had happened. He had passed through groves of clattering concertina wire, gashing himself but only slightly.

He sat and watched the owl sleep. His anger grew in him and he considered ways to scale the walls to get at the owl. It was a high, treacherous climb, an impossible climb, with an angry raptor at its zenith. Some vestige of the instinct toward self-preservation kept him from trying it. Still, he wanted revenge. He deserved it. He had not much savored the idea of the possum, particularly with no cookfire to roast it over, but now that it was gone it seemed like a bounty beyond estimation. He had devised the wire snare, had hidden it beneath the straw, baited it, lain for hours under the foul-smelling couch. He had caught the possum, and it had been his to eat until the owl messed in. He hated the owl. He would unhesitatingly have killed the owl with his bare hands, with his teeth if necessary, had the owl been within his reach. He found himself wondering what owls tasted like.

"You bastard," he called up to the owl. He stood beneath it. He cast around him for something to throw at it and found a short plank. He threw it, but his arm was weak and the missile fell far short of its intended mark. The owl opened one eye, resettled itself, closed the eye. Peanut shouted up again. "You thief!" he yelled. He wanted to wake the owl. He wanted to drive it away.

Yukon heard shouting from the direction of the grand ballroom. Finding the Mingos near the stockade, he signaled that they should follow him. He took his M16 off safety and proceeded into the gloom. He pointed the rifle at the figure of the man who stood shouting up at the owl, from time to time throwing a piece of trash at it. He seemed unlikely ever to hit it.

"Stop that," Yukon said. The figure turned to face him. It was a young man, he saw, malnourished and dirty. He blinked when his gaze fell on Yukon. The Mingos stole into the room. They raised their rifles, awaiting the order to open fire. The red dot of a laser sight bobbed on the young man's chest, rose to his forehead, dropped to his torso again.

"That owl stole my possum," he said. He was nearly in tears. "The possum was my dinner."

"Mr. Tannhauser likes that owl," Yukon said. "He's taken a shine to it and the way it hoots late at night. If you manage to hit it, it will mean a world of trouble for you."

"My possum, the bastard," the young man said. He was openly bawling, tears shining on his sallow cheeks.

"What's your name?" Yukon asked.

"Peanut," he said, brightening perceptibly. "That's what people call me. Say, have you got any food on you? Or water. I'd take a Coke too if you have one. I'm awful thirsty."

"No, Peanut," Yukon said. "I don't have any food on me, or Coke either. But we've got water, if you want some."

"That'll do," Peanut said. "I guess they'll feed me down at the jail, won't they?"

Yukon blinked. "The jail?"

"Sure," Peanut said. "Aren't you guys with the police?"

The expression of bewilderment on Peanut's face was so pure that Yukon lowered the muzzle of his rifle and laughed and laughed. It had been some time since he had found anything so funny. He howled with laughter. Watching him, the Mingos took their sights off Peanut too, and the most dangerous moment in Peanut's uncertain life had passed. The Mingos were not men much given to hilarity, but watching Yukon in the throes of his amusement, they surrendered to chuckles as well. Yukon's mood was infectious.

Last of all Peanut, who did not know what was funny in his predicament at all, joined in the general merriment in order to be polite. And the sound of the four of them laughing was loud enough that it stirred the sparrows and swifts among the rafters and drove them twittering out into the daylight, and forced the great horned owl to turn his noble head until he faced the cracked discolored plaster of the wall.

30

"I hate to see you this way, I really do," the sheriff said. "I mean, I've talked to other guys the way I've got to talk to you, but the renowned Wallace Claymaker ending up in this fashion? I never featured it in my wildest dreams."

They were together in Sheriff Faktor's office at the county jail. A vicious game of two-on-two basketball was going on outside. A couple of the guards had been inveigled into playing a pair of the inmates, and there was a bitter rivalry between them. A running body slammed into the other side of the cinderblock wall, and everybody in the room—Sheriff Faktor, Claymaker, the lanky deputy, two of the deputy's subordinates—flinched at the impact. The game paused for a few seconds and then continued, from the sound of it as vigorously as before.

"Tell you the truth, I never did either, John." Claymaker, by twenty years the oldest man in the room, was the only one of them who called the high sheriff by his given name. He sat, apparently comfortably enough, in the sheriff's own wooden desk chair, which had been pulled into the open center of the room, under the unshaded glare of the overhead light. The lamplight shone on his thick silver hair. It occurred to the sheriff to ask him, Had his hair always been that color? Even when he was a little boy? It had remained the same remarkable metallic shade for the many years the two men had known each other: a shade not like old-man gray, drained of some other pigment. This rich sheen was a color all its own. He did not ask the question.

Wallace was secured to the office chair, wrist and ankle, by plastic industrial zip strips, high-density toothed fasteners that could be tightened but not loosened. Shipping companies used them in varying sizes to bind bundles of pipe, coils of wire, steel rods, planks of wood, ingots of aluminum. The Dwyer County Sheriff's Department had recently acquired the smallest variety of the strips for use in restraining their prisoners. In practice, the officers had found the zip strips to be the fulfillment of everything they had seemed to promise: lightweight, practical, a highly effective replacement for conventional unwieldy metal handcuffs in every way. A well-equipped deputy could carry a dozen or more of them easily in his pocket and immobilize the same number of suspects; they made no noise, did not clank together when silence was a virtue; they had no locks to be picked or broken but had to be cut off the subject who was manacled by them. Entirely satisfactory. Wallace tested his strength against the bonds and found them secure.

"I believe you're making a problem for yourself," he said. The cigarette in his mouth, one that the sheriff had given him, jigged up and down as he spoke. The lanky deputy stepped forward, took it from between his lips, and tapped the overlong ash into the ashtray that sat on the sheriff's desk. He put the cigarette back in Wallace's mouth, and Wallace drew on it, expelling the smoke in twin fuming jets through his nostrils. "Thanks," he said to the deputy, who nodded.

"I believe that you've made an error in judgment that will lead to unhappiness all around," Wallace said to the sheriff. "I believe your thinking is clouded by emotion. By fear, I mean, and I think you should reconsider." His eyes were swollen and surrounded by blackening proud flesh; his nose had been broken during his arrest. He spoke with difficulty through split tender lips. His shirt and pants were flecked with his blood. He blinked worriedly in the relentless light. He had been hooded and locked in an isolation cell for two days.

"I am unhappy, Wallace," Sheriff Faktor said. "Unhappy about all of this unpleasantness. Don't ever think for even a second that I'm not profoundly unhappy." He paused. "But I'm not scared." The harsh light gleamed on the dome of his bald skull. His deep-set eyes were shadowed.

"Not fear, then," Wallace said. "I chose the wrong word. Anger, maybe, is closer to the mark. Tell me if I'm right." He had smoked the cigarette down to its filter, and the lanky deputy took it from him and flicked it, still burning, into the ashtray. When the deputy raised the pack to inquire whether he might want a second one lighted for him, he shook his head, then changed his mind and indicated that he did want another. The deputy slipped a cigarette from the nearly full pack and placed it between Wallace's lips, taking care to avoid the hurt places, the cuts and scabs. He held a light to the cigarette's tip. When Wallace had puffed sufficiently to get the cigarette burning well, he returned his attention to the sheriff, who loomed before him.

"Anger is closer to it, yes. You acted like a stupid kid, and you've almost ruined us all."

"The bastard was chasing my wife bare-assed through the woods. You think I'm going to stand by and watch that kind of a thing take place? He looked like he wanted to hit her with the helicopter skid."

"Dreama's a big girl," the sheriff said. "She doesn't need you to take up arms for her, bare-assed or not."

"She's my wife," Wallace said.

"Yep. It's a fact. She's your wife." Silence.

Finally Wallace said, "You know, Mr. Tannhauser isn't going to stand for you beating on me this way. He'll be coming around here asking questions after a while."

"After a while," the sheriff said. His tone was meditative. "After a while can seem like a pretty long time when you're tied in a chair. After a while can be too long to wait when somebody else is swinging a stick."

The cigarette in Wallace's mouth trembled visibly. He seemed to know that he was betraying himself, the depth of his terror. He knew it from the look of contempt that came over Sheriff Faktor's face, from the way the lanky deputy looked away from him; but he didn't know exactly how he might be doing it. His voice took on an unaccustomed urgency. "Look," he said. "You don't want to tangle with Mr. Tannhauser these days. He's got some important people in camp to see him, heavy hitters, and they brought artillery with them."

The sheriff's eyebrows lifted. "That where you got the popgun you used to shoot at the Fed? That's a nice little addition to the department's weapons locker. My thanks."

"And plenty more where that came from. Mr. Tannhauser will eat you alive for tearing me up this way. I'll forget it if you let me go right now. But one minute longer and next thing you know the Mingos'll be bearing down on you with a grenade launcher."

"You know what I think, Wallace?" the sheriff said. "I think you're getting old, and I think you've overplayed that Tannhauser card of yours. Here's how it lays: Tannhauser will do what Tannhauser must do. But with that DEA man flitting around, you're a liability, you're a loose cannon. I can't let you walk, and I sure as hell can't let you talk, a man with an irresponsible, uncontrollable temper like you've got."

Wallace stared at him. He wished desperately for the ability to gnaw through his limbs like an animal. He wished that his hands and feet would just drop off, so that he could be free of the confining zip strips, even if just for a minute, a second. He tried to compose his features into a mask of uninterest, but the jittering cigarette continued to give the secret of his terror away.

"And I'll tell you something else for free, old man. Old man with a young wife. I'll get to Tannhauser before the DEA does. By the end of the week, Mr. God Almighty Himself Tannhauser will be gone from the face of the earth. Expunged. His person, personnel, operation, equipment, and every living memory thereof eliminated. Tabula rasa." He made a sweeping motion with his right hand. "Erased," the sheriff hissed. He gestured to the lanky deputy, who took up a clipboard from the desk. The other deputies watched, standing at parade rest, their hands folded behind them, their feet apart. Their patent leather uniform shoes shone with a high gloss. Outside, the basketball rebounded off the loose, rattling backboard. "Write down the following," the sheriff said. *"Prisoner slain in cellblock altercation with unknown other inmates. Inquiry pending."*

Taking that as their cue, the two deputies stepped forward, sliding wooden truncheons from their wide leather equipment belts as they did. Wallace closed his eyes. The nightsticks rose and fell, rose and fell with the mechanical efficiency of valve lifters, finding with each blow the vulnerable parts: elbow joints, knees, shoulders, collarbone, groin, the tender back of the neck. The impact of the sticks against Wallace's flesh sounded much like the bouncing of the basketball on the nearby court. Wallace struggled manfully not to scream, and by the time he could stay quiet no longer he didn't have the energy or the ability to make much noise.

After a few minutes, Sheriff Faktor laid his hands in an avuncular fashion on the shoulders of the deputies. He moved them out of the way and stood in front of Wallace, reached down, and, putting a palm under his chin, turned Wallace's battered face up so that he could look into it. The steel-colored hair was matted with blood; hard to tell what its hue was now. "You know, Claymaker," the sheriff said, "I never liked you overmuch. But that girl you married—I admire her." He smacked his thick lips. "When you've left us, I believe I'll have to pay a condolence visit to little Dreama."

He stood back, and the deputies moved in again, swinging their clubs systematically, in precise synchronization. One of the sticks, upraised on its long backswing, nicked the light bulb overhead. The thin glass of the bulb gave off a high musical note but, surprisingly enough, did not break. The blow set the light to swinging on the short length of frayed electrical cord from which it depended. The shadows of the deputies, moving across the room in diametrical opposition to the oscillation of the bulb, kept rough time with their judicious strokes. At length, they stood back.

The sheriff surveyed the results of their handiwork with a critical eye. Squatting, he retrieved Claymaker's still-burning cigarette from the floor, where it had fallen. He held it between his thumb and forefinger, squinted at it in close inspection, made as though to stub it out beside the butt of the other in the ashtray. He changed his mind and instead put the only slightly exhausted cigarette in his mouth, drew a lungful of smoke, exhaled. "Well," he said, gesturing at Claymaker's slumped form, "that's a pretty nasty mess."

Outside, the basketball swished through the net. "Two points," someone, inmate or guard, shouted triumphantly. The gallery was evenly divided in the cheers and catcalls that followed, and play quickly resumed.

31

The hefty girl wiggled her tight-skirted hips in what she must have considered an alluring fashion. She bared her teeth and licked her full, sensuous lips. Peanut concentrated on her mouth, which he considered the only truly desirable part of her. Her mouth and maybe her auburn hair, which fell past her waist. Her hair looked like something a man could really get his hands into, heavy and oily-textured. Probably not even her real hair, he reflected glumly. Probably pulled out of a horse's tail somewhere. A curling wisp of it hung in her face, and she blew a breath at it, puffing her cheeks comically. All of her movements were too large, melodramatic.

She backed away, holding up one hand in a warning gesture. "Whoa up there, cowpoke," she said. Her voice was loud, the plosives harsh. She wore a low-cut top decorated with large cloth flowers. Her breasts threatened to free themselves from the blouse's insubstantial restraint. The movements of her heavily rouged, sensual mouth seemed strangely at odds with her words. Seemingly from nowhere, a cowboy appeared. Or rather, a man dressed in a cowboy costume. Part of a costume. He wore riding chaps, a gunbelt and holster, a polka-dotted neckerchief, and a drooping ten-gallon hat. He advanced menacingly on the girl, taking long slow strides.

"Fuck her! Fuck her!" somebody behind Peanut shouted. It sounded like the copilot.

"Don't worry. He will," somebody else—Yukon, probably—replied.

The cowboy backed the woman up against the footrail of a big brass bed. He turned to the side, revealing himself as hugely endowed. The size of his engorged penis apparently awed and frightened the girl; she put a hand to her mouth, and a grating screech filled the air. Peanut giggled. The cowboy snatched his Colt Peacemaker from its holster and with its barrel pretended to strike the girl a stunning blow on her forehead. She toppled onto the bed and lay in an untidy heap, skirt rucked up around her waist, her legs parted, unappetizing dimpled thighs on display. The cowboy dropped the revolver to the floor and climbed onto the soft mattress with her, straddling her prostrate form.

"Get it, hoss!" the copilot shouted. Peanut tried to ignore him, tried to concentrate on what was there in front of him. Something exciting. Something different, at least.

With a soft ripping snarl, the image of the cowboy coupling with the unconscious girl came unhinged. It rolled rapidly upward and tilted, flickering in and out of focus. Then the picture was gone entirely and the sounds of sex with it, and Peanut could hear only the soft *slap slap slap* of the broken end of the film against the take-up reel. Everyone in the assembled group groaned. A square of bright white light from the projector covered the tarp tacked to the outside wall of the cottage.

"Not again," the copilot said.

"I'll fix it," Yukon told them, rising from the seat he had made of some half-filled sandbags. He went to look at the old sixteen-millimeter projector, which sat on a wheeled dessert cart salvaged from the wreckage in the grand ballroom. Extension cord after extension cord stretched away from the projector, linking it to the generator behind the cottage.

In the distance, a hoarse voice called, "O my God I cry in the daytime but you do not hear. And in the night season and am not silent." The voice was faint, at the edge of audibility. Only a shift in the wind brought it to the ears of the group clustered around the makeshift movie screen. When the film was running they couldn't hear it at all.

"He does, you know," Peanut said, smiling at his own joke. "Cry during the day and the night."

The voice came again. "I am a worm and no man. A reproach to men and despised of the people."

Peanut laughed. "That too," he said. "Where did you all get this guy from?" No one answered him.

"Movies under the stars," the pilot said. "What a great idea. If only we could get to see a whole movie at one time."

"I know I know I know," Yukon said, working furiously at restoring the picture. "It's just Ernesto used to run this thing, and I don't have the least idea about it. He was a projectionist at a porno theater in Mexico City, and he really knew his stuff. He said it was a nice place really, very plush. He said they got all the best American porno down there, and Swedish and all."

"Mexico City?" Tannhauser asked. With Yukon's help, he had dragged a couch, the paisley one under which Peanut had watched his Vienna sausage trap, into place for movie watching. "I thought Ernesto was from Guatemala, not Mexico." Tannhauser sat with an arm around the girl Paloma. She had moved away from him during the film, and he tugged her toward him. She came without protest, her hands limp at her sides, face turned downward. Her skirt slid up as she scooted along the couch, revealing legs dappled with florid bruises and knotted flesh. Tannhauser dragged her onto his lap. She had made them a meal earlier, and a great slab of roast boar sat cooling on a tarnished serving platter beneath the movie screen. A long carving knife was sunk to its hilt in the meat. Flies walked on the pork and on the haft of the knife.

"Mexico, Guatemala," Yukon said, shrugging. "It's all pretty confusing to me." He flipped a switch on the movie projector and the gears ran forward, but the film didn't catch on the cogs. The picture was blurred and fuzzy, unwatchable. "Damnation," he said, and turned the machine off again. He returned to his frustrated tinkering, pulling loops and fistful of film off the reel, muttering under his breath.

"Why don't you fix it?" Tannhauser said to Peanut, reaching over and poking him with a forefinger. Peanut was perched on the edge of the couch farthest from Tannhauser and the silent Paloma, and the push almost dislodged him. "You're Ernesto's replacement, after all," Tannhauser said.

"I never fooled with any projectors before," Peanut said. "Never was much call for it."

"Maybe you better learn," Tannhauser said. A warning in his voice carried clearly to Peanut. "You know," Tannhauser said, as though he were just musing aloud, "if Ernesto hadn't had the misfortune to bleed to death when he did, I never would have taken you on. I'd have thrown you to the Mingos, and you'd be lying out in the woods right now, at the bottom of a grave that you dug yourself."

"I know it," Peanut said. He cast a fearful glance at the Mingos, who crouched together hunter-style at the edge of the group, rifles braced stock-down against the ground. They always went armed. "And I'm grateful. To you and to that fellow Ernesto. Which is not to say I'm glad he died, but just that the position happened to open up when it did. I've always had good luck like that somehow, my whole life. I mean, I know that if it hadn't—" He ran out of words at last.

Tannhauser said, "Of course, Ernesto didn't dig his own grave. We had a crew of his people to do that."

While Yukon struggled to rethread the film and set it running again, a murmur went up among the workers, many of whom, men, women, children, hung from the windows of their collapsing cottages to watch it. One of the kids was tossing something to the hounds that hung around the compound, and the dogs were standing flat-footed, snatching the morsels out of the air. New dogs showed up all the time, as many as two or three a day. They were drawn in by the smell of food, and there seemed to be no end to the supply of them. The dog treats that the kid threw were pink and they squeaked as they hurtled through the air before disappearing into the maw of one dog or another. Peanut saw that they were baby rats: blind, hairless, and shriveled. The workers chatted excitedly among themselves. Intermingled with their words, the distant shouting voice said, "My strength is dried up like a potsherd and my tongue cleaves to my jaws."

"I wish," mumbled Peanut, who seemed to be the only one any longer aware of the yelling.

"What is it?" Tannhauser asked the copilot, who spoke a little Spanish. "What are they saying?"

The copilot stared wide-eyed ahead of him as though the film were still running, as though it continued to run in his head for him alone. The pilot sat on the ground next to him. The copilot licked his lips. "I was just trying to make that out," he said. "I believe they're debating whether she wanted it, from the caballero, vaquero, whatever, the cowboy. Was she excited about it, or was she forced."

"He hit her in the head with his gun," Peanut said. "Do you imagine she wanted that?"

"They mean the actress, not the character. Was she paid to do what she did, or did she have no choice?"

"This is America," Tannhauser said. "Everybody has a choice. It's a free country. You tell them that."

"I don't think the film was shot in America," the copilot said. "At least, the words don't fit their mouths very well. I believe the English words must have been dubbed in over some other language, don't you?"

"Well, still, it was shot in some sort of a free country, you can bet. Do you think they have X-rated movies in Cuba? In Russia?" Tannhauser snorted in derision at the idea. "I don't think so."

Bodo spoke up. "They do," he said. "In Russia, at least. A group of young thugs distributes them. The Lubertsy gang. And I would think that they have lewd films in Cuba too."

"Probably the same ones, imported from Russia," Toma said. He and Bodo sat side by side in straight-backed chairs that they had brought from their cottage.

"Naked Russian women," the pilot said.

"Ouch," the copilot said.

"Actually, the girls in the few films I've seen there were quite beautiful," Bodo said. "Young housewives from the suburbs supplementing their incomes, their rations. The Lubers probably paid them in dollars. And the films weren't bad." He waved a hand at the blank screen. "Not as sophisticated as this, perhaps, and with a gloomier outlook," he said, "but still quite impressive."

"Sophisticated?" Yukon said. He had the film threaded and felt confident that it would run to its end unaided. "What's so sophisticated about a cowboy screwing a dancehall girl? I don't see it."

"I was attempting a witticism, Yukon," Bodo said. "A small one, I admit. A sarcasm."

"I wasn't aware that you made jokes, Bodo," Tannhauser said. He was massaging Paloma's shoulders, kneading the flesh between his powerful hands, working it like dough. Bodo thought that the process looked more painful than pleasant for Paloma, who said nothing. She did not look at Tannhauser, at any of them.

"Not often, Mr. Tannhauser."

Toma added, laughing, "And not well."

"No," Bodo said. "Not well."

The projector whirred to life again, and the cowboy and girl sprang back into their places up on the tarp. The girl was on all fours, having recovered from the jolt to her head, apparently, and naked but for a black lace garter belt. The cowboy sat astride her bare back, pretending to ride her, whipping her into a frenzy with a braided hank of her long hair. When his wild antics failed to dislodge the hair from her head, Peanut decided that it must not be a wig, that it was indeed her own hair, and real. The realization improved his mood substantially.

"I wish she was skinnier," he said to the group at large, "but she's doing okay."

"Hell, I like fat girls," the copilot said. "Lots to grab onto, lots to explore. And they are so *grateful.*"

"Fat women almost always smell like food," the pilot said, and it was impossible to tell whether he thought the tendency a virtue or a vice.

The picture rippled disconcertingly as a passing breeze shook the loosely fastened tarp. The wind brought with it another sentiment from the distant shouter: "I am poured out like water," he yelled, his voice waning in strength and intensity, "and all my bones are out of joint. My heart is like wax, and it is melted in the midst of my bowels."

"Jesus but he has a morbid imagination," Peanut said. "Bones and wax and bowels. How does he make that stuff up?" There were several cowboys on the screen now, and a few more of the hapless dancehall girls, these as substantial as the first. The girls were yelling, whether with pleasure or agony it was impossible to tell, their voices like shattering glass through the movie projector's cheap speaker.

"It's not his imagination," Bodo said.

Peanut could not hear him well over the noise of the movie: girls whining, cowboys grunting, the smack of sweat-slick flesh against flesh, the overworked springs of the bed which creaked to the syncopated rhythm of the choreography of thrashing bodies. "What did you say?" he asked.

"I said it's not his imagination. He's making nothing up. It's verses of a psalm. From the Christian Bible." When Peanut continued to look baffled, Bodo gave up his explanation and returned to watching the film. Beside him, Toma was humming a nameless tune under his breath, apparently greatly amused by everything that he saw.

Yukon had a stack of short reels of film piled on the dessert cart. They lay in their flimsy tin canisters one on top of another, and he showed them in the order in which they came into his hand. He showed them all, and before each one he had to do battle with the ill-natured projector. Several of the aging strips of celluloid broke as he showed them, some more than once, and had to be mended. A couple of them got stuck and the heat of the projection lamp melted them, the frozen image browning and bubbling, curling away from the center in an instant.

He showed a film about some college girls, who were dressed in bell-bottoms and thin tie-dyed shirts draped with love beads and peace symbols. They sat around on satin pillows in what was ostensibly a dormitory room, sucking on gnarled roaches ("The *product!*" the copilot shouted.) and talking hip to one another, considering acts of lesbianism. Peanut liked them because they were skinny. Emaciated, almost. The Vietnam-era film carried an antiwar message, or perhaps not: in the end, a group of outraged ROTC recruits broke into the room and molested the women. Perhaps it was an antidrug message.

There was one called *Hollywood Starlet* from the fifties, and another in black-and-white about a long-limbed farmer's daughter, a group of traveling salesmen, and a Packard with poor shock absorbers. Tannhauser swore that the daughter in the movie was played by Ava Gardner, had to be Ava before she made it big in legitimate films, he said, but no one else in the group really knew very well what he was talking about, or else they couldn't see the resemblance. There was an Army documentary about the prevention of gonorrhea and a short silent film from the twenties about a Chinese man who branded a white woman because she owed him money.

There were others too, at least a dozen more, the colors faded and the film stock grainy, but for Peanut they blended into a single seamless narrative of violence and subjection to violence, about lust and fluids and exaggerated body parts. All those parts moved together in a garish sea: breasts, lips, buttocks, hands, genitalia, armpits shaven and unshaven. Soon it became impossible to differentiate one image from another, they whipped by so fast, the plots (when there were any) streaming past too quickly for strict comprehension, but comprehension was not the point anyway and he soon abandoned his attempts at it. Bruised flesh, swollen flesh, humping squirming flesh. At one point someone was killed onscreen, and he had the impression that the death was real or the others thought it was real, and that they yearned to be shocked by the spurting blood but were not.

None of it looked like anything you might want to touch, none of them looked like people: they were not people but they aroused him, the blood beating in his loins until they ached, singing in his brain. He leaned his head against the lumpy back of the paisley couch, closing his eyes for a respite, but the film went on behind his eyelids, the bodies headless now, the detached heads gape-mouthed and eyeless, the bodies still copulating, still pulsating with simulated life as the whirring of the projector, the background roar of the generator, the laughter and shrieks and sighs of the players, the mumbling foreign conversation (like birds) of the workers, the occasional sharp cry of protest from the psalmist, all came together to make the quavering, petulant, ineluctable soundtrack of his dreams.

When he awoke, Peanut found that he had been abandoned. He raised his head from its reclining position on the couch, the muscles of his neck stiff and tender. Everything was in its place: the chairs, the sofa, the sandbags, the screen, the projector, and the canisters, coils of brittle film spilling from them. The projector was silent, as was the generator. The audience was gone. The workers had vanished from the windows of their cottages.

He was alone, he thought, utterly alone on the mountain. He had spent the last several days wandering by himself through this ruined place, and his fevered mind, his reason unseated by fear, loneliness, sheer hunger, had invented all those people: Tannhauser, Yukon, the unfriendly Mingos. He had conversed with the ghosts of his own imagining. He had been taken at gunpoint before no one, no twelve-fingered minor-league potentate with angry eyes; had not been made to beg, weeping, for his life, had not bleated out his anguish at the thought of his own small extermination; had not been asked for the reason that he should be spared and come up with no answer except *Oh my god oh my god don't kill me mister I don't want to die not die;* had not been told that perhaps he would make an acceptable mascot; did he know what a mascot was? That humiliating question had never been asked.

It thrilled him, the freedom to think that all of these things had never occurred. How much else, then? How much else of his past that was hateful to him could he safely relegate to the realm of nonexistence? All of it, perhaps. He sat on the paisley couch, a man with an aching neck and no past. It was not long before dawn.

With a feeling of crushing disappointment, he heard them soon after, Tannhauser and the rest, calling out to one another on the far side of the encampment. He rose and made his way toward the shouting voices. As he passed the workers' cottages, he could hear those unknown people inside as well, sleeping, talking together in hushed voices, panting as they made love. So they had returned too, or had never been gone. Still, in the face of all evidence, he could not shake the feeling, the holy feeling of the lack of a history and all the possible futures that the lack portended.

He crossed the compound, past the armory and ammo dump, the hulking main building, the long mess hall filled with the low buzzing of flies. Behind the refectory was a great drift of offal: split bones, intestines, hides, hooves. The heads of a number of wild hogs peered up out of the mess. The other men seemed always to be off hunting the boars, or watching porn flicks, or screwing the screeching brown girls. Peanut wondered how they found the time to raise the vast pot crop that Tannhauser was always going on about. The size of it, the potency.

Flawless, he called it. *Absolutely fucking flawless*, with his arms spread wide and his face turned upward as though he were somehow inspired. Peanut figured that the work details, which the Mingos marched off into the woods each morning and brought back at dusk, were the key. But most of the men had lately been taken off those crews and put to work lengthening the airstrip. More of them all the time. Peanut didn't know what exactly to make of it.

Beyond the refectory he found Tannhauser, the Mingos, and the fliers gathered around the psalmist. A couple of hounds were there as well, crouched on their haunches, their thin tails whisking the dusty ground. Tannhauser had another dog, one of the new ones, at his side. It was a malamute with blood-colored eyes, and it strained toward the psalmist, gnashing its white teeth, its jaws covered with milky slobber. Tannhauser kept it back with a hand on its ruff. It made little sound as it struggled against the hold he had on it. The psalmist, who was shackled with several lengths of light chain to the tallest of a trio of charred posts, kept his eyes on the malamute. His bare feet, hard with horny calluses, and his legs to midcalf were filthy with the ashes that clung to him. His lips were moving, but he said nothing aloud.

"It was a popular sport in Europe in, oh, the seventeenth century, I guess," Tannhauser said. "I bet that guy Bodo could tell you something about it. He seems to know a lot of things. They called it bear-baiting."

"Where's Yukon?" Peanut asked.

"They would chain a bear out in the public square, chain it to a post like this one, and then let dogs loose on it. The bear would tear up dog after dog, sure, but you let enough dogs in, pretty soon that bear's going to get tired."

The psalmist had a little leeway in the chain that attached him to the post. Though he was manacled hand and foot, he could slide one foot toward the other with a slow, crabbing motion. Now he moved away from them, turned his back on them. The malamute followed him with its crazy heated eyes.

"Where's Yukon?" Peanut asked the pilot.

"Gone to bed. He's got a fight coming up."

"Fight?"

"Fistfight. Some sucker from the valley. It's tonight. You could probably get to see it if you wanted. The rest of us will be hiking down."

Tannhauser had followed the psalmist in his half-circle around the post. He said, "What's your name, boy? Why don't you tell me your name?"

The psalmist said, "Those are my dogs." He pointed with one of his fettered hands at the hounds. Peanut saw that the hand was swollen and scabbed, probably some bones broken. It hardly looked like a hand at all. The guy's hair was long and crusted with filth. He was bearded and dressed in rags, and as thin as a beggar.

"I had the weirdest dream," Peanut said. "This place was here, but none of you were."

"Not anymore they're not your dogs," Tannhauser said to the psalmist. "These dogs hunt wild hogs for me during the day, and they're my dogs when they're doing it. Not long ago I saw one of the little boys in the compound feeding them, and then they looked like they were his dogs."

"They're my dogs."

"I thought maybe I'd been up here by myself the whole time," Peanut said.

"What's your name, boy? You plan to die without telling me." Tannhauser let his hold on the malamute slip.

The big dog lunged forward, teeth clicking savagely together only inches from the ragged psalmist, who leaned forward until his face was not far from the malamute's. "Dogs have compassed me," he said, spitting out the words. The malamute strained to get at him, and it looked like Tannhauser was having a hard time holding it back, and enjoying his difficulty. "The huntsmen are all about me. The assembly of the wicked have enclosed me. A band of ruffians rings me round. They have pierced my hands." He held up the wounded hand, rotated it as though for Tannhauser's inspection.

"Did you ever have a dream like that?" Peanut asked.

The pilot told him, "No. I never did."

"What's your name, boy?" Tannhauser wanted to know.

"I am a hermit. I am God's anchorite. I have nothing to do with you. With any man."

"You wish you had nothing to do with me," Tannhauser said. "Who are you spying for? For God, I bet. God doesn't want to see what goes on here. God has no interest. What did you see? Did you see the flames? What did you see? Answer me!"

God's anchorite was not fazed by the furious tone of Tannhauser's questioning. He turned away again, his stride this time taking him to the full limit of his tether. His bonds clanked and clattered on him. "Many bulls have compassed me," he said. "Strong bulls of Bashan have beset me round."

"Do you know," Tannhauser said, and his tone was calm again, "where I got this dog from? This big rabid bastard I got here beside me?" The anchorite did not face around or answer. "I found him running in the woods with a pack of others. Wild dogs, feral. The worst kind of scavengers. The others I shot out of hand, but this one here—as my rifle sights settled on him, they just seemed to pass him over. And he came to me. When the others were dead or dying, twitching with the lead of my bullets in them, I called him and he came to me. He does whatever I tell him to."

"Save me from the lion's mouth," the anchorite said. "For you have saved me from the horns of the unicorns."

"Unicorns?" the copilot said. "What the hell's he talking about?"

"A unicorn in the Old Testament means literally an Assyrian ox, as I recall," the pilot said. "But I think now he's using it as a metaphor."

"For what?"

"For the Mingos, don't you imagine? Although what the original psalm-writer might have meant I can't tell you. My old man might could, but I can't."

"Your old man the monk. Could be we're the lions."

"Not you and me, we're not," the pilot said. "Tannhauser, maybe, but not you and me."

"Get him," Tannhauser said, turning the dog loose. The malamute leaped, fangs bared, a hideous growl ripping out from deep within its chest. The anchorite hunched, obviously expecting to be bitten, but the malamute had gone elsewhere. It hit one of the hounds with its broad chest, knocked it sprawling. Then it clasped the hound's throat in its wickedly strong jaws. The hound that it had chosen was the male, and a fine spray of urine lifted from between its legs. It curled its tail tight. It whimpered, choking.

The anchorite appealed again to heaven. "Deliver my soul from the sword," he called, "and my darling from the power of the dog."

The bitch hound stood apart from what was happening between the malamute and the male hound. It wrinkled its long sensitive snout, backed up a couple of steps. It flicked its ears at the sounds, back and then forward again. Finally, it whirled and ran to another part of the compound.

"Take me instead," the anchorite pleaded, this time speaking directly to Tannhauser. "Set your beast on me."

Tannhauser shook a reproving finger at him. "Now what do you think I am?" he said. He bent and grabbed a handful of the malamute's ruff again. When he pulled it away from the twitching bloodied body of the male hound, it resisted for a moment and then came to him. It was breathing quickly, and it ran its tongue across its richly tinted chops. "I was talking about *bear*-baiting. I wouldn't try something like that with a person." He began walking away from the shackled anchorite, tugging at the malamute's leash, and the others followed him. As he went, he called back over his shoulder. "I mean, what exactly do you think I am? Some kind of an animal?"

32

The Ford pickup jounced along the washboard road at a high rate of speed, and Goody steadied himself against the dash panel to avoid being tossed around inside the cab. He tried various handholds and found none of them satisfactory. "Mr. Inchcape?" he said.

Inchcape kept his eyes forward and trod the accelerator more firmly. The racket of the truck's loose fixtures increased. A dented red gas can clattered toward the back of the narrow bed, bounded off the tailgate, and began to make its way forward again. Tonto, who sat in the truckbed, didn't even spare the can a glance as it caromed off the metal panels near him. He rested his massive head against the rail of the bed, his long hairy ears blowing like flags.

"Mr. Inchcape?" Goody said. He raised his voice to carry over the noise of the truck's engine, which howled in low gear. "Who's the opponent?"

Inchcape considered for a moment. "This here's what you call a corduroy road," he said, as though it were the trail they were following that interested Goody and not the man he was scheduled to fight. Like Goody, Inchcape shouted to make himself heard. "It's just logs laid down in the mud, side by side. It's a cheap way to make a road. Rides like hell, though." He spared Goody a look. "There's a lot of these roads that run around up in here, and they ain't on any map, either. You'd be surprised where some of them roads goes." He turned back to his driving.

The truck hit a spot where two logs had shifted apart from each other, leaving a gap like a missing molar in a row of teeth. The Ford took a brief nosedive, came up again. The back of Goody's head rapped against the rear window, hard enough that he thought either his skull or the glass plate might fracture. The gas can clanged hollowly against the forward bulkhead of the truck bed. Though he was a small man, smaller than Goody by thirty pounds or more, Inchcape seemed not even to rise up in his seat.

Goody blinked his smarting eyes and leaned close to Inchcape to make his question unmistakable. "Mr. Inchcape," he said again. Inchcape's right ear was large and filled with stiff gray bristles. Close to him in the narrow space of the truck's cab, Goody got a whiff of Inchcape's scent. It was not an unpleasant smell, as he had thought it might be. Rather, it was chemical and antiseptic, an odor almost of turpentine. "Who will I be fighting?"

Inchcape grunted. Goody thought he might refuse to answer, but the old man smiled and said, "A hump." He paused, and then elaborated. "A kid, most likely."

Goody caught himself on the truck's next leap and was just able to avoid cracking his head against the thin metal roof. Inchcape followed the truck's pitching with a fluid ease, as though he were not jointed together out of bone like other men. He was like a rider on his horse. "You mean you don't know who," Goody said. He tried not to let anger creep into his voice. "I thought you could tell me some things about him. You said you'd find out."

"If Tannhauser said he'd bring somebody, he'll bring somebody," Inchcape said. He negotiated a curve in the road without slowing, and the truck's rear wheels flirted momentarily out from their intended bearing. Inchcape corrected and the truck came back to the true. "He won't get nobody good, though," he said, with a crafty look at his passenger. "Nobody good as you." He reached across the seat with a crabbed hand and patted Goody's knee. To Goody it felt as though a bird had fluttered there briefly. "You'll give him the shove, don't you worry," he said.

Goody made no reply, looking out the window at the passing vista. The log road ran hard along the verge of a high drop-off. The valley beyond the ridge was filled with rising mist, which the evening sun could not penetrate. After a few more minutes of the rough ride, in which Goody banged his knees on the underside of the dash and caught the knuckles of one hand against the gearshift, he said to Inchcape, "Could you slow it down a little, please? You'll kill us before we get there."

Inchcape eyed him briefly. "You driven this road before?" he asked. Goody admitted that he had not. "Well, I done," Inchcape said. "We'll get there. I'm like Tannhauser: if I tell you somebody's coming, then here they come." He said something else, his underjaw working the words viciously, but in the noise Goody missed what it was.

"And tonight it's me," Goody said.

"That's right. Tonight it's you."

"Well," Goody said, "when Tannhauser brought people before, what kind of people were they?" He thought that he had heard the name Tannhauser before, but he couldn't recall in exactly what connection. Did it have to do with Dreama? He had not seen her since the day at the cave, and later at his house. She had said she might drop by but had not. He wondered if she would come to the fight, and whether Claymaker had been turned loose yet.

"Losers. Plug-uglies. And children a couple times, under age. Sometimes it's a criminal that he brings."

"Criminal?"

"He's got an in with John Faktor down at the county jail, so every now and again he brings up a felon." Inchcape went on. "Man-slaughterers, a few of them, but mostly just drunks and dopers and bad-check artists. That like. He had him a giant Mexican wetback name of Jesus for a while, would pretty much just beat people to death. Got so I was betting on him myself there toward the end, against my own men. Show you how bad it got."

"Sounds pretty bad." He remembered Faktor, talking while his deputies went into the cane to fetch out the body of Billy Rugg.

"Tannhauser and Sheriff Faktor thought they had a real thing going, didn't they? Thought they had the tiger by the balls. But then their guy killed a guard at the lockup and landed at Fallston, upstate, so you don't have to worry it's him. Just be some dumb hump, most likely." Inchcape settled back into his seat.

Goody brought up the hand that had struck the shifter and flexed it, closing it and then opening it, slowly. He watched the tendons in their subcutaneous working. He stretched out his legs against the floor of the cab and wedged himself into immobility as best he was able. He pictured himself as he would be that evening, wearing dark cotton trunks, skin sheened in sweat under the lights of some hastily fabricated ring. He pictured himself throwing short shoulder-height jabs, snapping them out from the center of his chest, leading with his left, ducking and bobbing to stay out of trouble. He pictured himself saving up his right, the big right hook, to finish with. He didn't think about the mystery of his opponent when he could help it.

A couple of miles farther on, Goody noted that the noise in the truck was less violent than it had been earlier. Looking around him for the reason, he saw through the rear window that the gas can was gone from the bed. A layer of flotsam—old monkey wrenches, spark plugs, a length of timing chain, ignition wires, c-clamps, a great shoal of corroded fencing staples, some grease-clotted items to which he could not put a name—shifted on the floor around Tonto in an unpredictable shivering tide, but the battered can had vanished. He didn't mention its disappearance to Inchcape, reasoning that they might well come across it on their way back to town, later. Inchcape switched on the headlights to cut the deepening gloom.

"Are we nearly there?" Goody asked. He had to urinate, and the truck's vaulting made the need an agony.

"We'll be there directly," Inchcape said. Then he asked a question that Goody missed.

"What?"

"I wanted to know, are you scared?"

"No," Goody said.

Inchcape grinned. "I always ask them that on the way up here, and they always ever one tell me no," he said. "Boy, if I was about to get punched in the face by some stranger, I guess I'd be pretty scared."

"Maybe I am, then," Goody said. "A little."

Inchcape stole another look across the truck's cab. Goody wondered what he could see in the dim wash of the dashboard lights. "Yes, you are," Inchcape said. "You carry it okay, though."

"I'll give you a good fight, Mr. Inchcape," Goody said.

"Sure you will," Inchcape said. He made a move as if to pat Goody's leg again, but Goody shifted slightly away and he did not. "You rest a minute now. Collect your thoughts."

Goody leaned his head back against the vinyl top of the seat and tried to ignore those brief gravity-free moments when the truck sailed

up from the surface of the road. The pressure of his full bladder had
become a dull ache in his kidneys. While he adjourned, the log trail
left the high ridge it had been following and began passage across a
broad forested plateau. Great silver maple trees and oak, cherry, and
black locust arched their heavy branches overhead. The spaces between and around their broad trunks were richly overgrown with
brush, and cicadas shrilled in the bracken.

Goody shut his eyes and tried to imagine himself as a sketched
figure, a man of simple lines and circles, an animated character: a
creature made of vectors moving over a frictionless plane. He willed
himself to imagine the functioning of his ideal body, a figure perfect
in struggle. Again and again, though, he managed to conjure only a
vision of the shadowed leafy tunnel down which he and Inchcape
traveled.

The corduroy road became a deeply rutted dirt path down which
Inchcape guided the truck. Shortly the trees on either side of them
thinned out, the forest walls falling back, and they found themselves
in a clearing of several acres' size. A few wooden outbuildings clustered around a frame house. Inchcape wheeled the truck around and
parked on the far edge of a group of vehicles gathered outside a large
barn. It was a prefab building, a Quonset hut made of corrugated tin.

"This here's Little Edgar Musser's place," Inchcape said, switching off the truck's ignition. The engine dieseled for a moment and
then shuddered into silence. Goody shook his head, unaccustomed to
the quiet. "You'll meet him here after a while," Inchcape said. "Just
don't say nothing about his weight. It's kind of a sore spot with him."

"I'll watch myself," Goody said. He wrestled briefly with his
door. He tugged at the handle, which levered noisily under his hand
and then would not return to its place, and he butted at the door with
his shoulder.

Inchcape, who had headed for the lighted entrance of the barn,
returned to the truck. "Don't do it like that," he said as Goody
battered against the doorframe. "You got to lift up on it." He gestured with his hands and shoulders, a shrugging motion. Goody
tugged at the armrest and lifted the weight of the door against its
reluctant hinges. It swung open and hung wide of the side of the
truck, like the broken wing of a bird. Goody left the vehicle and
pushed to close the door. It wouldn't latch. "Leave it," Inchcape
said. He turned back toward the barn, and Goody followed him.

"What about the dog?" Goody said, gesturing toward Tonto.

"What about him? He'll sit there until we come back. We're late already without worrying about him," Inchcape said. They threaded their way among the cars, which were parked at haphazard angles on the cracked mud plain of the barnyard. It was an eclectic assortment, made up of great long American sedans and station wagons and lift-kitted four-by-fours with their knobbed all-terrain tires, musclecars and work trucks covered with dust. There was a county sheriff's car, a late-model Chevy Caprice with bubble lights on top and a scatter-gun clamped to the dashboard, which Goody figured must belong to the jailer, John Faktor.

"Probably they're all waiting on us," Inchcape said. He picked up his pace, and Goody stumbled against the bumper of a cherry Nova SS. He muttered a curse.

"Move just like a cat, don't you," Inchcape said, appraising him with narrowed eyes.

"It's dark," Goody said, but Inchcape wasn't listening. He stood examining a loose row of gleaming motorcycles heeled up on their kickstands near the barn door. The warped rectangle of light that spilled from the barn picked out chrome detail-work on all the bikes: extended tailpipes, motor covers etched with the Harley-Davidson logo, long graceful front forks and shiny narrow fenders. A few notes of mournful music escaped from the barn. He heard a few voices, mostly men's.

"Them fairy-boy bikers," Inchcape said to Goody in a stage whisper, motioning toward the motorcycles. He held an open hand to his mouth as though to shield his words from other listeners. More loudly he said, "Sometimes they bring money with them, and some-times they don't."

Goody pushed past him into the barn. The space under the curved metal ceiling seemed enormous, filled with light and smoke and moving bodies. A crowd of men gathered around a bar. It was made from sheets of splintery plywood set up on sawhorses, and a squat, barrel-chested fellow handed out warm beers and pint liquor bottles and packs of Camels that had no tax stamp. He made change from the deep front pocket of the canvas apron that he wore. A couple of men in expensive clothes—narrow silk neckties and jackets of an exotic cut, despite the heat—stood not far from the bar. They were deep in conversation, pulling from time to time at the bottles of beer that they held. They looked out of place, and slightly uncomfortable to be where they were.

In another part of the room, an old man sat atop a tall stool, plucking at a Dobro that he held cradled in his lap while several couples square-danced diffidently around him. They moved on a decking of raw pine boards, and every now and then one of them stumbled on the uneven surface or scraped a foot to free it of the sticky clinging sap that oozed from the planking. Though guided by no caller, they executed their patterns of circles and promenades with efficiency and little apparent joy. The women wore checked skirts held out stiffly by crinoline petticoats, and the men wore tall wide-brimmed hats. The old Dobro player cranked his head mechanically from side to side as he performed, and Goody saw revealed on one pass, partly hidden by his dark spectacles, the pale meniscus of one of his dead eyes. Some rough-looking men in leather jackets, who Goody figured were the bikers, leaned against a wall of the place, smoking and watching the dancers, their expressions serious.

"Who's this?" A great fat man hauled himself off a folding chair near the door and set himself squarely in front of Goody and Inchcape. He had loose, thick lips, and his small eyes were nearly lost in the doughy flesh of his face. He wore a Hawaiian shirt covered with pictures of orchids done in wild, unnatural colors, and a pair of pants that closed with a drawstring.

"Hey, Little Edgar," Inchcape said, pushing Goody forward for the fat man's inspection. "This here's my boy."

"And who the hell are you?" the man said, glaring at Inchcape.

Inchcape gulped, seemingly at a loss for an answer. "Hell, you know me, Little Edgar," he said finally.

"Oh," Little Edgar said, without enthusiasm. "It's old Inchcape. I like to didn't recognize you there for a minute."

"That's okay," Inchcape said. "I disremember my own self every now and then, it seems like."

Little Edgar looked Goody up and down. "Is this your fighter?" he asked Inchcape, who nodded. "He don't look nearly big enough to be a fighter, does he? I thought maybe it was your grandbaby or something that you were bringing up here."

"He's plenty big," Inchcape said. Little Edgar grunted and waddled off. He moved with a queer shuffling gait, his broad flat feet turned out at angles as though his hips pained him. A couple of other men had come over to where Inchcape and Goody stood. One of the pair was tall and well proportioned; the other was stockier, with a slick shaved head over which he was continually running his hands. Faktor. "Hey, Mr. Tannhauser," Inchcape said in a low voice to the tall man. He began to edge past the pair, and Goody followed him, sticking close. "Hey, Sheriff."

Faktor put a restraining hand on Goody's arm. "Heavenly days, Inchcape, what is it you've brought us?" he said. Goody noticed that he wore a pistol cinched high up on his right hip. "I know you," the sheriff said to Goody. "I'll place you here in a minute."

Tannhauser laughed. He was wearing a tight shirt of some material that shone all over with soft highlights, and fawn-colored trousers. His clothes fit him as though they had been tailored to his body. Goody resisted an urge to reach out and feel the cloth. "We thought you weren't coming, Inchcape," Tannhauser said. He had a pleasant voice.

"I came," Inchcape said. "Just got a little bit of a late start is all. When I say I'm coming, I'm coming."

"Well," Tannhauser said. "When you lost so bad so often. How do you keep it up, I wonder?"

Inchcape looked down, said something about *ringers* under his breath. Tannhauser and Sheriff Faktor just watched him. Their attitude was not friendly, but it was not unfriendly either. Behind them, in the middle of the barn, a ring about twenty-five feet on a side had been marked out with bales of straw. A couple of kids in sweat clothes slapped recklessly at each other inside it. A few men watched them, making catcalls and yelling out what sounded to Goody like insults.

"What's this?" Goody asked Inchcape, gesturing toward the kids. One of them took a hesitant round kick at the other, and his foot sailed sloppily over his opponent's shoulder. The other kid made a rough footsweep and dropped the kicker on his rear.

Inchcape didn't answer. Tannhauser shook his head. "Opening card," he said. "Some of these little jerks think they're kick-boxers. They've seen too many movies." The kids in the ring were at it again, but most of the hecklers had drifted off and were watching the dancers or standing at the bar.

"No one said anything about kicking," Goody said.

"Don't worry, nobody's going to kick you. Say, you want a drink?" Tannhauser asked Goody.

"I need to use the toilet is what I really want," Goody said.

The sheriff said, "There's a set of jakes out back. Or you can just go anywhere out there. Little Edgar's not particular."

Goody started for the rear of the barn, where a door led out into darkness. "You ever fight before? Professionally, I mean," Sheriff Faktor asked him as he walked away.

Goody paused to answer. "I had some bouts various places. None in this county, though."

"Do any good?"

"I was sixteen and oh." Goody considered telling them about the man that he had killed in the ring but decided that they would not be impressed.

"That's okay, then," Tannhauser said. He and the sheriff were nodding at each other. Inchcape stood apart from them, a hangdog look on his face. "That makes the fight better. You'll maybe stay upright a little while. Some of those guys Inchcape keeps bringing, they topple right over on their faces at the first and never get up again until the fight's finished."

"I'll be back in a minute," Goody said.

"Don't worry," Sheriff Faktor called after him. "We won't start without you."

Goody crossed the wide sawdust floor of the barn. When he passed the two boys in the ring, they were clinched, shoving each other back and forth across the space. There was no referee to separate them, and they seemed unlikely to do it themselves, so Goody climbed over the musty straw bales into the ring with them. He put his hands on their shoulders. "Break," he said.

Surprised, they looked up at him. Their faces were very much alike, features blunt and square in the shadowless light from the lamps overhead. They were pretty nearly the same size, had the same athletic build. Goody wondered if they were brothers. "What?" one of them said. The other one blinked. They had stopped shoving.

"Break," Goody said again. He slapped them on the back. "Let go of each other. This isn't how you do it."

The boys relaxed their grip, and they stood apart with something like relief. They wore no gloves, and their hands were wound with strips of tape that looked cruelly tight to Goody. One of them had a little smear of blood on the white tape around his right hand, and the other boy wore a small drying trickle of the stuff under one nostril, like half a mustache.

"Okay," Goody said. "Now go to your corners." When they looked baffled, he pointed out a corner to each. "Go over there and sit down a while. Take a breather." They did it. "Good job," he said to them. "Now, when you're ready, come out fighting. None of this hugging stuff." He laughed and left the ring, the two kids breathing raggedly and watching each other behind him.

He walked out of the barn, and it took his eyes a few moments to adjust to the gloom. When he had accustomed himself to the low light, Goody made out several structures shaped roughly like telephone booths or like large refrigerators standing in a short row. The jakes. Two of them were blue fiberglass Port-O-Sans and the third was made from unfinished boards. He strode to the nearest chemical toilet and put his hand to the latch on the door. He heard a soft moaning and took a couple of seconds to verify that it came from the john where he stood. He listened, prepared to go to another. The moaning went on, and it was definitely edged with pain now. Goody rapped on the door. "You all right in there?"

The moaning stopped. The person in the toilet shouted, "Go the hell away!"

"I just wanted to make sure you're okay," Goody said. "The sound."

"Can't you go away?" the occupant wanted to know. There was a note of pleading in his voice. "Just leave me be."

"Sure," Goody said. "I never wanted to bother you."

"Well, you are," the occupant said, "whether you meant to or not."

Goody moved down to the next in the line of jakes, the second Port-O-San. Finding the door closed, he was disinclined to knock in order to find out whether it was in use. He passed on to the third, the wooden one. Its door stood slightly ajar. He passed inside and pulled it shut behind him. It did not latch, but rather wedged itself closed in the doorframe. The interior had a less permeable quality of dark than the outside. A diffuse glow penetrated the cracks and fissures of the walls, and that was all. Goody waited for the light to pick out details in the cubicle, for his eyes to become further sensitized, but no such thing happened. He unzipped his jeans and shuffled his feet delicately in front of him, hoping that they would encounter something, some sign of the hole that he knew must be there. They did not.

His need was urgent, and the odor of the jakes was monstrous. It spoke to him of maggots and rot and Billy Rugg's corpse. He found himself shaking his legs as he urinated, holding his feet off the ground one after the other to make sure that nothing was crawling up them. The chinks in the privy walls admitted planes of light that bisected the stream of his piss. He could hear the hollow sound of it sprinkling unseen wood. He seemed to urinate forever. When he was finished, he left the outhouse, casting an uneasy glance at the first one in the row of them. Its door was still closed, and Goody thought he could make out a thin moaning sound emanating from it. He hurried back to the barn.

The kids were gone from the ring when he got there, and the dancers had congregated at the bar. The blind man sat astride his stool, but he had stopped playing the Dobro. Somebody had given him a bottle of beer, and he raised it to his lips and drank. The Adam's apple bobbed in his skinny throat, and sizable air bubbles rose through the amber liquid. He lowered the bottle and smacked his lips, seeming to look straight at Goody through his black glasses. He belched mildly. Goody sought out Inchcape.

"When do we get to work?" he said. He cupped his right hand inside his left, cracking the knuckles, limbering the hand up.

"Listen," Inchcape said. "I don't want you getting a sudden attack of the nervous stomach in the ring or nothing. I don't want you laying down on the job."

"Why would I do that?" Goody asked.

Inchcape eyed him suspiciously. "It's been known to happen," he said.

"What's been known to happen?" Faktor asked, draping an arm over Inchcape's shoulders and the other over Goody's. "What are you all talking about so seriously here before the big fight?" His breath carried the scent of beer.

"Mr. Inchcape's just reminding me that I need to put up a quality fight," Goody said.

"Oh, you will," Faktor said, and his tone was breezy. "I know you will." He applied pressure to the arm that was hooked around Goody. "Did you find the toilet out there okay, good buddy?" he said. Before Goody could reply that he had, Faktor said, "So, what do you think of our little facility?"

Goody was momentarily at a loss for words. Then he said, "Well, I've fought in worse places. Some better, and some worse."

"Sure you have," Faktor said. He made a little feint with his left

hand in Goody's direction, but Goody stood passive. The sheriff
seemed disappointed that he hadn't made more of a reaction. "You
wouldn't know it to look," Faktor said, gesturing around him, "but
this place has a history to it. Jack Dempsey fought some exhibition
bouts here. He fought three local guys, two rounds apiece. He was
passing through the area and thought he'd make a little extra cash.
You never saw anything like Dempsey, and I haven't either. They say
he could have taken on those guys all three at once, he was that
tough. They never stood in a ring before with anybody like him."

"And never did again, I bet you," Tannhauser said. He had come
up to them while Faktor was talking.

"That wasn't here," Inchcape said.

The sheriff nodded. "Not here exactly," he said. "Not this building. That was a wooden grandstand about half a mile away. They
called it the Palace. It was built in a little hollow, what they call a
natural amphitheater. It had split logs for benches. Split logs raised
on planks."

Inchcape said, "It burned."

"To the ground," Faktor said. "I wasn't around then, but Edgar
Musser was. His dad ran the place. Old Man Musser died in the fire,
along with a bunch of other people from around here. They say a
fellow that was mad at Musser poured kerosene all over the timbers
of the stands and lit them up during a big fight. There was folks
climbing on each other's backs to get out of there, but they bottled
up at the door and a mess of them suffocated. They say it was that
ninny Floyd Askins set the fire, over money he had lost on a dogfight
the night before. Floyd liked to bet on the fights: dog, man, chicken,
whatever. He'd of bet on a catfight if they ever held such a thing. Old
Man Musser pulled a pistol at the end and started shooting people to
get them out of his way. He never made it out, though. I was just a
kid then. Were you hereabouts, Inchcape?" the sheriff asked.

"I was there. I was at the Palace that night."

"How come you ain't dead, then?"

"Not everybody died. I was out in the back getting a drink when
the whole place went up. I could see the fire rising. People climbed
the scaffolding of the stands like they were spiders. They hung up
there above the flames and then they dropped off when it got too hot
to breathe. By the time the bleachers collapsed, there was nobody left
on them."

"Did Little Edgar's daddy shoot people like they say? Trying to get out," Faktor asked.

"I heard some shots but I never did know where they come from. It might be it was just pine knots exploding in the fire. Still, you never know what a person will resort to when he craves to survive."

"So Dempsey fought up here," Goody said. "Anybody else famous?"

"Sonny Liston did," Inchcape said.

Faktor snorted. "He never."

Inchcape raised his chin a few degrees and went on. "Big black nigger with fists the size of a pot roast. He beat one man into a coma and then killed the man's brother when the brother climbed in the ring like a fool. They put the one dead brother in a pit in the woods and covered him with lime. When the other brother finally died, they put him in it too. The lime melted them away to nothing." Inchcape looked at Faktor defiantly, waiting for him to say it was a lie. The sheriff appeared not to notice his gaze. Inchcape said, "They tried to call this place the Palace when Little Edgar opened it up, but the name never took. It died with the old man."

"Little Edgar," Goody said. "That's the fat guy on the way in?"

"He wasn't always fat like that," Faktor said. "He was a track star in school, if you can feature that. Pole vault, standing broad jump, hundred-yard dash. He's still got a bunch of the old records in his name down at the high school. Edgar Musser. He didn't get fat until later."

"So what do they call it now?" Goody asked. When the other men looked puzzled, he said, "The place. The barn. If they don't call it the Palace."

Inchcape looked to Tannhauser, who shrugged. "Nothing, I guess," he said. "Everybody knows what you're talking about when you talk about it, so what use is it in a name?"

Tannhauser turned from them and bellowed toward the crowd around the bar. "Hey, Yukon," he shouted. "Get your ass over here." Inclining his head toward Goody, he said in a confidential tone, "That's my boy. I thought you'd want to meet him. You're going to go around and around with old Yukon. Wait'll you get a look at him."

The crowd of drinkers parted, and Yukon stepped over to where Goody and the other men were gathered. He was a tall man, half a head taller than Goody, broad across the shoulders and through the chest. He had a lengthy torso but a little bandy pair of legs. He wore his blond hair long, in the manner of television wrestlers. He had on a rough blue shirt, the seams of which strained against his biceps, and jeans and a pair of thick-soled brogans. He grinned as he approached, rolling his muscular shoulders. His grin broadened when he saw Goody.

"Whoa," he said. "Who's the pipsqueak?" Tannhauser and the sheriff grinned back at him. Inchcape seemed to want to vanish. He drew his head between his shoulders as though, turtlelike, he would pull it within his body altogether. To Sheriff Faktor, Yukon said, "He knows karate or savate or ju-jitsu, some shit like that, right?" He looked at Goody and laughed. "You got a club on you or what, bud?" he said.

"How much do you weigh?" Goody asked Yukon. When he got no answer, he turned to Inchcape. "How much does he weigh?" Inchcape said nothing.

"I go about two-ten," Yukon said finally. "Sometimes more, sometimes less. What do you care?"

"Well, Christ," Goody said, "I'm a cruiser-weight, maybe light-heavy if I eat a big dinner. You've got forty pounds on me."

The men around him were silent. Then the sheriff said, "He thinks he's in the Madison Square Garden, I guess."

Tannhauser said, "Marquis of Queensberry's rules are what he wants."

Yukon said, "Pussy." He had something tattooed on the backs of his hands, a pair of words. They looked like prison tattoos to Goody, homemade, blue ink painstakingly worked under the skin with a heated needle. From where he stood, he couldn't make out what the tattoos said.

Inchcape drew Goody to one side. "You can take this guy," he said. He sounded unconvinced himself.

"You've got to be kidding," Goody said. "Look at him. I'll never get inside his reach."

"I've seen him fight. I'm glad it's him tonight. He's easy." Inchcape was hissing his words, desperate to convince. "Check out the legs. He's got no legs."

Goody looked. Yukon's legs were certainly slender and bowed, and uncommonly short. "No legs? You mean they're fake?"

"No, no." Inchcape shook his head. "I mean there's no meat on them. No muscle. I think he had polio or something when he was a kid."

"Polio? Do people still get polio?"

"Or something. Maybe it was rheumatic fever."

"Then it would be his heart that's bad. Rheumatic fever gets you in the ticker."

"It could of got his heart too. He could drop at any time, probably."

Goody considered. "All right," he said. "But if he's taking me apart in there, you throw in the towel." Inchcape looked at him without comprehension. "Give up. Surrender," Goody told him.

Inchcape nodded enthusiastically. "You bet," he said. "That's what we'll do. If it goes bad."

The two of them returned to Yukon and his backers. Sheriff Faktor said, "Here to default?"

Tannhauser pointed at Goody's face, at his scarred cheek and the welt on his nose. "Look at those scars," he said. "This boy's a fighter. He won't forfeit anything is my bet."

Yukon sniffed. "Scars just mean you got hit," he said. "Anybody can get hit." His own face was largely unmarked, his nose long and straight. Except for the legs, he was a handsome man.

"Let's get to it," Goody said.

Inchcape clapped him on the back. "That's my boy," he said. Tannhauser shrugged at Sheriff Faktor, the gesture meaning *What did I tell you?*

33

Tannhauser found Bodo near the bar. Bodo held a sweating bottle of beer in his hand, but he appeared not to have drunk very much. Toma was nowhere to be seen, and that made Tannhauser feel a little better. Toma was twitchy, his hand always hovering, it seemed, near the pistol that he wore concealed under his suit coat. It was best that Toma not be a part of the upcoming conversation.

"Looks like we're set," Tannhauser said, forcing his voice into a facsimile of friendliness. "The fight'll be starting here anytime. The fellows have just got to change into their fighting togs. I met the guy that Yukon will be tearing up. He seems pretty sturdy, so it might get exciting."

"Fine," Bodo said. He lit a cigarette, took a swallow of his beer.

"Listen," Tannhauser said, "now that we've got a minute alone, there's a couple of things I'd like to discuss with you." He moved closer to Bodo, as though to shield him from the crowd and protect their conversation.

"There are a couple of things I need to bring up with you as well," Bodo said. "I too have been waiting for the correct moment. Is this it, then?"

Tannhauser grinned. "I can bet they're the same things."

"Possibly."

"You believe you're pretty cagey, you two foreign guys, you Europeans, but I can tell what you're thinking."

"Europeans?"

"Well, aren't you? From the way you dress, the way you talk and all, it was what I figured."

Bodo smiled. "Toma and I like to think of ourselves as transnationals. Or rather, as supranationals, if you see what I mean."

Tannhauser didn't indicate whether he saw or not. He said, "I've been watching you real closely, keeping my eyes open. We're not necessarily all dummies over here, whatever you may think."

"Of course not."

"You're wondering," Tannhauser said, eager to go on now that he had begun, "why you haven't seen any marijuana since you've been at El Dorado. Why I've not so far taken you on a tour of the patches out in the woods around the compound. I've been promising a lot but not, so far as you can tell, delivering. You're beginning to get worried about your investment, both past and future. Is that right?"

"The question has crossed my mind. From time to time."

Tannhauser took a long breath, and then another. Bodo waited, patient on the surface, for the explanation. He took another mouthful of beer, another drag on the contraband cigarette.

"The crop has failed," Tannhauser said at last. He made the pronouncement all in a breath, quickly as though it were one word, and it took Bodo a moment to separate the syllables from one another, to sort out their meaning in his mind, despite the fact that he had expected some statement very much like it. "There'll be a harvest, as promised, but it will be—" Tannhauser paused, as though searching for an appropriately descriptive word. "Minimal."

Bodo pitched his cigarette to the floor and ground it beneath the sole of his soft leather shoe. It smoldered in the damp sawdust. He put his hand in his pocket and found there the cool solid weight of the chandelier crystal. As the pilot had predicted, its sharp edges were quickly eating away the lining of his pocket. He fingered the collection of raveling threads, ran his nails across the faces of the crystal teardrop. His voice was calm when he spoke. "We'll be departing, Toma and I, immediately we arrive at the compound. You will see to it that the armaments we brought are returned to the airplane."

"Wait a damn second," Tannhauser said. "Hear me out."

"Promises, Mr. Tannhauser," Bodo said. He shook his head. "You may consider our participation in your little venture withdrawn, effective immediately. The experiment is at an end."

"Hang on there, Bodo. We've just gotten on an operational footing, and this is a temporary setback. Something in the soil we didn't count on, the variety of seed, some weakness in the strain. Most of the plants failed to germinate at all. And those that did, the majority of them aren't growing anything like they should. Next year, next harvest—"

"Will bloom, or will not, without our support. We do not contribute aid to charities. I thank you for your candor, Mr. Tannhauser. Now I would like to see your friend Yukon fight. To the death, is it? Or just for money?"

Tannhauser moved in on Bodo, his face mottled with rage. Bodo took a step away, but Tannhauser grabbed a fold of his shirtfront in a large fist and drew him back. Bodo looked around for Toma, who was nowhere to be seen. "Now listen here, you goddamn wog," Tannhauser said.

"Wog?" Bodo was bewildered. "I'm not a wog, unless I misunderstand the meaning of the term." Tannhauser shook him. Bodo was shocked by the sheer physical strength of the man. The crowd around them began to notice the altercation and to draw closer.

"The crop failed, that's right, but do you know why it failed?" Tannhauser gritted his teeth. "Do you have the least, the vaguest, the *faintest* idea why?" Bodo shook his head. Tannhauser seemed to regain some control. Noticing the people around them, the citizens in their square-dancing clothes and the bikers in their leathers, he released Bodo's shirt. When he spoke again, his voice was low. "Because there's something up there, something in the land that killed it. Something buried. And I've puzzled it out. I know what it is."

"The former inhabitants seemed to be able to grow what they liked," Bodo pointed out. "In fact, before you made your management change, your takeover, they were turning quite a tidy little profit. We were beginning to take an interest in them some time before we heard of you. Frankly, you seem to have destroyed a thriving industry with your unorthodox methods."

"Forget the hippies, will you," Tannhauser said. "Forget the dope. We're talking about something completely different here. We're talking about bigger game."

"Indefensible methods," Bodo said.

"Will you forget that?" Tannhauser was nearly choking on his rage and frustration. "That's done. What you've got to know is, there's a ship buried deep in the mountain up there. A ship, and it's poisoning the soil."

"A ship? You mean a boat of some sort."

"I don't, and you know I don't."

"Noah's Ark, perhaps?"

"I mean a spaceship. A life-carrying vessel from beyond the stars. It crash-landed up there I don't know how many hundreds of years ago. I know about it. I've done research. Indian legends tell it. The trees were laid down flat for miles around. A flash of light, the intense killing light of a nuclear explosion. They thought the world had come to its end. I know it all."

"You're out of your mind," Bodo said. "Plainly. Must I listen to more of this tripe?"

"It crashed, and it poisoned the land, and nothing that grows up there now is normal. All of it's distorted, mutated, changed. It's a kind of radiation. We have to mount a huge excavation. Dig our way down to it, uncover it, discover its secrets. Listen to me. Since I started looking for this thing, others, powerful others, have taken an interest in it as well. They're preparing to come for it, to usurp the work I've already done, elbow me out and destroy me. Do you understand? Are you listening? Do you hear what I'm telling you? I've got to fight."

"These forces that you mention. They are—?"

"The National Guard. The Army. The FBI, NSA, CIA. The whole damned intelligence alphabet. They've sent out spies, feelers, helicopters to circle around, satellites to take photographs, and the big push comes next. Shock troops. Commandos dressed in black cat suits, hoods over their heads, with only slits for eyes. Combat knives. Blowguns. Piano-wire garrotes. A full-scale assault. We've got to be prepared."

"Spies." Bodo felt trapped, cornered, in this room full of strangers. He spotted Toma, finally, in conversation with a great fat man to whom Bodo had been introduced early on in the evening but whose name, whose function, he could not recall. He motioned that Toma should join them.

"That's right, Bodo. Spies." Tannhauser leaned close to Bodo, peering at him, examining him minutely. "They've attempted to infiltrate, but so far I've managed to foil them. I believe I have. They've

devised a race of synthetic men to dwell among us and to learn
everything that we know."

Toma reached them, pushing through the edges of the crowd,
which had begun to thicken near the ring in expectation of the fight's
beginning. He had a worried look on his face. He heard this last, and
his expression of concern increased. He was on the edge of taking
some action. When he approached Bodo, Tannhauser moved to block
him. Bodo made a motion with his hands, a subtle signal that Toma
read as *Stay close, but don't interfere unless absolutely necessary.*
Toma hung back.

"These synthetic men," Bodo said. "They derive from the organi-
zations you mentioned, or from the extraterrestrial ship?"

Tannhauser smiled, a crafty smile. "That's a good question. From
one or from the other. Does it matter? And who's to say? The end
result is the same. They're among us, and we have to take steps to
ensure that we succeed and they don't."

"You're making poor decisions, Mr. Tannhauser. You might want
to take up another line of work."

"They're beautifully made, the synthetic men. You have to admire the craftsmanship. They've been around for years, in one variety or another. At times it seems like they're all I've known, that
everyone around me was one. There are probably some of them here
tonight, in this crowd. You don't know. You can't know, because it's
impossible to tell the difference between them and us, unless you've
learned the way how. And it's not an easy way. There is no easy way.
They've got wires made to look just like human nerves, insulation
that looks like skin. A computer made out of spongy material to
simulate the brain, steel that is just like bone. But there's one thing
that they haven't been able to synthesize yet, though I know they're
working on it, and that's the human heart. When they get that, we're
done for.

"In the chest of each synthetic man there's a little bellows, a little
gray plastic bellows that runs and runs and keeps the coolant—coolant just like blood, identical in every important respect—flowing." In
the vicinity of the ring, a great clanging, the fight timer's bell, commenced. Tannhauser did not pause in his tirade. "To know the difference, you have to tear them down. You have to shred your way
through the fake skin, strip it away, flay them with combs of iron,
straight through the fake bones, fake nerves, destroy it, melt it with
fire, climb straight on into the chest cavity, slash your way to the

heart. It takes a strong man to do it. Then, and only then, can you know the true nature of the subject."

Toma said, "The fight. Bodo?" When Bodo stepped past Tannhauser to go to the center of the barn, the big man made no move to stop him. He was breathing heavily with the exertion of his speech. He stood staring at the spot that Bodo had vacated.

"Are you synthetic, Bodo?" he asked. "Are you synthetic, or are you a living, breathing man?" No answer. Toma and Bodo disappeared into the crowd. "I know why you're leaving. I know," Tannhauser said. And then, loudly, so that everyone in the barn turned to look at him for a moment, "I know about you! I know exactly what you are, even if you don't!"

34

When he asked where he could change out of his street clothes and into his trunks, Goody was pointed back to the jakes again. He chose to disrobe in the shadow of the barn near the toilets, rather than inside one of them. He leaned against the building with one hand to pry his boots off, and the cool tin side of the structure gave slightly beneath his palm. After removing the boots, he stood straight again, and the metal uncrimped with a hollow booming sound. Yukon followed him out into the barnyard, and Goody tensed himself for trouble. Then he saw that Yukon also carried trunks and tennis shoes. Yukon said to him, "They tell me your name's Goody." Goody nodded. "What's that?" Yukon asked, smiling. "Some kind of a cookie?" He laughed and made for the first of the jakes.

"I wouldn't go in there if I was you," Goody called out. Yukon jerked open the door of the toilet, which was empty. "There was somebody in there a while ago," Goody said. "When I came out here before." Yukon went into the enclosure without looking at him.

Goody unzipped his jeans and pulled them off, stripped out of his shirt and undershorts. The dirt of the barnyard was fine and warm under the soles of his feet. He shifted them in the dust, sifting it through his bare toes. He did an impromptu little dance, enjoying the unaccustomed feel of his nakedness. Inside the barn, the blind man had taken up his Dobro again and was at work grinding out a mournful ballad. Goody hardened the muscles of his body against the night air, enjoying the play of light from the barn doorway on his skin.

In eighth grade, Goody had seen pictures of men who fought in the nude. An English teacher showed them to his class, telling the students that most of the people in these slides were Greeks, they were the original Olympians. They were statues made of marble, the men in those pictures, and they huddled over one another, held each other, twisted arms and legs and necks to gain advantage, but to judge from the look of their smooth bland faces it was all an exercise without pain.

Goody watched, fascinated, and the breath caught in his throat to see their grace. He thought of himself on the football field in his clumsy pads and the helmet that squeezed the sides of his head and muffled his hearing, of the faceguard that obscured his vision; or crowded with a lot of other boys on the smelly wrestling mats in the gym, in his headgear and mouthpiece and the ill-fitting, evil-smelling wrestling uniform that was like an old-fashioned bathing costume. These men in the slides fought without obstruction or impediment. They were able to see clearly; in picture after picture, their vision was fixed on some distant horizon point. What was happening there, where they looked? Maybe the gods were fighting. Even the faces of the defeated Olympians were unperturbed and beautiful.

By the fifth or sixth slide, the girls around Goody started to giggle and whisper together, and he grew uncomfortable with the larger-than-life figures thrown in such bright colors against the white classroom wall. Still, he couldn't take his eyes from them. He heard little of what the teacher was telling them, about the warrior spirit, about shields on which corpses were borne back in honor, about democratic forms of government. In the back of the darkened room, some of the boys laughed and then shouted, "Faggots!"

The teacher (what had his name been? Goody couldn't remember) tried to go on with his lecture. The disturbance in the back of the room continued to grow, and soon he switched the lights on. The boys back there, Goody's teammates, chanted "Faggot, faggot," in unison, and they directed it at the teacher. He came down the rows of student desks, past Goody, who sat unmoving in his seat. The teacher was a small neat man in a tweed jacket with leather patches at the elbows, high forehead gleaming with sweat, light from the overhead fluorescent light panels flashing off the lenses of his little round glasses. He went straight to the two biggest malefactors, a pair of oversize brothers named Tuggle.

He took the Tuggles by the backs of their necks and lifted with a surprising strength, and they came up out of their seats like unwilling puppets. The desk of the larger of them went over with a bang, spilling the couple of schoolbooks the Tuggle carried with him, some comics, a chewed pencil, a round canister of wintergreen snuff which spun on the floor for a moment and then came to rest against a fat red gum eraser. The teacher said he would bash the Tuggles' skulls together if they continued to struggle against him. He was trembling, and he hissed his words, little flecks of spittle striking the Tuggles and causing them to flinch. "You can't do that," someone said to him, some better friend of the Tuggles' than Goody. The teacher smiled, a grisly smirk that stretched slowly over his features. Goody thought that the Tuggles had gone too far this time, and that the teacher was going to go too far as well. The Tuggles were the size of full-grown men, but their limbs gangled loosely from their torsos; they hadn't developed the coordination that would allow them to pit themselves against an adult.

"Let us go, you homo," the smaller Tuggle said. He was nearly blubbering. The teacher didn't look back but propelled the Tuggles out of the room and down the hall. One of them bleated out "Queer bait" and the other managed an unintelligible syllable, and then they were all three gone.

But the last slide was still there on the wall, pale in the wash of overhead light. It was a detail from a Roman frieze, though Goody did not learn that fact until later, and in it two nude muscular men faced each other, rigid and unreal in their proportions. They were not wrestling but standing apart, their hands wrapped in iron-studded leather bands. One of them was in the act of striking the other. His open hand connected with the jaw of his opponent. They were not wrestlers. They were boxers.

The boxers stayed fixed in their place until one of the class pets, the one who always ran the film projector and the overhead transparency projector and the record player and the slide projector, shut the lamp down, taking that frozen image with it. The class clapped when the picture flickered and then vanished. They all applauded, except for Goody.

He dug his heels into the ground and flexed his leg muscles, curled his arms up and held the hands in front of him. He jabbed, ducked, jabbed, cut the empty air with his fists. His clothes were forgotten beside him.

Yukon emerged from the toilet, the bundle of his clothing and his brogans in one hand. He had a gaudy red robe thrown over his substantial shoulders, and his long hair was caught up behind his neck in a wide rubber band. He stood regarding Goody in silent disbelief for a moment, shaking his head. He said, "Get a move on, peckerwood," and trudged into the barn, where he was met with a smattering of applause and a few cheers and whistles. Goody listened for razzing but heard none.

He stooped and groped around him, pulling on his jockstrap and his cotton shorts. Something fluttered from the pocket of his shorts to the ground. He picked it up. A scratch-off ticket. The picture of a pig was printed on it. He tucked the ticket back into the pocket from which it had come and slipped his feet into the canvas tennis shoes that he wore to fight in. He had no robe. When he looked for his boots, he could find only one. He spent a few moments looking for the other, turning short circles in the dust, knowing that the boot was in plain sight, had to be, but evading his gaze somehow. He finally found it, half in and half out of the light. He proceeded into the barn, where Mr. Inchcape and Edgar Musser and Sheriff Faktor and Tannhauser expected him; where the crowd gathered; where, above all, Yukon awaited him, massive arms cocked, fists held ready.

There were brief introductions to the crowd, which milled listlessly outside the straw-bale barrier. The man in the canvas apron, the bartender, called Yukon a champion, and Yukon held his arms up over his head, making twin victory signs. The bartender asked Goody his name, and Goody told him, telling it to him again when the man looked confused. The bartender repeated it to the crowd and moved off to stand among them. Goody had thought the man would serve as referee, but there was apparently not to be a referee. Goody was used to that. It was okay with him.

A man with a tire iron in one hand, the timer, rang a dinner triangle and suddenly Yukon was there, rushing across the ring, windmilling his fists, pressing Goody from the start. He threw a series of haymakers, none of which connected solidly, chipping away instead at Goody's arms and shoulders. Goody tucked his chin in, covered up, and moved away from the big man, backing, using his longer legs to stay outside of the sweep of Yukon's crushing arms, his idea to keep Yukon leaning forward, just off-balance, his center of gravity somewhere five or six inches ahead of his toes.

The crowd was largely quiet. From time to time someone shouted Yukon's name, and there was always the hum of conversation from the rear of the loose circle of watchers. As he retreated, forcing Yukon to the outside of his orbit, Goody kept an eye peeled for Mr. Inchcape, but he couldn't find him among the unfamiliar faces. Tannhauser was there at ringside, sitting in a folding chair looking perturbed, and Goody saw Sheriff Faktor moving through the crowd, talking and gesturing. He seemed excited. For a second, Goody thought he saw Wallace Claymaker's profile, and involuntarily he searched for a glimpse of Dreama.

While Goody watched the crowd, distracted, Yukon caught him with one of those wide looping punches. His fist smashed into Goody's left cheek, and Goody tasted blood as the teeth on that side cut the soft flesh of the inside of his mouth. Their hands were tightly taped; they weren't wearing gloves. The rough adhesive strip left a burn on Goody's face, and two of Yukon's knuckles split and bled.

Goody tottered from the impact of Yukon's fist, and the air around him seemed to sparkle briefly. Yukon, drawing himself back for a second blow, the finisher, moved in a cocoon of light. Through an effort of will, Goody righted himself and covered up. For just a second, he saw the underside of Yukon's jaw, the sharp point of the mandible, the skin there stubble-covered and pale beneath the hair. Yukon was exposed, not screening himself as he ought to have been doing, and Goody readied his hand, the big right hand. All of his knockouts had come from that hand, the correct use of it, and he had broken the china-fragile metacarpals and the bones of his fingers nearly every time he used it.

He eyed the window in Yukon's defenses, the narrow space between the hairy over-developed arms where his fist would go, perfectly placed and perfectly timed, released from its protective station near his collarbone and launched like an arrow, like a missile, the body following in the arm's trajectory, putting a deadly momentum behind it. Yukon would reel. Yukon might fall. But if he didn't? Goody saw the opening widen slightly and then abruptly close as Yukon guessed where Goody's attention was focusing. Goody shook his head, cursing, swearing that he would keep his eyes from the crowd.

Yukon was sure of himself, grinning, and he came at Goody all stops out, throwing hook after hook, not inflicting much damage but not discouraged. Goody stepped back and then snapped a left jab at Yukon's upper arm, driving his knuckles into the solid flesh of the biceps. Wear the arms down. That was where Yukon's advantage lay, in the power and reach of his arms. The jab made contact, and Yukon looked surprised. He had not known that the little man could punch. Goody jabbed again, and again, peppering Yukon with a series of strikes, the upper arms, the neck, the temples. He popped away at Yukon, and the crowd pressed forward against the bales. Goody pushed Yukon until the big man was leaning awkwardly backward over the straw boundary, practically in the crowd himself, almost a spectator.

There were faces all around Yukon's, like flowers in some bizarre arrangement, and when Goody swatted Yukon in the right eye, a little blood flew from his knuckles and spattered a woman, one of the gingham-clad square-dancers. She was leaning down and shouting in Yukon's ear, shrieking at him. "Get him, get up and get him," she screamed. She wiped absently at the pinpoints of blood on her cheek, and the stuff came away on her fingers, mixed with the black smear of her mascara. The boys, the amateur fighters from the early part of the evening, were there too, watching the action but with little apparent interest. Goody completed the volley of blows, snapping the left hand out, and Yukon sat down on a square bale. Dust puffed up from under him, and short pieces of straw. His mouth hung open with surprise, and Goody closed it with a careful right. He prepared to put Yukon away.

The bell rang the close of the round. Goody didn't believe it and prepared to press his lead, but Yukon's handlers, Tannhauser and Sheriff Faktor and some others, fans, pulled the stricken fighter away to his corner. The timer, who had his metal triangle set up near Goody's corner, ran his tire tool vigorously around the inside of it. The triangle clashed and clanged, and the sound of it echoed among the steel rafters of the barn. A couple of swifts, disturbed by the din, left their nests and darted on knife-sharp wings along the curve of the roof, finally finding the door and departing into the night.

Goody retired to his corner. He sat and listened to the hubbub around him, looking for Inchcape and failing to find him. The bikers were gathered behind him, and they talked quietly, their leather clothes creaking, sounding as though it was a group of saddlehorses back there. They conversed for a while, and then one of them came forward. He tapped Goody on the shoulder. When Goody didn't turn, the biker poked him again, more insistently this time. Goody swung around to face him.

The biker was a large man with a beard. Under his jacket he wore a black T-shirt imprinted with the Harley logo and the words *Born to Ride.* "Hey," he said, "is this guy just warming up on you or what?" Goody said nothing. The biker continued. "Because we heard he was really something, superstrong, but he's not showing us much. We thought he'd take you apart first thing."

"It's still pretty early in the fight," Goody said. "Just the end of the first round is all." Reconsidering his response, he said, "But I don't think he'll take me apart. I think I'll hold him off. I'll drop him if I can just wear him down some."

The Harley driver grinned regretfully. "Sure," he said. "But you know what they say. A good big man'll beat a good little man every single time." Goody didn't have a reply. "Anyway, we just wanted to know," the biker said. "We've got other places we could be, if it ain't going to get exciting pretty quick."

"I don't think he's got any surprises for me," Goody said. "I think we've seen everything he's got. No technique."

The biker went back to his cronies. "He says that's all there is," the biker told them, and they muttered discontentedly among themselves.

Round two and the crowd was insulting Goody, shouting at Yukon to catch him, catch him and break his neck. Goody backpedaled around the ring. Yukon slammed him twice in quick succession, bone-rattling shots, one to the head and one to the ribs. He had a slow swing but he was powerful when he connected. He didn't get overconfident when he made contact. Goody had taught him something, frightened him in the first round, and now Yukon was careful. Goody could feel his battered ribs creak with each breath.

A thread of blood trickled down the bridge of his nose, leaking from a cut on his forehead, but it didn't run into his eyes. He continued to watch for another opening. When he looked at Yukon, he felt hot. He ceased to want to move away, but he knew he couldn't go toe to toe with the stronger man and so he kept moving. "Okay," he said, to keep himself going. "Okay." Less than six minutes in the ring and already he was tired. Out of shape. Out of training. It was like six hours anywhere else, doing any other kind of back-breaking work.

Just beyond the reach of Goody's fists, Yukon slouched like an ape. He was talking to himself as well. His mouth moved, his thin lips twisted. "Cookie," he said, or something like it. His eyes were glazed. Goody tried not to laugh at what it sounded like Yukon was saying, tried to concentrate on Yukon's feet as the big man shuffled forward. Yukon's feet were small, like his legs, and he telegraphed everything with them. He set himself up solid before he struck a blow. He had no footwork. Goody could cap a man with no footwork, but he had to tire him out first.

Yukon lurched forward and Goody skipped back once again. He came near the ring barrier, and rough hands reached out and clutched him. He was surprised to feel them against his sweat-slick skin. He shook them off, striking back into the crowd with his elbows, and the hands fell away, but then they grabbed at him again, shoving him this time. "Get out there and fight, you dumb son of a bitch," somebody said, and a solid push to the middle of his back sent him stumbling into the center of the ring. He slipped and fell to one knee in the sawdust, catching himself with his right hand. He pushed himself to his feet, and Yukon was upon him.

Yukon hit him in the face, and through the haze of heat and shock from the blow he struck out in reply. Yukon grunted, swung. Goody knew that he could not move away from Yukon without suffering terrific punishment on the way out of the radius of Yukon's reach. He caught Yukon's blow against his injured ribs, countering as best he was able. The two men traded blows in the open ring, Goody relying always on his left hand, using his right only infrequently and cautiously, never finding the opening that he wanted. The skin of his hands opened and bled, and the skin of his forehead and his chest, over his bruised breastbone. His lips were split and swelling, and with one of Yukon's hammering blows he felt his left cheek give way. He wanted to scream but did not. Yukon came on strong. Goody refused to back down. His heart belted along, racing so that he could hardly breathe. He wondered where the bell could be, why it didn't ring. He felt his knees loosening, the joints turned to poorly packed sand, but he wouldn't let himself fall.

When the opening came, he almost failed to believe it. It seemed to happen very slowly. Yukon threw a careless hook at him and missed, and the momentum of his blow drew him sideways. He stood unsteadily, out of balance, at a right angle to Goody, his profile perfectly presented. Without thinking this time, Goody lashed out with his right hand.

He hit Yukon on the hinge of his jaw and forced the jaw back into the flesh of Yukon's neck, jamming the bone into the big bundle of nerves there. The stroke was a strong, clean one, and Goody felt elation sweep through him just as his hand broke. Yukon's jaw shattered as well, and the eye that Goody could see was wild, rolling in its socket. Then it turned up, showing only the white of the eyeball, and the lid closed down over it. Yukon tilted, slumped, fell full-length in the sawdust, the way a chest of drawers tossed from a window might fall. He didn't even put his hands out to catch himself.

Goody stood over his ruined opponent, sucking his breath painfully between his teeth, holding his right hand very still. When the timer began to rattle his triangle, Goody was not surprised. He went to his corner and sat on the scratchy straw, watching Tannhauser and the sheriff and some others gather around Yukon. They dragged him to his place, cursing him, exhorting him to pull himself together, shake it off. They poured a bucket of water over him.

Goody spat blood onto the sawdust and examined the way the wood chips clotted in the liquid. He stirred them around with his foot. It occurred to him to wonder again where Inchcape was, and why he had no corner man. He wanted water to rinse the terrible taste out of his mouth. He looked around, but no one offered to help him. He could hear them talking.

. . . couple of good exchanges in there. Real pretty . . .

Old Yukon used to could fight, but I don't know about him anymore.

. . . little skinny kids. It's them bantamweights do some damage, not these big old . . .

. . . watched on the tube the other . . .

*   *   *

When the bell rang for the third round, Yukon staggered into the ring like something risen from its grave. Goody couldn't believe what he was seeing. Yukon wagged his head back and forth, and his mouth was strangely set, the broken jaw sagging distinctly lower on one side than the other. Yukon made his way across the ring, and Goody dutifully rose to meet him.

When he was a yard or so away from Goody, Yukon threw an arm stiffly out. Goody sidestepped the blow and tapped Yukon on the ear with his unbroken hand. Yukon's head wobbled on his corded neck, and his extended hand dropped. He stood dumbly in the same spot, not attempting to preserve himself at all. He moved his wrecked mouth as though he were trying to say something. Goody said, "Jesus, Yukon, why don't you just sit your ass down?"

Yukon wheeled at the sound of Goody's voice. His eyes were shot through with streaks of blood, and they fixed their wavering gaze on some point well beyond Goody's figure. The flesh of his face was growing mottled from the beating he had taken. He struck out at Goody, who slipped the blow. His other fist took Goody in the midriff, and Goody's breath hooted out of him. His throat closed down, and he gagged dryly.

Yukon picked up speed, coming after Goody, who, bent and staggering, scooted as well as he was able away from him around the ring. Yukon threw simple combinations at him, most of which missed. The few punches that landed took their toll, though, and Goody felt the fight begin to slip away from him. One of his eyes was closed now, and he could feel the other beginning to swell. There was no one in his corner to slit the puffed flesh of his eyelids and give him some relief; no one in the barn that he could trust with a razor blade. He held his broken hand to his chest and fended off Yukon's crushing blows as best he could with his good one, his left, waiting for the round to end.

The fight finished swiftly in the fourth round. When the timer rang his triangle, Goody stood up from his seat and strode to the center of the ring. Yukon lumbered out to meet him. The two of them stood facing each other, swaying slightly. Yukon stared at Goody with pain-filled animal eyes. He took a great shuddering breath and prepared to renew his onslaught.

Goody hit him. The lefthanded blow took him in the middle of the forehead, and Yukon's head rocked back on his neck, tipped back until his ponytail hung straight down between his shoulder blades. His eyes dimmed, staring straight up into the dark spaces of the barn's vaulted roof. He stood that way momentarily, like a ship hesitating in unendurable equilibrium before it slides beneath the surface of the sea, and then he went down. He landed on his back, jaw hanging awkwardly loose, arms outstretched on either side of him. His muscled chest hitched, hitched again, and began a steady heaving, as though he were deeply asleep. The tape had unwound itself from around Yukon's hands, and Goody could make out the words imprinted there in sloppy script: KICK, read the letters on the back of the left hand and, partly obscured beneath the raveling band on the right, ASS. Kick ass. The tape was discolored with blotches of Goody's blood.

Goody drew his left hand back. He did not examine it. He had recognized the sound it made when it connected with the hard dome of Yukon's skull, and the shock of agony that had proceeded up his arm. It was broken. He crossed his fractured hands in front of his body and went to his corner and sat. He ignored the people rushing past him, pushing against him and against each other to get to the fallen Yukon, to touch him, to get a look at him, perhaps to dip their handkerchiefs in his blood. They were for the most part silent as they went to the spot where he lay, not bothering to shout at him or coax him. They knew that he was not going to rise to fight again.

35

Even before the fight ended, even as Goody was readying himself for that final blow to Yukon's battered head, Sheriff Faktor was on his way out of the arena, the lanky deputy following close behind him. The sheriff moved quickly for such a heavy man, not speaking until he had pushed his way through the crowd, which was pressing toward the ring, compacting itself against his progress; not speaking until he had made his way past the blind Dobro player, who sat plucking a quiet tune, seemingly for his own amusement; not speaking until he had left the barn behind, had passed through the ranks of vehicles and was seated behind the steering wheel of the county patrol car.

"Tonight," he said. For a while the deputy thought that the word was all the sheriff planned to give him, and the single word was enough. He knew what he had to do, the raid he had to prepare. Sheriff Faktor cranked the car to life, jerked it into gear, and executed a wide sliding turn near the barn door on his way out of the hollow. People were trickling out of the place already. The county car narrowly missed running down a couple of the motorcycle drivers, kicking a pall of dust over them as it passed. They swore and shook their fists, but Sheriff Faktor seemed not to notice.

As the cruiser rumbled down the corduroy road toward the valley, the deputy broke the silence, saying, "Tonight, then."

The sheriff said, "Did you see that punk taking Yukon to the cleaners? I lost some money on that little puke, and so did a bunch of folks. I'm surprised if Yukon isn't dead by now, or at least revisiting parts of his youth."

"His youth? What parts?"

"The parts where he didn't know how to talk and he couldn't go to the can by himself. What was his name again? The fellow that put the hurt on him."

"I don't recall," the deputy said. "Some of the people in the crowd were calling him Cookie, I heard, but I doubt if that could be right. Did you ever before hear tell of a fighter named Cookie? I never did."

"I heard of one named Coffee. They called him Instant, if you can feature that. Instant Coffee. Pretty decent fists on him, the time I saw him fight."

"But still. Cookie."

The sheriff grinned. "Tannhauser must be out of his mind. People used to say for a while, when he first came up here, that it wasn't just partners, him and Yukon. They said he was sweet on Yukon, though nobody ever said if Yukon returned the feeling or not. That Cookie fellow will be lucky to get out of there alive and in one piece."

"I don't think he's in such hot condition himself, either," the deputy said. "He looked like he was aching pretty bad by the end. So maybe he won't notice whatever they do to him so much."

"Oh, he'll notice all right. Tannhauser will make sure he notices."

They were silent again. The sheriff's concentration on the road before them sharpened momentarily, and then he relaxed again. "Thought I saw something," he said. "But it's just an old gas can somebody pitched into the weeds."

"I hate when people do that," the deputy said. "You'd think they could just hold on to their stuff a little while and haul it to the landfill and get rid of it that way, wouldn't you?"

Returning to his original thought, Faktor said, "So, it's tonight. Friend Cookie took out Yukon, so we got one less worry to deal with. Tannhauser will never think to look for us on his doorstep tonight, I bet."

"I guess not," the deputy said. "You looked like you were pretty good buddies in there. You looked like you were close as brothers."

"We are pretty good buddies. It's just he's put me in an awkward position, with this DEA man whizzing around. He'd never pack up and leave, so we've got to make a move against him." The sheriff rounded on the deputy. "Don't you ever think I enjoy this, hear? It pains me to have to do what we have to do. But sometimes you've just got to bite the bullet."

The deputy laughed. "Or somebody else does," he said.

"That's right. Which, by the way, makes me think: issue to every man as much ammunition as he can carry. From what Claymaker said, we may run into a real shitstorm up there at El Dorado. And tell them all this: after we're done with what we're doing, nobody, but nobody, lacking a county uniform walks out of there alive."

The deputy made a note, the pen bobbling over the page on his clipboard as they made their way along the rough road. Behind them, a cluster of independent headlights like one-eyed animals, the motorcycle gang, began to gain ground. When he had finished writing, the deputy looked up expectantly. "Anything else?" he asked.

"One more thing," Sheriff Faktor said. "Tell them I pay a bounty of five thousand dollars to the man that carries directly to me that cocksucker Tannhauser's head."

36

"Do you figure he's all right?" somebody asked.

"I don't know," somebody else said. Goody recognized the voice but failed to put a name to it. "I'm no doctor. He looks pretty bad."

"Not near as bad as old Yukon, though," the first man said. "He's in some hard shape. He looks like a slab of bad pork."

"Goddamn," the second man said. "Goddamn. I'd never of let Yukon fight if I knew it was going to turn out this way."

"You can't see this sort of thing coming. That's why it always takes you by surprise," the first man said.

Much of the fight crowd had dispersed. The bikers had hopped onto their hogs and ridden away, their exhausts roaring and popping like machine-gun fire. The square-dancers had followed, talking among themselves. Goody sat in his corner, hands crossed on his lap, head down, eyes closed. He was concentrating on not being sick. He had managed to pull his shirt on, but not to button it. His pants had defeated him utterly, and he still wore the shorts and tennis shoes he had fought in. He waited. He was waiting for Mr. Inchcape to come and get him, but it didn't seem like Mr. Inchcape was going to come.

Goody kept on waiting. The blind man plucked without energy at his Dobro.

"Hey, you," said the first man. He turned to the second. "What the hell's his name? I forget. Are you okay?"

The second man said, "Look here." He put a hand under Goody's chin, tilted his head up. Goody opened his eyes to slits. They would not open further. The man held his hand up in front of Goody's face, waggled it back and forth. It was a large hand. "How many fingers am I holding up?" He continued to wave his hand.

Goody counted, then recounted. "Six," he said.

The man took his hand away. "Hell, he's all right," he said.

"Let me see that again," Goody said.

"What," the man said.

"Your hand."

The man held his hands out for Goody to examine. He held them still this time. There were six digits on each of his hands, twelve altogether. An extra pinkie sprouted from the outsides of the hands, down near the wrist where no finger should be. The surplus fingers were small, like a toddler's, with glossy pink nails. When the man closed his hands and opened them again, the supernumeraries flexed weakly as well. The other man giggled, a dry, nervous sound.

"I never saw anything like that before," Goody said. His voice was thick with mucus, and he spat into the sawdust, trying to clear his mouth of the stuff.

"Me either, except for me," the man said. It was Tannhauser, Goody realized, his vision clearing somewhat. Had he noticed Tannhauser's strange hands before the fight? Too concentrated on his own, he guessed.

"I was born with a tail, too," Tannhauser told him. "Little thing no bigger than your nose, right at the end of my spine. It was twisty, like a pig's tail. The doctor who delivered me took that off. He wanted to take the fingers, too, but my father wouldn't let him."

"Why did he want you to have extra fingers?" Goody asked.

"He thought it was a benign mutation. Fingers are something a human being has, so the more the better. Tails are something an animal has, so it had to go." Tannhauser laughed. "He used to call me *Homo novus*. He was a big believer in Darwinism."

"Monkeys have fingers, Mr. Tannhauser," the other man said. Tannhauser ignored him. "Apes got them on their hands *and* on their feet."

"How many toes have you got?" Goody asked. He looked up at Tannhauser. The tall man's image swam before him, so he looked down again.

"Just the normal complement," Tannhauser said.

"I believe I've got a detached retina," Goody said. He carefully cupped his injured hands over his eyes, one and then the other. "Everything looks funny to me."

"That could be a concussion," Tannhauser said. "It can take your vision a while to collect back into a single thing again, when somebody really rings your bell. And yours got rung tonight. I saw it happen."

Goody closed his left eye and looked up at Tannhauser. Then he opened it, let his swollen right eye fall shut. "Goddamn," he said. "I'm blinded. I can't see out of this eye."

"That's a shame," Tannhauser said. "You wait until the swelling goes down. That'll take the pressure off, and you'll be able to see again, probably."

"Or the retina might reattach itself," the other man said. "That happens sometimes. Otherwise you got to have surgery on it." His voice was high, his tone abrupt. He sounded as though he were impatient to leave. Tannhauser bent down to kneel next to Goody. His shoulders were broad, and his short blond hair was streaked with gray.

"Listen here," Tannhauser said. "Did you hate the man you beat?" The lights of the barn were still on but the place was nearly empty. The bartender in his heavy apron moved back and forth behind the makeshift bar, loading full and half-full bottles into cartons, hauling the cartons to the trunk of a white Chevy Impala that was parked near the barn door. The Dobro music stopped; a young woman had come to get the blind man, was leading him toward the barn's exit.

"Hate who?" Goody said. "I don't hate anybody that I know of. Some folks I like better than others. Who doesn't?"

"I'm not talking about some folks or others," Tannhauser said, "I'm talking about Yukon." He held his hands up before him, balled into fists. The little fingers twitched rhythmically, as though with his pulse. "The guy that maybe you've killed."

Goody drew himself up a little. "I didn't ever think about him, really," he said. "I get mad when I'm in the ring, but I'm not sure it's at the guy I'm fighting, really. Yukon himself—I didn't hate him in particular or have any other strong feeling. I wanted to beat him. I wanted him to fall down. If he dies, I never meant he should. He kept getting up." The long speech had taken most of his remaining strength. He wished that these two men would make their point, whatever it might be, and move on.

Tannhauser shrugged. "You got to admit, though," he said, "that it was your fists on him. Nobody hit him but you."

"No," Goody said. "Nobody hit him but me."

"So the responsibility lies with you. You have to make an accounting for what you did."

"Sure," Goody said. "Okay." He was still experimenting with his eyes, closing one and then the other. The air seemed to be full of dark bits of trash, motes that floated in and out of his vision.

"You freely admit your guilt? Here in front of Peanut and me?"

Goody took a moment to answer. He had to gather his thoughts. His head had begun to buzz nastily, and he felt a deep weariness descending over him. "I'll admit it, if that's what you want me to do," he said. "It was me and him in the ring."

"It's not what I want or don't want. It's what you did or didn't do. Now, did you mean to kill him?"

Goody shook his head, and then regretted the motion. He was tempted to stretch out on the straw bales, but he was afraid that if he went to sleep, he might not wake up again. "I never meant to kill anybody," he said. "But I wouldn't have stopped hitting him just because I thought he could die. Is that what you need to know?"

Tannhauser grinned. He had white teeth. There was a slight space between his two top front incisors, and the tip of his tongue showed red in the gap. "That's what I need to know," he said. The man who stood behind him sighed and shifted his weight, anxious to be gone. "And now I've got one more question for you."

"And that is?"

"Do you know what your heart looks like?"

"I've seen pictures, I guess," Goody said. "In textbooks and all."

Tannhauser shook his head. "Not *a* heart. Not just *any* heart, but yours. Do you know what your heart looks like?"

"I've seen x-rays. One time when I was in the service they took some chest x-rays, so I guess my heart was in there somewhere."

"So you're saying you've never actually seen your heart? Clearly and unmistakably?"

"I guess I haven't."

Tannhauser looked him up and down, studying him. "I bet you haven't, either," he said. "I'll just bet you haven't, and wouldn't want to." He walked away. The other man followed closely behind him, and Goody thought that he heard Claymaker's name mentioned. He was thirsty, and his throat ached. He lowered his head again and went back to waiting, the high-pitched buzzing in his head his only company.

Inchcape finally returned. When Goody asked him for a drink of water, he went away again and came back after a few minutes, a can of beer in his hand. "This is all I could find to give you," he said, holding the can up for Goody's inspection. "It was setting in a mess of ice slush at the bottom of the cooler. I thought about bringing some of the ice water but it was all full of bugs and stuff. You wouldn't have wanted it. Plus there was nothing to carry it in."

Goody licked his dry lips, watching the can that Inchcape held. Droplets of water ran across the side of the can and collected against Inchcape's fingers, finally running in a slow stream off the bottom edge of his hand. "That's fine," he said. "That'll do." He kept his blinded eye closed, but still he felt dizzy and sick.

Inchcape popped the beer open, and foam billowed across the top of the can. The old man sucked the foam away and then looked guiltily at Goody. He extended the beer. Goody reached out his right hand, winced, drew it back. Inchcape looked at him. "Can you not take it?" he said.

"No," Goody said. "My hand's broken."

"The other one too?" Inchcape asked, gesturing at Goody's left hand. "Both of them clear busted?" He whistled. "Ain't that something," he said in a low voice. "Broke both hands and still won the fight." He looked at Goody a moment longer before sitting next to him on the straw bale. He held the beer can up to Goody's mouth. When he tilted it, the stream of beer came too quickly, and much of it spilled down Goody's chin and splashed on the skin of his bare legs. The mouthful of beer was bitter, and it stung the lacerated flesh on the insides of his cheeks. He rinsed it around his mouth, trying to note which of his teeth felt loose, glad to find that none seemed to have been dislodged altogether. He spat the beer out, gestured to Inchcape for more.

Inchcape eyed the beer that Goody had expelled. The puddle quickly soaked into the sawdust floor. "Lots of blood in that," he noted. Goody nodded. Inchcape brought the can to Goody's mouth again, and the cold metal clicked against his front teeth. Goody leaned his head back and gulped greedily at the beer. Inchcape put his free hand to the back of Goody's neck to steady him as he drank.

When the beer was gone, Inchcape set the can on the floor and crushed it beneath the heel of his boot. He flicked the lopsided metal disk across the room away from them, and it skipped along the soft floor, skittering in the end beneath a cobwebbed collection of hand tools that leaned against the wall of the barn: shovels, mattocks, single- and double-bitted axes, a manure fork, its tines coated in a sheath of rust and its handle soft with rot. Inchcape stood and took Goody by the arm, helping him to stand, and the two of them started for the barn door. "We'll get you down to the emergency room at the hospital in the valley," Inchcape said. "Get those paws fixed."

"Do you know if that's where they're taking that guy Yukon?"

"I don't," Inchcape said. "I don't know what they might be doing with Yukon. They were none too happy about him getting beat, I do know that."

"Because he'll need to get that jaw set, and we don't want to run into his people down there. I don't ever need to see Yukon again, I don't believe."

"No," Inchcape said, "you're right about that. Me neither. He'll be looking for you when he gets back on his feet, though."

"You don't think he's had enough of me?"

"Not Yukon," Inchcape said. "Not the Yukon I know. You've got on that boy's shit list for all time, I'd say." They made their way slowly outside, Goody stopping frequently to rest, leaning heavily on Inchcape for support.

"I guess you won you some money on this one," Goody said. He gritted his teeth against the nausea that swept him in lingering waves. Inchcape's grip on him loosened, and he nearly sat down on the ground.

"Not so much as you might think," Inchcape said. His tone sounded regretful. He pulled a slim sheaf of bills from his pants pocket and held it up. "I got your purse from Musser. That's pretty much all we leave here with."

"But they were all Yukon fans here tonight," Goody said. "They had to have bet on him."

"Sure they did," Inchcape said. "I did it myself." Goody stopped for a moment, but when Inchcape tugged at him he continued his shuffling advance out of the barn. "You can't blame me," Inchcape said. "I got nervous when I seen that you didn't want to fight Yukon, so I hedged my bets a little. Nobody would of thought you could win it. Yukon's so much bigger than you." He brightened. "Still," he said, "we'll make it up next time. Now I know what you're made of."

They were out of the barn, part of the way to Inchcape's truck, which was parked alone in the barn lot. Tonto stood in the back, a great hairy silhouette, watching their approach. Behind the truck lurked the gross figure of Edgar Musser. He seemed to be waiting for them, but when he saw them approaching he turned his back and walked with his strange swaying gait to the porch of his house. He sat there, smoking and watching them, the end of his cigarette glowing orange, a small angry fire in the dark.

Goody shook his head. "No sir," he said. "No, Mr. Inchcape. I don't think so." This time it was Inchcape who stopped. He stared at Goody, who said, "I believe I'm done fistfighting for a while."

"It's your hands," Inchcape said. "They've got you worried. But they'll heal. You'll see. We'll get you a couple of casts and they'll be good as new here inside of a month. You'll be threading needles before you know it."

"Maybe," Goody said. He was too tired to argue.

Inchcape opened the difficult passenger door of his truck and helped Goody inside. Tonto sat down in the bed. Goody sank into the seat, dreading the return drive.

"Anyway," Inchcape said, "where's a guy like you get money, anyhow? From fighting, that's where." He slammed the door closed and waved the purse money through the open window. "How long do you think this will last you? Not long, that's how long." He was growing angry as he spoke. "Think you'll get a job flipping hamburgers? Think you'll pump gas for a living? Think that'll pay to fix your car? No," he said. "No, you'll be fighting again. Believe me when I tell it to you." He walked around the front of the truck and climbed in.

"I believe you," Goody said. He said it to calm Inchcape down. The old man didn't reply. He twisted the key and stepped on the starter. The truck ground to life. "Mr. Inchcape," Goody said, but Inchcape didn't look at him. He turned the truck around to face the egress, hauling the big stiff steering wheel around hand over hand. Soon they were bumping their way over the log road. "You might want to keep an eye out for your gas can," Goody said. "Unless somebody already picked it up before us."

Inchcape did not look at him. "What's that?" he said. His tone was sharp. He had been continuing the argument in his head and could not imagine what Goody was talking about.

"Keep an eye out for your red gas can that you've got. It bounced out of the truck somewhere along the road."

Inchcape looked around, bewildered, as though he expected the gas can to materialize there in the cab of the truck with him. Finally he craned his neck around and examined the bed. "I'll be damned," he said. "It's done gone."

"I told you that," Goody said.

"When?" Inchcape asked.

"Just now."

"No. I know you told me just now. When did it bounce out of the truck?"

"On the way up here, before the fight. It was on that last stretch of road where you were driving so fast. I heard it flying around back there and then I didn't. When I looked for it, it was gone."

Inchcape leaned forward, sweeping his gaze from one side of the road to the other. He slowed the truck, the better to search for the missing gas can, and Goody was grateful. "Why didn't you tell me?" Inchcape said.

"I don't know. You seemed like you were in a big hurry, and it was just a gas can. I never thought much about it. I'm lucky I remembered to tell you about it at all."

"Well," Inchcape said, "I wished you had told me."

"I wish so too," Goody said. "I never thought it would be such a problem for you."

"It's not a problem," Inchcape said. "It's just I hate to lose something, and I hate to have to try to find it this way."

He maintained the truck's creeping pace, and they continued on, moving slowly along the ridge. Inchcape hunted for the can along the jerry-built road and beneath the surrounding underbrush, which was only dimly illuminated by the truck's canted headlights. Goody, sitting beside him, tried to relax, and as they rolled along he managed to catch brief snatches of uneasy, dream-filled sleep.

37

Inchcape found himself standing in front of his tenant house. It was less than an hour until dawn, and the sky was already beginning to lighten in the east, the blackness there turning purple, the sky shiny as the skin of an eggplant. Inchcape's legs hurt, and his head swam with hunger and fatigue. He patted his pants pockets with his free hand, his left hand, hoping to come across a candy bar, some piece of candy, to satisfy the craving he had for something sweet. He had nothing, nothing of the sort that he was looking for.

(He had stopped, left the truck to pick up the gas can. Heard voices. The exhaust that curled from the Ford's tailpipe was dyed red by the taillights, and in that blood-colored radiance he saw men. How many he could not tell. They surrounded the truck. They had guns, M16s. They took him. Took Goody.)

In his right hand he carried the gasoline can that he had retrieved from the side of the road. It was heavy; from the weight of it he guessed that it must be nearly full. Gas weighed—what? Eight pounds per gallon, nine? Figure nine pounds. That made it nearly forty-five pounds on the right side, and he found himself leaning in that direction, straining to straighten himself. He was breathing heavily, his thin chest hitching under his shirt. "I'm not a well man," he said aloud. The sound of his voice in the lonely yard surprised him. It was, in fact, the voice of a man who was not well. It was a weak, trembling voice. An old man's voice, an old man who had been up all night and who carried in his right hand a very heavy can of gasoline. The stench of it, so heady, like fresh-ground coffee, like tobacco, rose to his nostrils.

(He found the gas can caught, upside down, in the branches of a little hawthorn tree by the side of the road, a dozen yards from the place where he had stopped. The hawthorn tree was in bloom, but he could not tell what color the flowers were; it was too dark. He pulled the can loose from the limbs, carefully to avoid embedding the tree's stickers in his hands. Was that before or after he heard the voices? If after, why take the can? Make it before. He began the short walk along the road back to the truck and to Goody and then he heard the voices. Angry, belligerent voices, making demands. The truck's headlights cast a glow in front of it, and figures moved there, a cordon of armed men stretching across the road.)

He held the can out before him as though he were offering it to someone. His arm trembled with the weight of it, and before long he had to let it drop back to his side again. He set it down in the yard, massaged the bones of his sore right hand with his left, picked the can up again. The gas sloshed from side to side within it, making the can pitch and wobble. A little of the fuel spilled from the open spout, spattering the toes of his shoes. He moved his feet, scuffing dust onto them. The dirt caked on his shoes. He tried to whistle, but his lips were dry and chapped, and he made nothing but a hissing noise. His tongue seemed inclined to stick to his teeth. He settled for tuneless humming instead, waiting for dawn to come. A bird chirruped loudly in the big maple that stood in the yard and went silent again, back to sleep. A light breeze stirred the nearby canefield. The cicadas shrilled endlessly. The cycle of their noise resembled the hunger sound that he heard in his head, an edgy rhythmic whine. He tried to drown the noise out with his humming, but he could still hear it. He wished for a cigarette but knew from the previous inspection of his pockets that he had none.

(They did not know about the passenger door, how hard it was to open. They shouted, demanded that Goody get out. He heard the door rattle and knew that Goody couldn't lift the door to open it, with his hands broken. They were about to shoot him, shoot him where he sat in the truck, when somehow he shouldered the door

*open, broke the latch to do it. They rushed him, dragged him out,
struck at him. Someone was screaming—Goody, it was Goody, of
course, who else had reason to scream?—"My hands my hands you
bastards my hands!")*

The house was perfectly dark, perfectly quiet. He strained to
make out a figure behind the windows on his side, but the glass was
black. There was nothing. He laughed at himself. *You are one crazy
son of a bitch. If there's nothing, then you don't have to be scared to
go inside. If there's nothing, then you don't have to go inside at all.*
He took a step toward the front door.

The phone rang. He listened to it, its small shivering bell. It was
loud, shatteringly loud in the morning quiet, and he wondered if the
sound could be coming from inside his head, if he had somehow
added this intermittent ringing to the constant hum. His legs
twitched, with weariness and the desire to run. Run away. Who could
be calling Goody at this hour? Only family called at this hour, and
only to tell you that somebody might be dying, was dying, had died.
Goody's family. He supposed that there was one. Had to be, somewhere. Everyone had a family. The phone continued to ring, not
inside his head, no, inside the tenant house. Someone who wanted to
talk to Goody. Or talk to him. How could they know that he was
there, standing out in the yard, out in the dark, the predawn chill?
The phone ceased its ringing.

*(They had not known about Tonto lying in the truck bed. The
huge dog, abruptly awakened, had roared and lunged, jaws gaping,
lashing out at the gunman nearest the truck bed. The gun had come
up, flame licking from the muzzle. And afterward the voice: "Whoa.
Just a dog, man. Just a dog is all. Jesus you motherfucker busted caps
on a dog. Capped a fucking dog." Laughter all around. He had run
then. Or had he shouted? He had shouted, too late to stop anything
but still he shouted, and the gunman turned on him. He had taken
off, red pencil of laser light stabbing out from beneath the barrel of
the gun, imprinting its bright hot spot on him, his back, the empty
gas can bouncing at his side. He tripped. Something hurtled at great
speed through the branches just overhead. Leaves and twigs, clipped
from the branches above, pattered down on him. No one pursued as
he scrambled on all fours through the underbrush.)*

And the gas had come from—where? He had not carried the full
gas can all the way back to Goody's house, down off the mountain.
The thing was not possible. It had been light *(empty? near empty?)*

when he found it in the branches of the hawthorn. There was a fifty-five-gallon drum of gasoline in the shed at his own house, across the farm, but he did not recall having gone to his place on the way here. He did not recall having tapped the drum for this small amount. He did not remember having come here at all, but here he stood. His hands smelled of gas. His clothes reeked of it. He stank as though he had bathed in the stuff.

A couple of bats wheeled across the yard, nabbing moths out of the air, the light of the moon washing silver over their hairy bodies, frosting them with it. The moon was well above the horizon. Its light would reveal him to anyone who waited in the house, who crouched by a window, looking out. The moon would show him up, standing like a target in the yard, can of gas at his side.

(Jumpy motherfucker busted caps on a dog. My hands you bastards my hands.)

He would not enter the house until dawn.

"Okay, you bitch," he said. He soaked the mattress. The bedsheet was gray with many washings, and it turned a darker color when the gasoline touched it. "You got another one." He walked backward through the house, the gas can upended, the vaguely pink gasoline gurgling out. He irrigated everything: saturated the clothes that hung in the closet, the shoes beneath; the few poor furnishings; the jump-rope that hung over the back of a chair in the living room; anything that might burn, or that might be caused to burn.

(And always there was more gas, there seemed to be no end of it. Surely there could not be so much in the can, surely this was more than five gallons oh much much more.)

He doused the kitchen until the peeling linoleum floor was awash and, backing out of the house, splashed great gouts of it on the walls, on the unevenly painted patches. He half expected the gasoline to act as a solvent, to melt the paint away in those places, melt it away but leave the dried blood: the handprints underneath. It did not, and he went out into the yard.

(And was something—someone—following? Oh yes, it—she—was. The poor revenant hobbling along the worthless corridors, hovering just at the edge of his perception, like a reflection far back in a dirty mirror. He tossed gas, fountains of gas, but at what? Could he really see anything? No. But like the constant buzzing of hunger in his head, it—she—was there.)

Led a trail of gas across the yard to the Pontiac. So glad to be outside, and the air smelled sweet and pure to him in spite of the bitter stink of fuel. Stopped at the car as though puzzled about what to do. Raised the gas can and brought it down on the starred windshield of the car. Once, twice more. The rounded side of the can dented, turned concave. The glass under it went milky, fractured, bulged inward, finally surrendered to the blows and slithered out of its frame and into the car, lying in a splintered sheet across the steering wheel, the dashboard, the transmission hump. He poured the remainder of the gas into the Pontiac's interior, where it sank deep into the cloth seats, splashed the vinyl of the dash, pooled on the floorboards, dribbled through the several pinholes in the rusted sheetmetal. When he was finished, he tossed the crimped can—suddenly light; it had emptied itself, exhausted its supply finally—through the smashed windshield as well. And he paused, at a loss.

What to light it with? All that gas, it had to be touched off. Else why was there gas everywhere, throughout the house and a track of it, shallow gleaming rainbow-streaked puddles of it stretching across the yard, if not to burn? He peered into the car's interior, but the cigarette lighter was gone, its socket empty. He thought of the house, but he would not go in there again, even with the sun climbing into the sky, another hot golden day. Not now that she knew what he intended to do. Not now that there was no more gas, he had no more gas to fling at her.

In desperation, he patted his pockets. And came up with *(a miracle?)* a book of paper matches. Had he not checked his pockets only a short time before, while he waited for the sun to rise? And had he not failed to find any matches, any thing, at all? But he had been looking for candy, then. He had been checking his pockets in a desire for sweets. Not matches. Not for a slim book of matches, so easily overlooked. *Union 76,* it said on the outside. *Strike with cover closed.* There were seven matches left in the book.

The first popped with a white flame, sizzled, went out. The second likewise. The sulfurous head of the third came off the matchstick when he struck it and adhered to the book instead, burning a small black-edged hole in it. The fourth lit and burned, the small pale flame climbing swiftly up the paper stick toward his fingers. He held it to the heads of the three matches remaining in the book, and they blazed into life. He felt their combined heat against his skin and reflexively pitched the matchbook away from him, onto the front seat of the Le Mans.

The car went up like a torch, exploding into flame with a concussive *thump*. He was showered with chunks of flying safety glass, and stepped back, shielding his eyes from the terrible glare, the heat. His skin felt dried, as though it might crack. Near-invisible flame marched across the yard, hopping from puddle to puddle, crossing the doorstep, hungrily entering the house. He stood expectantly, waiting. Waiting on something. Some sign.

(All right . . .)

And noticed that he too was enveloped in the colorless blaze. He held his hand up and watched the shimmering wave of flame run across the skin. It made his complexion look slightly blue: some trick of refraction. His eyebrows were gone; his hair was gone; but he felt no pain at all. He took a step, and the fire took a step with him. It had his shape. It covered him.

(. . . you bitch.)

The windows of the house blew out, all of them at once. Flames shot from the empty window frames. The house fire made a rushing sound, like the wings of many thousands of lifting birds. He felt heat, but still no pain. His lungs toiled, straining to filter oxygen from the air. His clothes began to blacken and fall away from his body. His vision dimmed, and as light waned he saw movement in the canebrake. Dead eyes, thin denim-clad legs, withered lips drawn back from long yellow teeth. Billy Rugg. And Inchcape knew with a stab of infinite regret, the painful knowledge of things left undone, that he ought to have burned the field of rustling cane as well.

He took another step *(Toward the house? Or away? He could not tell)* and another, before he stumbled, and fell, and lay without moving in the dirt of the yard.

38

Dreama held the pay phone's receiver to her ear, listening to the unanswered ringing. A car roared past the narrow gravel turnoff and the phone booth, a sedan headed north, and its headlights lit up the Bronco parked at a careless angle not far away, shone blindingly through the glass of the booth, and passed on. She groaned with released tension. Within the earpiece, the phone continued to ring, a tiny insect buzzing.

What, after all, had she hoped for? Goody would not rescue her; he could not. Rescue her from what? She wasn't sure. She only knew that Wallace was gone and she was alone, and frightened. The close air of the booth smelled of urine and mold. The overhead light and the fan seemed to be broken. She was glad not to have the light on her, but she regretted the lack of ventilation. The phone line clicked, and she thought for a moment that it had been answered. She took a breath to speak, but there was no one on the other end. The ringing went on as before.

She replaced the phone on its hook and opened the door of the phone booth just as a car pulled into the cutoff. A sedan, southbound. Had the northbound car seen her, turned around, and come back? It looked like the same vehicle, but it could just as easily be

another. Someone waiting to use the phone. The car sat on the
gravel, facing her, headlights on high beams. She squared her shoulders and began to cross to the Bronco, forcing herself to take normal
strides. One, two, three, four. A dozen. Half a dozen more.

"There she goes," the lanky deputy said. Beside him, Faktor stirred
in his seat.

"Yes," he said, "there she goes."

They sat and watched her move toward the Bronco. One of the
deputies in the back seat gave a long low whistle of appreciation.
"Pretty lady," the other one said.

"We'll take the Bronco with us," Faktor told the lanky deputy.
"We'll dump it on the way to El Dorado. You follow in the prowl
car." He moved to open the door of the sedan.

One of the deputies in the back seat shouted, "She's tipped to
us!" Dreama had given up her slow, almost dreamy pace. She was
running, headed for the truck. The deputies slammed open their
doors and made for her at top speed, the heavily built sheriff lumbering along in their wake.

Eyes wide, Dreama sprinted the last few feet to the Bronco, the
chunky sandals flying from her feet, first the right, then the left, hard
soles pounding against the gravel, muscular legs driving her forward.
Her body had never failed her. Never.

Reflected in the shiny finish of the Bronco's door, she saw the twin
pinwheels of the sedan's headlights and, between them, distorted and
elongated, pale as the belly of a fish, pale as a ghost, the image of her
own torso. She could not make out the reflected images of the men
who had emerged from the sedan. Two yards away from the safety of
the truck now, still running, slipping in the gravel. One yard. The
pistol was in the glovebox. She tried desperately to recall if it was
loaded. She stretched a hand out, fingers yearning for the metal of
the door handle, the onrushing footsteps of her pursuers only yards,
feet, inches behind her.

She pulled at the door handle, and the door swung easily open.
She threw herself across the seat, was clawing at the latch of the
glove compartment, when rough hands reached in after her, caught
at her clothes, tangled in her hair. She thrashed, flailing out with her
long sharp fingernails. She screamed, and a callused palm covered
her mouth. She bit it and drew blood. The bitten man cursed and

cuffed her. She scrambled away from him along the seat, toward the passenger door, but another man was there already. He took her by the shoulders and pushed her to the middle. She was sandwiched between them. They were shoving at her, crushing her. They were large hot men. She knew that they were speaking, barking at her or at each other in harsh tones, but in the confusion of voices within the Bronco she could not understand what was said.

A man in the back seat took her by the hair and yanked hard. Her head came back against the seat and she stared up at the white plastic cover of the dome light. Something cold was laid against the skin of her throat. Something sharp. The man who had her by the hair leaned close to her ear and said, unmistakably, "Quiet." She quieted. The others obeyed as well, the man on her right and the one on her left. She could hear their ragged, excited breathing. She had the sense that there more men standing outside the truck, looking in through the windows at her.

"All right," the man in the back seat said, and the man on her left started the Bronco and put it in gear. There was something familiar about the voice. If she heard him talk more, she was confident, she would know who he was. She wasn't sure whether she wanted that bit of information or not. They pulled out onto the road, accelerating. What was that against her neck? She pictured a skinning knife, its short triangular blade pressing against the big vein just below her jaw. She was very careful not to move her head. The agonizing tension on her hair eased, but she did not straighten her neck. She continued to gaze upward at the dome light.

"Honey," the man said, mouth close beside her ear again. She could feel hot breath against her skin, and the reek of his stale breath carried to her nostrils. "Honey," he said again, and she knew who he was.

"Sheriff," she said. "Sheriff Faktor." She endeavored to make her voice pleasant. "Where are we going?" she asked.

"Honey," he said for the third time. He moved the knife blade in long sweeping strokes, up and down the length of her neck, like a barber stropping his straight razor. He pricked her with the point of the knife, and she squeaked in distress. The man in the passenger seat laughed. He jammed a knee into her side and began to paw at her. He tugged at the thin cloth of her skirt.

"Honey," the high sheriff said yet another time, and he interposed his head between Dreama and the dome light. She could make out only the lower half of his face, the broad expanse of his nose, his mouth, his thick lips. "Sweetie pie," he said to her, "you need to know this one simple fact: that your troubles are only now, just at this very moment in time, beginning."

39

"Meet your death," Tannhauser said. "Meet Renny."

Goody did not know when they stopped walking. With every stride he had taken through the forest on their way to this place, he had sworn that he would not, could not, take another, that the step just accomplished would be his last. Let them shoot him for stopping. Let them. He would ask them to do it. He had sworn that a hundred times, a thousand, ten thousand, and now he had stopped, they had allowed him to stop. He felt as though he were still moving at forced-march pace. His neck was bent, his vision fixed on the ground a pace or two ahead of him. With an effort, he raised his head to look at Tannhauser.

"Meet Renny," Tannhauser said again. He indicated a muscular young man who stood beside and slightly behind him. Renny was solidly built, with dark eyes, dark skin, a shock of unruly dark hair. He wore tattered clothes and sneakers.

The men who had snatched Goody from Inchcape's truck—the Mingos with their rifles cradled in their arms, the pilot and copilot, Peanut—stood ranged around the triangle formed by Goody, Tannhauser, and Renny. They were in the grand ballroom, in a space relatively clear of clutter and wreckage. Yukon, jaw askew, eyes blank, sat slumped in a salvaged easy chair. His red robe had been draped unceremoniously over him.

Goody held his hands at waist level, crossed at the wrists. They were badly swollen, and the pain of them had become something else now: a tide that rose like water in his body, that reddened his vision, that made him weak and sick. He felt bloated with it. He wanted to weep.

"Mr. Tannhauser," the pilot said, stepping forward. "We're pretty tired, and Bodo tells me that we're supposed to leave as soon as it gets to be light. I think we'd better beg off of this exercise, if that's all right with you." The copilot nodded his head in agreement. The Mingos were impassive.

Peanut said, "It has been kind of a long day, I guess. I wouldn't mind getting a little shut-eye myself, tell you the truth."

"If I don't get some help soon," Goody said, "I'll never use my hands again. And your pal Yukon there looks like he could use a doctor's skill too."

Tannhauser ignored them all. "Renny is my new executioner. He's the man who is going to solve all my problems for me from here on in. Somebody doesn't do what he should? Show him to Renny. Somebody betrays the cause? Show him to Renny."

In another part of the camp, a hoarse voice shouted, "They gaped upon me with their mouths, as a ravening and a roaring lion."

"Yukon does look pretty bad," the pilot said. "I think he may need brain surgery or something. A neurosurgeon. I've heard about fighters who get hurt that way, and some of them even die in the ring. He may have a blood clot on his brain or something. Pressure."

"Do you know that all the rulers of all the great kingdoms of earth have had one man that they could trust? One single man. The man who was not a jailer, not an army officer, not a bureaucrat, not a hunter: an executioner. All of the viziers, the seneschals, the advisers, the cabinet members—they're nothing like a pair of hands, a single pair of remorseless hands, that will kill when and whom you tell them to. Execution, properly performed, is an art; its use can cause realms to be saved, when in its absence they would have fallen. That's been the problem here: lack of a strangler. That's been the failing at El Dorado."

Renny's uneasy gaze roamed over them and around the ballroom in which they stood, a room in which he had never been allowed before. The workers imagined among themselves that it must be a room of fabulous splendor. He looked at Goody, and when Goody met his eyes he looked quickly away. Goody felt a sudden unexpected start of sympathy for the man, who plainly hated to be where he was.

"And this guy," the pilot said, indicating Goody, "he never did anything wrong, really. Not that I saw. He was just in a fight, and he happened to win. What was he supposed to do?"

Tannhauser looked balefully at the pilot, who went silent. "Did you see what he did to Yukon?" He gestured at his broken lieutenant. "Yukon, who stood by me, always and at all times. Yukon, whose feet you are not fit to wash. Yukon, my right hand." With this last, he held up his literal right hand and looked from it to Yukon's slumped figure, as though somehow comparing the two. "This is not a tribunal. There's no need of a trial, or your testimony, or your opinion. What do you know about wrongdoing? What do you know about what this man did wrong?"

The pilot seemed to shrink into himself at the verbal onslaught. Still, the copilot heard him muttering under his breath. "Nothing wrong."

Tannhauser turned his attention back to Renny. He clapped him on the shoulder, and Renny flinched. "All right," Tannhauser said. He shoved him toward his victim. Goody's head felt heavy on his neck, and he longed to look away, but he kept his eyes steadily on the man who, according to Tannhauser's plan, was going to execute him. For what? The people around him were obviously insane.

"Do it," Tannhauser said. Renny stood, his hands clenched into fists, a few feet in front of Goody. He swayed slightly. His breathing was rapid and uneven. "Strangle him." Still Renny did not raise his hands to Goody's throat. Goody blinked.

"Does he know what he's supposed to do?" Tannhauser asked the copilot, the only one among them who knew any Spanish. "Did you tell him?"

"I told him," the copilot said. "As best as I could. They didn't teach us much vocabulary about strangling and such in high school. Plus it was a good long while ago. I'm pretty rusty."

Finished with a night of hunting, the horned owl swept on its strong wings back into the room, entering through one of the long glassless windows. It circled three times over the group of men before settling onto the head of its cherub. None of the men looked up. It closed its eyes and settled its large head against the soft feathers of its breast, composing itself for sleep.

"No voy a pelear con usted," Renny said. He addressed the words to Goody, who could not guess at their meaning.

"I might have got some of the details of it wrong when I told him," the copilot said. He sounded nervous. "He might not have understood me exactly. Our Spanish teacher that we had at home wasn't much. You know the first thing she taught us to say in class? She walked into the classroom, right up in front of us at the blackboard, and she told us to repeat after her. Then she said, *Es hora de pagar.* And we all said the same thing back to her, just like she said it. *Es hora de pagar.*"

"What's that mean?" the pilot asked.

"*It is time to pay.* Isn't that a hell of a thing to teach a bunch of seventeen-year-old kids? It's time to pay. Where are you going to say something like that? Working for a Mexican collection agency, shaking down campesinos?"

"A whorehouse, maybe," the pilot said.

"Right. That's the kind of thing they're preparing you for in public school anymore. Job in a foreign bordello is all you're fit for."

In the same steady, confident tone that he had used before, Renny said to Goody, "No quiero pelear." His voice was quietly assured, as though his mind were unequivocally made up. He looked Goody in the eyes now, and Goody returned the look. He was grateful for it. It told him that whatever else might befall him in this place of abandoned buildings (and nothing much good, he thought, could come about in such surroundings), he had nothing to fear from Tannhauser's executioner.

"I don't think he's going to do it," the copilot said to the company in general. Then he said, "I think that means he's not going to strangle him for you, Mr. Tannhauser."

"That's that, then," the pilot said. "I guess we can get some rest after all." The sun was rising, and its weak light slightly lifted the gloom of the ballroom. He turned to leave and found his way blocked by the imperturbable Mingos. "Hey," he said, weakly. "Hey."

"I can argue with him some if you want," the copilot said, "but to tell the truth, I don't think I have the words for it. And he seems pretty determined."

"I suppose you're right," Tannhauser said. "I suppose he must have missed my meaning somehow. Renny." He snapped his fingers, and Renny ceased to regard Goody in that steady way, looked at Tannhauser instead. Tannhauser motioned that he should stand out of the way, and Renny did so. Tannhauser looked at them, his eyes bright. "That leaves us the problem of the man who killed Yukon." Goody remained standing in the center of the group, his knees locked so that he would not fall. He knew that if he allowed himself to fall, none of these people would pick him up, and the dirty trash-strewn floor was no place to lie.

"Yukon's not dead," the pilot said.

"He's not?" Tannhauser said. "Look at him. Just look at him."

The pilot did. Yukon had slumped further in his seat, and his head rested against his shoulder. His right eye was glassy and unfocused; his left was closed. The material of his robe was soaked with blood and saliva. His breathing was stertorous, and seemed to slow even as the pilot watched. "Well," the pilot said, "he's not technically dead, anyhow."

"I need someone loyal to me to take care of the problem," Tannhauser said. "I could do it myself; I could have the Mingos do it; but I'll make this a test. To find out what you're all made of."

He looked to the pilot, who said, "Murder the guy? I can't—I won't . . ." While he struggled for words, Tannhauser turned his face to the copilot, who blanched.

"I fly some, and I navigate," he said. "I don't strangle."

The gaze moved on to Peanut, who nodded enthusiastically. "Okay," he said. "I'll give it a shot. I never tried anything exactly like it before, so I don't know how I'll do, but I'm game to try."

"Peanut," Tannhauser said. "My man." He clapped Peanut on the back. Peanut beamed. He stepped up to Goody, flexing his hands. He and Goody were of a height, and Goody tried to engage his eyes, which flicked from side to side, up and down, moving always, seeming never to light on anything for long.

"You're going to kill me?" Goody asked.

"What?" Peanut seemed taken aback that Goody had spoken to him.

"You plan to kill me," Goody said. "With your hands."

"Don't sound so superior. What did you use on old Yukon over there? Or was it somebody else that cleaned his clock so?"

"I don't mean to sound superior. I don't mean to sound any way at all. I just wanted to ask. I just wanted to hear you say it."

"Well, you've asked. Now shut the hell up, will you?"

"I never heard you say it yet. These others wouldn't say it, and they won't do it. And I still haven't heard you say it."

"Say what?"

"That you're going to strangle me to death."

Peanut shrugged. "Okay," he said, his tone affable. "I'm going to strangle you to death." To Tannhauser he said, "Would it be okay for him to be on his knees or something? I think it would be better for my grip that way."

Tannhauser nodded, and the Mingos stepped forward. They struck Goody savagely behind the knees with their M16s, and his legs folded. He had not thought he could feel further pain, but the blows made his joints burn and ache. Something, some ligament or tendon in his right knee, separated. With a gasp he went down, kneeling in front of Peanut, face on a level with Peanut's belly. "Thanks," Peanut said. He was looking at Goody when he said it, but he must have meant to thank Tannhauser, or the Mingos. He laid his hands on Goody's collarbone, thumbs and fingers spread wide.

"At least Yukon was standing up when he got his," Goody said. Peanut could feel the vibrations of Goody's voice in his hands. "At least it was two of us in the ring, facing each other like men. My hands are broken. There's nothing I can do against you."

"What do you want?" Peanut asked. "You want me to wait until your hands heal?" He looked around at the others in amazement. "He sounds like he wants me to wait for his hands to get better so he can punch me." He giggled.

"Get on with it," Tannhauser said.

From the other side of the camp, the anchorite's words carried to them. "Be not far from me O Lord," he cried. "Hasten to help me."

"And when you're done with him," Tannhauser said, "I believe I'll sic you on that noisy son of a gun chained to the post out back of the mess hall. If you don't mind too much."

Peanut tightened his fingers on Goody's throat. He wrapped his long fingers around the back of Goody's neck and dug his thumbs and the heels of his hands strongly into the column of Goody's esophagus. The spongy rings of cartilage there threatened to give way. Goody coughed and tried to throw himself backward, but the Mingos were behind him again, holding him up, pressing him forward into Peanut's sweaty grasp.

Goody gagged and fought. Blood rushed to his face. He tried to keep his teeth closed tight, but his tongue forced them apart, protruding dryly from between his lips. His lungs spasmed, and he flailed his arms, oblivious to the pain in his broken hands when the

Mingos seized him by the elbows and pinned them to his sides. "Peanut," Tannhauser said. His voice came to Goody's ears as though from a great distance above or below. "Mascot no more." Goody tried to puzzle out the words, but he could wrest no meaning from them. There seemed to be no words left in him, only a deepening isolation to which he could put no name.

He had closed his eyes when Peanut touched him, but now, without his volition, his eyelids rose. The lids opened wide, wide, wider than they had ever opened before. He had not recovered the vision in his left eye, and now his right seemed to be failing him as well. Peanut loomed before him. The field of his sight expanded and contracted with the fitful beating of his heart. The world was edged in black.

Brilliant light bloomed suddenly in his head, followed by a popping sound, and then a whole series of explosions, one after the other, perfectly repeated. The light, which was green, seemed to push back the terrible darkness, and the pressure on his throat lessened. The others in the grand ballroom were shouting, but their words carried only faintly across the booming of his blood, its flow renewed and vigorous in his ears. His arms were released, and his neck, and he toppled to his side. Pieces of loose parquetry rattled beneath him. He lay still as sight and sound returned to him, and with them sensations, largely of pain but also of the currents of the air that passed along the floor of the ballroom, of the smells of the place, smells of mildew and bird droppings. He coughed painfully and spat up onto the floor.

Outside, sporadic gunfire crackled. Someone shrieked repeatedly, a single nonsense syllable, and then ceased abruptly to make any sound at all. At the perimeter of the camp, a blazing tripflare burned itself out and dropped to the ground. Another immediately followed it, rising lazily into the air and hanging there, shimmering, its color an intense lime green.

When Goody was able to bring himself to a sitting position, he found that he was alone in the grand ballroom. Alone, that is, but for comatose Yukon in his easy chair. It sounded to Goody as though a firefight was in progress outside, and he stayed low to the ground, crawling on his elbows and knees to the comparative shelter of a pile of loose boards. He lay behind them, panting, gathering his strength about him. Yukon moaned and raised a hand, set it back on the arm of the chair.

"Still kicking, eh, buddy?" Goody said. His voice was harsh and weak, and it pained him to talk. His throat felt raw, swollen and constricted. It hurt him to draw breath. The skin of his neck was hot to the touch and ridged with the bruised impressions of Peanut's fingers. As if in answer to Goody's words, Yukon grunted again. At the same time, he voided his bladder and his bowels, and a nearly intolerable stench rose from him. He murmured to himself like a man in the thrall of dreams.

Raising himself to look over the heap of boards, Goody saw someone crouching behind an upturned table not far away. The figure looked up, and their eyes met. It was Peanut. He rose when he saw Goody looking at him, and Goody tensed himself, clambering to his knees and then, with a terrific effort, to a standing position. His injured right leg throbbed. He waited for Peanut to approach, to try to finish the job that he had begun earlier. Alone, he would not find it so easy this time.

Peanut shrugged. He giggled nervously, a dry sound that came from the back of his throat. He lifted his hands and held them, palms out, toward Goody in a gesture of helplessness, of apology. Goody took a step toward him, and Peanut took a step back. His giggling died away, but he shrugged his shoulders again, and yet again, as though he could not stop himself from doing it. Goody took another step, and Peanut backed away. Still Goody came on. He did not know what he would do when he reached Peanut, but he knew that it would have to do with his forearms and his elbows and his knees and his feet, every undamaged striking surface left to him in the absence of his hands. He knew that it would have to do with his teeth.

Seeing Goody advance with his limping gait, Peanut retreated across the floor of the ballroom until he ran into something, a steam table or some other heavy object that refused to yield to him. He turned and scrambled over it. Goody came after him, growling now, though the sound hurt his pinched vocal cords badly. And the two of them, pursuer and pursued, passed out into the open compound, where a battle raged, where tracer rounds laced the air with their fiery trails, where star shells popped and pressure mines detonated, leaving behind them in the ballroom the slowly deliquescing Yukon.

40

Bodo and Toma had taken on the unpleasant job of reloading the Dakota themselves, as no help seemed to be forthcoming from the pilot and copilot, or from any of Tannhauser's people. Toma had wanted to force the others, at gunpoint if necessary, to perform the arduous task of repossession, but Bodo had stopped him. A dozen times already they had made the trip from the makeshift armory to the DC-3, bearing the heavy crates between them, and they were not even half finished. Their hands were blistered, their arms sore. They sat on a couple of the crates that they had dragged out of the building, smoking, and Bodo considered the merits of abandoning the whole project.

"In any case," he said, "we don't want to overload the aircraft. We'll want it to be light, to lift in as short a length as possible."

"Absolutely," Toma said. "Do you think he'll try to stop us?"

"With that madman, anything is possible," Bodo said.

Toma mopped at his face with a white linen handkerchief. The handkerchief grew limp with the heat and the moisture of his skin. He took a last drag on his cigarette and pitched the butt onto the ground. "I suggest that we stop right here." He stood, and at the

same moment a glowing flare rose above the line of trees at the edge
of camp. The flickering light gave to the narrow features of his face a
shifting, alien look. He shook his head, sighing. "Those tripflares,"
he said.

"Yes," Bodo said. "Those flares." Several times in the past week,
flares had gone up, signaling an incursion of some sort, and Tannhauser and his people had armed themselves to meet the threat, only
to find that nothing was there, that the flares had fired as a result of a
change in temperature, in humidity, or through some fault in work-
manship. Sometimes wandering wild hogs set them off. And Peanut
had described hitting a couple of trigger wires, maybe more, as he
blundered into the camp in a daze of hunger, and the flares, as well
as the Claymores that should have cut him to ribbons, had not dis-
charged. The multiple failures of their weaponry pained and humiliated Bodo.

A bullet took Toma in the center of his chest, shattering his ster-
num and exiting in a welter of blood and bone from a point between
his right shoulder blade and his spine. It was a high-velocity .30-
caliber rifle round that hit him, and he staggered backward with the
force of the impact. The look on his face was one more of surprise
and puzzlement than pain or fear. He leaned against the wall of the
armory. When he drew a shallow breath, air whistled through the
hole in his breast.

"Toma," Bodo said. He half-rose from the crate where he sat,
extending his hand as though to offer help. His tattered pocket lining
finally gave way, and the heavy chandelier crystal that he carried slid
through the hole and down his pants leg, dropping from it, bouncing
painfully off the toe of his shoe, and tumbling, unbroken, to the
ground. Toma looked at him, but there was no sign of recognition in
his widened eyes. Gunfire had begun to crackle all around them, rifle
fire, pistol fire, the high-speed popping of the M16s. No more seemed
to be coming their way, at least momentarily. "Toma," Bodo said
again.

Toma slipped down the wall to a sitting position, and the stones
behind him were stained with his blood. The handkerchief that he
had used to wipe sweat off his face slipped from between his numb
fingers and fluttered to the ground. He tried to open his jacket with
his right hand, failed, tried again, got it this time. He slid the Beretta
from its holster and pointed it before him, but the weight of it was

too much, and his hand fell into his lap, loosely gripping the butt of the pistol. His breath whined hideously in and out of him, but not through his mouth or nostrils.

Bodo knelt beside him, thinking that there was most likely nothing he could do. He knew something about chest wounds, and this was a bad one. That Toma, faithful Toma, sweet Toma, should die in such a place and in such a way—he could hardly bear it. He reached under his own jacket and pulled out his pistol, the exact replica of Toma's. He checked the clip and found it full, worked the slide to run a round into the breech. He did not know precisely who might be attacking the compound, but he intended to make them pay.

The sniper who had shot Toma seemed to have found them again, and a bullet whined off the stone side of the armory, spinning off into the sky. A second tugged at the sleeve of Bodo's suit jacket, passing through near the cuff and leaving behind a pair of matched ragged holes, entry and exit, but leaving the arm inside whole. A third hit the crate behind which he crouched, throwing up a flurry of splinters. A fourth dug harmlessly into the ground beside him. He held the pistol tight in both hands, braced his elbows on the rough top of the crate. He closed his left eye, peering at the trees along the polished barrel of the pistol, looking for movement that would betray the enemy, waiting for the next bullet, for the muzzle flash that would reveal the sniper's location.

Toma was the gunman. Toma who loved his pistol, who felt it as an extension of himself. Bodo cursed Toma for leaving this duty to him. He squeezed off an ineffective shot, followed it with another, knowing that he was wasting ammunition. Toma would have chided him for shooting at nothing. "Wait your target," he would have said. "You have to *think* the bullet home, and you cannot think of that which you are unable to see."

Bodo fired and fired, and soon the Beretta was empty, the slide back and locked. A curl of smoke licked up out of the breech. He swore and leaned over to Toma, plucked the pistol from his unresisting hands. He extracted the full clip from Toma's Beretta and was preparing to slip it into his own when a bullet struck him in the right cheek, immediately below the eye. He fell back, his shoulder driving the tear-shaped chandelier crystal, still whole, into the ground like a tent spike. He curled tight into a ball behind the sheltering crate, his brain a ruin, and died even before Toma did.

*   *   *

The gang of deputies, a dozen or more of them, came heedlessly on. Their booted feet trod tripwires, and the occasional warning flare rose smoking into the sky. They were heavily armed, struggling through patches of jangling concertina wire that cut them and tore at their clothes. They beat at the troublesome stuff with the butts of their rifles, sliced its razored strands with bolt cutters, and swept through the compound's defensive perimeter.

41

Peanut scurried between the cottages, dashing this way and that, bobbing and weaving to avoid being shot. He rounded corners on all fours, froze when he detected motion. He was determined to survive, whatever conflict was raging at the compound, whatever hostile force had arrived to do away with Tannhauser. He was determined to escape the place.

Behind Peanut, keeping him always in sight, came Goody. He hobbled along, his wounded leg swinging out awkwardly from his body. His breath was ragged, his lungs burning. He would be damned before he let Peanut escape him. As he swung unevenly along, he came under the sights of any number of Sheriff Faktor's men, but whether because they deemed him an unworthy target or because they thought from his bold manner that he might be one of their own, they passed him over in favor of other, more difficult targets.

42

The Mingos laid down a withering cover fire, and Tannhauser dashed across the last few yards of open space to reach the porch of his private cottage. He climbed up onto the porch, shouldered the door open, and entered. He strode into the house, and a slim figure, unseen by either him or the Mingos, stirred from the shadows in the hallway. The door swung abruptly shut. The Mingos concealed themselves in the shrubbery outside the cottage and waited for him to emerge.

43

Renny ran to the workers' quarters, bullets kicking up dust at his heels, buzzing past his ears with an awful keening sound. The air seemed to be full of them. He was hit, fell, rose to his feet, went on. He clutched his burning side, and his hands were covered with blood. Another bullet struck him in the back as he came within sight of the cottages. He fell again, for the second and final time, the cry of outrage stifled even as it rose in his throat, a terrible image the last that he saw: the image of a crowd of men, men in uniforms, leaning in through the windows of the squalid cottages and the stockade; and the sound, the shooting, the noise and flash of their pistols, *pop pop pop*. And the screams. And the exultant shouting. "Like fish in a barrel. Fish. In a barrel!"

44

Loomis saw the flare rising and pointed it out to Carmichael. It was dawn, and they were done for the day. Carmichael was tired from looking at the ground and inclined to dismiss the light. Loomis would not turn away. Then a second flare rose, and Loomis said, "I believe that's over at El Dorado."

"Maybe the hard guys in action," Carmichael said. "Let's go see."

As they approached, the helicopter skimming along at treetop height, they both saw the orange light of the tracers that zipped back and forth across the open ground. It was like nothing Carmichael had ever seen before. It looked to him as if the men on the ground were playing at some strange game, the rules of which he might never divine. They darted from building to building, crouched, running, belly-crawling. They hid themselves behind whatever objects they came upon: walls, crates, outcroppings of stone. And though they sometimes managed to hide themselves from their adversaries on the ground, Loomis was pleased to note that they were all, aggressor and defender alike, plain to him as he hovered above them.

45

The copilot wondered whether maybe they should try to wait a little longer for Bodo and Toma.

"No way," the pilot shouted over the revving engines of the *Domini Canes.* He stomped the right rudder pedal, braked the right wheel, ran the left throttle forward, and the big plane came slowly about, one hundred and eighty degrees. Its broad wings shadowed scattered crates of munitions, their deadly contents strewn about on the packed dirt of the airstrip. The fliers had pitched as much of the stuff out of the plane's cargo hatch as they could easily put their hands on, to lighten it. They had ripped away the camouflage netting. They had speedily unchocked the wheels.

The copilot looked out at the brief runway. At the far end, a barricade of thick trees. The clearing crew had forced the forest back in that direction, had cut the trees and, for the most part, left the sawn stumps in the ground. They had been working by hand, and building an airfield without the aid of even a single crawler was slow work. "Can we do it?" he asked. He looked around them. None of the attacking force (he could not guess at their identities, but he had no doubt that the slackly defended compound would be successfully overrun) had so far found the clearing or the airplane. No sign of Bodo or his pal, either. What had he called the guy? His gunsel.

"We have to," the pilot said. He took both throttles up to full, keeping the wheels braked. The Dakota shuddered, and the blue smoke of burning oil fumed off the bucket-size pistons of the twin radial engines. "No choice." The props were a spinning blur. He ran the flaps out to twenty degrees. He hoped the added lift would suck the wheels free of the airstrip's soft dirt.

"Here they come!" the copilot shouted. Running figures emerged from under the iron arch that led from the airfield to the resort grounds. They wore dark uniforms and campaign hats and carried rifles. The Army? The copilot could not tell. When they saw the airplane, a couple of them raised their rifles and began firing. The copilot could not tell whether the bullets were finding their intended marks.

The pilot released the brake, and the Dakota began to roll down the strip, slowly at first, then gathering speed. The packed earth rumbled under the hard rubber tires. The copilot stood by, ready to raise the wheels the second that the pilot gave him the signal, the second that they were airborne. Retracting the landing gear would give them precious extra airspeed. He watched the pilot's face intently.

Faster and faster. The wings began to catch the air, and the Dakota's tail wheel lifted from the deck, dropping the nose. "We're going to make it, we're going to, going to, make it," the pilot said under his breath. He repeated himself as though he were offering up a prayer. He struggled with the stiff yoke, striving to keep the airplane from bounding down the runway as the Dakota was prone to do, keep the tail wheel off the ground but not too far off, get the weight of the plane off the mains until it was ready to rise without stalling, rise above the trees and away, above the mountains and away, free of the confining earth. Pieces of netting clung to the wings and fluttered from the fuselage, but the control surfaces were unimpeded by the stuff.

The copilot looked from the pilot's face to glance ahead of them, past the nose of the plane. The rampart of the forest was terrifyingly close, the trees seeming a hurdle that they could not possibly clear. The Dakota lumbered along, unshakable, the air-speed indicator rising, rising, but not fast enough, he thought. At last, when it was not possible to wait a moment longer, the pilot hauled back on the yoke, and the *Domini Canes*, like an ungainly long-legged bird, staggered into the air.

The copilot brought the wheels up. For a breathless instant, the plane ceased climbing, fell slightly back, and the copilot believed that they were going in on the belly. He had yanked the landing gear too soon, pulled the wheels out from under the still-rolling plane. Then the Dakota began its climb again, over the raw stumps at the end of the runway, and barely, miraculously, over the trees beyond. The branches of the tallest of them made a terrible battering racket against the belly of the plane as it passed over, but they could not drag it down. "Oh man," the copilot said. Still they were not clear. The bulk of Little Hogback reared up before them, a green-covered wall. On the ground, the rifles of the high sheriff's men cracked uselessly.

"We're okay," the pilot said. He briefly scanned his instruments. "Airspeed good. Oil press good. We're golden." He sounded relieved and excited. As they approached the mountainside he smoothly banked the plane, the tree-stubbled slope sliding away close under the starboard side. He brought the plane around again, already considering his heading, his destination. They were low on fuel and would need to replenish the supply soon. Two hours was pushing the envelope.

They cruised over El Dorado, gaining altitude, breathing more easily, recovering from their close escape. They both looked down, recognizing in the growing light of morning the buildings where they had spent their time, taking in the rising smoke, the spreading flames, the sprawled bodies below. The copilot recognized Bodo lying next to a small building, the armory, he believed, and figured that it had to be Toma's body slumped next to him. He felt bad about leaving them behind. He pointed a finger, picking them out for the pilot, who turned his head and consequently failed utterly to see the darting, hovering shape of the Defender helicopter as it crossed the path of their flight.

46

"Watch watch watch!" Carmichael shouted as the gleaming cargo plane thundered toward them. The words were useless as a warning, he knew; they were what you yelled as the speeding car in which you were a passenger careened off the clifftop and began its fatal plunge, as you felt the press of the crowd behind you shove you inexorably off the edge of the train platform, as the toddler chased the ball into the path of the oncoming truck. He had an impression of something painted on the front of the plane, a dog or an animal of some kind, done in garish colors, and of the whirling blades of a propeller that seemed aimed straight at him. Loomis was frozen at the controls. His mouth gaped. Carmichael thought forward in time to the coming crash, the helicopter gyrating wildly, pirouetting as it died; thought of the smoking crater they would leave, the strewn wreckage. This was a story, he thought, this thing that was happening to him. This was a story they would tell forever back at DEA.

The port wing of the plane dipped at the last moment, as though it would pass under them and thus avoid catastrophe. Instead, it bisected the helicopter's fuselage, crushing the Defender like a toy. The smashed helicopter dropped from the air as a stone drops, turn-

ing end over end. Its wreckage fetched up at the edge of the compound. Jet fuel spurted from its ruptured tank, ignited, burned.

The stress of the midair collision snapped the Dakota's wing spar,
and the port wing, with engine attached, separated from the plane at
a point near the body, both wing and still-turning motor dropping
into the forest below. The venerable Douglas DC-3 then spun and
flamed, broke, descended swiftly and uncontrollably through the
lightening morning sky into the dark canopy of the trees, shedding
parts as it went.

47

Goody had somehow lost track of Peanut. Tannhauser's erstwhile executioner had vanished into thin air. One minute he was loping along, apparently believing himself free and clear, and the next he was gone. Goody had trailed him out into the woods surrounding El Dorado, leaving behind the sounds of the battle that raged there. Gunshots carried to him only faintly now. Not long before, a great silver plane that looked like something out of a World War II movie had roared by overhead. He had glanced up at it, and when he looked down again, he found that Peanut was missing from view. He moved on in the direction he had last seen Peanut taking, wary of an ambush.

And found a hole. A hole about three feet across, roughly circular in shape. It appeared that the opening had previously been covered over with bracken and sticks and leaves, and that the flimsy covering had given way when some unwary foot trod upon it, plunging that person into the void. Plunging Peanut into the void. Goody chuckled. He crouched down to peer into the hole. It had no bottom that he could make out.

"Hey," he called. He knelt in the thick carpet of weeds that grew around the lip of the hole. The ground was grainy and soft beneath him. When he leaned close and shouted into the opening, his voice did not echo, but instead simply disappeared into the cavity. Its size, he guessed, must be vast. A huge pit. And how deep? Bottomless, potentially. "Are you in there?" he called. It hurt him to shout. He could not be wrong. Here Peanut had met his end. Here, in the famous caves of the county. Maybe he would end up as a mummified exhibit for some future tourists to gawk at.

Goody waited. No reply. As he was rising to leave the place, a faint voice rose up from within the earth. It called to him. "Sorry," he thought he heard, and "out." It had to be Peanut's voice. Who else's? *Sorry. You bet you're sorry. Sorry son of a bitch. Choke me, will you.* He crept closer to the edge, cupped his hand to his ear.

"Come again?" he shouted down. "I didn't exactly hear you."

Again the garbled voice. "Fell." Gasps. "Got to pull." Peanut was fighting for the breath to speak. Had he been injured in the fall? It seemed likely. How sweet. "Can't keep."

"What?" Goody said. "You'll have to speak up a little louder. It's hard to make out what you're saying." He laughed. What could he do for the guy in any case? Even if Peanut had been his best friend, he had no rope. He had no block and tackle to save him with.

"Water. Can't." The voice from below was markedly weaker, the pauses between syllables longer. "Swim."

"You say there's nobody down there to strangle? You say you're unemployed now that you're trapped in a cave? Well, I'll be." Goody sat back on his haunches.

The ground under him gave a little. Suddenly nervous, he shifted his weight, felt the soft dirt move again. The place where he knelt was, he saw, distinctly lower than it had been, distinctly lower than the surrounding surface and rapidly sinking. He stood quickly, putting all his weight on the balls of his feet, and with a noise like a human sigh the earth beneath him collapsed, pouring into the abyss.

Goody could no doubt have saved himself from falling if the bones of his hands had been whole. He would have reached out and laid hold of great handfuls of the tough sedge that sprouted all around the hole, and carefully, hand over hand, being exquisitely careful not to uproot the stuff that gave him so tenuous a hold on light and air, drawn himself up and out of the pit. Or he could have snagged the low overhanging branch of a great leafy chain tree that grew nearby and clung to it, bobbing as he hung on to its resilient wood, bouncing gently over nothingness while the whole edge of the hole roared downward, peeling off the sides in widening concentric circles until the entrance had doubled, trebled, nearly quadrupled in size. With a working pair of fast, deft hands, there were a dozen ways in which Goody might have kept himself from falling.

But as it was, he could only slap with his ineffectual paws at the churning soil, swat at it as it ran like sand, particle by particle, clod by clod, stone by stone into the mouth of the chasm, taking him with it. He fell through the air, turning and turning, and he had no way to tell as he descended how many times he spun or how far he fell. He only knew that it was a long way down, an endlessly long way, and that falling into darkness was akin to sleeping and having no dreams.

48

It was not Tannhauser who emerged from the cottage, as the Mingos had expected, but Paloma, the girl whom Tannhauser had taken for his own. She pulled the door slowly open and stepped out onto the porch into the early morning light, apparently unafraid of the firefight raging around her. Her face was puffy, swollen with bruises, and her wrists and ankles were chafed and raw as though she had been tied and only recently gotten free. Her thin cotton shift was covered with blood. It adhered wetly to her slender body. In her right hand she held a long carving knife, its cutting edge and broad blade dark with the stuff as well; in her left she held something small, pale, anomalous. An animal?

The Mingos looked at each other, at a loss as to what action to take. They watched Paloma as she crossed the porch and climbed down the three wooden steps. At the bottom she turned to face the cottage and called in through the door, "Ya tengo tus dedos, monstruo, hijo de puta!" She held the pale thing, the things—there were two of them—aloft and pitched them onto the porch, where they bounced and skipped lightly across the weathered boards.

They were . . . what? Grubs. Horribly pale, fleshy, an inch long or less. Mice. Cocoons. As one, the Mingos identified them: fingers.

Tannhauser's fingers, his supernumeraries. The knife dropped from Paloma's hand to stick point downward in the dirt, and she began walking again, not lifting her feet off the ground. She wore no shoes. She had passed the shocked Mingos, had almost managed to evade them entirely, when they came to themselves again. They stood, their M16s leveled at her back, prepared to cut her down with their raking fire.

A rifle cracked, and first one Mingo and then the other heeled slowly over and dropped. They lay one atop the other like split lengths of firewood. The first had been shot through the neck and the second through the lungs. "Goddamn," a voice said. It was the lanky deputy, and he stood up from behind the bush where he had been crouched. "I think I got them both with one shot." Paloma tottered off in the general direction of the main building. She tacked like a sailing ship that moves against the wind.

"I believe you did, Saberhagen. I believe you did." Sheriff Faktor stood as well and clapped the deputy on the back. Throughout the compound, much of the gunfire had ceased. The squads of deputies were going from building to building now, mopping up. The sheriff was confident of his victory. He was sure of it. He strode over to the inanimate Mingos and prodded them with his foot. "I've wanted to see these guys laying dead for some little while," he said. "I knew they wouldn't die one without the other."

Saberhagen came over so that he could admire the corpses as well. "Just like Frank and Jesse James," he said.

"Or like Jim and Cole Younger," Sheriff Faktor said. "Or two of the Daltons, but I can't remember which two right now." It was incredible, how he had managed to sweep Tannhauser's people before him. What a rout. And as a side benefit, the DEA man had even managed to get himself dead, knocked from the sky by the wing of Tannhauser's own airplane. Faktor had seen it happen, had needed to scramble to avoid being killed by the plummeting debris. It was almost too good to be true.

"Now," he said to the deputy Saberhagen, "you manage to plug Tannhauser like that, and you'll be a fortunate man."

"Plug Tannhauser?" The voice was loud in the near-silence that had come over the compound. "Has Tannhauser come unplugged? That you need to plug him?"

Sheriff Faktor and his deputy turned to face the speaker, who stood on the porch of the cottage. They froze. It was Tannhauser. He

towered over the two men, his head nearly touching the low beams of
the porch roof, his eyes wide and staring. Like Paloma, he was
steeped in blood. The stuff soaked his shirt and his pants and stained
his teeth. It dribbled from his mouth when he spoke.

"I ask you," he said, "has Tannhauser come unplugged somehow?" His hair stood up from his head in great electric tufts. He held
the LAW on his shoulder, unlimbered and fully operational. He
peered down its length through the simple sighting system at Sheriff
Faktor. His eleventh and twelfth fingers were gone, and blood from
the stubs spotted the tube of the rocket launcher. The sheriff held up
his hands, dropping the pistol that he carried. He motioned for the
deputy to do the same, and Saberhagen laid his rifle on the ground at
his feet where, if he wanted, he could stoop and grab it up again
quickly enough. He hoped quickly enough.

"Hey, Tannhauser," Sheriff Faktor said. He strove to sound calm
and reasonable. The bore of the LAW seemed incredibly wide to him
as he looked into it. He had looked into the muzzles of pistols before,
and once the maw of a ten-gauge shotgun, but this was something
different altogether, this thing in Tannhauser's hands. He imagined
that he could see a faint shaft of light playing over the head of the
rocket that sat within the tube, ready for launching. He imagined
that the rocket knew him and would seek him out. "You don't want
to shoot that thing."

"I don't?" Tannhauser lifted his eyebrows. He was remarkably
steady on his feet for a man who had been gutted.

"No," the sheriff said. "It would be a bad idea."

"I don't know," Tannhauser said. "Do you think it might not
work or something?"

"It might not," the sheriff said. "You might squeeze the trigger
and nothing would happen. The rocket wouldn't come shooting out
of the barrel. And then where would you be?"

Tannhauser frowned and seemed genuinely to be concerned.
"The fellow that brought it to me—a fellow that your people have
killed, by the way—showed me how to use it. Pull this pin, extend
this, move this arming lever. It's all pretty simple. I believe I got it
right."

"But if you didn't," the sheriff said. He would not move. He
willed the deputy beside him not to move either. "Are you going to
take that chance? If you do, you're a dead man."

Tannhauser laughed bitterly. "I'm a dead man anyway. In case you didn't notice, that bitch that just ran out of here has opened me up pretty good. Ripped me right up the front with a butcher knife. I can feel my insides moving outward. It's a damn peculiar feeling. Plus my fingers are gone." He looked down at his hands and then back up, too quickly for anyone to take advantage of the lapse in his attention.

"We'll get you fixed up." The sheriff was willing to promise anything, staring into the depths of the rocket launcher. "We'll get you doctors. They'll patch you back together. And we'll hunt her down, the cunt that did this to you. Hunt her down and bring her your head on a platter."

The deputy made a little hissing noise between his teeth. Tannhauser narrowed his eyes and tightened his grip on the LAW. "You'll what?" he said.

"Bring you *her* head on a platter. I was confused. I'm sorry. *Her* head, to *you*. Of course that's what I meant, you know that."

"I don't know anything anymore, it doesn't seem like." A couple of the other deputies had moved into view of the porch, and one of them braced his rifle against a couch that sat out in the open between Tannhauser's cottage and the next one over. He planned a head shot. Clean. To the temple. He was a marksman. He had killed Bodo and Toma a little bit earlier. Such shots were his specialty. It occurred to him to wonder whether Faktor had been speaking literally when he talked about wanting Tannhauser's head. He wondered if a shot to the skull might prevent his getting the reward. He held off a moment. "Like, for instance," Tannhauser said, "I didn't know you were planning anything like this. This here. What you did to me and my people."

Sheriff Faktor tried to control the marksman with telepathy, force him to move in, to take his shot carefully and perfectly. He did not like having his fate in the hands of one of his people this way. He was sweating in the heat. "I admit," the sheriff said, his voice shaking, "that I made a mistake. And I'd like to make it up to you. Pull my people out. Promise full protection. Full restitution." He tried with his eyes to command the deputy to pull the trigger, to put Tannhauser away.

"A mistake," Tannhauser said. His gaze roamed over the wreckage of his compound: the slumped bodies of the Mingos; the cottages where the workers lay piled in their murdered numbers; the smoke that rose from the burning helicopter and, farther off, the Dakota. He nodded his head. "Yes, I believe you made one in coming here. A big one."

He squeezed the trigger of the LAW just as the deputy fired. The rocket, unleashed, soared from the launcher, gathering speed as it traveled. The heat of its backblast, venting from the open rear cover of the LAW, seared and bubbled the ancient coat of paint on the cottage's veranda. The sheriff had no time to move, no room to dodge, before the heavy antitank round hit him in the chest. Its high-explosive charge did not detonate. Instead the rocket broke his ribs, bored into his vitals before the brief charge of its solid fuel burned out. Hydrostatic shock stopped the beating of his heart. The rocket's force threw him backward, and he could not even scream as it drove him along, his boot heels dragging behind him in the dirt.

The marksman's bullet caught Tannhauser cleanly in the left temple, lifted off the bony top of his skull and exited that way. He plunged sideways, his heavy body crashing through the light railing around the porch and landing in the dirt of the yard. The tube of the LAW landed on top of him.

Sheriff Faktor's death convinced Deputy Sergeant Saberhagen that it was time to withdraw from the field. He gathered his men together, and found that other than the sheriff, there had been only two casualties among them, one of those fatal. He and his people fashioned stretchers for the wounded man and the two dead and bore them solemnly away from the compound, toward the valley. They hauled the dead sheriff along the difficult trail, heedless of the still-smoking warhead buried in his chest, unmindful of its potential for explosion.

They left alive at El Dorado only the anchorite, who yelped and capered and strained at the far end of his chain, endeavoring to keep himself from the raging fire started by the helicopter's fuel; and Yukon, who yet breathed in the damp, dark interior of the grand ballroom, eyed suspiciously and hungrily by the great horned owl; and Paloma, who wandered among the ruins, looking vainly for something: looking for her family, which was no more; looking, perhaps, for her own lost self.

49

Peanut was cold. He had been cold since he came slipping through the surface to this place, ever since he had plunged into the water that was black and who knew how deep and it was frigid, frigid beyond knowing. His wet heavy clothes clung to him, not insulating him at all, dragging him down.

Had he heard voices? A voice? He had, but it had long ago ceased to call to him. He had shouted, but the voice had given him no answer. It had ceased, as had the light. It was pitch black where he was and, except for the rush of his own blood, the uneven hooting of his own breath in and out, silent.

He did not swim well, had never learned to swim as other kids seemed to have done; or had they always known? He had been afraid to try, afraid to leave the shore, to leave the place where his legs could reach the sandy bottom, the rough, reassuring bottom. His brothers and his sister had swum like fish; they had seemed to love it. They loved it more because he could not do it; loved it more, and him less.

One December, when he was nine, the ice on the skating pond not far from his parents' house had given way beneath him, and beneath a bunch of the other skaters as well. They had been skating out in the middle, where they had been warned not to go, where the ice was brown and thin, and it crackled under them as they flew over it, made delicious crunching grinding noises. Water shot up in miniature geysers from the cracks in its gritty surface. You had to skate fast over the thin places, or they would break; that was the thrill of it. And somehow he had not skated fast enough, his legs had been insufficiently strong, and a great stretch of the poor ice had disappeared into the dark water. It had swung open under his scrambling feet and weak ankles like a trick, like a hidden trapdoor.

Most of the kids had gotten only their feet, or their legs up to the knees, wet, or had been caught almost immediately by friends stretched on their bellies at the soft edges of the gulf, and they had soaked in the cold water for not more than a few seconds, and shortly they were sitting by the bonfire on the shore, wrapped in dry blankets, stripped of their skates and their heavy soaked socks, drinking from mugs full of the hot chocolate they had carried along in plaid Thermos jugs. They had brought marshmallows to dunk in the cocoa. The fire burned hot, and their wet clothes steamed.

Somehow he had not been caught and pulled to safety. Somehow, he had been allowed to remain in the water longer than anyone else. Because he had been the first to fall through the ice, because he had not been quick and strong, and because he had brought grief on them, he would have to get himself out of the jam. He wore clunky baby skates with twin blades because he could not stand up on the regular skates with only a thin single blade, like the blade of a knife: slow skates, retard skates. He was an object of fun; they would not put themselves out to rescue him. That was the way kids operated.

They did not understand *(did they?)*, as he did not, that it wasn't funny, it was pathetic and cruel, it could be deadly to leave a little boy swimming in the freezing water for any length of time, any time at all. They did not understand that he couldn't swim. No, they did not understand, simply were not aware until later, when it had been forcefully explained to them by the use of such exotic terms as *hypothermia. Anoxia. Hypoxemia.* Exposure. Then they had hung their heads in shame and understanding.

He had splashed and kicked and tried to call out, barely keeping his nose and mouth above the surface of the water. His clothes, his heavy clothes pulled at him like hands drawing him downward. When he opened his mouth wide to scream, the water rushed in with its gunmetal taste, and he became afraid that it would fill him and weigh him down and drag him under. When he grasped at the thin broken border of the ice to pull himself out, it crumbled like old glass in his grasp, sharp serrated edges cutting him, gashing his fingers to the bone. And many times, he could not count how many times, his head had slid beneath the still skin of the water and he had thought he would drown.

The last time that he slipped under, he had felt his body go neutral in its buoyancy. He hung where he was, the tips of his fingers clear of the water but no other part of him. It was silent there, silent and dead. Shortly, it did not seem cold. The water had heated to the temperature of his skin, or his flesh had cooled. More comfortable, either way. An unsuspected current caught hold of him, like a breeze, and he wafted sideways, the clear noncolor of the water overhead replaced with the blue sheen of ice. His upraised fingertips traced the rippled icesheet that covered the pond, finding the hairline cracks and crevices in it over which he and his friends had sped on the polished steel blades of their skates. Only he had not sped fast enough.

As he drifted, neither rising nor falling, he kept his eyes upturned, watching for the flash of those blades, wondering whether the skating had resumed. The workings of his mind seemed to be slowing, flattening out. No excitement, no anxiety, no fear. He had thought, vaguely, that it would be interesting to watch the skaters from that angle. The wide-twirling skirts of the older girls. The white cotton of their panties. The ice overhead grew thicker and thicker as he drifted, slowly blocking out more and more light. Soon he was covered by blackness. And he died.

He told the girl who saved him that he had died. She was an eighth-grader, four years older than he, a great lumpish girl when on land, thick-legged, slack-bellied, red-headed, with a pale, unwashed complexion that was always a riot of pimples, blackheads, every variety of painful eruption and swelling. She had a lifesaver's badge, though, and in the water she was as graceful as a seal, her unruly coppery hair plastered against her sleek head, her limbs strong and sure as she smashed through the ice and stroked down to him, raised him to the surface, forced the brackish water from his lungs, pumped breath back into him, violently. She bruised his ribs, possibly broke one, and every time he breathed while it healed, the pain of that tightly taped fracture was a reminder of her.

She had not wanted to be remembered. He followed her. Pursued her. Bought her things when he had any pocket money, which was not often. Trinkets from the five-and-dime. Plastic combs. Beads. Brightly colored pencils with overlarge erasers. She never showed the slightest interest in these baubles. Only in the chewing gum that he bought, which eventually was the only thing that he bought, when he saw that it was all she wanted. Cinnamon-flavored gum. Her breath smelled of cinnamon. The strong scent seemed to emanate from her pores after a while. She was always chewing.

He must have bought her a thousand sticks, two thousand, more, over the years that he courted her, the three years before she vanished. She took the chewing gum from him, but ungraciously, as though she suspected that this time, *this* time something would be wrong with it: it would be laced with garlic salt, or onion flavoring. Joke gum. He adored her.

She never spoke to him. Almost never. All she ever said to him was "I never broke any ice to get to you." She said, "You weren't under the ice. That's just a dream. You panicked and swallowed some pond water. You were floating on the surface, and I grabbed you by the hair and dragged you in. That's all." She said, "At the time, it seemed better than just letting you die."

Then she vanished. A number of stories, some complementary, most contradictory, circulated. Her father, estranged from her mother, had kidnapped her and taken her to Ohio to live with him. Her father, a drunkard, had beaten her to death in a rage and had buried the body, afterward running away to Ohio to escape justice. Her mother, a well-known local prostitute, had sold her to a white-slave ring. She had gotten a lot of money because the girl was, as everyone knew, a virgin. Her mother, an inveterate gambler but a poor one, had sold her into prostitution to pay off debts. The girl herself, despondent over a failed love affair with an older man, a divorced man, a drunkard, a gambler, had hopped a freight train on the fly, had ridden it all the way to Portsmouth, Ohio, where her father lived. She had tried to hop a rolling freight but had missed her hold and fallen, to be crushed beneath the rumbling wheeltrucks. She had intentionally thrown herself in front of a freight train and been ridden down. Her belongings had been found in a rucksack left in a rental locker at the bus station in Akron, Ohio. Her dismembered body had been found in a rucksack. Her limbs, but no head. She had left behind her nothing, not even a note. She had left behind a note that explained it all, but her mother, distraught, had destroyed the note. She had left behind no note, only a pile of plastic junk, baubles that were junk to other people but had meant the world to her.

Her name had been Evangeline. Peanut did not know what had become of her. Or did he know? The mystery of her disappearance had gone unsolved, as he remembered it, or it had been solved but he had not been privy to the solution of it. Evangeline. Her eyes had been very blue, luminously blue, as she swam down to him, the fine red hair on her arms and legs trapping glistening bubbles against their slender shafts, globules of captive air that trembled and swung with the motion of her arms and legs.

He had ceased to thrash. He floated, arms out, head thrown back, in perfect suspension. It was hard to know what direction was up and what was down, whether he was on top of the water or under it. The darkness prevented his knowing. Every time he drew a breath, it was a surprise to him that he took in air. At any time it could become water. At any time he could drown, and he thought that most likely he would not resist. He seemed to be in a river, caught in a fast-moving silent river, and the river moved only under its surface. Its surface was glassy, perfectly calm, but underneath it tugged and pulled at him with a force that he could not refuse or deny.

Or so it seemed. He knew that darkness changed things, made them seem what they were not. He thought that if he had a lamp, or if the earth opened up and afforded him the light to see his true situation, it might be completely different from his perception of it. It might surprise him in some way, perhaps in a large, a substantial way. It delighted him to think that he might be surprised at how he stood. His situation, however it changed, whatever it was, had ceased long ago to astonish him.

He was a hopeful person. He never gave up hope, that was his hall-mark. Just as it was his hallmark not to struggle against the inevita-ble. And a river, a river in which you were caught, a river that swept you along and afforded you no idea of its depth or its width, its speed or direction, that seemed to have no bottom and no banks, comprised for Peanut a whole and complete notion of the inevitable. He could not swim, he could not strike out for a destination and had no desti-nation in mind, but he could float. And a river, even an underground river, had a destination. It was bound to come out somewhere. Wasn't it?

His legs tangled in something. A projection of rock. His ankle was caught, his ankle and his thigh clamped in an angle of rough stone, caught as in a vise. His legs were cold, all of him was cold, frozen, and he found it hard to think what the rock might mean. Was it a shelf onto which he could clamber and thus be safe? Was it entirely underwater? He stretched out his hands to touch its surface, to see what he could understand of it. Its surface was slick and his hands were numb and the rock defied his idea of exploring it. His fingers slipped uselessly over the formation.

The current tugged at him, trying to bear him along as before, and his leg slipped deeper into the crevice of the rock that held him. It caught him fast. He found his head underwater. Water rushed up his nose and, when he opened his mouth to shout, down his throat. It forced itself into him. He pushed to no avail against the entrapping stone. It would not yield. Shortly he gave himself up to it. The river came out somewhere. It had to, did it not? Perhaps he was still moving, moving toward that eventual light. Perhaps it was very near.

He had an instant of hysteria near the end, just before his brain shut down, just before he opened his nose and mouth and drank in the water. He struggled and fought, bashed his hands against the rock. He wept, and there was no one to hear him. That was the worst of it. He had not known that it was possible to be so entirely alone. The world had always seemed so crowded to him. Crowded house. Crowded classrooms. Crowded gymnasium. Crowded dormitories. Crowded mess hall. Crowded cellblock. If you died there, in any of those places, you did not die alone, no matter how you died. His loneliness pressed against him; or perhaps it was the water.

Evangeline, he thought, growing calm again. He did not understand where he was. He believed that he was under the ice again. That he was still under the ice. The tight cap of her water-soaked hair, which was not red underwater, which was black under the ice. He would have gone with her, wherever she had gone. Evangeline. She had clawed her way down to him, the blue of her eyes like unearthly beacons under the water. Where was the ice? It should have been cold against his fingers, he should have been able to press against it, to test its thickness.

The cold water, he thought. The cold water would preserve him. As long as it flowed, he would remain. For a hundred, a thousand years. Refrigerated. Perfectly preserved beneath the sheet of ice, waiting. And the water came roaring in.

50

Goody struck water. He did not know how far he had fallen, but the sharp slap of liquid against his skin when he hit it, the chill of it, instantly energized him. He struck out for shore, some shore, swimming strongly and swiftly, afraid lest the frigidity of the water should cause his muscles to cramp and swallow him down. He was driven to find some solid place onto which he could climb. As he swam, he bumped into something, some heavy bobbing object, and he thought it might be Peanut. Peanut drowned and dead. He could imagine the pop eyes, the mouth drawn and slack, drooling water, the cool limbs splayed and contorted. He reached out to push the thing away and was suddenly afraid that he might put a finger into one of those dead eyes, that dead mouth. He shoved at it with his foot, and it floated off, borne away on some unseen current.

It did not take him long to reach a pebble-strewn beach. He lay face down, gasping air into his straining lungs, moving his arms and legs to restore circulation. He feared going into shock. He looked back the way he had come, expecting to see light shining down from the hole through which he had fallen. He hoped that it would show him the height of the room, the shape of its roof perhaps, maybe even faintly illuminate the surface of the lake or pond into which he had plunged. There was no light at all.

He blinked, passed his hand before his eyes. No light. He could not see. He flipped over to lie supine, fearful of rising. There might be something overhead, some ledge or sharp projection that would brain him if he raised himself up. There might be a chasm to his right, his left, into which he would plunge if he so much as shifted. His mouth tasted acid. His stomach churned.

He did not know how long he lay in that paralyzed state. Seconds, minutes, hours. Finally, it was the fact that he was hungry that inspired him to move. Hunger seemed to him a positive sign. Time had not stopped. His cells had not ceased to function. He was still alive and human. He raised his head, and it encountered no obstacle. He rose to a crouch and then, slowly, to a standing position. Feeling a breeze from behind him, and imagining that it meant an open passage, a way out of his entombment, he began to follow the current of air.

He walked with his tender hands held out before him, like a blind man or a sleepwalker, moving along in perfect dark. He shouted from time to time, partly to hear a sound, even if it was only his own voice, and partly to try with echoes to steer himself away from obstacles. He moved in terror of running into something, bashing his broken hands against it. They felt overlarge, like a pair of clumsy mittens, and hot.

The way seemed to be clear. As far as he could tell, he walked in a hallway approximately the size and shape of a subway tunnel. The footing was gravel, and he occasionally splashed through frigid fast-running streams. The streams were most often shallow, but sometimes the water climbed to the height of his thighs, his hips, and the weight of the flow against his body threatened to push him off-balance and sweep him away. His clothes clung wetly to him, and the feeling of them was unhealthy and uncomfortable. He had hoped that the exertion of walking would help to dry them, but the air was full of moisture, and they remained damp. His shoes made a squishing noise when he walked.

When he saw the shaft of light, he at first took it to be a trick of his vision. To his weakened gaze, the light seemed as concentrated as the beam of a laser. It looked like a solid thing. He was almost afraid to reach out and touch it lest it should burn his skin. He had no notion of how long he had been underground: a timeless period spent wandering in the tunnels, passing from chamber to unseen chamber. His stomach rumbled, reminding him that he had not eaten since before the fight. The fight, which seemed to him to have taken place a year ago, no, a century ago, and on another planet entirely from this one.

The shaft of light was near the floor of the cavern room. It seemed to emanate from a fault in the cavern wall. He bent to it, and as he reached out his hand to touch it, his broken aching fingers encountered water. The water ran crystal clear, invisible to him but for the ripples that he had caused. He bent to the pool of water and drank. The water was full of minerals and tasted faintly metallic, but its effect on his strained throat was remedial. He raised his dripping face to catch his breath before lowering it to the surface of the pool again. He sucked the water up with his lips, lapped at it like an animal. He ducked his whole head underwater. And saw a peculiar thing: inside the duct that led to the surface, there seemed to be living things. Plants. Waving stems of grass. The brown furry heads of cattails. He reached down the channel toward them and found that he could not touch them. They were reflections, shadowy holographic images thrown by some process unknown to him onto the slick calcite that lined the pipe. He watched them waving as in a faint breeze, his head immersed, until his lungs felt ready to burst. He pulled his head from the water, shaking it from side to side so that droplets flew from his hair in a fine spray. He gasped for breath.

As soon as he was able, he inhaled deeply and thrust his head into the shallow water again. He gazed at the pipe where the reflected plants waved and thought that he could see other things there: the top of a stripling willow tree; thin reeds; stormclouds racing swiftly across the sky; wildflowers in a riot of colors. The pipe, he thought, must feed a stream on the surface. He stretched his arm out to its fullest length and thrust his hand down the tube. His fingers slipped easily over the slick calcite. His arm blocked the light, leaving him in darkness. His hand did not leave the water; he did not have the reach to put his fingers into the open air.

Obscurely disappointed at his failure, he tried to withdraw his arm from the channel. It would not come. It was wedged fast. Already a high, thin whining had started up in his head, warning him that he must breathe soon or lose consciousness. It was a sensation he recalled from his session with Peanut. He tugged at the arm, but something—the pressure of the flowing water—held it tight in the narrow space. He was going to drown in this place, this pit, this blackness. Drown in eighteen inches of clear water. He forced himself to relax. Then, his lungs an agony to him, his brain screaming for air, for light, he heaved against the vacuum that had him pinned. With a loud sucking noise, his arm came free, and he sat back beside the stream. Light flooded into the room again.

After a few minutes, he considered putting his face to the water again, to catch a last glimpse of the plants on the surface, but he decided against it. Instead, he tested his eyes: first the right, which saw plainly, and then the left, which revealed nothing.

It took him quite a while to bring himself to leave the room that contained the brilliant light. He waited for night to come to the outside, watching as the beam of light swung across the room. It occurred to him that perhaps he could make some sort of clock out of the sweeping branch of daylight, some way to track the passage of days while he dwelled underground. He knew that such a time-telling method would be useless to him, but his mind refused to stop turning over and over the possibility of the contrivance. Rocks to mark the hour, the quarter-hour, the minute. He could watch time slip away. When the light went gray, shading into the black of night, the black of the cavern, he rose, shook his stiff limbs in order to warm them, and went on his sightless way.

He began measuring time by the growth of his beard. He had always been one to hair up pretty fast; he had frequently been compelled to shave twice a day to keep his appearance neat. Now, as he roamed among the rock walls, shuffling his feet to prevent, if possible, a plunge into some invisible fissure, he ran his hand over his chin and cheeks from time to time to see what new amount of hair had sprouted there. Sometimes there had been little or no detectable growth between these examinations, sometimes a great deal. Did hair grow differently when you were starving? he wondered. Did the body slow its output of such nonessentials to conserve its remaining energy? He suspected that it did but could not be sure. All told, he believed that he had been underground not less than forty-eight hours and not more than seventy-two when his blinded eye regained its sight.

He was not able to guess how it had come about, but it seemed to have happened gradually. At first he began to see vague shapes in front of him: the humps and jagged edges of broken rock. Then he was able to make out the walls of the cavern tunnel on either side of him, and soon enough he saw distant elements of the cave as well, saw them as though they were lit by clear daylight. He assumed it was some glow that emanated from the cave walls, some phosphorescence deep within the stone itself. But when he covered his eyes, always anxious to check the wounded left, he found that he could see perfectly well with the damaged eye and nothing at all with the whole one.

It was a peculiarity that he accepted without question. It seemed to his advantage to do so. Now his steps were sure. He did not stumble over stray boulders, did not trip and fall when he encountered a slide of pointed, splintery shale. Instead, he was making good time along the apparently endless tunnels of the cave system, even if he had no notion where he might be headed.

He entered a dry section of the cave. Water no longer dripped from the walls. Streams no longer wended their mercurial way underfoot. The temperature had risen as well. It was the fourth or the fifth day of his confinement. He could feel his body beginning to consume itself, weakening as it broke down the precious protein of his muscles in an effort to survive. He had passed through hunger, beyond it, but he had not left thirst behind. The craving raged in him as he passed through the dry place, and there was no help for it. He did not sweat, and he no longer urinated.

He passed through a chamber where lava dripped from the walls and ran in fiery rivulets across the floor. Flames reached up from the flowing streams of molten rock. The air seared his lungs. When a tongue of magma spread itself in his path, he did not bother to step over it but waded through instead. He expected to feel pain when his feet hit the seething stuff, but there was no pain. He shook the lava from his tattered sneakers and marched on.

He passed through a chamber hung with trembling sheets of ice. A screaming gale rendered him deaf. His breath frosted as it left his mouth, caking on his cheeks, freezing the hairs of his mustache. When he spat, experimentally, the tiny ball of saliva froze solid before it hit the floor. It spun there before him, perfectly globular, a bright marble sparkling in the light that was no light. Sparkling in the light that radiated, he imagined, from the damaged tissue of his martyred eye. When he reached the center of the vast room (a walk of some hours' duration), he threw his head back and he howled. He could not hear his own voice but he screamed as loudly as he was able, and the great membranes of ice that clung to the walls, the floor, the ceiling of the place, trembled with the sound of his voice. They quivered and tinkled like crystal, and the thousand distorted reflections that he saw of himself in those walls, some as tiny as mice, some a hundred and fifty feet tall, all those reflections shimmered and pulsed. He screamed again, more loudly this time, and the whole arrangement came crashing down, burying him in its frozen debris.

He passed through a chamber where the dead congregated. They had been waiting for him, it seemed, and when he entered the room they turned their heads as one to stare at him. They watched him with their hollowed eyes as he moved among them. They parted to open a passage, a passage three feet wide, no wider, and their numbers packed the edges of the boulevard. Dirt clung to them. Gray mold bloomed in the folds of their winding-sheets. Their flesh was blood-less. He was afraid at first that they would reach out and touch him, that they craved something from him and would try to take it by force, but no one among their multitude so much as extended a hand in his direction.

As he passed through the divided horde, he sometimes caught a glimpse of a familiar face, a feature that he recognized: the line of a nose, the angle of a chin, the tilt of a head. He saw a man whom he knew but to whom he could not put a name. When he paused to call out, to find the name, the man, who was tall and muscular, nearly nude, turned his back and seemed to melt into the crowd. He saw a man with long yellow teeth, his legs twisted and odd and clumsy beneath him, and this time the name came to Goody's lips—Billy Rugg—but in that place he did not dare to call it out. He saw a woman that he knew as well, a woman with mud and gravel caked in her thick dark hair, but she showed a similar disinclination to con-verse with him. As he motioned toward her, she drifted quickly away, and he dared not follow her lest the dead close their foul ranks upon him.

When he reached the far side of the room and prepared to leave it, the massed dead seemed to lose interest in him and began once again to visit with one another. Their voices were high and squeaky, and though they were speaking a language that he knew, he failed to understand even a single word.

He entered a room where the walls were lined with the impressions of petrified bones, layer upon layer of them like lines of indecipherable typescript rising to the stone ceiling above. The fossil remains at the bottom were small, nearly microscopic, clustered in colonies like air bubbles, the rock as porous as sponge.

Above those were the bones of the lower vertebrates, and then larger animals, and larger, rising up perfectly in a reverse pyramid of size and complexity, the striations like an illustration from a high school science text, an illustration of the relentless march of evolution. He looked carefully, but nowhere in the elaborate ladder was the form that he knew, the human form, the bones of man. Trilobites, amphibious lizards, the curved teeth of the tyrannosaur, the light chicken-size bones of the pterodactyl, sharks, monkeys, eohippus, all else. He made his study of the walls (wonderful how thirst had at last ceased to plague him) and moved on.

There was little strength left in him when he reached the shore of the subterranean sea. It stretched away as far as he, with his new faultless vision, could see. The vaulted roof stretched upward in a perfect dome shape, its apex lost in shadow. This, he knew, was the place that he had been seeking. He had passed through all of the other rooms simply to reach this one, this final one. Beyond this, he knew, there were no others. Here, ranged around the shore of the still black sea, was a lost metropolis.

The mud-colored city was built almost entirely on the vertical. Its tall slender habitations rose from the gently sloping shore almost to the arched stone ceiling; the tops of many were hidden in the high shadows. The walls had a strange texture to them, as though they were made not of masonry but rather of something less substantial than concrete or steel, some papery substance. He imagined that if he put his hand to the material it would be crushed by his crude touch. The exceeding lightness of it accounted for the ability of the ancient builders to set these soaring buildings against their stone sky.

He was tempted to walk among the buildings, to stroll through the city, but his desire was frustrated by the fact that there were no streets at ground level. Its avenues were airways, passable only to winged men. The designers of the city, its inhabitants, the city itself, were all long dead. That much was obvious. Once, perhaps, the place had been a hive of activity, the air full of the fibrillation of wings as the creatures that lived here fluttered from one elevated doorway to another, landing on delicate insectile legs, lighting briefly, springing into the air again. Once, perhaps, but not now.

Instead of exploring (for really, what was there to find in any case? Only more evidence of what he already knew, and would never communicate to another living person), Goody sat himself down on the noiseless shore and stared out over the inert body of water, waiting for the time when his unearthly vision would fail, when his body would have consumed itself entirely and he would cease to be.

51

Goody sat on the rough beach and drowsed.

As he slept, the denizens of the degenerate city opened their eyes, eyes a handspan apart, and emerged from their high towers, stood at the brink of their manufactured valleys, and spread their squamous wings. Their feathery antennae moved this way and that. One after another, they took to the air, wonderfully light wings folding and opening, propelling them speedily, gracefully, from every corner of the vast outspread city along the network of their aerial avenues.

He woke. One of the creatures stood before him. It was an impressive example of its weird kind: many-legged; as tall as a man, and as broad. It regarded him out of expressionless faceted eyes that glittered like jewels. It moved its wings, so like a moth's, great curved sails covered in silver scales, and the scent of damp earth was borne to him. He saw that each wing bore a pattern, dark lines like rivulets of spilled ink against the silver background. And as the wings twitched, back and forth, he thought that he could make sense of the pattern. Its lines had the look of bone, an inverted bowl of bone; a skull. From each broad wing a perfect death's-head, worked in silver and black, stared at him with blank empty eye sockets. The creature took a tentative step toward him, clawed limbs outstretched. When he took a protective posture, it chittered nervously and fell back, awaiting reinforcements.

He heard them as they came, squealing and crying in high-pitched voices that were not unlike the voices of the dead. The multitude of their wings agitated the air. They came along the beach. They skimmed the water. They came at him from every side, and he threw up his maimed hands, crossed his arms at right angles before his face in a useless defense, pushing at their packed bristling frantic bodies, striking out as they greedily probed his flesh with their long pointed sucking proboscises, shouting in fury and despair as the jabbering, flapping mass of them poured over him and bore him down.

52

Dwight was checking the cave for stragglers, as he did every day at closing, when he came across the ragged man. The fellow was standing at the black iron railing of the Veil of Tears. The Veil of Tears was now called Swan Falls, and the face had been transformed by a new configuration of lamps into the semblance of a large bird with wings outspread. The man, who sported an unsightly growth of untrimmed beard and whose shorts and shirt were frayed and soiled into shapelessness, had nonetheless the air of the familiar about him. Dwight, who rarely forgot a name, was sure that he knew him. He touched the man on the shoulder. "Hey," he said gently, "time to go. All tours are over. You know you shouldn't be back here."

The man turned slowly—exquisitely slowly—to confront Dwight. He rotated his whole body, as though his neck were frozen and it was impossible for him to turn his head. He looked down at Dwight, and his face was terrible to see: swollen and bruised, one eye milky and washed out, the other overbright, darting about wildly as though to compensate for the loss of its twin. But the bruises were not the worst of it. The flesh of the man's face was covered in sores, reddened oozing sores like some sort of a terrible pox. The red bubos blanketed his chest, too, what Dwight could see of it under the unbuttoned shirt. His legs were similarly marked. Dwight recoiled from the sight of him.

"This," the man said, and his voice was a harsh croaking in his throat, little more than a whisper, "used to be a face."

"That's right," Dwight said. "But we've been doing a little remodeling. It's a swan now." The man looked as though he had been bitten. Bats? Askins would shit if he learned that bats had swarmed one of his tourists. Such a thing had never happened before, that Dwight knew of. All the bats had supposedly been flushed out of the caves a long time before. He himself had encountered very few of them in his time below, and those had been meek and timid, huddling close against the rock. He was relieved to realize that it was not his problem, no longer his problem at all.

"It's not a swan now. It's nothing now," the man said. He coughed a little. He was cruelly thin, the ridged lines of his rib cage visible beneath the skin of his chest. He said, "The earth is hollow." He said, "It's full of terrible things."

"I know," Dwight said. Something, a slip of paper it looked like, lay crumpled on the floor at the man's feet. Dwight could see part of a picture that was printed on it: a smiling pig. Scratch-off ticket, he realized. Not a winner, apparently, to judge by the manner in which it had been pitched away. He sighed. "Listen," he said. "It's my last day. As of a quarter of an hour from now, I'm no longer employed here. Don't ruin my last few minutes on the job, will you? Let's go." He put an amiable hand on the man's shoulder, to guide him out.

The man ignored the hand, turned back to the lighted waterfall and the swan. His lips were moving, but Dwight could not tell what he was saying. Dwight pulled at him, but he would not come. Despite his decrepit appearance, the man was quite strong. He bowed his head, and his shoulders shook as though he might be crying, but no tears came to his eyes. "All right," Dwight said. He had no desire to fight with the scarred guy. It wasn't his cave anymore. What did he care? "You stay here if you want. Me, I'm going topside." He moved off.

The man did not make a reply. His shoulders continued to hitch in that pitiful way, and he was openly sobbing. Dwight decided that he had been mistaken in his earlier impression. He did not know this man, had never met him. He came back to the railing and took a fold of the man's shirt between his fingers, and this time when he tugged, the man came with him.

"That's the way," Dwight said as they left the grotto. "Come right on." He made a clicking sound with his tongue, the sort he might make to urge a horse onward. He uttered a constant string of low, soothing noises. The man continued to follow him docilely, and together they threaded the cavern's narrow meandering pathways, leaving behind them the darkness and the sound of endlessly rushing water.

about the author

Pinckney Benedict grew up and continues to live on his family's dairy farm, not far north of Lewisburg, West Virginia. He studied creative writing at Princeton University with Joyce Carol Oates and at the University of Iowa. His first collection of short stories, *Town Smokes*, was published in 1987. It was followed in 1992 by another collection, *The Wrecking Yard*. Mr. Benedict is the recipient of the Nelson Algren Award, given by the *Chicago Tribune*, a James Michener Fellowship from the Writers' Workshop, and a fellowship from the Bread Loaf Writers' Conference. In the spring of 1993 he was the Thurber House writer-in-residence at Ohio State University, and he can be heard from time to time as an essayist on National Public Radio's "All Things Considered."